Bitch Spray

A Team Crosspatch Novel

Contents

Nettle Lane

There was nothing particularly unusual about that Sunday evening. It was mid-October, so yes, it was chilly out. The wind was still blowing in gusts, but the rain had moved on in that part of Kent. The remaining clouds rolled swiftly across the face of the moon, casting shadows that flitted silently across the garden surrounding the 'little cottage', as Laura liked to call it. Other people might have laughed a bit at that description, but to Laura Handley-Davison it was just right. It was certainly nothing like the enormous house she'd grown up in.

She loved her house, had put her soul into it, making it not only beautiful but a haven in her busy world. A haven for her husband too, she had hoped. And it was, or at least it had been. But she wasn't deriving much comfort from it tonight. She was alone and fretting. Ian had left in a towering temper. *Stupid, stupid man!* She kicked at the carpet angrily. She'd been pretty furious too, of course. *So unnecessary. So stupid!* She had been pacing restlessly in front of the fireplace, a tumbler of whisky in her hand. Now she took a long draught, sighed and slumped down on the sofa, pulling the dramatic black kimono she was wearing more tightly around her, stretching the brilliantly embroidered crane on the back taut across the tension in her shoulders.

She was at a loss as to what to do, how to put everything right again. Really what was the point in bickering over - well - trivia? *Oh God!* She adored her husband. Was miserable when they were at odds. Stretching her hand out towards the fire, she let the memories come flooding in. The gentleness, the laughter, the passion. She shook her head, half smiling, half weeping. Such exciting days, such glorious evenings! They hadn't even made it up to the bedroom half the time. Tangles of clothes and limbs and passionate love - right there in front of the fire. She sat up abruptly. These weren't old memories, she told herself. One of them was going to have to compromise. Would it be so difficult for it to be her?

Outside, the wind gusted, rustling the leaves in the trees, and echoing hollowly in the chimney. She gave a shiver, suddenly chilled. She crossed to the sideboard, topped up her glass and drew back the curtain. Shadows seemed to flutter across the lawn. Was that someone out there? She wished she had Luna with her tonight. Nothing like a dog to keep the horrors at bay. She shrugged. What she needed was a hot bath, essential oils, and soft, sentimental music. She punched in a selection on the house system, an old Acker Bilk album, the safe all enveloping sounds of her childhood. The gentle sound of his clarinet followed her up the stairs to the bathroom.

Taking out a box of rich, perfumed oils, each in its own miniature bottle, she studied the labels – *patchouli and lavender? Inner contentment? Perfect. One capful? Not enough!* She emptied the entire bottle into the water and breathed in deeply as the room filled with scented steam. Slipping off the kimono, she stroked the embroidered crane briefly and held it to her cheek, then let it fall to the floor. Dimming the lights she took a match from the cabinet, lit the candles on the shelf above the bath and stepped in.

She lay back, letting the water settle around her. Warm, slick, and expensively perfumed, it soothed the day away into the shadows and let the gentler, candlelit ambiance prevail. She stretched her legs and flexed her feet, seeing but not really observing the long toes that rested against the tap, pink now with the heat of the bath, perfectly pedicured a deep blood red. She breathed out the frustrations of the day and closed her eyes.

She was still on edge. Ian had been so angry. Furious. She huddled back down into the enveloping warmth, breathing in deeply, taking comfort from the aromatic oils. This could be resolved. No. It would be resolved. She would sort it out. A small private smile echoed the beginnings of arousal, anticipating his relief and delight. It really wasn't so difficult. She'd phone him. He'd be home tonight. She stretched out a hand for her glass, took a sip of the golden, peaty whisky, then reached for her eye mask, slipped it on and closed out the world.

* * * * *

He eased the door open. All too easy. The spare key hadn't been hard to find, under the pot by the garage. People were so naive, so stupid. He knew the dog was in kennels tonight, a pedigree bitch, ready to be put to the stud dog in the morning. Looking around to assimilate the layout of the house, something caught his eye on the shelf by the door: "Bitch Spray," he read. He picked up the aerosol, and his lips twitched in an unpleasant smile - *how very appropriate.*

He moved lightly. Over the haunting tones of a clarinet, all was quiet. He climbed the stairs, silent as a ghost. At the end of the corridor, a bathroom door was ajar. He could see her in the mirror, relaxed, dreamy, and unsuspecting. All his.

Laura had heard and seen nothing, and suddenly it was too late. The mask was ripped from her face, and there, leaning over her, was a gloating, taunting, seemingly giant head haloed by the candles above. As she opened her mouth to scream, he put the canister to her lips and pressed. Bitch Spray. It choked her and she fought for breath, jerking and writhing, lifting her arm to hold him off. No chance. He reached down, gripping her throat, hauling her straight up out of the water, her fingers scrabbling at his hand, trying to escape. Oh yes. She was all he had imagined. With a terrible smile he brought out the knife. A long blade, perhaps eight inches in length. A flaying knife.

Laura's horrified stare fixed on the knife lazily circling towards her stomach and her struggles became ever more violent. Greased by the oil in the water, she slipped out of his grasp, but as her flailing feet hit the bath, they too lost purchase and down she went, hard, hitting her head violently on the side. Her body convulsed, then lay still and limp in the water; no fight left in her.

He stared for a long moment. Then, as if galvanized, he cursed loudly and lunged for her again. No! She couldn't die now! He hadn't even started! Tearing his gloves off he pulled her up by her hair, felt for a pulse. Not there. No breath from her mouth. She'd cheated him! His rage exploded in an unstoppable orgy of violence. The knife lashed out, stabbing, tearing, again and again, a ghastly compensation for the deprivation of her pain and morbid terror that should have carried him to ecstasy… until, quite suddenly, he was sated. He slumped back, limp and damp, against the wall, pulling his gloves on again, slowly. As his eyes cleared, he looked at the room.

Laura lay silent, violated in every way and yet inviolate now, beyond pain. Her face was peaceful, but her torso was barely recognisable as such. Her legs were stretched out, long and elegant, her toes flexed against the taps, her scarlet nails almost invisible against the blood red of the water.

He blinked. Reality returned, pushing back the frenzy. He was exhausted. He was also, he was surprised to realise, a bit afraid. These were uncharted waters. He sat for a moment, thinking, then pulled out his mobile. Punched in a number. It was answered after a short delay and without waiting, he spoke, his voice hoarse…

"It's done," he said. "Over. She's dead. Now you play your part," and hung up. Wearily he started to clear all traces of his presence. They'd know she'd been killed, but he wasn't in the habit of leaving anything that could be traced back to him.

* * * * *

Ian was on stage when the call was made, playing a different man in a different time, wielding weapons, maiming, and shedding blood with no terminal effect, in a scene that would be tidied and replayed, with all participants up again and then out to the pub for a congratulatory drink. But when he retrieved his phone after the rehearsal, he would step into a new reality, one that could never be swept up and tried again.

* * * * *

Rehearsals were going ahead as usual. The routine, the noise, the controlled chaos as the scene stuttered into being, with actors' innovations and the moulding and polishing of the director's hand, always intoxicating, working like a drug. The outside world, the real world, receded and was lost, swept aside, and forgotten in the rush of fantasy. It was taking a little longer than usual for Ian to lose himself in his part, but as the actors worked, the play took hold. Snatches of the dialogue were resonating more particularly with him that evening as he let his grasp on himself lessen and instead absorbed the thane's reality.

The witches' voices seduced and unsettled him as never before, hinting at change, but more than that: reward, immediate advancement. They'd have a triumph on their hands. He'd be the star, the king. He knew it. *But at what cost?* He threw up his hands, saw the dagger there, before him, red with blood - flung the thought away. The king he loved, to whom he'd sworn his fealty, safe in his care - what was he thinking? Then Laura's face swam up before him pushing the gentle Duncan aside, and he stumbled a little, hesitated, lost his way.

His wife. He'd sworn to cherish her! Yet still the taunting voice of the lady of the castle tore at him. He heard derision in her words, questioning his courage, strength, and action. Was he a man? Was he? By God he was!

I dare do all that may become a man;
Who dares do more is none.

Where was Laura's loyalty? She'd sworn to cherish too - more - to obey. It was her duty to help him, not stand in his way, defying his authority, his ambitions. His hands again - he lifted them and felt the dagger - heavy, dripping blood. He gagged. So much blood. But still the voices whispered in his ear, tempting, taunting. The future was his, wasn't it, but for Laura, the doubter, the stumbling block?

The mists swirled, the witches cackled, and, as Macbeth, Ian felt himself grow, to tower above other men. Bony fingers pointed the way and doubts faded. Untouchable. He was untouchable. He felt something mystical reach out to pull him through those mists. Duncan, the king - Laura - they had merged now, and his loves and loyalties were swept aside as the world turned red, a sea of gore through which he strode to glory.

"If it were done, when tis done," he spoke the line and his whole being thrummed to the conclusion, *"then t'were well it were done quickly."*

* * * * *

Ian was inordinately proud of his theatre. He'd played most of the major London theatres in his heyday but since making the switch to owner-director as well as actor he had had to work his way up through venues that were little more than parish halls. Now, here he was in The Classic, charming and esoteric, a converted Edwardian Bank, in spitting distance - his words - of the West End, public transport and after-theatre dining that didn't cost your soul.

Younger actors straight out of drama school were welcome at The Classic, usually starting out as very poorly paid box office clerks, ushers, and the occasional, extremely attractive script assistant. Ian liked the feeling of giving them a foothold on the very slippery ladder that most aspiring actors would never actually manage to climb. Several of his young team had though. He called them 'The Chameleons', because of their ability to transform themselves, to morph from faceless spear-carrier to black toothed addict and back to ingenue. Alison, or Ali as she preferred, was one of these.

After joining the troupe the previous season, she had done her time as usher, face in the crowd, chorus dancer, walk-on and had just been given her first named role. It was tiny: The 'Waiting Gentlewoman' who calls the doctor to Lady Macbeth. Scarcely on stage, many of the major characters had only the vaguest notion of who she was. But when she wrung her hands, you believed in her distress even as her mistress uttered some of the best-known lines in the play.

She was an uncomplicated person, open, friendly, and easily amused. She'd read English at Bristol before going on to drama school and she studied seriously each of the plays they put on. She expected to work hard at her chosen profession; she found it a delight. She adored what she did.

She'd been floating on air since being given the role and while she was only on in the final act, she was happy to help backstage throughout the rest of the play. She handed a soldier a sword, held number 3 witch's cardigan and commiserated with her about how cold it was during rehearsals. A very modern adaptation, Ian's witches didn't wear much. They really didn't need their blue makeup, the drafts on stage handled that. She did what was needed but also spent quite a lot of time sitting in the warmth of the curtained corridor of the wings, just observing and learning and worshipping from afar.

In her eyes, Ian could do no wrong. She had been a huge fan of his when he'd been with the Royal Shakespeare Company. Fliers from the Royal Court, the National and the Old Vic had been tacked up inside her desk at school, one showing Ian's face in sinister, shadowed profile, one his back bent under a prosthetic hump, another his head crowned in a fairy wreath. She'd applied to join The Classic pretty much straight out of drama school and now refused to hear a word of criticism against him.

"Yes, some of his earlier plays when he parted company with the RSC were… difficult. But they were ambitious and… brave! You must admit, brave!"

To her, it was Ian's hand that had reached down and pulled her up onto the professional stage. She felt that his eyes were on her, and she could count on his loyalty and support.

She really didn't know Ian.

To him she was almost faceless. He had no individual impression of any of his chameleons really. They were simply puppets. Coming alive under his fingers, they would live and die at his behest, and he would cut the strings, toss them away, without a shrug if they failed to live up to their perceived potential, or if someone better came along. What he saw in Ali was not a person, but a body that could make itself frail and small or transform, stretch somehow, into a much taller, determined figure. He saw a face that broadened, lengthened, tightened, or flattened at will. Eyes that shone with pleasure or darkened in misery or anger; hair that could be a deep, lustrous red one day and dry, limp, and mousy the next. He scarcely remembered her name.

Called in to rehearse, it had been a long and disappointing Sunday. Ian had been 'off' in some way. She couldn't put her finger on it, but the rest of the cast had picked up on his disconnect and were also not quite on point. The constant stops and starts had been frustrating and tiring but suddenly the atmosphere changed. Ali sat up. The timbre of the actors' voices changed. The pace picked up. She was electrified, fascinated. Ian had caught fire and was carrying his cast along with him. She couldn't wait to get on stage, to be a part of it all.

Just behind her a phone vibrated and then rang. Not too loudly, but the spell was broken, and she realised that while no one on stage had heard it yet, they soon would. Ian absolutely forbade the use of phones during rehearsals. If it broke his concentration now, there would be hell to pay. She looked around, found it, and grabbed.

"Come on," she growled, "come on. Switch off, damn you. Switch off!" But before she could find how to switch it off, a voice crackled through at the other end. *Oh God*, she thought, *switch off!* She didn't want to hear; her cue was coming up any minute. But a few words did half register.

"… Done… Over… Dead… Play your part." Her brain refused to understand…

"What the hell…?" she mouthed to herself. Then it finally switched off.

That's weird... Did he say…? He can't have meant... Wrong number? Must be. It's got to be a prank or a joke… Whose phone is it anyway?

"Hey! Gentlewoman," came a hiss from the wings. "No more waiting."

Ali pushed the mobile back where she had found it and promptly forgot about it. She closed her eyes, breathed out the present and became her part. She seemed to grow, to straighten and to age just a little. She joined Duncan, who was playing the Doctor of Physic, and together they stepped out onto the stage.

"I have two nights ***watched*** *with you,*
but can perceive no truth in your report.
When was it she last ***walked****?"*

Then together they observed the Queen of Scotland as she paced through her castle trying in vain to wash imaginary bloodstains from her hands - an accessory to, an instigator of unnatural deeds.

At the end of the act the dead were resurrected, the villains congratulated, and everyone milled around laughing, giddy and relieved that it had finally gelled and gone so well. Ian's Macbeth had positively reeked of blood tonight! He laughed at their enthusiasm, still high on adrenalin and not yet back in the real world.

"You lot go ahead," he said. "I'll join you for a nightcap – order me a whisky."

"You coming?" asked Duncan and Ali nodded.

"A quick one, but I'm bushed. I didn't think it would be a full run through. I thought we were just doing a tidy up. It's much later than I'd expected."

"Yep. Got the wind under his tail, our Master, and couldn't stop." Duncan was already halfway out of the door.

"Get a move on, Gentlewoman, or they'll close on us." She shrugged on her coat and grabbed her bag and was following when she heard Ian's voice.

"Where the fuck is my phone?"

She hesitated. "There's one just behind the wings," she called as she ran to catch up with the others.

It may not have been his phone, she thought. *If it was, he'll see when the call came in and realise what happened. I'm sure as hell not going to tell him what I thought I heard. He'd think I'd lost the plot!*

The pub was not only still serving when they got there, it was hopping. A perfect fit to their mood. Success had been snatched from the jaws of terminal boredom and they could sense a hit in the making. The drinks developed into celebrations and then looked set to turn into an all-night roar for those with the stamina to move on to food and clubs. Ali laughed and teased with the best of them, but when Ian arrived, blown in on his own post performance high, a hint of shadow touched her. She really was tired. She wanted to be home, in bed, with Tom. She downed her drink, mouthed a quiet goodbye to Duncan, sketched a half wave at the others and made her escape. It suddenly seemed a long way home and she was unusually aware of the darkness in the side streets and shadows on the main thoroughfares.

She'd texted Tom earlier to let him know that things were running late, so she wasn't surprised to find the flat quiet and mostly dark when she got in. He'd left side lights on for her, and a plate in the kitchen with a post-it-note on it. He'd drawn a large arrow and angled it so that it pointed to the microwave. In the corner - very small - was a *wry smile* emoji and a question mark - and a *x*. She gave a snuffle of laughter. Actually, she was starving. Risotto al funghi - perfect. It went down fast.

There was another post-it on the bathroom mirror reading simply 7.30. *Damn!* That meant he had an early start in the morning and would really prefer not to be woken. Ali had learned that adrenalin-fuelled enthusiasm when she got in from the theatre just didn't work for Tom. His job was also built around glamour and dreams, but in the more practical world of the automobile. Tom took the Grizabellas of the auto trade and brushed them with stardust, magicking their gleam and lustre back into being, and fitted for the 21st century. The extravagant emotions of the thespian world weren't for him. Ali loved his pragmatism and good sense. He grounded her.

She'd really wanted that good sense tonight. The voice on the phone had spooked her and she wanted Tom to exorcise it for her, laugh it away. Well, it would have to wait. She stripped off, made do with a lick and a promise and slipped into bed. His body next to her, warm and heavy with sleep, was going to have to be comfort enough for now. When she woke, he was gone. More post-its, giving her his schedule for the day and plans for a theatre free evening with a question mark. All with the tiny *x* in the corner that still raised her heartbeat a fraction and the corner of her mouth a little more, the ghosts of yesterday forgotten.

*   *   *   *   *

A New Start!

Susan Cross shivered as she got out of her old Polo in the Centre's parking lot. The heater wasn't working again so it had been a chilly drive. She knew it was probably time she replaced it with something newer, but she was fond of it. She tightened her coat against the wind.

It was a bright, sunny morning, but the warmth of the Indian summer they had been enjoying seemed to have leached away with last night's rain. Still, it looked promising and the temperature could come up quite quickly if the sky stayed clear.

Over by the entrance, she spotted someone waiting for her. One of the "M&M's", the nickname that had attached itself to her two DC's, Sean Murphy, and Stuart MacLean. They were both just over six feet, a policeman's height, she thought, and both with fair hair and blue eyes. Not for the first time she wondered how Sean came by that colouring from an apparently Irish ancestry. *Perhaps his mother had Nordic blood.*

This one, though, was Stuart, whose Scottish ancestors she had decided must have tried their luck as mercenaries in Eastern Europe after Bonnie Prince Charlie's ill fated 'forty-five' rebellion.

"'Morning, Ma'am," said Stuart as she stepped onto the pavement. "We've got an early one today – sounds nasty. Sean went off about half an hour ago with the FP. She seemed pretty keen to get there. Anticipating a challenge perhaps."

How very different her life was now. Could it really be just three months ago that the DCI had walked into DI Featherstone's second floor squad room and pulled her career out of the toilet? Her mind drifted…

*   *   *   *   *

"Hullo! Something's up."

The hiss from a neighbouring desk had Susan looking up with interest when Detective Chief Inspector Robert Gordon entered the squad room. Everyone else in the room had clocked him too, a strong looking man dressed smartly in a well-fitting navy suit. Dark hair just starting to show silver along the edges, he looked both distinguished and successful.

Well, she wasn't assigned to him, so it was someone else's headache. She had enough troubles of her own. She sighed as she looked back down at the file on a spate of robberies at mid-range jewellery shops that had been plaguing the channel towns along the coast over the past few months.

These should have been handled locally. It's far too early to pass them up to Region.

A report had gone out detailing the items stolen, and a quick local response had found none of it turning up in known pawnbrokers' or antique dealers' stock. None of the usual informants seemed to know anything either. She sighed again. It was pretty obvious why Featherstone had assigned them to her. Another opportunity to put a failing mark on her file.

It was the sudden silence, followed by a discreet cough that had made her look up - straight into the face of the DCI, who had come to a halt in front of her desk.

"Sergeant Cross," he said. "I'd like to see you in my office. Now, if you wouldn't mind?" He turned and walked back towards the door, scarcely waiting to see if she was following.

What have I done now?

Gordon led the way up the stairs to the third floor and into another squad room, this one marked 'Major Crimes Unit'.

Susan saw a squad room similar to the one they'd just left – if somewhat larger. Several young men were sitting at desks, tapping away at computers, and another was talking quietly on the phone. There were two glass-walled offices down each of the two window sides, sandwiching the DCI's office in the corner. Gordon moved straight behind his desk and gestured towards one of the chairs facing him.

"Close the door, would you?" he asked in a quiet voice, "and have a seat." Sitting down behind his desk, he studied her. He knew from her file that she was in her late twenties. The picture there showed a bright, vibrant young woman, with expressive green eyes. The woman now sitting opposite looked neither bright nor vibrant. She was quite tall, but hunching over, making herself appear shorter than she was. She looked trim and fit, an attractive woman, but was she deliberately muting her looks? She was all greys and browns, charcoal grey slacks, a light grey shirt, and a long, slate grey and brown cardigan. Her hair was light brown now too, no blond highlights as in her photograph, and pulled across her face as if to hide it. But those surprisingly keen green eyes were unchanged and were looking back at him questioningly. She sat silently, waiting for him to speak. There was an air of hopelessness about her that made him unusually brusque.

"Sergeant Cross," he said. "You passed the sergeant's exam with flying colours six months ago. You were brought up to Region in the expectation you would soon be leading one of our teams on significant cases. But your DI has you working minor cases that shouldn't even be handled at Region. He claims that you are a disappointment and unlikely to progress any further. Why is that?"

Susan waited quietly. She had dreamed of a career as a police detective since she was little more than a child. It had all started so well too. Was it ending already?

"That wasn't a rhetorical question, Sergeant." She could hear irritation in his voice. "Your career path should have you working on important cases where your ability would be a major asset. What has happened to the nascent superstar we thought we were getting?"

"I don't know what to say," she said finally, flatly "Wouldn't DI Featherstone be the person to answer that?"

Gordon waited a moment, clearly hoping for a little more. When he went on his voice was gentler. "I've been looking at your staff reviews, Sergeant. DI Morley in Maidstone rated you as highly capable. It was his opinion you would sail through the exam - as you subsequently did. In fact, you passed with the highest marks in this entire region. Now I am being told that you are unlikely to achieve much at all. What has happened to you?"

She sighed. "I really can't say, Sir. I don't get along with DI Featherstone's people - or with DI Featherstone, for that matter. I just don't," she said tiredly and with a faint touch of bitterness. "I asked DI Featherstone to assign me more challenging cases, but he said I had to prove that I was ready." Gordon remained silent, one eyebrow raised in question. "Oh," she added, "there may have been a bit more to it than that, but nothing that I haven't come across before. I hoped I could just wait it out."

"I see", said Gordon, and he was pretty sure he did. Silence reigned while he continued to look at her appraisingly, that eyebrow still raised. "You don't want to add anything to that?" She hesitated, then shook her head. "I see," he said again and silence descended once more. Then he had sat forward again, and for the first time, surprised her.

"Damned if I'm going to waste an officer of your potential," he said almost angrily, "I'll make up my own mind as to which appraisal is correct. Morley's or Featherstone's. You came with stellar recommendations. You may simply be in the wrong place to display your ability." A pause, then "I'm transferring you to our group up here on third, where I can monitor your progress myself." She blinked.

"DS Jones has moved on to the vacant Inspector position in Folkestone, leaving his team short of a leader. I want that to be you. DI Morley reckons that you are up to it. Says he can't understand what's happened. But he tells me I won't regret this, so don't let either of us down. Your appointment to Major Crimes takes effect immediately."

Susan sat up, those green eyes suddenly wide.

"Don't expect to have much personal time over the next few weeks. I want you signed up on a couple of external courses. You'll be handling tougher, much more public cases, so you need to get your interpersonal skills dusted off. You'll need them to motivate and lead your team, and for dealing with the public and the press.

"Clear out your desk in Featherstone's squad. Hand over whatever you were doing to DS Smith. Then come back and see me. You will be in the office at the end, on the right. You can introduce yourself to your team tomorrow. There are just two of them at present, but you'll find both are very good. Their personnel files will be on your desk." He paused and leaned forward again.

"You may feel that you're being thrown in at the deep end." He shrugged. "You are! You're six months behind where you should be. I'll be watching you carefully, Susan. Don't disappoint me."

She sat quite still, looking at him blankly. "I thought I was being fired," she said. She felt dazed, like a rabbit caught in the headlights of an oncoming car.

"Not yet," he said, amused. "Get your things. Come back and see me at 16:00."

She gathered her wits, got up and made for the door. Turning back, she smiled and her whole face lit up, the woman in the photograph shining through.

"Thank you, sir. You won't regret this. I won't let you down."

The difference between DCI Gordon's squad and Featherstone's had been dramatic. The DCI didn't accept minor crimes. Those went straight back to the local stations with suggestions on how they might proceed. His staff had no time to waste on the small stuff. In just a few weeks she'd already worked two suspicious deaths, and the staff - especially her own two detective constables - were grades above Featherstone's in competence, in attitude and in their sheer work ethics. That made an enormous difference to how a case could be handled.

*   *   *   *   *

"Sergeant?"

She shook herself out of it. "Sorry, Stuart. What was that?"

"I asked if it would be your car or mine, or both?"

"Oh... We'll take yours. Pick me up at the front in a few minutes, will you? I need a coffee. Still a bit sleepy this morning."

The DC nodded and set off across the car park. Susan turned and hurried inside, making for the coffee shop near the main entrance. This was one of the many advantages of working in one of the new model Police Centres where, in a bid to present a friendlier face to the public, small coffee shops had been built just off the reception area with a barista serving a variety of drinks and snacks; easily accessible and attractive to both public and staff.

Susan hurried in. Since joining Major Crimes, and particularly since resolving two killings, she had become a familiar face, and the barista knew exactly how she liked her coffee.

"Good morning, Sergeant Cross," he said smiling. "You are looking good this morning! I think you have new hair? Si? And those brighter colours suit you."

She smiled. "Thank you, Sergio. The usual, please. Make it a large one. We've just had a call out."

"The one near Tonbridge?" he asked, as the steam whistled and bubbled in the pot of milk. "Everyone has heard about that. It is bad, I think."

"Well, I don't know yet" she said. "But it sounds like I'm going to need that coffee!"

"For you, Sergeant! On your tab?"

"Yes please, Sergio." She waved her thanks and hurried out. Stuart's smart little Peugeot was waiting, and she pushed her coat and briefcase over into the back before lowering herself gently into the passenger seat, careful not to spill a single drop of her coffee. Sitting back, she took a sip.

"Oh God!" she sighed, "I needed this... OK, Stuart, let's go".

* * * * *

"Late night last night, Ma'am?" Stuart ventured, a bit hesitantly. He was still a little unsure of his new DS, even after several weeks on her team. She seemed to be a good person to work with. She had certainly proved herself competent on the two cases they'd handled. What's more, she was more than willing to give her team credit for the results. But still… There were those rumours, supposedly from people she'd worked with before, and how had she earned the nickname 'Crosspatch'? He hadn't found her difficult or bad tempered, but he was still going to tread carefully - especially if she *was* sleeping with the DCI as the rumours suggested. Not that he'd seen any signs of that, either, unless that was the reason for the late night.

Susan took another swallow of her coffee, shut her eyes, and sighed again. "Yes. I'm taking a night course in 'Personal Communications Skills' at the local college. The DCI wants to be sure that I can open my mouth without offending anyone, I suppose. It's to do with the poison about me that's bubbled up from DI Featherstone's bunch." She gave a short laugh and took another sip of coffee. "When this one's finished, it's going to be 'Public Speaking'. So there will be quite a lot of late nights in the next few weeks. She laughed again, "But he's the boss. He can send me on any course he wants."

"I'd have thought he'd be pretty pleased with what you've done so far, Ma'am." He flicked his eyes across to her and chanced a smile. "I haven't had anyone commiserating with me about my 'new sergeant' recently… well, other than your previous lot. They just can't seem to let it go. Those idiots are starting to look a bit stupid."

"Thanks. But one messed up case and it'll all start again. So, let's make sure we get this one right. What do we know so far?"

"Right," said Stuart. "999 got a call about eight o'clock, a woman screaming blue murder! There had been sightings of a vagrant prowling about the area the night before, and she'd wanted to warn her neighbour to lock the house if she went out. She tried phoning. No answer. Her friend's car was there, so she thought she'd pop over and talk to her directly. The front door was open. No sign of her in the garden, so she went in and as no one was around downstairs either, she went upstairs and found the body in the bathroom. Blood everywhere apparently. She started screaming, and couldn't stop… Exchange called out a Panda from Tonbridge. They confirmed a DB in the bathroom and have contained the scene.

"The FP went out right away, and Sean went too. Her team will be a bit behind them."

As he finished, his phone beeped with an incoming text. "Could you get that, please, Ma'am?"

Susan pulled the phone from its mount, saw a new text was showing, and opened it.

"It's Sean. He hopes we both have strong stomachs. Nice! How far out are we?"

"Ten minutes on the GPS. Nettle Lane. One of those quiet little roads outside Tonbridge. Expensive. What my father used to call the Stockbroker Belt."

"If it was the prowler, he probably hasn't got very far, and we can wrap this up quickly. But I have a feeling it's going to be more than that."

*   *   *   *   *

Team Crosspatch

Stuart's Peugeot hurried down the country lanes, a small blue light flashing above the roof and reflecting off the tall hedges towering high along the banked edges of the road. It was part of the charm of this part of England: a rural setting, but barely five minutes from the town of Tonbridge, on one of the main routes to the coast, with an excellent train service that linked into the centre of London in under an hour.

Which is what makes it so ruddy expensive, he thought. They passed picturesque cottages, old farm houses and a few more modern buildings with straight lines, dark red brick and lots of glass. Any one of those would swallow his whole salary for the next ten years, he thought, and still leave him with a massive mortgage! He shrugged, *not for me*, and then he grinned, *well not unless I robbed a bank!*

"We must be nearly there?" Susan shook her head and took a long drink of her coffee. *Wake up*, she told herself. *Wake up!*

"Almost," said Stuart, and sure enough they came around a bend to see a group of cars pulled up onto the verge outside a sizeable property on the right. The gate was open, and a uniformed PC signalled to them to pull into the drive. There was a smart Lexus hatchback outside the garage, and Stuart parked next to it. Susan recognised one of the two other cars as Sean Murphy's Subaru.

The PC approached. She was small, almost slight, wearing a uniform that looked brand new and freshly starched.

"Sergeant Cross?" she asked as Susan struggled up and out of the little car. "I'm PC Varma. DC Murphy asked me to keep an eye out for you. He and the FP are up at the house."

Susan thanked her and walked up the drive, past the double garage, to the front door. Ellie Richardson, a slim, usually elegant lady, was crouched on the doorstep in pale blue crime scene coveralls, her face almost grey in the sunlight. DC Sean Murphy, was standing beside her, also wearing the required coveralls, and looking just as pale and shaken. They both looked up, but there were no welcoming smiles.

"Morning, Ma'am," This from DC Murphy. "A bad one."

The FP pushed herself up from her seat on the front steps. "Hello, Susan," she said grimly, "One of the worst I've seen."

Susan looked down at her, concerned. "It must be bad if you both needed a breath of fresh air!"

Ellie nodded and gave something that tried to be a smile. "You can have a good look before I start. My team isn't here yet."

Stuart walked up behind Susan and passed her a crime scene pack. Plastic booties, a blue plastic jumpsuit complete with hood, and surgical gloves. He suited up too. Quicker at it than Susan, he walked over to the door and picked up a spray can lying discarded by the step.

"Bitch Spray," he read. Turning to Sean, he asked "Was there a dog in the house?"

"Haven't seen one. What's that?"

"It's 'Bitch Spray'. If you have a bitch in heat, you spray it on her when you take her for a walk. That way you don't wind up with a pack of dogs following you all the way. It disguises the smell. Someone here has - or had - a dog. Or rather, a bitch. It's not something just anyone would have."

"God, where do you get all this from? Glad I'm on your side on Quiz Night!"

Stuart grinned. "We haven't been beaten yet!" Then to Sergeant Cross, "Should we take a look, Ma'am?"

He went in first, looked towards the stairs, and went up carefully. Susan was a few yards behind with Ellie and Sean. Entering the house, she was struck by how attractive it was. It had clearly been put together by someone with considerable talent. She went into the dining area first. A quiet, simple part of the larger, modern, open plan room with a long, limed oak table and chairs for eight. Nothing flashy. Just nice. She put her briefcase on the end of the table and turned back to the stairs.

She reached the top just as Stuart lurched backwards, gagging. Aware she was watching, he cleared his throat noisily, said "Right, then," and strode back into the bathroom, Susan right behind.

It was like stepping into a nightmare. The house had been spotless, well ordered and comfortable; the bathroom was anything but. And in the chaos - a body in the bath. A woman, very attractive from the neck up, stared sightlessly at the far wall, her face half submerged. From the shoulders down there was nothing easily recognisable. No shape, no form. Just torn flesh, meat, bone - *oh God, are those intestines*? - in a chaotic mash to the top of her hips. Splashed with blood, the legs seemed otherwise untouched; one with the knee slightly bent, the foot jammed under the tap, the other straight out - the foot over the end of the bath, scarlet nails shocking against scarlet water. No wonder the neighbour hadn't been able to do much more than scream!

Susan slowed her breath, steadied herself and looked around. The blood on the floor would have splashed from the bath, but over near the basin, there was a large smear of blood on the wall. Closing her eyes, she pictured it... The killer raging, hacking at the victim until he'd exhausted himself, then falling back, sitting, slumped against the wall, getting his breath back. Then what? There were words scrawled on the mirror, **'Fuck all rich pigs'**, apparently written in the victim's blood?

Oh great! *Well, that's a pretty pathetic attempt to lead us down a blind alley.* But it couldn't be ignored.

The murder weapon? No doubt at all this was murder. If they were lucky, the knife would still be in the bath, but she doubted it.

She saw the burned down candles on the shelf above the bath, the little bottle of oil still on the cabinet, the whisky tumbler, the discarded kimono, the elegant crane now trampled in water and blood. In the near silence, she could hear a tune wafting quietly through the house. *Is that really Acker Bilk?* Before her time, but she knew it. "Stranger on the Shore." It had been one of her grandfather's favourites, he'd played it for her often when she was a child. Poor woman; she'd been treating herself to a quiet evening at home, unaware of the horror closing in.

A shaving kit on one side of the vanity unit, two toothbrushes, two glasses … there'd be men's clothes in the wardrobe. *She had a partner… husband maybe, but she'd been alone… or had she? Things to look into.*

"OK," she said. "Let's leave Ellie to her job here. We'll regroup downstairs. Sean, check the bedrooms. Evidence of other people in the house, please, and look for any signs of burglary. Stuart, you take the downstairs rooms. We'll need to know all the ins and outs of this poor woman's life. I'll give the DCI a quick update."

Susan headed back down the stairs, turning into the dining area at the bottom. She sat down at the table, opened her briefcase, drew out her tablet and keyed in her initial thoughts on the case. Pulling her mobile out of her pocket, she almost dropped it when it suddenly vibrated in her hand and the DCI's ringtone sounded. She answered.

"Good morning, Sir. I was just about to call you. I'm on site at Nettle Lane."

"Morning, Susan," from DCI Gordon. "Yes, I know about it. I'm trying to establish some basic facts on the case at this end.

"The address gave us the probable name of the victim. Laura Handley-Davison is listed as the owner. You'll need to confirm that as soon as you can. You probably recognise the name… No? She's the 'Laura' behind the boutiques of that name. I put a routine query into the National Database to download whatever we know of her.

Her husband is Ian Davison, well known as an actor and director in the theatre world. But, as soon as I put her name in, a number of flags went up and within minutes I had DCI Crawford of the Organised Crimes Division at the Yard on the line."

"Organised Crime? Really?"

"Yes. Although the lady herself hasn't triggered any suspicions, her father is Sir Gerald Handley, and it turns out that he *is* under watch. He's a senior director at one of the Investment Banks. They haven't been able to pin anything on him, but they are certain he's in bed with one of the London mobs. Davison is on the watch list too - associated with the same mob. Crawford doesn't believe Davison is actually aware of the connection though. Something to do with unorthodox financing."

"Interesting!"

"Yes. Crawford is worried that if the victim is Sir Gerald's daughter it might cause ructions amongst the local gangs. He's not going to step in and take over the case, but he wants to be kept in the loop. If you do unearth connections to Organised Crime, I'm sure he will get involved. We'll play that as it comes. For now, he wants all reports copied to him, but his interest is to remain confidential. Your team needs to be aware that some very violent people may be involved, though."

"The killer was certainly extremely violent, Sir."

"Yes. Worrying. I'm making you joint SIO on this. I'm going to take an oversight role, but I want you to keep me updated daily on the direction and progress of your investigation. Now tell me, what do you have so far?"

She was silent for a moment, assimilating what she'd just been told.

"Well, it seems to have been staged as a 'burglary gone wrong'," she started. "There are reports of a tramp seen skulking about the neighbourhood yesterday, and the neighbour who found the body certainly assumed that he must be the killer. But there's no sign of forced entry into the house, nor of burglary. If it *was* a burglary, the intruder knew exactly what he wanted, and made sure not to disturb anything else. But the murder wasn't careful or methodical. This was rage and... butchery. It looks personal to me." She paused "I recommend that we make a show of following up on the tramp story but start investigating elsewhere. We need to know a lot more about both the victim's and her husband's background to see what else pops up. For starters, where was the husband?"

"That's a good approach, Susan. Let the killer think we've bought the 'Tramp' theory. It'll keep the phones in the incident room buzzing for days, though! Keep me informed of everything you find. I'll have PR issue a statement that we are investigating a suspicious death, and that we're looking for a vagrant who has been seen in the area as a 'Person of Interest'.

"I'll handle notifying the husband for you, wherever he is. As soon as you have a positive identification, have someone call me. I'll get on to it. That will save you a few hours, and I do think we need to move fast on this. There's going to be a lot of pressure building up to get a result here, both from the press and top brass. I'm afraid it rather puts you in the spotlight."

"Understood. We'll get the positive ID. And we'll keep you informed, Sir.

"Thank you," she added, before punching out. Then she called up the stairs to M&M to join her in the dining room.

"OK," she said as they sat down," I've spoken to the DCI, and he has some interesting things to add. Most important, the victim's name raised some flags in the PND, so we have to be careful. As far as the press are concerned, we're going to roll with the idea that it was a tramp who got in last night. We'll play up the message left on the bathroom mirror - so someone with a deep chip on his shoulder!"

Both DCs nodded. It was the obvious first step and gave them cover while they looked for something shadowy in either Laura's life, or her husband's. Someone had been very upset with Laura. Very upset indeed! Would that tally with the possible violent gang connection? They sat at the table for a good half an hour, swapping theories of what it could have been.

"Where's her husband?"

"Don't know, but it won't be difficult to find him. The man lives in the public eye."

"Do either of you know anything about him?"

Sean, an avid theatre buff, did.

"I've kept an eye on his career - he's something a bit different. He was a really well-known actor a few years back. Looked to be on track to be a leading light in the Royal Shakespeare Company. There was talk of TV and films, but he turned down at least two good roles. Said he wanted to keep to the stage. But he was also attracting a reputation as someone who didn't take direction well. Then he went quiet for a couple of years before re-appearing with his own theatre company. They did some very avant-garde plays, but even with his name behind them, they didn't go down well.

"I went to one. Very posh and intellectual, but frankly the play was boring. Too clever by half. I didn't bother so much after that. I heard he went broke, but his wife bailed him out. Since then, he's been doing mostly classics and seems to be getting by.

"When you think about it," he said, "he owes Laura. No reason for him to want to get rid of her, surely?"

"I don't know," said Susan. "Gratitude can be a hair shirt - it chafes. If Laura kept reminding him that she'd had to bail him out and he'd come to resent it, that could be a motive.

"Anyway, interesting background. Sean, you take that one. It sounds as though you might have connections that can give us some insight into what's going on at the theatre. Stuart, you take a look at Laura's business affairs. See if anything smells off there. But a warning; stay clear of anything to do with her father, Sir Gerald Handley. If anything relates back to him, stop right there, and bring it to me! The DCI is handling anything that may involve him. Apparently, he's a bigwig with one of the Investment Banks, and wields a lot of clout."

"Right."

"Gotcha".

"I want to see how the search for the tramp is going. I'll grab a ride back to the Centre with one of you later, but I'm going to look around a bit before we leave. First though, one of you go round to the neighbour who found the body. She was apparently a friend, so ask if she can give us a positive ID. If she can confirm it is Laura in that bath, please phone the DCI directly."

"I'll do that", said Stuart, getting up. "I could use some air."

Standing up, Susan stretched. Good thing she didn't have another class tonight. She'd need her wits about her while this case was hot - and it would likely get *very* hot before they closed it out. A violent mob hit made sense, given the state of the body, and yet she couldn't shake the sense of something closer to home. They would all need to be very careful, indeed.

"Look, go together. Just on the off chance that we do have a violent killer lurking around, no one should be on their own. I'll borrow PC Varma from outside."

She walked out into the front garden. The sun was bright and it was already quite a bit warmer. She breathed in the fresh air, gratefully. Ellie's team had arrived and put up their tent in the middle of the lawn. The FP was with them. Susan walked over.

"Are you going to bring the body out?" she asked.

"Yes, we're just discussing it. It's going to be a job to get all the bits together for the autopsy, Susan. He's pretty much cut her in half."

"Any preliminary conclusions, Ellie?"

"Well, she's been throttled, but I don't think that killed her. The signs for that aren't showing. Indications are she was simply stabbed many, many times. I'd say a really big knife, probably with a serrated edge on one side. Any of the wounds could have been fatal. The killer will have been right-handed, probably very tall and very powerful. I'm sorry I can't be precise right now. I can't even venture at a time of death because the bath water would have been hot to begin with. I've taken measurements, and I should be able to give you at least an approximation once I get everything back to the mortuary. Oh, I've arranged to use the one in South London. I may need some help piecing the body back together. It could take days! I'll have everything in my report, and I'll get it to you just as soon as I can."

"OK. Let me know when you're ready. I'll come by when you have something definite. You didn't find the weapon in the bath, did you?"

Ellie shook her head. "No. Bastard must have taken it away with him. He's either dumped it somewhere else or it's miles away by now."

Ellie took Susan by the arm and lowered her voice. "There's something about this killing that's ringing bells, Susan. Not sure what it is. But it'll come to me."

"What? You don't think he's done this before? I know it's not your job to say but you've seen so many different killings, and I know you're a bit of a detective at heart."

“Mmm…” said Ellie hesitantly. “Do I think he’s done this before? No. I’d say this murder is unique. I follow what’s been happening around the country, and I’m sure there hasn’t been another like this. But something is nagging at me. Give me a day or two to think about it.” She turned back to organising the process of removing the body.

Susan looked around. There was a different constable controlling traffic along the lane now. He was sitting on the bank under the hedge. She walked towards him and waved him over.

“Miss?” he asked. “If you’re parked along the lane, you need to move on now. There’ll be a press release this afternoon letting everyone know what’s happened here.”

“I’m DS Cross, Constable,” she corrected him. “I’m the SIO on site for now, and no, I’m not parked along the lane. I understand that a search has been launched for the tramp who was reported loitering around here. Who’s organising that?”

“Crosspa…? Ah... Er, Sergeant Davis is running the search, but he went back to Tonbridge to get things organised from there, Ma’am. He left me and PC Varma to keep traffic moving and to check around the area to see if the tramp dumped anything when he ran away.”

“I see,” said Susan. “And have you found anything?”

“I sent PC Varma to check the ditches and look through the dustbins along the lane. I’ve been keeping the traffic moving along here.” Susan looked up and down the empty lane.

"Well you've certainly managed to keep traffic moving, Constable. Don't you think it might have been better for the two of you to keep together with a killer on the loose?"

The constable looked at her in consternation. "Well, there's no sign of him. I expect he's miles away by now, I mean, why would he hang around?"

"A fair question, Constable, but a dangerous assumption." She sighed. "Which way did she go?"

He hesitated, then pointed further on down the lane. "That way."

"Thank you, Constable", she said. "Please resume your duties. We wouldn't want a traffic jam, would we?" and she set off down the lane.

Around the corner she came to another cottage, older and much smaller than Laura's, with a bleached brown thatched roof, and a small front garden. There was an elderly lady pottering about, apparently unfazed by the dramas around her and quietly weeding a flowerbed that looked as if it hadn't seen a weed in years. *It's like a bloody postcard*, Susan thought.

"Excuse me," she called, "have you seen a policewoman come by?"

The lady looked up from her flowerbed. "Oh, hello dear," she called back. "Yes, she was here only a little while ago." She got up slowly and walked carefully over to the gate. "She wanted to look through my dustbin. It was about the murder. She seemed to think the tramp that killed poor Laura might have thrown something away here. I let her look

- she asked so politely - but I told her that if I were a killer on the run, I'd want to dispose of my weapon a little further away. I suggested she try down the lane a bit. There's a lay-by further along with one of those big steel containers for rubbish in it. We always get rid of anything nasty there because the dustmen don't empty our bins very often and it's hard to keep the lids on all the time. Foxes, you know... The smell can get quite overpowering." She finally stopped for breath.

"Thank you. That's very helpful. I'll go and see if she's down there," said Susan quickly, making her escape before the would-be Miss Marple could speculate further. And some minutes later, there it was, the lay-by, and as she'd been told, a large yellow skip. There was no sign of PC Varma, but as she got closer, she heard scuffling noises coming from inside. Smiling to herself, she got up on her toes and looked in. There, of course, was PC Varma, her uniform no longer so crisp and new.

"What are you up to, PC Varma?" she asked." You look like a Hollywood swamp monster!" Constable Varma looked up at her.

"I'm looking to see if the murderer has thrown anything away," she said rather stiffly.

"Have you found anything?"

"Well, yes, I think I have," came the surprising reply. "There's a jacket here, and a shirt, and they're all covered in blood - well, I think it's blood. It looks like someone tried to hide them underneath this rotting ... stuff."

Susan was suddenly hyper alert. “Well done, Constable. Can you pass them out to me?”

PC Varma shoved a couple of evil looking heaps aside - *Oh God,* thought Susan, *I don’t even want to think about what that could be. It smells awful!* - and stood up. She pushed a jacket and a blue shirt out to Susan. Sure enough, both were stiff with dried blood - *ugh, not all dried* - and something unspeakably revolting was draped around them. It stank. She took them gingerly and laid them down by the hedge.

“Can you get out?” she asked.

“Yes, I think so,” came the reply, and Varma launched herself upwards in a surprisingly strong leap, grabbing the edge of the skip and rolling over the top. But as she did so her safety vest snagged a hinge on the top, putting her into an uncontrolled tumble. Susan lunged forwards and managed to catch her as she fell but couldn’t maintain her balance and they both went down in a heap. Untangling themselves, they got up and looked at each other.

“PC Varma,” said Susan, “you’re a mess.”

Varma looked down at her once pristine uniform and then looked back at her “I’m really sorry Sergeant Cross,” she said, “but there’s a lot of it on you too, now!” The two women looked at each other for a moment and then burst out laughing.

“Right”, said Susan. She was feeling a little lightheaded, *Blood sugar running low!* “I think we need the cavalry, don’t you?”

“The cavalry, Ma’am?”

"I'm going to call my team to get down here and help," she explained. "It won't take long."

She hit DC Murphy's quick dial number. "Sean?" she asked breezily when he answered, "It's Crosspatch. I'm at a lay-by, a quarter of a mile or so down the lane. I need you with your car. Bring several extra-large evidence bags and borrow a couple of blankets from the medics. Oh, yes... And you can bring that idiot constable who is pretending to control traffic in the lane, too. I've got a much better job for him."

* * * * *

Sean looked across at Stuart. "That was Crosspatch… She called *herself* Crosspatch, mind… She wants me to take my car to a lay-by down the lane. She wants evidence bags, and blankets. She must have found something."

"Sounds like it," said Stuart. "What else did she want?"

"The constable who's poncing around out front. Says she has a job for him."

"I'll get him, and I'll follow you as soon as I confirm the victim's ID to the DCI."

* * * * *

DCI Gordon hadn't been wasting any time that morning. He'd set aside Conference room 3 as an incident room and arranged for extra phones and computers, one with an extra-large screen. He'd co-opted DC Dave Crewe from Bob Stevenson's team; He also had two competent uniformed staff, Helen Jarvis and Scotty MacPherson, to man the phones, and help with any research they needed, and he'd arranged for others to do the same after hours.

The first thing was to check CCTV to see if it could show where the victim's husband had been at the time of the murder. There were no cameras on Nettle Lane, but if he hadn't been at home then he may have been at the theatre - and there were sure to be some near there. He set Constable Jarvis to reviewing camera locations to see if they could find any sign of him.

Davison's new production was to open in barely two weeks so despite it being a Sunday, the cast had been rehearsing, and had run late that night. PC Jarvis found a camera that picked up the alley to the side of the theatre and gave a good view of the stage door. Shortly before 9:30 pm the actors were seen streaming out and along the road towards a pub. Ian Davison followed shortly afterwards and joined them. Further follow up through two other cameras showed he had stayed there with them until they all emerged again and set off in several directions. Probably too late for Davison to have got home and murdered his wife.

*   *   *   *   *

The Police are here!

Ian had spent the night at his old flat - or what was left of the night after the last of his cast and crew had slumped across the table and slurred a need for home. He had kept his flat in Pimlico as an in-town stopover and he used it regularly during runs or periods of intensive rehearsal. He'd sent a text to Laura's phone earlier in the evening.

"Really sorry darling, late one tonight. Staying at Dolphin Square." He didn't know whether she had picked it up or not. He'd always played the part of the loving husband well, as he did all his roles. He swallowed two aspirins, drank a mug of water, and wove his way to bed.

Not enough hours later his alarm went off. His head told him that the celebrations had been good. He got up carefully and put a pod in the Nespresso machine on his way to the loo. Two espressos later he was ready to face the world. He defrosted a croissant from the freezer and started to chew. Memories were surfacing, and with them came the feeling that something was not quite right.

"Christ!" He was suddenly wide-awake. He grabbed his mobile from the docking station, stared into it and it came to life. No messages. Nothing from Laura or anyone else. He walked over to the window, looked out and thought. He finished the croissant and wiped his hands on his dressing gown. Then he picked up the phone again and went into recent calls. There had been a call, but not a missed one. His phone had been answered while he'd been on stage. The call had lasted 13 seconds. Who the hell had it been from? Who the hell had taken it? He tried calling, but there was no answer, and after a few pointless attempts, he gave up and left a guarded message.

"Hey!" His voice upbeat and casual. "All good? Speak soon." Then he braced himself to take his usual cold shower, struggled into black jeans and sweater and joined the crowds on the underground. He was at Elephant and Castle before he'd done much more than open the Guardian and scan the headlines. *Nothing to frighten the horses there*, he thought, relieved. When he nodded a cool 'Morning Phil' to the stage door man and went through to his office he was almost back to his usual self.

They hadn't done notes after the rehearsal last night, so he called them all onto stage and started going through them now. No one was surprised that the earlier scenes were being found wanting, but they listened and nodded and tried out a few of his revisions and were getting through it all at a good pace. It was well into the afternoon when Anna, his latest decoration, came down through the stalls to the stage and pulled him aside.

"The police are here, Ian!" It was the best line she'd ever had, and she was delivering it rather well. A hint of nerves, discretion in front of the cast, but efficient and compelling. "They need to speak to you. Now."

There was a sudden silence and then a buzz of noise. Ian leapt to his feet and shouted. "Take a break everyone. I'll just check what this is about. Be right back," and he was off, taking the steps two at a time, Anna in tow, asking her, urgently if she knew what they wanted.

DCI Gordon and DC Crewe were waiting in the foyer. Gordon recognised Davison immediately. He and

Elizabeth had seen him in a Pinter production a few years earlier; rather a good one. He hadn't changed much. Gordon put out his hand, aware that what he had to say was about to change this man's life forever. It was never easy to break the news of a death, harder in the case of murder. He gave his name and introduced his companion.

Davison looked at the two men and smiled. It was an open, trusting smile, slightly hesitant, a question and concern behind his eyes.

"How can I help you?" he asked. "Shall we go into my office? Coffee?" He half turned… "Anna, could you…?" Gordon nodded very slightly and followed him through into a simple room, with a desk and several chairs pushed back at random. They sat and as quickly as he could, he pushed through the usual precursors to the grim finality of his announcement. Davison stared and for a long moment, there was silence.

"I'm so sorry." Gordon spoke simply, but the emotion in the words was palpable. *If it were Elizabeth, if he were the husband being told his wife was dead...?*

"How? When? You're sure - no mistake?" It was a scene that rarely differed, despite the people and the circumstances. But then shock would begin to take over and that was less predictable.

"Is there anyone you'd like to call, Mr. Davison?" the DCI paused.

Davison had pushed himself up from his chair. He looked older than he had just minutes ago, his hands shook a little as he grasped the edge of the desk and leaned against it. His voice failed at first, then he coughed a little, straightened up and appeared to be trying to smile. He shook his head.

"You understand, also, that there are certain questions we must ask in these situations? I know they may seem cruel, but they are necessary." Davison nodded. "Can you tell us where you were last night, sir?"

"Of course, yes. We were rehearsing quite late. We were all here, and then we dropped by a local pub afterwards. Celebration, you know. Things were starting to come together. Then I stayed at the flat." He saw the question in their eyes.

"I have a flat in town," he clarified. "I stay there when things get late." Then he seemed to run down, sag a little, looking lost.

"Can you give us the address, Mr. Davison?"

"What? Oh, yes, of course. Just ask Anna." Looking around, he seemed to register where he was. "Look, we're in the middle of a rehearsal. I'll have to speak to the cast." Anna had reappeared with a tray of coffees - she was standing quite still in the doorway.

"Anna." He turned towards her, and she started, visibly. "Leave the coffees. Get them back on stage for me darling? And then give the Inspector the address of my flat in Pimlico." He was suddenly fizzing with energy. He reached out to Gordon and grasped his hand. "Is that all for the moment? I'll be here when you need me, Inspector – no - Chief inspector, wasn't it? - I'm sorry. Shock."

His eyes glistened, but his handshake was firm again as he clenched his teeth and lifted his chin. "I'll – well. I'll just be here."

They watched him walk slowly and then pick up speed as he made his way back to the stage. Gordon tapped his constable lightly on the back and nodded in the direction of the door. After a few minutes the two policemen moved up through the auditorium towards the foyer. They stopped behind the stalls to watch and listen. The DCI hadn't detected anything false or unexpected in Ian Davison, but the man was a superlative actor, wasn't he? The husband was always a suspect when his wife was killed… and all too frequently proved to be the killer. He wouldn't be, in this case, but that didn't mean he could be ignored in the investigation.

"Well, David", he said quietly to DC Crewe, "what do you think of him?"

*   *   *   *   *

Davison felt the eyes of his actors and crew on him, agog with curiosity. He walked slowly, climbed the steps onto the stage, embraced them all with a glance and said simply.

"My wife is dead. Laura. She's dead. They came to tell me."

There was a silence as their breaths were drawn in and then a tsunami of sound as they reacted to his words. "Accident?" he kept hearing through the babble of concern, "Crash?"

Duncan stepped forward. "My God, Ian, was it an accident?"

"I don't know" he said, disjointedly, then "No. I don't know. She was killed!" - The puppet master with his own strings cut. "Someone killed her." And as the words left his mouth, he saw a momentary flicker of a different horror in one of their faces. Saw her pupils contract and widen in a nanosecond. What was her name? Ali?

She looked away immediately, her face as distressed as they all were. But was her distress different? Why? Was she the one who had answered his phone last night? Heard the message?

What bloody message? What did he say?

In fact, that connect between news and realisation hadn't been instantaneous. Even as Ali thought she recognised the truth, her loyalty and just her every day practicality screamed out in resistance. Denial. *For God's sake, this is life, not fucking Hollywood. It's Ian! ... Ian, for Christ's sake!* But when her eyes flicked unwillingly back to him and Ian's eyes met hers, he thought that here was his Banquo. Could she bring him to ruin?

"Guys!" He said, his voice wavering and cracked, "Guys - give me five. I'll be back." He flung up a hand. "I want..." and then the tears came. Great gulping sobs. Wet, snot filled sobs. "Just give me five," and he ran for his office, pulling his phone out as he went. The door slammed.

* * * * *

There was silence on the stage. They looked at each other in consternation, and then suddenly the bubble burst and everyone was talking at once.

A few minutes later Ian came out of his office. He summoned up his training and slowed his pulse, breathing more normally now. He looked at the phone in his hand, hesitated, then put it back in his pocket and readied himself to face his team.

"We're almost there" he told them "We open in barely a fortnight." Jitters and emotion were to be expected. "You're probably expecting me to call it off."

They were. He could see it. Now was the time for Harfleur, for Agincourt. It was time to rally the troops. He dropped his voice into confessional mode and they could see the effort it cost him to go on.

"I've made mistakes, guys," He looked crushed. "We were this close," and he raised a thumb and forefinger a centimetre apart. "Really, this close to losing it all." He paused to let the implications sink in. Job losses, if nothing else; a long future of cleaning houses, washing up. He went on. "But Laura knows - Oh God, she *knew* - how important this was to me," he caught himself, "shit - how important *you all* are to me. She wasn't going to, but I begged her!" Truth is always helpful in a lie… "This is Laura's play guys. She bailed us out. We can't just let it…" and the word came out in a rush of emotion, "… die."

He turned away, then back again. He knew he had them.

"I'm may have to be away, perhaps a lot. Understudies have to be prepped. You're going to have to double up." He stopped, looking around. "Duncan - number 2 to Macbeth and," he hesitated, bit his fingertip and narrowed his eyes… "Ali?" He looked her squarely in the eye. "Yes. Ali. I want you to be number 2 to the Queen." The other major parts were given their failsafe stand-ins and he sent Anna out for sandwiches and coffees.

"Double shots," he shouted after her. "Triple. We all bloody need it! OK, people, let's get back to work."

They did a quick run through - first characters, then first understudies and then the new ones. He drilled them hard, and gradually the surreal, embarrassed shock of it all began to fade and the play took over once again.

Ali was reeling. *God, I really thought… when he told us…* But there was no time for thought or speculation. Second understudy? OK, not much, but understudies almost always had their opportunities and she'd be working directly with him. No chance of him missing her now.

No. No chance at all.

She was working through the lines with him, one on one, when Ian's phone chirped. He glanced at the message, then looked at his watch. It was getting late.

"OK people, let's call it for today. Back tomorrow, 10am sharp. If I'm not here, go on without me. I'll get here as soon as I can." There was a moment of confusion as people shook themselves out of their imaginary world, looked at each other and then began a general bustle back into the green room to find the coats, hats and boots they wore in the real world.

*   *   *   *   *

Alarums and Excursions

Susan was sitting down by the hedge, taking a moment to assess the situation. It was pleasant with the late morning sun on her face. *If only it didn't smell so vile!*

"Sergeant Cross," said PC Varma, who had been wandering up and down the lay-by. "I'd say there was a car parked here for a while quite recently. There are tracks along the hedge from the tyres where it's still a bit muddy from last night's rain and look… there are some cigarette-ends in the hedge as though someone had been sitting here in their car, chain smoking while they were waiting for something."

"You're right," Susan said, getting up and coming over to join her. "We'll have forensics gather it up and photograph the tyre tracks. You never know…" She looked around. They were out of sight of any of the cottages along the lane, so it wouldn't have been seen by anyone further up the lane. "Our person of interest may have arrived by car, which puts the kybosh on the tramp theory. This may help put someone at the scene last night. Good work!

"Don't let the cavalry drive over those tracks. Here they come…" DC Murphy's Forester drove up and they unloaded what he'd brought from the back of his car.

"Give us a moment Sean," Susan told him. "We're both in a revolting state and we're going to need those blankets. We can't stay in these clothes." A few minutes later PC Varma's uniform was in one evidence bag, and Sergeant Cross's jacket, shirt, and slacks in another and the two women were swaddled in blankets and sitting in the back of the car. The bloody jacket and shirt were bagged too.

"Can you drive us back to the Centre? I have a change of clothes there. PC Varma? Do you have anything at the Centre you can wear?"

She shook her head. "I'm from the Tonbridge station."

At that moment Stuart's little Peugeot pulled in. If he was surprised to find his sergeant dressed in little more than a blanket, he didn't show it.

"Stuart", she called, lowering the window. "We're heading back to the Centre. PC Varma found a bloody jacket and shirt in the skip. Ask forensics to get down here and photograph the tyre marks in that patch of dried mud and have them collect the cigarette ends in the hedge near them. Then make sure everything goes in for DNA analysis. They may be evidence we can use later. Oh, and get that PC into the skip… If the jacket and shirt were dumped there, then maybe the murder weapon is in there too! I'm sure it's easier work than controlling traffic along this busy lane!"

Stuart gave her an odd look… "Right you are, Ma'am. I'm sure he'll appreciate that."

She turned to Sean. "OK, we need to pick my briefcase up from the cottage, and then back to the Centre. I'll update the DCI on the way".

"You're going into the Centre like that?" asked Sean, eyebrows disappearing into his hairline.

"Ah…" She looked at herself and PC Varma. "Yes, I suppose it would be a bit difficult to live that down. All right, we'll go to my place. My younger sister stays overnight sometimes, and she leaves a change of clothing there that should fit PC Varma. We'll go there, shower and change, and then you can drive us to the Centre."

Her phone vibrated… "DS Cross," she answered without looking to see who was calling. "Ah, hello, Sir. I was just about to call you. I'm inbound to the Centre, but I have to nip home on the way to shower and change.

…

"Oh, I'm - ah - not wearing much more than a blanket at the moment, which would set tongues wagging at the Centre.

…

"Yes sir, there is a story behind that.

…

"Well - the short version is that PC Varma found what we believe is the killer's jacket and shirt in a skip a little way from the cottage. Unfortunately, she had to search through some really revolting rubbish to find them. Then she almost fell getting out again, but I caught her…

…

"Yes, I got covered in it too.

…

"Well, I'd say it'll be at least two hours before I'm back at the Centre…

…

"Yes, I see, Sir. That's probably best. I'll see you tomorrow then."

"That was the DCI", she said, looking a little pink. "Ian Davison is in London, so he is already heading up there now to inform him of his wife's death." She paused. "He seemed to find this situation funny." Looking across at Sean, it was clear he did too. *The rotten…* Well, she supposed it was PC Varma and herself that smelled rotten… *OK, so it was funny... A bit…* "If this gets out at the Centre, Sean Murphy, it'll be you in the next skip we have to search!"

"No problem, Sergeant" he replied in a rather strangled tone.

"Oh, for heaven's sake, go ahead. Laugh if you must… Get it out of your system!" There was a burst of laughter from the driver, who proceeded to chuckle for the next several miles, even after stopping for Susan's briefcase at the cottage. Disgusted, she turned to see that PC Varma was smiling too!

"And what are you grinning at, PC Varma? You were covered in far more of this stuff than I was."

"I'm sorry Sergeant Cross, but you are so unlike what everyone says you are. You're supposed to be mean and surly. They call you 'Crosspatch'… But you're not like that at all."

"Oh… Well… I can be as mean as anyone else under the right circumstances, Constable. But it doesn't help teamwork, or getting people to… well… work with you, does it?" PC Varma shook her head. "So, tell me, what are you called when you're out of uniform," she grinned "which you very clearly are?"

"Um, Sandeep, Ma'am."

“Well, Sandeep, this idiot driving us is DC Sean Murphy. He’s part of my team, and although he clearly has trouble with his sense of humour, he can be quite useful. The other DC who we left at the lay-by is Stuart McLean, and I hope by now he’s dumped your fellow PC deep into that skip, digging for the murder weapon. Serves him right. He should never have sent you off on your own when there was the possibility of a violent killer in the area.”

“Oh, I didn’t mind. I can look after myself.”

“That’s hardly the point, Sandeep. If there is any possibility of a violent suspect being in the area, no-one should be wandering off alone.” DC Murphy’s chuckling seemed to go over a speedbump.

“What?”

“Oh, nothing really, Ma’am. It’s just that I was wondering how you got down to that skip without being on your own?”

She looked at him, grinned again and then said primly “I was on my way to join PC Varma. I was not alone.”

“Of course, Ma’am.”

Susan laughed. Then she looked at the two constables and made a quick decision. “Sandeep, would you object if I asked the DCI to have you seconded to Team Cross for the duration of this case? We’re going to need some extra people, and you've already made yourself very useful. She grinned. “There may be other skips…

“Unlikely, I hope… but you’d have to be based at the Centre for the duration, and I warn you,” she wasn’t smiling now, "I have some detractors there. If you work with me, you could become a target too."

PC Varma looked back at her, her eyes bright. "That would be wonderful experience Sergeant. I'd be proud to work with Team Crosspatch."

"Team...? Yes... Well, I hope you'll continue to think that. You will have to pull your weight, you know - just like my other two jokers."

"They seem to be surviving, Ma'am."

` * * * * *

"Ma'am! Sergeant Cross!"

It rang out plaintively. Susan looked out of her bedroom door. There was PC Varma looking miserably uncomfortable in a short, flared yellow skirt, and a startling electric blue blouse. She looked about thirteen! "I can't wear these, Ma'am. I look like a teenager!"

"Nonsense, you look fine. No, seriously, just wear it long enough to get through the rest of day." *She looks adorable. All that shiny, raven black hair!*

"Ma'am! Sergeant! I can't go into the Centre looking like this. I'd die of shame! My uncle works at the front desk there, he'd tell my father."

Susan sighed. "It's OK, Sandeep, we'll go in the back way from the staff car park."

"Ma'am, by the time we get there many of them will be going off shift. They'll be coming out there. They'll *see* me."

Susan decided that she'd better give in on this one. There were limits to the constable's fearlessness, it seemed. *Oh, for a photograph! But she'd probably kill me…*

"OK, Sandeep, we'll stop somewhere you can pick up a pair of jeans. Yes, not usually allowed I know. We're less picky about that at the Centre. But we do need to keep moving…"

* * * * *

"Will this do, Sandeep?" asked Sean, pulling over to the curb. Susan looked up from her phone where she had been texting DC McLean for an update. They were outside a smart looking boutique.

"Yes, it's fine. I've been here before," said Sandeep. "They have nice clothes, and their prices are good," and then... "Oh! Sergeant, it's a Laura's!"

So it was. "Well, then, Sandeep, let's take a look." Susan's phone started vibrating again, and a moment later, the DCI's ringtone sounded. *Damn.* "Both of you go in. I have to take this. Have a look round. I doubt there's anything off, but it'll give us the flavour of Laura's business."

Sean's expression showed exactly what he thought of shopping in general and women's clothes shops in particular. But this was work so he shrugged his shoulders manfully. "OK, Sandeep, let's see what we can see," and the two walked in. Susan was already answering her phone.

"Yes, Sir, we're on our way in. You're at the theatre? … They're rehearsing? ... And Davison went right back to it after you spoke? Really? I'd have expected them at least to stop for the rest of the day…"

She got her request in before he closed the call. "Sir, I'd like to add PC Varma from the Tonbridge station to my team for this one. She's already found what may be the killer's shirt and jacket, and what might well be further evidence too. She's bright, energetic, and not afraid of hard work, and I think we're going to need extra people before this is done…"

There was a question from the other end.

"Er, no Sir. She's cleaned up now. We're just getting her something to wear… Yes, Sir. I'll do that, of course…" But the DCI wasn't finished… "On CCTV? So Davison is ruled out. Ok. Good … We'll just have to look elsewhere. Yes. Compare notes in the morning? Yes sir. Crosspatch out…

"What? … I didn't say that. No. I'm sure I said DS Cross… Are you laughing, Sir?... No, Sir… Yes sir, I'm hanging up now," and she did. And she stood for a moment, a bemused look on her face. "I'm losing it!" she muttered, and pushed her way into the shop. What on earth was happening to her world?

"Here you are, Sean. This is what I need, and they're in my size." Sandeep held up a pair of indigo blue jeans. "Now for a top."

"I dunno, Sandeep. You look pretty good in that blue thing; it really sets off your hair and eyes." Sandeep looked at him, suddenly disconcerted, just as Crosspatch joined them.

"Yes, those will do nicely," she said, looking at the jeans. "Look, get a couple of pairs. The DCI has approved your secondment to - er - Team Cross for now. He said you can wear 'civvies'. I'll put them on my expense account. He'll approve it as long as it's reasonable."

The little constable was looking a little bewildered. "Thank you, Ma'am." She seemed to have lost track of what they were doing. "Right!" She grabbed DC Murphy by the arm. "Sean, help me find what I need," and she pulled him away into the depths of the shop.

Susan looked around, trying to get a feel for Laura's business. The boutique was fitted out in light wood, with mirrors making it seem larger than it was. The lighting was low, but warm and comfortable. Spotlights picked out displays showing suggested combinations of the clothes at hand. Effective and inviting. The divisions seemed to be by colour as well as style. It was mostly smart casual with a few more dressy pieces. Nothing startling, but very tempting. *I should have tried these shops before. This stuff is nice.* She looked at some price tags… *Not badly priced, either. No wonder they're popular.*

A sales assistant was walking over to her. A little shorter than she was, the person approaching her had dark, almost black hair cut asymmetrically across sharp cheekbones, a pale complexion, and warm brown eyes in an oval face. She wore a crisp, multi layered, white shirt, open at the neck, above dark burgundy trousers, showing both Laura's collection and her trim, gamine figure off to perfection.

"Susan, it's lovely to see you here. Can I help you with anything?" She was smiling, naturally friendly. Susan looked at her for a moment before she recognised her.

They'd met one evening at a pub not far from here. As neither of them had been with anyone else, they'd found a table together, had a friendly chat, and parted saying they should get together again. But that was in her Featherstone era, and she simply hadn't followed up on it.

"Hello Mandy. I didn't realise you worked here." She smiled back apologetically. "I'm with those two," she motioned towards the back. Where *were* Sandeep and Sean? Then she saw Sandeep step out of a changing room and… *twirl*. There was no other word for it! She was wearing the jeans she'd picked out, but still wore the electric blue top under a sharp little jacket. And there was Sean, propped up against the wall, watching her.

She was about to head down towards them when the door chimes sounded, and two men walked in. Shaven heads, t-shirts of a faded and indeterminate colour under heavily distressed leather jackets, the sleeves pushed back to show, darkly tattooed arms. Unlikely customers! What would they want here? She stepped back into a shadowy alcove between two high shelving units against the wall and watched.

Mandy moved in their direction, clearly nervous. "Can I help you?"

"Yeah, we're here to see the manager," said the first man. (*Thug #1*, thought Susan).

"I am the manager, Sir," Mandy replied. "How can I help you?"

"Well, we heard you stopped paying your insurance," he said, towering over her. "We've come to suggest you keep it in place, know wot I mean? There's a reinsta'ment fee, but you can pay us tha'… righ' now!" He leered at her.

Mandy stepped back, looking around rather wildly. "I'm sorry, I can't help you. All our insurance is handled through our head office!"

"It's like this darlin'," he said pushing up against her. "You've been on the 'ands off list for three years or more. This morning you got crossed off. That means you ain't paid, an' it's our job to sort it. So, we're gonna give your 'ead office some encouragemen' to... ge' back on the programme." He looked around. Sandeep was back in the changing room, and Sean was invisible, between displays. The other sales assistant had disappeared. Susan heard the back door close - she'd clearly decided on a strategic retreat, leaving her boss without any help.

Thug #1 gave the young manager a menacing leer. "An' I fink I'll star' wiv you!" He lunged forward and grabbed her by the throat, pushing her back towards the wall. "Let's you and me 'ave some fun!" The only response was a hoarse attempt at a scream and a frantic attempt to loosen the hand on her throat and stop the other that was ripping open her shirt.

Not on my watch you don't. Susan hit the emergency speed dial on her mobile; the call answered quickly.

She identified herself and gave the address. "Violent Robbery and assault in progress, two large white males. Requesting urgent and immediate back-up!" Then, leaving her mobile still connected on a shelf, she moved out of the shadows.

"Stop! Police!" When that had no effect, she lunged at the thug's back, putting him in a tight headlock and hung on. He let the girl go and whirled around trying to throw off the irritant on his back, but Susan was not to be dislodged as she tightened her hold trying to force him to his knees. She succeeded, too, but the second thug came barrelling across the shop, pushing displays in all directions. Grabbing her from behind, he pulled her up and off his partner, who stayed on his knees, hands to his throat, trying to get his breath back. Turning, he flung Susan into the shelves behind them, and punched her in the face as she bounced back towards him. He was moving in to do more damage when DC Murphy arrived.

"Police," he was shouting, "you're under arrest." The man responded with a wild swing, but Murphy stepped back and he missed. Moving back in again, Murphy sent a straight fist into number two's face. The man staggered back but did not go down. Instead, he re-balanced, charged and they both went down grappling.

Thug #1 was getting back onto his feet… Crosspatch was down on the floor, probably out of the fight. Mandy was down too, backed up against the wall, eyes wide, hand to her throat and screaming, hoarsely. Thug #1 looked towards the two struggling men and moved towards them.

"Stop," came a light, clear voice. "You are under arrest. Get down on your knees." He looked around. There, in the middle of the shop, in the aisle between two colourful displays, a small teenage girl was facing him. "On your knees with your hands on your head!" He stared at her, incredulously. *A girl? A bloody Paki, too!* With a hoarse growl, he rushed straight at her. She seemed to be moving back - but then she stepped forward again, launching herself into a high kick. His own momentum did the rest. As her foot connected, it was as though his head stopped while the rest of his body kept coming. His feet flew up into the air and he slammed into the ground on his back. Sandeep, landing lightly on all fours, was up quickly, stepping back, watching to see if he was getting up again. But he seemed to be out for the count.

The other one! Sandeep turned to look at the others. Sean and Crosspatch had thug #2 down, and were sitting on him, staring at her in shock! Both had obviously been in a brawl. Susan's face was swelling around one eye that was practically closed, and Sean's nose was crimson and bleeding. Both looked thoroughly rumpled. Mandy, still sitting against the wall, had stopped screaming, and was staring at Susan, with an expression bordering on worship…

They all looked back at Sandeep. Completely untouched, she wasn't even breathing hard, her eyes sparkling with excitement. "We got them, Ma'am! Ouch, he had a hard head though!" she said, limping slightly. "Ooh, Sergeant, that's going to be a real shiner! I hope it doesn't hurt too much!"

With a groan, Susan got to her feet. Sean was already putting handcuffs on #2.

"Well done, Sandeep! Have you got any handcuffs? No? Out to the car and get some then, quickly, before that one wakes up." Sean tossed her the keys and Sandeep trotted out. Within a minute she was back and was cuffing #1 with obvious enjoyment.

Susan looked at her, then gave her a big smile. "Was that your first arrest?" She nodded, a bit shyly. "I doubt there's anyone who's made a more spectacular one!"

Susan turned, went back to the shaking manager, and knelt down next to her. She was still breathing rapidly, clearly in shock.

"Mandy, we're police officers. We just happened to be here looking for a couple of things for Sandeep here, who managed to get her uniform all mucky, ("Hey!" from Sandeep). We're going to have to close your shop until our crime scene people have checked out what happened here, but I don't think it'll take long. Anyway, we'll look after everything.

"Sean, put the "Closed" sign up will you, and call the Centre. There should be a team on the way. I called it in when this kicked off. They'll need to pick up this pair, and we need a couple of paramedics, oh … and a photographer. This will all have to be documented."

She turned back to the woman on the floor. *God, I must look awful* - one eye was almost closed, and bruising was already showing - *enough to scare her out of her wits* - but she did her best to be calm and reassuring. "Are there any blankets here, Mandy? You've had a shock. You're getting cold. We need to warm you up."

"Up…upstairs."

"Sandeep?"

"Yes Ma'am, there's a staircase by the back door. I'll run up and see."

Susan sat down by Mandy and put an arm around her while they waited for Sandeep to reappear.

"There's a little flat upstairs Ma'am, with a nice gas fire and a kitchenette. If we can get her up there, she can warm up by the fire and we can make her a hot drink."

Susan looked at Mandy. "Is it your flat?" Mandy nodded. "Right, that's what we'll do then. Sean, can you carry her?"

"I should think so, Ma'am," he said, "she doesn't look as though she weighs much." and he got down on one knee and put his arms under her. Still frozen with shock, she was actually pretty much a dead weight, but they got her up between them, Susan following behind to help Sean keep his balance going up the stairs. They carried her into a cozy sitting room with a gas fire, and a comfortable looking sofa. The room felt bright and cheerful with lots of natural light setting off crisply pretty wallpaper. At the end of the room was a small kitchen with a fridge, stove and microwave, and a sink against one wall.

Sandeep was already lighting the fire, so Susan settled Mandy on the sofa, while Sean went into the bedroom to find a blanket to wrap around her. When that had been done and she seemed comfortable, Susan started to get up, but Mandy clutched at her arm. "Please," she whispered. "I'm so cold." Susan sat down again and put her arm back around the shivering girl.

"Sean, you go and wait for our people to arrive. I'll send Sandeep down as soon as they get here. Sandeep, do you think you could make Mandy a cup of tea?"

“Yes, of course, Ma’am,” and she bustled over to the little kitchen.

Susan felt the shock of the attack gradually recede as the warmth of the fire and the comfort of her arm around Mandy’s shoulders took effect and a few minutes later Sandeep came forward with a mug of tea.

“Both milk and sugar, Ma’am,” she said. “She’ll need it.” Susan coaxed her to sit up and take a few sips, and she started to show more signs of awareness as the tea slowly went down.

“I need to go down and see how DC Murphy is doing downstairs, Mandy. I’ll leave Sandeep up here with you. I’ll be back shortly,” and Susan got up. “Sandeep, look after her, will you? They’ll send a couple of paramedics since there’s been a fight, and I’ll bring one of them up to check on Mandy. They’ll want to give me and Sean a once over, and then we’ll come back up.” Mandy looked a little distressed, but she nodded, and Susan started down the stairs again.

The response team had arrived by this time. Two burly constables to take the handcuffed thugs into custody, and three others to document everything that had happened. Right behind them came the paramedics, unkindly amused to see the two somewhat battered officers. One took Susan into a changing room while the other sat Sean down outside. Both were stripped to the waist and received impressed ‘oohs’ and ‘aahs’ at the bruises. Sean’s were comparatively minor, but Susan’s were vivid where she had bounced off the shelves, with both her left arm and ribs already coming up in bright rainbows colours. Pain deadening creams were applied, and those were a great relief. There was some concern about Susan's nose, and whether she had any teeth loosened, but after some painful poking and pulling, it was just a case of more ointment over the worst areas.

"That must have hurt," was the comment, "But you're lucky. It looks terrible, but you came out of it quite lightly."

The two thugs were also checked over before they were taken away. Thug #2, who Susan and Sean had wrestled down together, had only superficial damage but Thug #1, who Sandeep had taken out, had a comprehensively broken nose. He objected quite violently to the paramedic's attempts to tape it up until Sandeep came down and told him to stop being a baby or she'd "do the same again, but with a different target," staring pointedly at his groin. Following which, he couldn't have been more cooperative.

Susan, in the meantime, had taken the other paramedic upstairs to see Mandy. Her throat was sore and bruised where the thug had gripped her, and she was still showing signs of shock. "You'll be OK," was the verdict, "but I'd suggest a really quiet night, and if you have any brandy, now's probably a good time." She looked at Susan. "She should have someone with her tonight. Perhaps a friend or relative who can come over and stay with her? I doubt she'll sleep very well for a day or two."

"We'll sort something out," Susan told her. "Sandeep, did you see any brandy in the cabinet?"

"No, only a bottle of cooking wine. There wasn't much else."

"OK, there's an Off License up the street. Take my wallet and go and get a half bottle of brandy and a nice red wine."

"Yes, Ma'am," and off she went.

"Sean," she said turning to him. "If there's no one else she can call, I'll stay with Mandy for a while to be sure she's OK. If I give you my car keys can you get someone on the evening shift to drop my car off here?"

"That shouldn't be a problem, Ma'am." He hesitated. Then said, impulsively "Could I just say, I think you've handled this brilliantly. That girl was half out of her mind - absolutely terrified - but you calmed her right down. No hysterics. Fantastic." Then he grinned at her. "The DCI should be pretty chuffed at how your interpersonal skills are coming along, Ma'am."

Susan laughed, appreciating the moment of camaraderie. "Someone had to do it, Sean."

"Absolutely, but it was still well done. I'll make sure we get your car to you tonight."

"Thanks. And Sean, thanks for getting that thug off me."

"We took him down together, Ma'am. Not sure either one of us could have handled him alone... Mind you, Sandeep would probably have made short work of him. Incredible, wasn't she?"

Susan smiled, then winced. "I'm awfully glad she was on our side. That could have gone wrong in the worst way."

"Do you think you can keep her on the team, Ma'am?"

"I'll certainly try. She'll be back in a minute... Can you give her a lift back to wherever she needs to go?"

"Of course, Ma'am."

Sandeep re-appeared with the brandy and a bottle of Australian red that she said the man in the Off License had recommended. It wasn't one Susan knew, but she wasn't about to be fussy. She took them both upstairs.

"Right," she said, smiling as much as her face would allow. "The doctor ordered brandy. I've also got what I hope is a nice bottle of Australian plonk, and I'm going to order a pizza. They want someone to stay with you tonight, so that's going to be me..." She hesitated, "unless, of course, you have anyone else you'd like to call?" Mandy shook her head.

"OK, I'm going to pour us each a stiff brandy, and later on, I'll order pizza. We'll have a nice quiet evening, and I promise you'll be safe. Now, what's on TV?"

The medic was right. The brandy brought the colour back into Mandy's face, and by the time they'd demolished the pizza between them (and half a bottle of what turned out to be a spectacularly good Australian wine) they nodded off together on the sofa.

Later that night Mandy woke up screaming. Susan was up in an instant, speaking soothingly and rocking her as she might a child. "It's all right Mandy... Hey, it's me! They're gone. No-one here but me, I promise!"

It calmed her enough for Susan to lead her across to the bedroom and help her into bed. As she turned to go back into the sitting room and make her own bed on the sofa, Mandy pulled her back. “Stay with me?” So Susan lay down beside her on top of the covers and slept with her till morning.

*   *   *   *   *

“Somewhere they can’t find me.”

(Paul Simon)

“Ali, can I have a word with you?” She looked up, a little surprised. “Wait in my office, would you? I just need to fetch something. I’ll be right back,” and Davison followed the last of the others outside.

Oh no, he must be having second thoughts about my understudying the queen. Shit! I thought it went really well. Glumly she finished putting on her boots - good solid biker boots which she wore to protect her feet on the tube in rush hour. She picked up her coat and wandered disconsolately back towards the office, past posters and props from previous productions.

Creepy, she thought, noticing a scaled down guillotine. *Why not just do that as a backdrop*? Hearing a movement behind her, she turned, expecting to see Ian hurrying after her. *Not Ian!* She gasped as an enormous man grabbed her and pushed her hard, face first into the wall, scraping her cheek against the plaster.

“No noise,” he grunted, swinging her around to cover the scream trying to escape her mouth. “You and me are going to wait until everyone has gone and then we’re going to have a good time!” His smile was feral, his eyes dilated.

Oh shit! He’s on drugs! He’s going to kill me! But no sooner had she had that thought than another took its place… *Sod that!*

She slumped forward as though in a dead faint and he put both arms around her to hold her up as excitement shot through him. "Oh yes," he groaned, but the groan shot up at least four octaves into a squeal of agony as Ali's knee came up with all the strength and precision of a dancer, right between his legs. As he folded up, she stepped back, but she wasn't finished. Her knee came up again, smashing his nose across his face.

"Stupid bastard," she swore. "I've practised that fight scene a hundred times." He was down on the floor now, his face a mask of blood, keening in the back of his throat as he rocked, grasping at his savaged testicles. He made a half-hearted grab for her foot, but adrenaline still sky high, she stepped lightly aside and then kicked him hard in the face.

Hah! Worked like a charm! She grabbed her coat,

And stopped.

This man had been waiting for her. Right outside Ian's office! His office, where he had sent her! Alone! The phone call burst into her mind again, crystal clear. "It's done. She's dead!" and all the shock and horror came back with it. Ian had driven it from her mind, convinced her that it could not be… But it could!

The monster on the floor was stirring again. She needed a weapon. Hurriedly she reached up to the guillotine and pulled. It was a lot heavier than she'd thought. She pulled sharply, harder, and it toppled down on top of him. "Damn," she muttered, sucking at her finger, which had been sliced by a loose nail as it fell. She turned and ran for the doors. She had to get to the police.

Outside, Davison, halfway down the alleyway, saw her burst through the stage door. She hesitated, saw him, and was off, running down the alley and out into the street. High overhead, a storm was gathering. The wind, gusting down the funnel between the buildings, kicked up the dust and leaves behind her as she ran. Ian ran after her, calling "Ali!" but she didn't pause. She turned into the street and in just a few yards she had merged into the mass of workers disgorging from an office building across the road. In seconds she had disappeared as the first drops of rain caused a forest of umbrellas to sprout over the swirl of commuters, all bustling towards home. She was gone.

* * * * *

She watched Ian from the windows in the pub where they had celebrated their successful rehearsal the night before. She'd stepped in with several others from the crowd intent on waiting out the rain and choosing to have a drink before heading home. Ian spun around on the pavement in the fading light, clearly frustrated, raking his hand through his hair, his eyes searching the crowd. Finally, he gave up and took off, walking briskly, back towards the theatre, stopping several times to look back, anger clear on his face.

"Hello, Ali," came a voice from right beside her. "Waiting for your boyfriend? From the look on your face, I'm not sure he's going to get a very warm welcome!" She spun round. A cheerful looking woman, probably mid thirties, in a smart, black suit had come up behind her, a glass of red wine in her hand. "That's probably how I look when I've wasted the entire afternoon explaining the business plan to the bunch of twenty-somethings the top brass have decided are our future." She shuddered. "God help us if they are. A glass of the house red? Go on. It's rough enough to smooth out even the shittiest day."

Ali smiled at her, relieved. "Madeleine! Thanks! I'd love one. It's been - hmmm - rather a stressful day." Madeleine gave her a grin, and went back to the bar, waving to the girl behind the counter, holding up her glass in one hand and indicating "two" with the fingers of the other. She was back in barely a minute, handed Ali a glass, and sat down.

"Thanks, Madeleine! You're right. This is exactly what I need." She took a large mouthful, and leaned back, keeping her friend between her and the window. Madeleine both worked and lived locally and was a regular here. They had met often and got on well, tucking up at a table in the corner and chatting comfortably about anything from the latest TV Bake Off to whatever else 'BJ' had bollocksed up since taking over from Theresa May.

"The man's an idiot," she'd said cheerfully. "Stuck his thumb in the EU's eye. Gave them the finger, and then thought they'd give him everything he wanted. Even a blind man could see that wasn't going to happen." Ali's point of view exactly. They'd shared opinions on most things and enjoyed setting the world to rights over a drink on the way home.

Madeleine chattered on quietly about this and that, recognising that her friend needed bringing down from whatever it was that was upsetting her. Ali had been listening while keeping an eye on what was happening out in the street. Suddenly she tensed and leaned forward. Outside Ian came back into view with the man who had assaulted her in the theatre.

She was pleased to notice that he was limping, obviously still feeling the after-effects of his brush with her knee… Ian was gesticulating, hands in the air, and she could see he was shouting, but the sound did not penetrate the cheerful rumble from inside the pub. Ali saw Ian point in their gencral direction and the big man turn and move towards them already yelling into his phone. She held her breath, but he flung past the pub and on up the road. Ian stood there for a moment, looking after him, then, throwing his hands up in the air again, he turned back towards the alley and the theatre. Ali waited, scarcely breathing, until both men disappeared into the dusk.

"That's your boss, isn't it?" asked Madeleine, looking out. "Nice looking bloke, but I don't like the look of his mate. Looks like a giant version of Boris with that mop of blond hair, and I'd say he had a temper on him. Was it you they were looking for, Ali? You want to be careful, Hun," she said as Ali got up.

"Don't you worry, Madeleine, I will be… very careful, now."

"Was it a "me too" sort of thing?"

"No. Worse." came the response.

"Shit! Well good luck."

Ali gave her a quick hug. "I'll tell you all about it, but not now. I've got to get home. Thanks though, and for the wine."

She ghosted out of the pub, watched both ways in case either Ian or "Boris" (yes, he really did look a bit like him) were still about and made her plans. There was a police station just off Walworth Rd. It was a bit of a walk, but not too far and the rain seemed to have stopped. *Carefully, though*. She didn't want to run into Boris along the way. So, she headed out cautiously, keeping to the shadows and avoiding the brighter areas lit up by the amber streetlights.

She made it as far as the next corner and stopped again. This was silly, *not* how to avoid being noticed. She stepped out more boldly, walking as though she hadn't a care in the world, keeping close to other groups, hoping she'd be seen as just one of the crowd, eager to get home. Now it was she who was watching the shadows for lurking menace, and that gave her confidence. It wasn't long before she saw the lights of the police station ahead. She went up the steps and through the front doors. *Safe*!

* * * * *

He had a problem. The girl was in the wind, and he had no idea of who she was or where she lived. Davison could get that information and they might need it later, but if she had gone to the police, she might already be out of reach. He needed someone on the inside who could find out.

Featherstone! He was at the Centre in Sevenoaks, which was probably handling the case. The investigation team there would want to hear what she knew. He knew the Inspector had been a useful source of information on police activities before. He might even be leading the investigation. He looked up the station number and called. They would probably have Featherstone return the call to him in the morning. He hoped that would not be too late.

"Good evening," he said putting on his plummiest voice as the station switchboard picked up. "I need to speak with Inspector Featherstone. It's really rather important. Is there any way I can get hold of him tonight?"

"You're in luck Sir," came the reply. "DI Featherstone is the duty officer tonight. I'll put you right through." *The duty officer? Yes!* Now this had possibilities. He felt his hunting instincts rise.

"Featherstone, it's Paul Lennox. Look, I don't want to tie up any of your lines at the station. Would you call me at this number as soon as you get a chance? I have something for you." 'Paul Lennox' was the code that told him it was Organisation business. He gave his mobile number.

It wasn't long. His mobile chirped. "Featherstone here. You chaps are bloody lucky I happened to be on tonight. What do you want?"

He explained. "There's a girl. She has information that we don't want spread around. It's critical. We think she has gone to the police already. If she has, you will probably be notified, as it may be of interest in one of the cases you have down there. A killing over near Tonbridge."

"The Nettle Lane murder? Yes, it's hot right now… No, I'm not on the case. The DCI kept it in his Major Crimes unit. He won't give me a look in."

"OK, pity, but it still leaves us a chance. We think she can only just have got to the police, so the call might come in tonight. If it does, will you get it?"

"Yes, it should come to me."

He smiled to himself. "If it does, try to get them to agree to you going to pick her up, right away. If you can get her, pass her on to me. I'll take it from there. If you can't, try to find out where she is and if, when and how she'll be brought to Sevenoaks. We may have to engineer an accident. Call me back on this number if you hear anything."

* * * * *

It was a fairly modern building, with tall glass doors leading to the glassed-in reception area and counter. There didn't seem to be much of a waiting room, just a metal bench where a rather elderly man sat gloomily nursing a cup of tea. Alison hesitated a moment but then marched up to the counter. The desk sergeant looked up, smiled at her through the glass screen, and asked what they could do for her.

"I need to talk to someone," she said, almost whispering. "I know who killed Laura Davison, and now they're trying to silence me!"

The sergeant looked at her for a moment and adjusted his microphone, wondering first if he had heard her correctly and then if she were pulling his leg. He decided to play it straight. "I see… Who was that you say was killed, Miss? Can you give me the name again?" he asked.

"Laura Davison. The wife of Ian Davison, the actor. She was killed … last night, at their home, I think. Somewhere near Tonbridge." It all sounded a bit dramatic even to her own ears. But the sergeant's response was almost disappointingly matter of fact.

"Ah well," he said. "That won't be in our jurisdiction. That would be the South East lot. You come through and talk to a constable, Miss. We'll need you to write up a statement, and I'll contact them and see what they want to do." He called over his shoulder to one of the shadowy figures beyond and in a matter of moments she was being led through a large open office filled with cubicles to a smaller space at the back.

"A constable will be over to get the details," she was told and sure enough a PC came out of one of the cubicles and walked confidently towards her. She was tall, maybe five foot ten or eleven and was in her mid-twenties, Ali guessed.

"Hello, I'm PC Pandya," she said smiling. "I'll just get a couple of cups of tea, and then we'll chat," and she disappeared away down a corridor at the back. Ali sat there quietly, willing herself to be calm, imagining herself a character in a film, a suspect about to be grilled by the police! No, sod it. This was not Hollywood, and she wasn't a suspect. She'd simply tell them what had happened, and then they could take over. She'd be out of it.

PC Pandya came back in carrying the promised cups of tea. *This must be a ritual*, she thought. *Do they always bring you cups of tea in police stations?* She took a sip. *Well, they may do, but they aren't very good at it!* Still, it was hot, and if it was a bit sweet, well, she didn't seem to mind that so much now. She'd begun to shiver. She pulled her coat tight around her and took another sip of tea. Yes, it was definitely hitting the spot.

"You're shivering," said Pandya. "Are you OK"?

"I think it must be shock. I was attacked." Concern etched itself across Pandya's face.

"Let's start with your name."

Still shivering, Ali replied. "It's Ali. Alison. Alison Johnson."

"OK, Ali, you say you were attacked. Do you need to see a nurse? Were you physically assaulted? Raped? We have a nurse here who can check you out and document any injuries."

"Raped?" shot back Ali, sitting up. "No. In his dreams perhaps! … But… oh shit! I think he did mean that. He… he grabbed me… said we were going to wait until everyone had gone and then have some fun! I got him in the balls though – so no, no rape. Definitely assault, though."

Pandya looked at her. Yes, her face was scratched, and some bruising was showing. "OK, let's start from the beginning. Just one moment." She walked through to the front desk and had a quick word with the Sergeant, then went back to her cubicle and came back with a small tablet. She sat down again. "Tell me what happened. I'll record the details."

The story came out gradually. The rehearsal. The phone call. The police arriving to tell Ian his wife was dead, then the rehearsal continuing until what? An hour, an hour and a half ago? Was it really only that? Then going back alone to Ian's office, and the attack by Boris.

"Who?"

"Boris - sorry - probably not his name, but he's got this mop of really blond hair - reminded me of Boris. You know, the PM."

Then the flight from the theatre, the pub, and finally to the police station. PC Pandya looked at her.

"This is a big man?"

"Yes. Huge!"

"Over six foot?"

"Easily. I'd say 6 foot 5, maybe 6. My head didn't even reach his chin."

"Heavy? Roughly?"

"Maybe 15 stone. Maybe a bit more. He's really, really big. But fast, too."

"Ali, you got away from a six foot plus, fifteen stone man who already had his hands on you?"

"Yes, I did. I've got his blood all over my knee. It's probably ruined my dress! There was blood on my boot too unless the rain washed it all away."

PC Pandya looked a little dazed. "Your knee? Dress? Boot?"

"Yes," she said. She stood up, opening her coat, and sure enough the skirt of her rehearsal dress was stained with blood and who knows what else. She held up her foot. There, the rain hadn't washed it all off.

"Right. I'm sorry, but we're going to need the dress - and your boots too - for our forensics people to examine.

We can find you some other clothes. Tell me again, he grabbed you?"

"Yes," and she told her story again, detail, by detail. "When he still tried to grab me, I kicked him in the face."

"With your boot?"

"Well, yes. I don't rehearse in boots, but I'd put them on to go home. But he was still moving so I pulled the guillotine down on top of him."

"The guillotine?"

"Yes. An old prop. It was outside Ian's office. I cut my finger on it." She held up her left hand, with a slightly bloodied cut on the pad of one finger.

"Then I realised that he'd been waiting for me. Ian sent me right to him. He must have had his wife killed. Must think that I know. What else could it be? He must have sent me back there to be killed too! I saw him with Boris afterwards, in the street." She was beginning to shiver again.

Pandya hit return and saved the statement and then stood up briskly.

"OK, let's get you changed. We'll take the dress and boots for forensics, but we'll find something else you can wear." She led the way down the corridor to a room near the back of the building where a middle-aged woman in a nurse's uniform was sitting. She looked up from the paperback she was reading.

"Anne, this is Alison. We need her dress and boots for forensics. I'll bag them, but can you find her something she can wear instead?" She turned to Ali. "This is Nurse

Ryan. She'll look after you. I'll go and see what I can do with your statement," and she turned and hurried back out of the room.

*   *   *   *   *

"She's certainly been in a fight, Sergeant, and her story sounds very plausible. We need to look into it." The desk sergeant turned round.

"I just got off the phone with Sevenoaks, Pandy. She's right. There was a murder, a nasty one, they say. A Mrs. Laura Handley-Davison. I spoke to their duty officer, a DI Featherstone, and he says that this Alison is a Person of Interest in the case. They want us to hand her over along with whatever information we have. He's driving up himself to pick her up, and listen, he wants her presence here kept quiet. Apparently, it's a very sensitive case. They're trying to keep the noise down to the minimum. I checked with the chief… he checked with someone else, a DCI at the Yard no less, and he says we should hand her over. He knows Inspector Featherstone."

"Did they want her arrested?"

"They didn't say. But she's definitely a POI, and they want to talk to her."

"Sergeant, she was attacked *here*, barely a mile or so down the road. Shouldn't we be investigating that, at least?"

"Chief says hand it all over to them. We have enough to do as it is, Pandy. If Kent decides she's not who they want, then maybe we'll look into it. But they seem sure they want her. Rather their budget than ours!"

Pandya looked rebellious, and it seemed she might argue the point. But her sergeant raised his hand and shook his head, and she thought better of it. "Understood," she said rather stiffly. "I'll get her statement typed up, and she can sign it, but I'll be off shift after that. She'll have to wait with Nurse Ryan."

"Pandy, I know you're keen to do some investigating, but leave it to the detectives. If the Sevenoaks end doesn't work out, we can send one of our lads around to check it out in the next day or so."

* * * * *

The call came just ten minutes later. Featherstone sounded excited. "She's at Walworth, up in London. I told them she was a Person of Interest in our case and that we wanted her ASAP. They're short staffed and were quite happy to let me take her off their hands. I'm driving up to get her now."

"Let me know as soon as you have her, and we'll meet. Try to clear the file on the net if you can, and no one will ever remember to find out what happened to her."

"This is going to be worth my time, right?"

"This may be the most important thing you've ever done for us. Yes, it will be worth your while."

He smiled. This would work. The girl had escaped him once, but he had her now. The hunt was on again! Featherstone didn't know it was an unauthorised job. No one was going to pay him, but then, he wasn't going to be around to ask to be paid either. As soon as he had his hands on the girl, Featherstone would be a liability he could do without.

*   *   *   *   *

"What's taking so long" asked Ali. "I've been here over an hour. Where's PC Pandya?"

"Oh, Pandy's shift will be over by now. She was just going to open a file and get all your info onto the net, and pack up the dress and boots for forensics."

They had dug out some clothes for her. Jeans - not too bad a fit - and sneakers, which they had made do with a bit of paper scrunched up in the toes. For the top she'd been given a tee-shirt and a sweat shirt with the Chicago Bulls' logo on it - *the Chicago Bulls? A baseball team? Probably.* At least she was a little warmer, and she rather liked the look, anyway.

"What's the delay?" she asked.

"They're waiting for a detective from Sevenoaks. They are interested in what you have to say. He should be here soon." Nurse Ryan settled back down to her novel.

PC Pandya had gone home? *Home! Oh God! Tom will be at home! Ian could look up my personnel record and see where we live. I need to call Tom, now!*

She grabbed her phone from her bag. "I'm just calling my boyfriend," she told the nurse as she punched in Tom's number.

She breathed a sigh of relief when he answered. "Tom, it's Ali. Where are you? It sounds noisy. At the pub? Thank God! Tom, listen." She glanced across but Nurse Ryan was oblivious. Still, she dropped her voice to a whisper, "… please listen, this is important. Don't go home. Wait for me. I'll join you there. Please Tom, don't go home!" She put her coat on and huddled up a bit on the chair pretending to be cold, then looked around at Nurse Ryan.

"Sorry. Where's the ladies?" she asked. The nurse looked up. "Just down to the right, near the back door, darling," and then she was immersed in her paperback again. That dastardly Lord Russell had been trying to get Lady Amanda into bed since page ten or so, and it looked like he might be about to succeed. What a disaster! The brave, hot headed young heroine would be ruined! Where was that handsome Mr. Benedict when he was needed?

Ali collected her bag and walked quietly down towards the back door. Another couple of steps and she was outside and moving purposefully away. Not the tube, she thought. Taxi? No. Uber. She had the App on her phone. Risky? Maybe but worth it. She hoped PC Pandya would forgive her for doing a runner, but she'd told them everything. She had nothing further that would be of interest to the Sevenoaks police. It all felt wrong, somehow.

Tom was with the two salesmen from work. He was a whizz at rebuilding classic cars, and they had just sold two that he'd worked on, so they'd brought him out for a pint or two. He hadn't expected Ali home until late. He was used to her irregular schedule and was fully supportive of her career, of course he was, but it wasn't always easy, and he'd welcomed a spot of company tonight. She'd sounded pretty spooked though. Not like her… Still, she was coming to join him. There were worse places to wait.

The Uber driver dropped her outside the pub and Ali took a careful look around. Nothing seemed out of the ordinary. Could they track her here? She'd called the Uber, paid on-line. Could the police track her through that? Could Ian's hit man? Was it just one hit man? Could there be a whole gang after her? She shook her head. Took a yoga breath. OK. Even if there was a gang, she should be at least a few hours ahead of them. She went into the pub to find Tom.

There he was, with two of his mates from work, over by the window. She waved and hurried over to him. He looked up, smiling, murmured an apology to his friends, got up, and guided her over to an empty table in the corner.

"Hello, Love," he said. "What's all the super-secret stuff about? You sounded really shaky on the phone!"

"Oh, Tom." For a moment it was all she could say. Then out it came in a rush. The whole story.

"They wanted me to wait for an Inspector from Kent or Sussex. He was driving up to take me off to the police station in Sevenoaks… Why the hell would they want to take me down there? I gave them my statement, and my address, so they knew where to contact me. Then I realised that Ian must have my address and he would give it to Boris…"

"Who?"

"The hit man."

"He's called Boris?'

"No… Look, I just called him that. I don't know – because he looks weirdly like Boris. Then I realised that you might be there, Tom. He was going to kill me; I know he was. I'm sure he killed Ian's poor wife! I thought he might kill you, too! … We need to get away somewhere for a while

– just till the police use my statement and nail the bastards. We should be safe then."

"Ali, love, this sounds crazy."

"I know it does. Maybe it is. But, please Tom, let's just disappear for a few days. Just because it's crazy doesn't mean it isn't real. That big bastard had a lock on me – see?" She pushed back her sleeve. "Look at the bruises on my arms. He was going to kill me, Tom. Please, just believe me!"

He could see she meant it. Could see the scrape on her chin – the strange new clothes. It was something out of a film script, not a gastro pub in Wandsworth, but crazy or not, this was Ali. If she really wanted to do this, well, that's what they'd do. He thought it would probably all have blown over by morning, but hell... It might even be fun!

"OK, then… No, wait! I don't have Simon this evening. I do have an E Type that Charlie wants me to deliver to Jermyn's in Hastings in the morning. Why don't we just drive straight down there? Maybe Clare and Ivan can hide us for a couple of days."

"Brilliant!" Ali's eyes were keen and shining. She was excited now. "Brilliant! Clare's always said she'd help me bury the body! She'll be so up to helping us. Let's do that… Wait, I'd better call her." She pulled out her mobile, and punched the number in.

A woman's voice answered, "Hello?"

"Clare, it's Ali."

"Ali, Hi! Not working this evening?"

"No. Look, Clare, Tom and I are driving down to the coast… No, not tomorrow. Now. We need somewhere to stay the night and we thought of you… Could we possibly?"

"You don't need to ask. You're sounding a bit hyper, Al. What's happened?"

"Nothing. Well, yes. We're in a bit of trouble. I'll tell you about it when we get there… Yes, we're still in London… It'll be after midnight by the time we get to you."

"OK, Ali. I'll wait up, just get here. Tell Tom to get a move on. But tread a bit softly when you come in won't you, so you don't wake Olivia? See you soon."

Ali looked at Tom. "All good. Show me how fast that E Type is!"

"Umm… ahh… You'll have to drive, Al. I'm not out of it but I've had several beers.

"Me? In a Jag? I hardly ever drive. How fast is it?"

"Quick. Probably not as quick as Simon. Not as sure-footed either. It's just two-wheel drive. You'll have to take it a bit easy. But it's all we've got!"

It was bright red, low and sleek, and looked about forty feet long! Ali got in and groaned. It was so low it felt as though she was sitting on the ground, and she couldn't see over that long bonnet in front of her. She'd be looking upwards at everything. The only way she could reach the pedals was by moving the seat so close to the steering wheel that her elbows jabbed into her ribs when she turned the wheel.

"Recline the seat a bit more. You'll have more room for your arms," came from Tom.

She tried it. "I can barely see out of the windscreen," she muttered. "This is going to be a disaster." She maneuvered the car out of the parking space carefully, giving lots of room at the front to allow for the invisible bonnet. Before pulling out into the street she took off her coat, wadded it into a cushion, and tried sitting on it. Yes, that gave her a slightly better view through the windscreen, although she still couldn't see the bonnet.

"Here goes," she said, and with a slight squeal from the rear tires she pulled out and accelerated carefully down the road.

Traffic was light, and before long they were on the M25, then the M26 and by the time they turned onto the A21 Ali was starting to relax. The car was fast, but it had good road manners, and once on the dual carriageways it purred along nicely. *Very nicely, actually. I could get used to this... With a higher seat, though!*

Ali glanced across at Tom. She knew he was sceptical about this whole thing – *Who wouldn't be*? But he had still set off with her on this – what? Flight from danger? Flight of fancy? Whatever it turned out to be, he had done that for her. God, he still made her stomach flutter and jump, even after all this time.

She'd known him since school, and she'd fancied him rotten even then. People often wondered if Tom were Italian, with his dark hair and golden skin tones, but she knew that these came from his mother, a vivid slip of a girl, a sprinter on the Malaysian track team, whose career had ended in the arms of an Irish entrepreneur. His eyes, an unexpected flash of deep and penetrating green, were pure County Offaly though.

She thought it was his smile that she loved best about him – it was certainly what had first attracted her to him. He was smiling now – a crooked, rather wicked smile – as he returned her sideways glance and slipped a CD into the disc player. He pressed the button, scrolled through the numbers and, finding the track he wanted, let it play. Ali wasn't as familiar with the 60s and 70's music he collected but this was a mutual favourite and she grinned as Paul Simon's opening bars whispered from the speakers, lightly, but spiritedly on an acoustic guitar. She recognised it, one of her favourites. She joined in on the chorus

"But I've got to creep down the alleyway," she sang…

"Fly down the highway," in Tom's light tenor…

"Before they come to catch me I'll be go-o-ne," she added before they both hit the last line…

"Somewhere… they can't find me!"

And for the first time in several hours, she laughed out loud.

*   *   *   *   *

Clare had been Tom's friend first. A tall, statuesque New Zealander, she was studying photography at the Royal College while he'd been dreaming up cars in Industrial Design. But when she met his girlfriend, the aspiring actor, a common sense of the ridiculous and love of the eccentric and the wild bound the two together as if they had shared a paddling pool at the age of two. Then Clare met Ivan at a gig. A songwriter, all black leather, skulls and studs, and she was gone, pregnant and ecstatic, joining the creative exodus from the crazy costs of London to the light and beauty and somewhat cheaper rents of the south coast. Not long afterwards, along came Olivia, a happy, smiling baby. Ali was godmother, (not Tom's thing), but work and even that short distance meant they didn't see each other nearly often enough.

It was well after midnight when they arrived in St Leonard's, but good as her word, Clare was up and waiting. Ivan was away for a week or so, locked up in a barn somewhere with his producer, writing the lyrics for what they hoped would be a Grammy winner. Olivia was fast asleep in bed, and Clare had been weeding out duds from today's fashion shoot. Ali was up to something, she could tell. She couldn't wait to hear about it.

"Come on through. Dump your stuff... Nothing? Never mind. I'll lend you whatever. Have you eaten? No? Spaghetti? Al Burro? Tom, grab the wine from the fridge will you - there's one open. I'd already started when you called."

She pounded the garlic, threw the pasta into the pan, a flick of sea salt and olive oil, about half a ton of butter, a generous screw of pepper and the meal was there. They were famished.

"Right." Clare sat down, picked up her glass and sat expectantly, looking at Ali. "Tell me."

Ali looked at Tom, and he smiled. "It's your story, Al. Far too complicated for me!"

"Well," said Ali, "We're sort of on the run! We need to disappear for a few days." Clare looked at her, waiting for more. When nothing came, she exploded.

"Alison Johnson, I want the whole story, not just a precis. You're 'sort of' on the run? Sort of? Who did you kill, and where's the body?"

"All right," said Ali a bit sheepishly. "You know the play I'm in? … it's opening soon… The Scottish Play… Oh you know, '*Macbeth*'." She gave it its name reluctantly. *Such bad luck!* Her face clouded over. "Well, I'm not going to be in it after all…"

Clare waited, then burst out. "Good grief woman! Stop it! For someone whose life is drama, you spend far too much time playing it down! What did you do? There's so much blood and guts in that play that even if you murdered half the cast no one would notice!"

Ali looked at her friend and sighed. "There was a murder last night, Sunday night, up near Tonbridge."

"Yes, I know. It was on the evening news. Ian Davison's wife…" Clare suddenly looked stricken. "Oh God, Ali, that's your play… You didn't?"

Ali looked appalled, in turn, but before she could say anything there was an interruption.

"Mummy! I woke up!" A little girl with tousled pre-Raphaelite curls and boys-own striped pyjamas looked accusingly at the adults as they sat over a bottle of wine around the long wooden table in the kitchen. "You didn't tell me Tom and Ali were coming."

Clare took her onto her lap and stroked her hair. "I know," she said. "I'm sorry if we woke you up. But Ali and Tom are having a bit of an adventure, so they've come down to share it with us. They'll tell you about it tomorrow. They've had a long day and they're tired - we all are."

Tom got up and held out his hand. "Come on, Ollie. Let Mummy and Ali finish catching up. I'll take you up and tuck you back in and you can tell me a bedtime story. Then we should probably all go to bed." Olivia looked at the three adults suspiciously, but then decided it was a pretty good offer.

"I should have a glass of wine first, though," she said.

"Watch it! I'll make you drink it!" said her mother, mock serious as she handed her daughter over. Olivia pulled a face and grinned, then she held her hand out to Tom and turned back to the stairs.

"OK, Ollie, remind me which way we go. I've forgotten where your room is!"

"Oh Tom! I showed you last time! You must remember!"

"Sorry Ollie. That was weeks ago. Come on let's go and find it," and Tom and a giggling little girl disappeared up the stairs with Olivia giving him directions.

"No, silly, *that* way," was the last they heard as the two rounded the corner at the top of the stairs. Serious again, Clare turned back to Ali.

"I know I told you I'd help you bury the body, but which body is it? They've already found Mrs. Davison. A tramp was seen in the area on Sunday evening. They think he did it. So, what did *you* do?"

Ali looked ready to explode. "Me? Nothing! It was Ian! He has a hit man. And now he's trying to kill me too!"

"Whoa… You've lost me. Start again." So Ali told her the whole thing - and it didn't sound any more rational this time around either. She shrugged, tired.

"I've given the police the whole story. If we can just stay out of the way for a few days while they round everybody up, everything will be fine. We'll be able to get on with our lives – what's left of them!" The realisation of what life would be after the murder was solved had suddenly hit her. "I suppose the play will be cancelled now. Shit, shit … shit! It was going to be so good. Ian's so brilliant, but if I'm right about all this, he's finished." She looked at Clare, eyes suddenly hard, and said, "He tried to have me killed too. How could someone so talented do something like this? Why? Honestly, it's as though he's actually turned into MacBeth!"

"I can't answer that," said a somewhat shaken Clare. "All I know is that you and Tom had better stay here until it's over. I really don't like the sound of this Boris. I think we'll just keep you out of his way. Keep all of us out of his way."

* * * * *

A Campaign of Lies

Susan slid out of her car. It was cold again but sunny, with the promise of warming up as the sun rose higher. October in England, she thought. Sometimes almost the most beautiful month of the year. But they were nearly into November. She hated November. Usually wet, dull, and grey with nothing of any cheer to relieve the gloom! *Perhaps not this year though*, she thought with a smile.

Mandy was going to keep "Laura's" closed today. She was still badly shaken but was putting a brave face on it. She would phone head office and discuss what had happened, but she was staying upstairs, warm and safe. Susan had promised to pop back to check on her when she could and had said she would pick up some supper and spend the evening with her again. Somehow the day seemed brighter, the sky a deeper blue. She realised she hadn't had a real friend since she joined the force, five years ago.

She looked over towards the staff entrance and saw that Sean had just arrived too. She walked over to him. *He's cleaned up well!* A bit of a bruised forehead, courtesy of a head-butt that fortunately he'd seen coming, and a bruise over one cheek. *That'll probably set a few more hearts aflutter,* she thought wryly.

She'd gone to town with Mandy's makeup, trying to cover the worst of the damage to her own face and a large pair of sunglasses helped too. Beyond that, she was limping slightly, but even the short walk across the car park helped to work off the stiffness. A long-sleeved polo neck, courtesy of Mandy, worn under her jacket hid vivid bruises down one arm from where she'd hit the shelves.

Well, she thought, *walking wounded we might be, but by God we're victorious ones! And wasn't Sandeep a surprise!*

"It's Savate," the young constable had explained. Her father and uncle had insisted that she learn to defend herself if she was to join the police, and it had to be something better than the standard police training if her small stature was not to be a liability. She had excelled at gymnastics at school, and her martial arts coach had recommended Savate, which was very gymnastic, as being her most likely strength.

I wonder if they knew about this in training. Of course, she hadn't seen PC Varma's service record yet but if Sandeep was to be on her team, she would. Perhaps there were more surprises there?

"Morning, Ma'am," greeted Sean. She was, guiltily, quite glad to see some stiffness around his mouth. She couldn't look like the only one who'd taken a hit! *I suppose Misery really does love company...* she admitted to herself. "How is Mandy holding up?" he was asking.

"Morning Sean. She's a lot better, but still shaky. I'll check on her again when I can. How did Stuart do yesterday?" She knew that M&M had planned to meet for a drink the night before, so he would know.

"He'll be here. He waited up at Nettle Lane while they finished the forensic sweep at the lay-by. Then he stayed on a bit longer because he didn't want to have to offer a ride to that PC you'd told to search the skip. Apparently, he stank to high heaven. He had a Panda there anyway, so he went off on his own in that. Stuart went straight back to The

Hole. He was there a bit before me, but as soon as I got there, he headed me off and we went up the road to The Swan's Nest. Feather's boys were at The Hole, and Stuart didn't like what they were saying."

"What was that?" she inquired.

"I'll let him tell you, Ma'am. Better you hear it first-hand."

Security at the staff entrance seemed surprised to see them. Entering the DCI's domain, they were met by a very bouncy PC Varma, looking younger than ever in a smart pair of jeans, and a short brown jacket over a cream shirt.

"Good morning, Sergeant Cross," she said rushing up to them, "and you too, DC Murphy," she added with a wide smile. "I have met the DCI. What a nice man! He told me to use one of the desks over there." She pointed over towards where Stuart sat, sipping his own steaming cappuccino.

"Sean, get Stuart. We'll meet in my office. We're seeing the DCI at 10.00 in the incident room, and we need to go over everything that's happened. You too, Sandeep." The two women moved down towards Susan's office. It wasn't the large corner office that the DCI had, but it was spacious enough; a far cry from the days when police stations were in cramped, ancient buildings with offices barely better than the cells below.

"Sergeant", said Sandeep in a low, conspiratorial tone, "The DCI is lovely. I can see how you fell for him. Anyone would."

Susan stared at her. "What on earth are you talking about, Sandeep? I ... fell for the DCI?"

"Well, everyone says you slept with him to get this nice office, but I can see how you must have fallen in love with him," she answered earnestly.

"Slept with him?" responded Crosspatch, flustered. "I …" But at that moment the M&Ms arrived. "I… er, right, sit down everyone. We've got a lot to talk about." She gathered her wits together. "OK... Those goons from the boutique are locked up downstairs?"

The three looked at each other. "Should be," said Sean.

Susan turned to the young Constable. "Sandeep, will you go down and tell the custody sergeant that I'll be down to interview them this morning?"

"Yes Ma'am" and she almost ran out the door.

"I thought we wanted to talk about the Nettle Lane case, Ma'am," ventured Stuart.

"Yes, we do, but something those thugs said just might link in with it. It was a 'Laura's' boutique, remember? We only dropped in to get Sandeep something she could wear back to the Centre, but we may have been incredibly lucky."

"Lucky?" asked Stuart. He was looking a tad sceptical. "If you call getting in the way of a wrecking ball 'lucky' then I suppose I could concede that."

"No that wasn't lucky, and if it hadn't been for Sandeep, it might have turned out very badly indeed. But one of them said something that might be a lead. He said he was there to persuade them to reinstate their insurance that had lapsed. The manager had no idea what he was talking about and said that their head office dealt with all their insurance." She paused. She had their full attention.

"It's pretty obvious that the 'insurance' was a protection racket. The classic 'Pay us to protect you from the nasty villains in the area.' Laura's' has a chain of about, what, 10 shops or more just across the south of the country? The 'insurance' on a chain like that would be considerable. Then suddenly their name was taken off the list of protected businesses. Those two must be a pair of their debt collectors. You don't get away with stopping paying for your protection. Now, just a day before, the owner of the whole chain was murdered. The news can't have filtered down that fast. Someone knew about it in advance; knew there was going to be a change in management and wanted to make sure the new team kept their cover in place... Are you with me?"

The two M&Ms sat there looking at her. Finally, Sean broke the silence. "We have been warned that a very violent gang might be involved, haven't we?" he said. She nodded.

"Bloody hell!" came from Stuart. "And you just happened to walk in on it? I take it back. That was incredibly lucky. A bloody great signpost to where we start looking, isn't it? Hah! Crosspatch takes one for the team! Ooops, sorry Ma'am," he said, then "I'm almost sorry I wasn't there!"

Sean looked at him. "Yes, well, you take my place next time we meet up with those bastards. Now I know why they call them hardheads. It's the literal truth!" he said, rubbing his forehead gently.

They were interrupted by PC Varma coming in at a run. "I'm sorry Ma'am. They let them go last night."

"What?" Susan leaped up from behind her desk. "No! Why would they do that?"

"I'm sorry. Ma'am. That's all the custody sergeant said."

"I need to look into this," Susan slammed her hands down on the desk, propelled herself out of her chair and she was gone. The two DCs looked at each other.

"Well, come on," said Sean and all three followed her.

She stormed down the hall, taking the stairs at breakneck speed, the others following more gingerly. Reaching the underground level, she burst out of the stairwell and charged down the hallway towards Custody.

"Who let those bastards from the boutique assault go?" she asked without preamble and the sergeant on duty looked up, visibly annoyed at the intrusion.

"The night sergeant, who else?" he answered, after a deliberate pause. "It's all in the custody book. He told me before he left this morning that the duty officer had phoned down to say there weren't going to be any charges, so when some posh lawyer turned up just before midnight demanding we either charge them or let them go, he let them go with her."

“He didn’t think to check with the arresting officer before letting them go?”

“Check with the arresting officer? Don't make me laugh! It was almost midnight. The word was that you wouldn’t even be in today as you were injured, and we couldn’t hold them without charges for more than twenty-four hours. Sgt Ballard did keep a record of their home addresses…”

The M&Ms came in followed by Sandeep. Susan turned to them. “Murphy, get the details on this. Maybe we can still find them.” Turning to the sergeant she asked “You said a DI okayed this? Which DI?”

“DI Featherstone, your old Guv. He was duty officer last night.”

“What?” and she was off down the corridor. Sean fancied he could see smoke coming from her ears as she went.

“Blimey, Murph,” said the custody sergeant, “No wonder they call her Crosspatch! I could think of other words, too! Is she always like that? I can’t understand what the DCI sees in her! Why did she get into that fight, anyway?”

“OK,” sighed DC Murphy. “Let’s just settle that one right now. I was at that fight last night. Those goons attacked the manager there. She called it in and tried to stop it. And without her I’d have come out with a lot more than bruises. One of those bastards had me down. She’d already been smashed into a wall, but she got up and came and helped me. It took both of us to collar him.”

"There were two of them Murph. What about the other one?"

Sean smiled at the memory. "You've never seen anything like it, Sarge! PC Varma here took him down on her own."

The custody sergeant looked at the diminutive PC and smirked. "Yeah! Course she did! Very loyal of you to stand up for your sergeant, Murph! But if you want to be believed, you'd better come up with something better than that. Word is that you pulled her out of it and took down the boys yourself. Everyone's a bit impressed! Sorry you've got her after Jonesy, though. You too Mac. You don't deserve a bitch like that." He shook his head in resignation. "Here you are," he said, bringing out the custody book. "Here's the details we have."

DC Murphy wasn't finished. "Dammit, Sarge," Sandeep looked at DC McLean. A quick flick of his eyes had her back out of custody in her sergeant's wake, leaving the two DCs to defend their leader. It was going to get noisy.

*   *   *   *   *

Susan marched down the hallway and slammed through the door into her old squad room. DC Monk looked up.

"Well, if it isn't the Prima Donna! Heard you got your bell rung good and proper yesterday, and you weren't going to be in today. What do you want?"

She looked around. Christ, she was glad she was out of this group. "Where's Featherstone?"

DC Monk sneered. "If you mean Detective Inspector Featherstone, he isn't here. He was duty officer last night and he had something important to follow up on one of his cases. He won't be in today. Should I tell him you want to see him? The DCI getting tired of you already? Heard he's got a new little Brownie, this morning," he finished with a leer. It died abruptly as Susan slammed both fists down on the desk in front of him, staring straight into his face.

"You really are a nasty little prat, aren't you? If you want to say anything about 'the Brownie', who has nothing at all to do with the DCI, try saying it to her face. She won't bother having you up for harassment. She'll just take you apart without even breaking a sweat! That girl's worth two of you! Hell, she's worth a dozen." She turned around and marched back up the stairs, leaving DC Monk slack jawed.

Where did all that filth come from? Susan had thought the rumours that had spread after her sudden transfer to the Third Floor had died down. Then Sandeep's naive remarks about the DCI came back to her too. *Bugger!* Clearly, they hadn't. In fact, they seemed to have become even more poisonous. Hadn't Sean said that Featherstone's group had been bad mouthing her at the pub last night? This wasn't just unpleasant for her, it could seriously damage the DCI's position, and after he'd rescued her from an intolerable situation. She sighed. She was going to have to talk to him…

She walked into her office and sat down. OK, losing the two thugs was unfortunate, but not a disaster. She doubted very much that they could track them down at the address they had given. Questioning the lawyer wouldn't help either. She would just claim Client/Solicitor privilege and say nothing at all. Fingerprints? Yes, they'd have those since they had booked them, and she would put a uniform on that to see what they might find. They would undoubtedly have form which would give them names, but chasing them down would waste time and resources. Better to start right back at the Laura's group head office and try to track the protection racket from there. If insurance was being paid, there would be a record. 'Follow the money'. With luck they would be able to follow it right through to whoever it was that had known about the imminent change of management there.

Sandeep came trotting back. She was looking concerned. "Where are the others?" asked Susan, who had calmed down a bit.

"They're coming. But they were arguing with the custody sergeant. He said you started that fight last night, Ma'am! Sean told him what really happened, but the sergeant didn't believe him. DC McLean kept trying to pull him away. I think he was afraid he might hit the sergeant, he was so frustrated. Who would tell the custody sergeant such lies?"

"You remember I warned you that people were saying derogatory things about me? You've obviously heard some of them. Now you see it in all its ugly realism. You even believed some of them." Sandeep looked at her.

"About the DCI? You aren't in love with him?"

Susan sighed. "No, Sandeep, I'm not. He's a first-class police officer, a great boss, and a lovely man. But he's also married, very happily as far as I know. I'll be forever grateful to him for getting me off the second floor, but that's all."

"Oh," said Sandeep. "I see. I'm sorry."

"Sorry? Why would you be sorry?"

"It is so romantic," she sighed. "It makes a wonderful story."

"Come off it, Sandeep! What would that make me? 'Crosspatch the Home Wrecker'? That wouldn't be romantic at all!"

"But it is." She put both hands on her heart and looked soulfully at the ceiling. "You love him, but you know it can never be, so you will never speak to him of the feelings of your heart! That's very romantic!"

"Honestly, Sandeep, what have you been reading? Pull yourself together! I respect him, I like him, but that's it."

Sandeep sighed again; her eyes dreamy. "It is romantic!"

This had to stop. "Enough! No more! I am NOT in love with…"

"10 o'clock in the incident room, Susan?" The DCI was at her office door. "I have a meeting upstairs first, but it should be over by then." He was off through the squad room to the stairs, leaving Susan once again more than a little flustered.

She shook herself and looked at Sandeep sternly. "Let's get back to real life, shall we? We have a particularly nasty murder to solve, a really vicious killer to find. Can we concentrate on that?"

Sandeep stepped back. "Of course, Ma'am. Sorry Ma'am."

"Right, let's go over what we know…"

* * * * *

Team Crosspatch were ready in the conference room, by 10.00. A few minutes later they were joined by DCI Gordon, who brought DC Crewe with him. Sitting down at the head of the table, he opened the meeting.

"Right. Everyone's here. This isn't the only case I'm supervising at the moment, and the other DI's also have a fairly heavy caseload, so I'll just say that Sergeant Cross will be the Senior Investigating Officer of this investigation on the ground. She will report to me regularly. Today's meeting is just for me to see that you have a viable plan of investigation, and that you all understand the need for absolute discretion throughout. All information to the press is to go through the Centre's press office and is to be cleared either with Sergeant Cross or myself.

"Sergeant Cross has requested to add PC Varma to the team for the duration of the case. She's been released by the Tonbridge station on a temporary basis. DC Crewe, here, is also on loan from DS Stevenson's team. His forensic accounting experience may be helpful."

Sandy haired, bespectacled, of medium height and dressed conservatively in a white shirt, grey suit and nondescript tie, Dave Crewe was a man who would blend in well in any office setting. He looked around. "Murph, Mac," he nodded to each. "Sergeant," nodding again to Susan. "PC Varma, no, we haven't met before, but I know Helen and Scotty." Sandeep nodded to him, but for once had nothing to say. Susan spoke up.

"PC Varma was one of the uniforms at Nettle Lane. She was the person who found our first pieces of evidence on the killer. It seems she's also our martial arts expert," she added with a smile.

The DCI broke in. "I heard about that. Opinions seem to vary on the truth of that encounter." He looked directly at PC Varma. "Are you telling me you took down a six foot plus villain single handedly? In fact, with your bare hands?"

"Yes, sir," she said matter-of-factly. "Well, not bare handed," she added, wanting to be accurate. "I kicked him in the face sir, and I had standard police shoes on. They're a bit awkward to fight in, but they deliver a very solid kick."

"She did, sir," added Sean. "It was amazing. I've never seen anything like it!"

"It really was." Susan.

"Well, PC Varma," said Gordon, "Let me add my congratulations, and my thanks for getting my people out of a difficult situation. Welcome to Team Crossp… Cross. A spectacular first arrest!"

Turning back to the group, he continued. "DC Crewe will give you the written report on our meeting with Ian Davison. We watched from the back of the auditorium for a few minutes as he addressed his cast. Apart from popping back to his office briefly he seems to have just got straight on with the rehearsal we had interrupted.

"Now, as I'm sure you're aware, the most common perpetrator in this type of murder is the spouse or partner. Accordingly, I had PC Jarvis search through the CCTV files to see if we could see where he was at the presumed time of the murder. She found him at his theatre until late in the afternoon, and he then joined the cast until late in the evening at a local pub. Unless the FP comes up with a much later time of death than we are expecting, he has a solid alibi. Which leaves the investigation completely open.

"So over to you, Sergeant Cross. What do you have so far?"

"Ian Davison may not have killed his wife, but someone did," she said, "very brutally. Why such violence? Who would have hated her so much, and why? The answer must lie in either their personal lives, or their professional lives.

"We have two separate lines of inquiry. One, the husband and his business. That's his theatre. DC Murphy is knowledgeable about the theatre in general, so I have assigned that line to him. We need to know everything about Ian Davison's life over the past year or two and we need a detailed look at his background and his finances. Was his wife in the way for some reason?

"DC's MacLean and Crewe have the line on Laura's. That's a bit more difficult, especially since we lost those thugs from the fight last night. They probably know who had advance notice of Laura's death. Still, we can perhaps work that one in reverse, by finding out who ‘protection’ was being paid to. It’s possible this could have been the result of Laura’s own business affairs. So, we have two people’s lives to track down; two sets of financials to go through.

“And we still have Ian Davison as a person of interest. He didn’t kill Laura himself, but could he have arranged to have her killed? That may show up in a review of his finances. It wouldn’t have been cheap, and hired killers don’t generally extend credit. So unless he has financial resources that we can’t access, it shouldn’t be hard to find.

“Other than the attack by an unseen and unknown ‘tramp’ we have little else, and we believe that is just a red herring. Tonbridge is following up on that. Other lines will undoubtedly appear as the investigations proceed, and we’ll look at them as they come up.”

Susan was winding things up. DCI Gordon sat back, pleased by what he was seeing. She was living up to the potential he had seen in her early record. She had stepped up and drawn her team around her. This was no longer ‘Team Jones’.

“Sergeant Cross,” he paused. “How is it those two thugs who attacked police officers were released last night?”

Susan flushed. “The night custody sergeant was advised by the duty officer that there would be no charges, so when a lawyer arrived demanding their release, he felt he had no option but to let them go.”

“The duty officer? On what grounds did he authorise the release?”

"He had apparently been told that I, or my team, had instigated the fight, and that it would be better to release them than face the probable resulting bad press, Sir. Wherever that story came from, it seems a lot of people believe it."

"And who was the duty officer last night?"

"DI Featherstone, Sir"

"I see," said the DCI. "Unfortunate." There was a moment of silence then, "I'll have a word with the custody sergeant. Perhaps he isn't aware that your call to the emergency line was recorded last night – all of it, including the fight. That makes is quite clear that your team did not instigate the fight.

"Let me bring you up to speed on the PR situation. Yesterday we issued a brief statement that a dead body had been found at a house on Nettle Lane, and it was updated with the victim's name late in the day once Davison had been informed. He has been notified of his wife's death, and so have her parents, Sir Gerald and Lady Handley. The Yard is dealing with any issues relating to Sir Gerald, as you know. Unless you disagree, Sergeant, I'll have the press office release an update confirming that we're still looking for a vagrant reported to have been in the area. I will have the press officer contact you if they need further details. I'll also remind them that either you or I are to approve all press releases on this case before they go out."

She nodded. "Thank you, Sir."

"One more thing you all need to be aware of. A warning came through this morning from the Security

Services. They believe ISIS is stirring things up again, and are pressuring their acolytes to attack police 'anywhere and everywhere'. Everyone needs to be aware and be on the alert." He stood up to leave.

"Ah… Can I have a moment of your time, Sir?"

"Of course, Susan. I was going to suggest the same. Let's go down to my office," and he led the way out. "What's on your mind?" he asked, as he settled down behind his desk. Susan sat across from him, acutely embarrassed.

"Sir, it's about the rumours that are circulating. They started when you pulled me out of DI Featherstone's squad." She blushed. "The story going around is that I'd slept with you to get this job," she finished in a rush. "Obviously that's untrue, Sir - I mean, you know it isn't true, and I'd never really met you before that day other than a brief introduction. And I wouldn't… but they're getting worse." She felt herself floundering, stopped and then said frankly, "I don't know what to do about it Sir, and I'm worried that it'll damage your career, if we can't stop them."

Gordon sat back and sighed. "Yes, Susan, I know about them. I had been hoping that if we both got on quietly with our jobs it would quickly become apparent that the story was baseless.

"You've done your part. You've buckled down to the job and you have become an excellent team leader. The team is now clearly Team Cross, and the team members have even taken ownership of the name of "Team Crosspatch" with pride. That's no small achievement, but you're right. The rumour mill hasn't backed off. Someone has it in for one or both of us, and I'm afraid I know who it is."

He paused for a moment and then continued. "You weren't here when I was promoted to DCI." She shook her head. He sat back for a moment, laced his fingers together and then tapped them against his lips before he continued. "There were three DI's here when DCI Thompson moved up to the role of Superintendent of the Cumbria Constabulary. All of them applied for the position. I was a DI in the Thames Valley force, in Slough. I applied for the job too, and I was selected. It's quite common to select from outside the local group when there are several local candidates. The theory is that it won't upset the chemistry of the local office the way selecting one and rejecting the others might. It makes for less infighting and local jealousies and it usually works."

She nodded and he went on.

"It doesn't seem to have worked here. While I have no difficulty working with either of the other two, DI Featherstone has waged a non-stop war of minimal cooperation. He won't go against a direct order but there has been a constant run of under the table criticism and questioning of anything coming down from the Third floor. I'm told he had the idea from somewhere that he was the preferred candidate and took it hard when he was not selected. I think it is almost certain that he is behind it."

He paused, and then carried on. "When I selected you for this job, it was apparent that you had problems with DI Featherstone. You have never made a formal complaint, and we can't investigate without one, but would you be prepared to tell me - off the record, if you like - what the problem was?"

She hesitated, clearly uncomfortable, but then out it came.

"You have to understand that this is something that I can't prove," she said quietly. "After I passed the sergeants' exam and was transferred here, I was assigned to DI Featherstone's squad." She sighed. "I was really looking forward to it and imagined myself working with a topflight team, but it turned into a nightmare. I was seriously considering leaving the police force when you intervened.

"DI Featherstone started by making a fuss of me. He told the rest of the squad that I was on a fast track to becoming a DI, and that they'd better 'pull their socks up' or I'd make them look bad. That didn't exactly make it easy for me to establish a good working relationship with the others. Then he decided to change the entire format of his squad.

"I was to work for him directly, rather than with a team. I was to be his 'executive officer', as he put it. I would be above the others but working under him."

She paused, took a breath, and hurried on. "He meant that literally. It was made clear that to get positive performance reports, and to be 'showcased' - his words - on the most important cases allocated to his squad, I was to be available at all times that he wanted me t... to service him." Her voice had dropped away but he could see the anger in her eyes.

"I refused, but nothing specific had ever been said where others might hear. He was always careful only to use innuendo. I had nothing to support any complaint I might make." She shrugged. "He seems to be very popular at senior levels. It would have been his word against mine, and I was the newcomer, an unknown quantity, and he'd made sure I wasn't exactly popular.

"He assigned all the DCs to DS Smith as one big team to handle what he considered to be important cases, and I became a solo DS assigned to clean up all the odd cases that he didn't consider big enough to require a team."

Gordon looked at her with respect. That had taken a lot of courage. "So, you refused, and as a result you wound up with poor performance reports and were shuffled off onto trivial cases and kept in the background," he said. "Susan, I am so sorry, and more than ever I'm glad to have got you out of there. I think this campaign might well be aimed as much at you as at me."

He paused. "Thank you for telling me. Let me think about it all for a day or two. We need to take some action to deflect these rumours now, and a reorganisation of the second floor is clearly overdue. But as you have observed, he has his supporters, including some influential people at the Yard. We'll have to move carefully.

"DI Featherstone was duty officer last night. Do you know where he is today?"

"No-one seems to know, Sir. Apparently, he received a call from the Met about someone they were holding at Walworth who was believed to be a POI in one of our cases, and he went up to London to bring them back here."

"That's not the job of the duty officer. Why wasn't a Panda dispatched?"

"I agree. It's strange, Sir"

"Mmm. I wonder. Do you know if Walworth did have a POI that we would want to talk to?"

"Not that I'm aware of, Sir. I have no idea who they had unless they have found our tramp. I'm hoping DI Featherstone will reappear shortly with whoever it is. But, of course, it could have nothing to do with this case."

"True. But in light of what we've just been discussing I'm rather concerned that he would take off without anyone knowing in more detail what it was about. Keep me up to date on that. Look, Susan, make a point of dropping in to talk to me at least twice a week. Don't just send a memo or a report. I want to be able to discuss your findings with you on a regular basis… But let's make sure it's somewhere we can plainly be seen to be doing no more than that!"

She smiled. "Yes sir, no locked doors!"

*   *   *   *   *

Doubting Thomas

Tom was up early that morning. He wanted to get the Jaguar off the street in front of Clare's house and delivered to Jermyn's. He'd been marginally surprised the previous night to hear that the murder was all over the news, but then, of course, he hadn't heard the news at all that day. He had gone straight to the pub from work. So, Ali wasn't imagining it. Perhaps Davison really had killed his wife - or had her killed. If he had, and he knew what Ali had heard on his phone he might well have turned his hired killer loose on her.

But that was all speculation, and anyway, Davison didn't know him. He hadn't been to any of the rehearsals. Davison didn't like hangers-on distracting his players when they were working, so why shouldn't he pop up to London and collect a few things they needed from their flat? He could pick up Simon while he was about it and square away a few days off with his boss. It made sense. It would give them more options if they did need to hide.

It was a glorious day, the sun, gleaming golden through the clear autumn air, picking out the tops of the waves in the Channel. But it sat low in the sky and as Tom drove along the seashore into Hastings, it filled the windscreen with dazzling, blinding light. He sat up higher and lowered the sun visor. Slowly, then. He couldn't risk putting a scratch on the beautiful work they'd done on the car. *Probably should have thought of that last night, asking Ali to drive all the way to St Leonard's!*

Jermyn's was a smallish operation. Just three repair bays with an office and storeroom attached. However, they had a formidable reputation in the field of servicing and repairing old Jaguars, and customers brought their cars from all over the country and beyond, threading their way through the back streets of Hastings to find them. The E-Type that Tom had brought down had needed some serious bodywork, and Jermyn's had sent it up to Classic Cars for them to finish the restoration.

It wasn't an unusual arrangement. The two companies sent work to one another regularly and Tom had been there before, so he had no trouble finding them. He dropped off the car, went back into the workshops to say hello to a couple of the mechanics that he knew, and then strolled up to the station. He was in luck, a train to Charing Cross was due to leave shortly. He could get off at Waterloo East, walk over the link, and pick up a train to Wandsworth Town. He paid for the ticket with his credit card – they might need whatever cash he had later – and while waiting, he picked up a newspaper. There it was. Front page news. He bought a copy and folded it to read on the train.

It was after the early morning rush to the city, so finding a section to himself, he settled back comfortably by the window and started to read. There really wasn't much. The actual story of the murder was brief and to the point; probably taken verbatim from a police press release. The tramp story was being run as the official line, although it was vague. There was no clear description other than that he was a 'big' man. The story went on to speak of Ian Davison and his triumphs on the stage, but also provided some information on the victim, who was apparently a successful businesswoman in her own right, and the owner of the chain of fashion boutiques named *Laura's*.

It seemed to Tom that either the police were barking up the wrong tree completely, or that they were just letting the tramp story run while they put together their case against Davison. Since they already had Alison's statement that was probably exactly what they were doing. He smiled to himself. This would all be over soon. Ali could stop worrying.

*   *   *   *   *

DI Featherstone had not been pleased when he arrived at Walworth to find his bird had flown. He'd scooped up her written statement, and cleared the file, but beyond that there was little to be done at that time of night. He drove over to Scotland Yard, where he was well known, and where he might find somewhere to put his head down for a bit. He managed to get three hours of shut eye and was up and ready to go as the regular day shift was arriving. He was waiting at the theatre when Ian arrived looking rather the worse for wear.

Bad coppers aren't necessarily bad policemen, they're just bad individuals - or weak ones. They want more and they want it to come more easily than it does. Adding a sense of entitlement and superiority can be a very dangerous thing. In Featherstone's case this was allied to a firm belief that he'd been cheated in his drive for promotion. He knew how to do his job and needed no prompting.

He found Ali's address in the personnel records at the theatre and went straight there. It was one of the newer blocks of flats, 14 stories high and overlooking the river. A flash of his warrant card persuaded the concierge to let him in. A few days' worth of post had been left on the counter in the kitchen. He leafed through it.

Mobile phone bills on the table. Useful. Ah, the girl was living with her boyfriend. Then the likelihood of their being together now was high. No sign of a hasty packing job. Toothpaste and 2 brushes in the bathroom… two razors and a packet of birth control pills.

Pulling out his phone, he initiated a search on Alison Johnson and Facebook confirmed that she was in a relationship with one Tom O'Malley. Tom wasn't a Facebook user himself but had an active Instagram account that gave a lot of coverage to Classic Cars of Wandsworth.

Worth keeping an eye on this place, he thought. They - or one of them - might well be back. Birth control pills? Probably would, then. He called 'Lennox' and gave him the address.

"Get down here. There's no one here now but we need to watch the place in case they come back. I know where the boyfriend works - I'm going over now to see if he's there. If he is, I'll insist that he comes with me 'to the station' and I'll bring him to you. If anyone knows where she is, he will. I'm sure you can make him talk."

Featherstone left the door on the latch and went back down to the foyer. Barely half an hour later a taxi stopped outside. An enormous man got out and walked up to the entrance where Featherstone let him in. The two talked for a couple of minutes, and then Featherstone came out and walked over to his car, a black BMW. Settling in, he put the address of Classic Cars into the satnav and drove off, following the directions.

*   *   *   *   *

Tom walked home from the station. He wanted to pick up spare clothes, and grab their basic toiletries and… maybe their passports? Their walking boots? Just enough for two backpacks. He was cheerfully congratulating himself on making the right decision to nip back up to London. No one had accosted him, no suspicious characters were loitering outside their building. Poor old Ali. She had certainly had a fright yesterday, but in the clear light of such a beautiful day he suspected she had over dramatised it all.

All the same, though… he'd seen it himself - front page of all the Nationals. Davison's wife *had* been murdered. And Ali's bruises & scraped chin … something was definitely going on. He'd watch himself.

He let himself in at the front entrance and took the stairs up to the flat, as he always did. Healthier to climb the three flights of stairs every day than to use the lift. He came out of the stairwell at the end of the corridor and walked past the lifts towards their door. He was about to put his key in the lock when he realised the door was on the latch! *What…?* Then he heard the toilet flush. Someone was in their bathroom… Without hesitating he turned and was walking smartly back the way he'd come when, just as he reached the lifts, he heard a voice.

"Oi, you!"

He turned. A man was standing in the doorway of their flat, looking at him. And not in a friendly way. A huge man. Six foot five? Six? *Bloody Hell!* Built like a tank, and with a mop of straw-coloured hair! Well, Ali wasn't the only one who could act.

“Yes? Can I help you?” he asked

“Who’re you then?”

“And who’s asking?”

“What’re you doing here?”

“I live here,” answered Tom, pressing the button to call the lift. Boris (*it must be Ali’s Boris*, he thought), advanced towards him threateningly.

“What’s your name?”

“And what business is that of yours?” said Tom, stepping aside from the lift which had conveniently just arrived. Out of it stepped an elderly couple and a bright-eyed Jack Russell terrier. Mr and Mrs Olsen from down the hall, just coming back from their morning walk.

“Good morning!” came from Mrs Olsen, a perpetually cheerful little woman. Smiling in greeting, Tom stepped briskly into the lift and hit the down button. The little Jack Russell had its ruff up and it was growling at the big man who eyed it warily and stepped back. The lift reached the ground floor and Tom was out and running for the back entrance, and out to the street. He didn’t stop running until there were at least two buildings between him and his own. Suddenly Ali’s near panic was all too real and - *For God’s sake!* - all too reasonable. *Christ… She put that brute down and escaped?* The story was now terrifying! He’d already tracked them to their home and had obviously been waiting for one of them to show up. If ‘Boris’ hadn’t flushed the loo just then, he would have walked right in on him! Somehow, he didn’t think he’d have got away as neatly as Ali had done!

It was time to think seriously about this. Yes, the police had Ali's statement and would be checking out Davison very carefully. But they might not know who Boris was, or where to find him. So he could still be in the clear, free to track Ali down. She might be the only person who could identify him. *Christ! We really do need to hide somewhere. OK. OK. So, what do I do?*

First, if they were staking out the flat, they didn't know where she was. In fact, they probably thought she was still in London. Did they have access to her - or his - bank account? His Visa account? He didn't know, but in case they did he'd draw as much cash as he could on the bankcard, and then use the Visa to buy a couple of train tickets to somewhere. Maybe Manchester. Buy some camping stuff, and a guide to the Lake District. Give them the idea that they'd gone walking up there on the Fells. Get the word spread at work that they'd gone up there for a week's hiking? Was it a bit late in the year for that? Not really sure, he thought, but 'Boris' might not be sure either.

* * * * *

'Boris' had moved aside to let the old couple past. He didn't want any trouble with dogs. They were noisy - far too noisy - and quick. Past experience told him to avoid them at any cost. But in doing so, the man he had wanted to talk to had disappeared down in the lift. He was just turning to go back to the flat when he heard Mrs. Olsen say "I wonder what Tom was doing at home so late in the morning? He must have taken a day off work."

He went in. Closed the door and suddenly realised what he'd heard... Tom... Tom O'Malley! He was back out of the door in a flash and, rushing towards the stairs, he saw the light on the lift button had gone out. Tom was already on the ground floor. He ran down the stairs as fast as he dared - someone of his size had to be careful… His centre of gravity was high, and the saying 'the bigger they are, the harder they fall' was apt. It could be painful if you lost control on stairs. He burst from the stairwell and rushed out of the front door. He looked in all directions but couldn't see Tom anywhere. Cursing under his breath, he turned to go back into the building only to find that the front door had closed… He couldn't get back in unless he smashed his way through, and that would bring the police in a hurry. He'd have to call Featherstone. Then he remembered he'd left his mobile phone on the table, in the kitchen, three floors up! He'd have to wait for someone else to go in or come out.

Nothing, *not one fucking thing*, had gone right since Manchester! Had that last woman put a curse on him as she died?

* * * * *

At the theatre, everyone was giving Ian a wide berth. The man himself was feeling almost desperate, blocked at every step. He'd tried walking into the Laura's Group head office in South London to speak to the Finance Director about his taking over as CEO. The woman had been very polite, very gentle, and offered their condolences. They had all loved Laura and they were devastated about what had happened. The board of directors was currently consulting with their lawyers concerning the succession issue. But surely, he must have known … Laura had left very specific instructions that in the event of her death her ownership in the company would go to her father, in trust…

He had also approached their bank to see about getting a second mortgage on the Nettle Lane house but had met with similar resistance. All legal procedures around a suspicious death had to be followed, and, of course, probate granted before he could have the land title transferred to him. Until then, they were very sorry, but they couldn't help him. And mortgage payments were still to be paid. Laura had always paid that…

And meanwhile his investors were demanding their money back...

Hang on, though ...

Were they? All he had had was a hurried interview with Bellamy, the man who'd introduced himself as coming from Georgiades. He realised he had panicked…

Shouldn't they have approached him more formally? Shouldn't he have spoken to his father-in-law? It was Gerald who had introduced him to them after Laura had bailed out the Classic.

"Don't depend on your wife for money, old son. Very uncomfortable. Talk to the professionals."

Ian had wondered whether he spoke from experience. But Laura's father? He flinched at the thought.

He had to call Georgiades. Ask for a delay... Pulling out his phone he checked his contacts list. Where was it? Then he remembered. This was his new phone. He hadn't transferred all his contacts yet. The shop he'd bought it at had offered to transfer all the information from his old phone for him, but he'd told them his old phone had been destroyed; crushed under the wheels of a taxi when he'd dropped it getting out. It had, too, but that had been a still older phone. So, he'd been transferring his contacts list manually, whenever he had a few spare moments, and it was taking him too long. He pulled out the old phone, brought up the number, bumped it into his new one and pressed 'connect'.

"Georgiades." An impatient tone.

"Mr. Georgiades. It's Ian Davison."

The tone changed. "Ian, good morning. I have just heard about your wife's death. I am so sorry…"

"Thank you, Mr. Georgiades." He paused, uncertain, then hurried on. "It's about your group's investment in the theatre. I know you want your money back, but it's going to take time. I can't raise the funds until all the legal proceedings with regard to Laura's death have been resolved. I need time." He was babbling. There was silence for a moment.

"Ian, of course. Terrible thing to happen." Then, in a worried tone… "But are you trying to buy us out? I have good reports about what you're doing, and we're not going to let you buy us out just when the investment looks like it may pay off!"

Ian paused for a moment, then spoke very slowly. "You sent that Bellamy bloke over to tell me you wanted all your money back! He said I had to come up with it now!"

There was another moment's silence. "No, Ian. We said we needed you to move faster. We cannot continue advancing you money for interminable rehearsals and other delays. My reports are that it is very good already, so please move things forward. That is what we asked. For you to speed things up. Money will be forthcoming as needed, but you must move the opening forward. As soon as possible! The investors say you are wasting their money with all these delays."

Ian was silent for a moment, stunned.

"Ian, please tell me this has nothing to do with the death of your wife?" The question was urgent, distressed.

"What?" *Oh God, this can't be happening!* "No! No, Mr. Georgiades. How could it be? I'm sorry, I've been in a terrible state ever since I heard the news. Hard to focus on anything."

"I understand, Ian. I am relieved."

Georgiades' voice reverted to its usual business-like tone. "Now, can you move forward on the opening? We are not concerned that the initial performances might not play before a full house! It will be enough to show that you can back up your promises!"

"Yes, of course Mr. Georgiades. We'll need to do some rush advertising, and I'll need to bring in the rest of the staff earlier than expected, but of course we can do it."

"Good, Ian. The investors will be very glad to hear that. But no more delays, yes? I'll have one of my people come around to coordinate that with you…" and that question again… "Ian, you are sure this is just a misunderstanding? It has nothing to do with your wife's death?"

"No, of course not, Mr. Georgiades."

"I sincerely hope you are right on that, Ian. You have no idea how bad it would be otherwise."

Ian sat back, a rollercoaster of emotions. *Oh God... What happened? He said they wanted the money. Now.* He'd threatened him. But he'd said he'd fix it… hadn't he?

Why hadn't Laura supported him? Why had she turned him down when he'd asked her to bail him out … suggested that her damned shops, the cottage, for fuck's sake, were more important than his theatre?

The witches - he could hear them cackling, feel the cold rising, the mists closing in, swirling red behind his eyes. His head ached; his heart was roaring.

O, full of scorpions is my mind, dear wife!

Laura! And for the first time, Ian really wept.

*   *   *   *   *

Georgiades sat back at his desk. What the fuck had Bellamy done? The Organisation had wanted that play open according to the original schedule, but Davison had put it off claiming he was not ready. Davison was never ready… "Almost there. A couple more weeks." After two calls that failed to get Davison to understand that there were to be no more delays, he'd decided to send in one of their enforcers - to get the point across. He remembered his call with Bellamy… the man had sounded a little vague about the job now that he thought about it… but he had an excellent record. When Bellamy said "do something" people complied. He got results. No "or else" needed.

But Bellamy had been essentially de-activated in the last couple of years after he got a bit too enthusiastic over a couple of jobs and made two unauthorised kills. Georgiades had only used him as no-one else was in position at the time, and as a messenger. Nothing else. He'd reported back "everything under control" on this one. What had he told Davison? What had he done? Heads would roll if it turned out that this had been the cause of Laura's death. And one of them could well be his own.

*   *   *   *   *

A bit out of his Territory?

Arriving at 'Classic Cars' Featherstone went straight in through the showroom doors and approached the receptionist at the front desk. She was good-looking, late twenties he guessed, with a mass of bright blonde hair and shiny red lipstick.

Flashing his warrant card at her, he growled "I'm here to talk to Thomas O'Malley."

"I'm sorry," came the reply, "I don't believe the Cat is in today. I'm not sure when he will be."

"The Cat?"

"Oh, the girls all call him that. You know, 'Thomas O'Malley'?" She wiggled her eyebrows. "I think he was delivering a car somewhere."

Featherstone clearly didn't understand.

She tried again. "Thomas O'Malley, the Alley Cat? The Aristocats? Disney? ... Oh, never mind."

Annoyed at being considered slow on the uptake, he growled again. "I'm here on official police business. I need to speak to O'Malley. If you don't know where he is, find someone who does."

She looked at him. He'd gone red, and she could swear his moustache was quivering. "I'll see if Mr. Crosby is in. Can I see your identification again?" She waited while the Inspector pulled out his warrant card again and gave it to her. She looked at it carefully and kept it.

"Just wait here, Inspector," and she got up from behind her desk and walked with a deliberate sway quietly and slowly up the stairs to the offices above and sauntered into Crosby's office.

Once past the door, and out of his sight her languid air disappeared. "Charlie," she said urgently, "There's a copper here. An Inspector Featherstone from the South-East Constabulary. Nasty type. Very growly. Demanding to see someone who can tell him where the Cat is. Didn't he go off to do something for you?" She handed him Featherstone's card.

Charlie Crosby looked up from the auction catalogue he'd been studying. In his early fifties, he was a fit, athletic looking man, his face ruddy beneath a greying mop of hair.

"A bit out of his jurisdiction, isn't he? What does he want with Tommy?" he asked.

"He didn't say. Just said he was on official police business and had to see him. He's implying that Tommy's been up to no good."

"OK Doris, I'll come down and see him. Let's keep everything wide open and public, so that he can't claim anyone's said anything they didn't. But we'll let him stew a bit."

* * * * *

Doris sashayed slowly back down the stairs. Featherstone was still standing at her desk and watched with growing impatience.

"Mr. Crosby will be down to see you in a moment," she said, handing him back his warrant card. "He's just on a call. Do take a seat," and she gestured towards some basic steel chairs over by the wall. Then she got a small bag out of her handbag and gave all her attention to re-varnishing her nails.

Featherstone sat down. Several minutes passed, then several more and still nothing happened. He got up, went up to her desk again. "Look here, I'm on…" and her phone rang. She looked at him, smiled, shrugged her shoulders as though to say "I'm sorry, but you know how it is…" and answered the phone.

"Classic Cars. Oh, good morning, Mr. James, so nice to hear your voice. How's that gorgeous Bentley of yours? You sold it? Oh, but it was such a lovely car… Ah! Well, I suppose I would have too, at that price. Are you looking for something to replace it?"

Featherstone, not used to being ignored, broke in. "I'm on important police business. Just get Crosby…"

Doris gave him an annoyed look, holding her hand over the mouthpiece of the phone. "Do you mind? I'm on the phone with an important customer!" and she went back to her call.

Charlie watched from the upper level with a grin. Doris really was a gem. She could deflate pompous, self-important prats better than anyone he knew. Better step in, though, before the copper had a stroke! He headed down the stairs and over to the Inspector, holding out his hand, a bright smile on his face.

"Charles Crosby, Inspector. I'm so sorry, I was on the phone with Sotheby's. They're looking for a valuation of three old Rollers for an estate that's going to auction. They've got a little gold mine there. Now, how can I help you? Doris says it's something about our Thomas?"

Featherstone, caught halfway into another rant, had to re-organise his thoughts quickly. "I think a murder investigation takes precedence over Sotheby's!" he huffed. "I understand you employ a Thomas O'Malley?"

"A murder? My goodness, surely not. Thomas is one of our restoration team. Excellent young man. A real artist. Royal college trained. I can't believe he's involved in a murder."

"He is a person of interest in one of our cases, Sir, and it's vital that I talk to him as soon as possible. Where is he?"

"How alarming, Inspector. Let's go and see George, the restoration team supervisor. Perhaps he'll know more about this." He smiled again and, without waiting for a response, took off through a door at the back, leaving Featherstone no choice but to follow.

As they went through the door, the hush of the sales floor was replaced with the harsh scream of air tools, the chug of compressors and the occasional bang of a hammer on steel echoing throughout the workshops. Charlie said something to him, but a compressor cut in just as he began talking, so the Inspector didn't hear a thing.

"What?" he asked.

Charlie leaned close and shouted close to his ear. "If you worked in here, you'd need ear protectors, but we won't be long. You'll be OK. This way," and he led the Inspector towards a small office set against the wall, built out of what looked like a large freight container. The noise lessened, as he closed the door behind him.

"George," he said to the man sitting at a desk beside a window looking out into the workshop. "This is Inspector…" Then to Featherstone, "Sorry. I'm terrible with names. What was yours again?"

"Featherstone, Inspector Featherstone."

"Right, I'll try to remember that. Feathers … turkey! Oh sorry, Feathers, yes… Inspector Feathers. Right, got it."

"George, this is Inspector Featherweight. He's looking for Tom O'Malley." Then looking out the window into the workshop, he muttered "Oh no, this won't do at all."

Turning to Featherstone, "Excuse me for a moment, Inspector, one of our mechanics is working on something we haven't been cleared to start yet. I'll be right back. I'm sure George can help you." He left the little office and hurried off across the workshop.

"Right, then," said Featherstone. He took out his notebook. "George what?"

George looked a little confused. He was not a tall man. His dark hair was greying around the sides, and receding in front, where a livid scar suggested he was no stranger to a brawl. Charlie had winked at him as he left the office. What did he want him to do? He glanced out of the window onto the workshop... *Oh... OK, play for time.*

"What?" he responded to Featherstone's question.

"George what? What's your full name?"

“Me? Why do you want my name? I haven’t done anything.”

Featherstone was getting exasperated. “I just need your name; in case we want to speak to you again.” For a moment, George appeared lost in thought.

“No, you’re not serious… You’re not going on about that complaint from 'Erbie Wilson, are you? Oh no, mate. It was his fault. He started it.” He thought about it a bit more, then a grin came over his face. “I did finish it, though. But you can’t blame me for that. Self-defence!”

“Just give me your name!” Featherstone’s voice had ratcheted up in volume.

“Ok, ok, no need to get upset. What’s the ‘urry? It’s like I tell my boys out there, don’t rush the job. Take it steady - do it right first time! We ‘ave a good safety record ‘ere, and we don’t want it spoiled. Puts up the insurance, I can tell you, if someone gets hurt.”

“Just give me your name. I don’t give a damn about your Herbie whoever.”

George’s smile was beatific. “All right then!” He grabbed a notepad from behind him and licked a pencil stub. “What was your name again? Inspector Freeweather? Can you spell that for me?”

“What?”

“So when Pete - he’s our local copper - comes by about it again, I can tell him that it’s been resolved by Inspector Free…weather. But I’d better have it spelled right. Ah, there we go. An inspector is higher than a constable, right?”

Featherstone felt he'd lost control of the situation. "OK, forget the names. I need to know where to find Thomas O'Malley!"

"Oh, Tommy. Why didn't you say so?"

"Never mind. Where can I find him?"

"I dunno…"

"What? Aren't you his supervisor?"

"Well, yeah, but he's not in today. Could be anywhere."

"Who might know where he is then?"

"Well, Charlie might. I think he was doing a job for Charlie today."

Featherstone burst out of the little office in a rage. Where the hell was Crosby? He'd put George on to him deliberately. He was going to haul him off to the nearest nick, he was going to charge him with… what? This wasn't his case. He couldn't.

He pushed back into the showroom. "Where's Crosby?" he barked.

Doris looked him up and down slowly, clearly unimpressed. "I'm so sorry, Inspector. Something must have come up. He had a visitor, and he went straight out with him. He did say that if George couldn't help you perhaps our assistant manager Mr. Brown might. I'll call him for you." Her smile was getting bigger.

Without waiting for a response, she pressed a button on her telephone and spoke into it. "Mr. Brown to reception, please." She smiled sweetly at the Inspector. "He'll be right out."

A few minutes later, a stocky man came out of one of the side offices, by which time Featherstone's temper was boiling over. Thinning brown hair, well on the way to grey, and a bushy 'salt and pepper' moustache adorned a round, cheerful face. He wore a tweed sports jacket complete with leather elbow patches, cavalry twill trousers and a pair of shiny, brown oxford brogues. Almost the perfect caricature of a 1950's car salesman! He smiled at the inspector. "Ron Brown, Assistant Manager." he said holding out his hand. "And you are?"

Featherstone sighed to himself. Here we go again. "Inspector Featherstone, South East Constabulary."

"A little out of your territory, aren't you, Inspector? Never mind, how can we help you?"

"I need to find Thomas O'Malley, one of your employees."

"My goodness! Thomas? I'm ever so sorry, but he won't be in this week. He took an E-type we'd done some work on down to Jermyns in Hastings today, and he's taken the rest of the week off. Making up for overtime, you know."

"I see. So, no one knows where he was going after dropping the car off in Hastings?"

"Not that I know of. Not really our business what he does on his own time, is it?"

"When is he expected back?"

"Not until next week at the earliest. Certainly, the week after that though. We've got a big restoration project coming in mid-November. Someone unearthed one of the '58 Le Mans Aston Martins - it may even have been driven by Stirling Moss! They want it restored to go to the big classic car auctions in Arizona or California. It'll bring in millions for the owner, especially if Aston can confirm that Moss or Brooks drove it. Tom will be handling it. Boy's a wizard when it comes to restoring cars like that."

"So, he may not be back for a couple of weeks? I need to speak to him urgently! Perhaps he's told someone at this place in Hastings where he's going? Can you give me the address?"

"Of course, anything to help. Doris, can you give the inspector the address of Jermyns in Hastings? Is there anything else we can help you with Inspector?"

"Any friends who might know where to contact him?"

"I'm sorry, Inspector. We try to stay out of our employees' private lives. Data Protection! Privacy, you know. I've probably overstepped the mark telling you as much as I have, but we always help the police if we can. I can say in all honesty that I just don't know."

"I see. Well, thank you for your help Mr. Brown. I wish I could say that all your people had been equally helpful. I could have been out of here half an hour ago."

"It's like everything else, Inspector. You need to talk to the right person, don't you? I'm afraid that's almost a law in our business. When you're looking for parts for old vehicles, you have to know who to ask! Can we interest you in a Classic? We could find you a nice Jaguar like Inspector Morse! Or perhaps a Healey 3000? I can just imagine you in a Sherlock Holmes hat and a big pipe in an open Healey. Most impressive!"

Featherstone nodded, turned away, but Brown was in pursuit. "No? I'm sure we can match you up with something that will suit! How about…"

"No, Mr. Brown. Please excuse me, I'm in hurry".

"A pity, Inspector… Perhaps next time? Well, do have a nice drive home."

Featherstone felt as though he had just pulled himself out of a sticky spider's web. Salesmen! Especially car salesmen! He walked out into pleasantly warm autumn sunshine and walked back to his car. Best go back and see if Lennox had had any luck at the flat.

* * * * *

Charlie and Tom watched him from outside the pub further up the road. "There he goes. Off to Hastings, with luck." He looked at the younger man seriously. "He may be an arrogant prick, but he really is a policeman, Tom. You'd better tell me why you can't just tell him your story."

Over cheese and pickles with a half of zero lager for Tom and a Guinness for Charlie, Tom told Ali's story. The murder was common knowledge, of course. There was nothing like a grisly killing to excite people in what was otherwise a week bereft of any significant news, and everywhere people were buzzing with speculation.

But Tom had details that the newspapers and radio didn't. He and Charlie both wondered why the official news was still talking about the hunt for an elusive tramp that everyone seemed to believe must have done it. Sales of expensive and exotic new door and window locks were soaring as were house alarms. For some, the murder was big business.

"Why did you warn me about the copper, Charlie? You could simply have pointed me out to him when I came into the workshop."

"He just didn't seem right. Set my teeth on edge. Doris felt it, too, and she's got a sixth sense to what people are. She didn't like him at all. I'd expect a Detective Inspector to be fairly civil. This bloke was rude, and he wasn't giving any explanations. Just demanding we tell him where you were. What's more, he's out of his area. If he was legit, he'd have stopped George's game right away - offered to interview us formally at the station. But I don't think he could. I think he's on the wrong side of the line.

"I asked Ron to get rid of him. Tell him you'd gone down to Hastings - nothing less than the truth - which should be a dead end for him since you're not there now. It'll be interesting to see who turns up down there asking questions, won't it? If it's the big'un you're telling me about, that'll show what side the inspector's on. Soon as we're done here, I'll get Geoff on the blower and warn him someone might be sniffing around down there."

"Yeah, but Charlie, Ali's still down there, in St Leonard's, right next door."

"Then you'd better get back, hadn't you? But it's going to take them a while to work out the details. They may already know you came back to London. This Boris does. Police could track your train ticket or pick you up on CCTV. But listen, if the wrong type turns up asking questions in Hastings, move… and don't tell me where you've gone." Charlie paused to take a pull at his Guinness, then continued.

"How're you off for cash? With a bent copper tracking you, you shouldn't use your bank card or any credit cards. He'll track them. Go and pick up a couple of burners – you know, prepaid, throw-away phones. And call Ali, get her to shut off her phone right away. Switch it off and keep it off."

Charlie thought for a moment, then pulled out his wallet. Leafing through it he pulled out several notes.

"Here, I've got two hundred quid and the same in Euros just in case. Use your bankcard and draw whatever else you can in cash. If they trace it back up here it'll only confuse them, but don't use that card down there or once you're on the move. With luck this thing will be over quickly - Ali gave a full statement at Walworth, so they should be closing in on the killer. But don't throw the cash around… Just in case it takes a bit longer than we expect. Tom took the money, nodded.

"Once you've got the burners, use one of them to phone me. Then I can call you to let you know what's happening. And keep Simon out of sight once you're tucked away. He's a bit too colourful. He'd be noticed. Pick up one of those car-covers and keep him under it."

"I don't know how to thank you Charlie. "

“That’s all right." he waved a hand dismissively. "Finish your lunch, then pop round back of the garage and get Simon. Don’t forget the burners and a car cover. Then you get down to Ali. Once I know who pops up in Hastings, we’ll have an idea of what’s happening. If it’s the big’un, you and Ali can make yourselves scarce. I’m going to go back to the shop and call Jermyn’s. Best of luck, lad. Nasty situation, but you’ll be OK.”

“Thanks, Charlie. And thanks for believing me, and believing *in* me.

“Eh lad, we look after our own. You’re a good sort and do bloody good work. We’ve got your back.” He walked over to the bar, paid the bill, and wandered over to the door, calling out “See you in a few days!” as he left.

It was good advice. After he finished his lunch, Tom went shopping. The car cover was easy. Two burners got him a couple of odd looks, but he paid for them, with cash, and left. Finally, he found himself some walking trousers and a pair of hiking boots in the Arndale Centre, and bought the same for Ali, plus hats and gloves. Lastly, two warm sleeping bags. This time he paid with his credit card and had the girl at the till write out an itemised bill. That should reinforce the idea that they’d gone hiking if anyone checked.

It was rather a bulky load, and he asked the sales assistant if he could leave it all behind the counter while he went to get his car. Since he’d already paid, and it was a good sale for her, she was happy to agree. Then Tom went back to ‘Classic’.

Parked behind the garage, Simon waited. A sleek, metallic blue, 1970 Jensen Interceptor, the only thing beside

Ali that Tom really loved. He sank into the contoured driver's seat, put the key in the ignition, and turned. Simon's big American V8 burbled into life, and he sat there, quietly warming up.

Named after Simon Templar, Leslie Charteris' legendary 'Saint', Simon was ready for adventure, just like his brother from the TV show of the Seventies. Tom had seen re-runs of the series and had promised himself one of those cars in his future. Simon had appeared at the garage three years earlier; old, broken down, and fit only for the breakers yard. Tom had been working there for just a couple of months but when he saw the car he didn't see what it was, but what it could be. Charlie wasn't interested. It would cost too much to restore, and Jensens had never been really popular with classic car collectors. There was a stigma attached to big American V8 motors that turned off the self-proclaimed connoisseurs. There was simply no money to be made out of it.

Tom wasn't going to let Simon be broken up though. He went and talked to Charlie. This was a job he knew he could do.

"Let *me* buy it," he'd begged. "I'll work on it on my own time. I'll pay for all the parts and materials I need. Let me show you what I can do." And Charlie went for it. He allowed him a small space in the back of the workshops, and he bought it from the owner for just a few hundred. Then he arranged for Tom to pay him back in monthly instalments. Tom had his car, and over the next year he spent evenings and weekends doing little but work on Simon.

He'd taken pictures at the start, and more as the work progressed. After six months Charlie knew he had a craftsman. He tossed in some time on the engine and transmission, and even paid for the upholstery to be replaced. When Simon was finished, copies of the 'before' and 'after' pictures appeared on the company's website as an example of Classic Cars' workmanship, and Charlie often took clients around the back to look at the real thing. And he kept his word. The car was Tom's.

Since Simon had appeared on their website, two more Jensens had come in for restorations, not to mention a number of Jaguars, Aston Martins, Bentleys and even some of the foreign exotics. Both Charlie and Tom were very happy with their side of the bargain.

Now, in Tom's mind, Simon was ready for an adventure befitting his namesake. Perhaps this would be the opportunity. Backing out of his space, Simon rumbled quietly out to the road. A quick stop to pick up his purchases at the Arndale and he was off cruising down the road to Hastings.

* * * * *

Featherstone found 'Lennox' waiting for him at Tom and Ali's flat. He was in a foul mood. "Bastard was here. I almost had him. But he got away and now he knows we're on to this place, they won't come here again. We need another idea. He could be anywhere!"

"I know where he's been," said Featherstone. "And I've got other ways to track him, but it'll take time. I need to get back to the Centre and spend some time on my computer.

“What we do know is that he went down to a place called ‘Jermyns’ in Hastings. He must have done that already and come back on the train. But since we don’t have anything else, you get down to Hastings and see what you can find out. Maybe he told someone there what he was going to do. In the meantime, I’ll find out if he owns a car, and put a trace on it. I’ll track his phones and his bankcard and any credit cards too. Those’ll tell us where he’s gone. But it won’t be quick. I’ll have to put in a request to his bank, and to his mobile provider - and the girl’s too. It could take two or three days. You might be lucky and get the answers straightaway in Hastings.”

‘Lennox’ didn’t like the delay, but he recognised that it was their best chance. It also gave him something to do. He was no good at just sitting around doing nothing. “Right, I’ll take your car. Gimme the keys!”

“No,” said Featherstone. “I need it, and we need to stay under the radar. If I lost my Beemer, I’d have to report it stolen, and that would put you at risk. Where’s your car?”

‘Lennox’ glowered. “Back near the theatre. It was quicker to grab a cab when you called. Just drop me at the station, I’ll get back up there and pick it up. Then I’ll head down to Hastings; find out where he went...” He cheered up at the thought. “Give me a bell if you learn anything.”

* * * * *

Behind every great man…

Susan had picked up a takeaway from the local Chinese after her class the previous evening and stopped by to enjoy a few hours with Mandy. Then it was back to her own flat for some sleep and a change of clothes. In the morning, she was in early and going over the operational plan for the "Nettle Lane Murder" as it was now being called.

Sean was off to start a review of the theatre and its operations, and to dig into details of how it was being run and financed, and she'd sent Sandeep with him. She could act as his runner while he interviewed all the people there. More importantly though, it was her job to hang around the players and be friendly, open, and helpful where she could in the hope that she'd hear some useful gossip. Sandeep was a little unsure, saying she had never been to the theatre, but Susan thought that in itself might be helpful.

Stuart and Dave Crewe were sent up to London to visit the head office of the Laura's Group and begin a review of their financials, aiming to track down and trace the protection money. Susan herself would continue the research into the private lives of Ian Davison and his wife Laura that she had started the previous afternoon.

Ian Davison. There was plenty of information on him. He had lived his professional career in a blaze of publicity and had obviously revelled in it. Laura Handley, on the other hand, had avoided the limelight except, inevitably, when in the company of her dazzling husband. Looking at the many pictures of them it looked to Susan as though Laura

Handley had been as much in awe of Ian Davison as any of the adoring fans clustered around them.

But there were also pictures of Ian with other ladies on his arm: his most recent leading lady; a newly 'discovered' actress he had sponsored; a well-known pop star. If it had been Ian's body found butchered in that bath, she would have taken a very good look at Laura. But it wasn't. Had there been a serious rival, someone who wanted Ian badly enough to want Laura out of the way? That might explain the sense of a personal motive. But a professional killer? Unlikely. A professional would have made a far cleaner job of it and would have killed her in a way that might easily have been mistaken for suicide or an accident. Professionals wanted to minimise the likelihood of a police investigation. Uneasily, she thought of Ellie's comments.

She was interrupted by a knock on her office door. She didn't know the woman waiting outside. She was attractive; tallish - about Susan's own height - bright and fresh looking, with clear blue eyes and honey-streaked blonde hair touching her shoulders. Impeccably put together in chinos and blazer she was smiling and self-assured. Should she know her? Puzzled, Susan got up, went to the door, and opened it. "Can I help you?" she asked politely.

"Sergeant Cross?" It was a quiet, musical voice. "Can I talk to you for a few minutes?" Susan looked around. The squad room had fallen silent, and everyone - yes, everyone! - was watching, apparently with bated breath! Whatever this was about, it seemed she was the only one who had no idea who this woman was.

"Of course," she said, stepping back and gesturing the woman into her office. Closing the door behind them she said "Please, take a seat," indicating the chairs on one side of the office by the small coffee table. She moved to the opposite side and sat down in turn.

The woman looked back out into the squad room and raised an eyebrow. "We seem to have attracted an audience!" Susan followed her gaze. Sure enough, everyone's attention remained riveted on her office. "I suppose", said the woman with another smile, "they're wondering if we're going to get the knives out!" Susan stared. *What?* The woman laughed and held out her hand. "Oh, don't worry. I'm Elizabeth Gordon, Robert's wife."

The world stopped…

And then reality crashed back into existence. Susan leaped to her feet. "Eliz…, Mrs. Gordon!" She couldn't take the outstretched hand! "Oh God, Mrs. Gordon. I'm so terribly sorry," she gasped.

Elizabeth still looked amused. "Really, this isn't a soap opera. Why are you sorry? Don't tell me you *have* been sleeping with my husband?" She cocked an eyebrow in mock question.

"No! No, I haven't!" spluttered Susan, "I wouldn't… really!" For a moment she was lost for words, and then clawed her way back to the moment. "But there are all these stupid stories, and they keep getting worse. They must have hurt you so badly…" She ran down and sat back in her chair, looking quite bewildered.

"Well, they might have," conceded Elizabeth, crossing her legs and smiling, "but I know Robert very well, and I *do* sleep with him. I think I would know if he started wandering. Besides, he told me about you from the start.

"He was delighted to have found a well-qualified female detective sergeant to replace Derek Jones." She leant forward to make her point. "It's been a priority of his to make better use of the women in the force. You know, we've met so many really bright women in comparatively junior positions, and seen lesser men promoted over their heads. He was a bit put off when he got a very poor report from DI Featherstone – spectacularly awful – but he went back and talked to your old superiors in Maidstone. Their assessment was so different that he just didn't believe Featherstone's." Susan gave a half smile at that. Elizabeth nodded and went on.

"When he requested your re-assignment, Featherstone tried to persuade him that he was making a mistake, but Robert is quite a stubborn man… It made him all the more determined to follow his own judgement, even though he hadn't really met you at the time."

She sat back and opened her jacket, completely relaxed, then smiled at Susan again. It was an understanding, rather rueful smile. "That was when the rumours started. You wouldn't believe how some police wives gossip. Really spiteful. I got several of those 'poor you' and 'I thought you should know' calls. If they were to be believed, you had been 'banging' my husband for weeks. But I know Robert, and I've never doubted him.

“Then, he came home yesterday and told me about how you were worried that it might hurt his career, and - I hope you don’t mind - he told me about how you had been treated in Featherstone’s squad. Anyway, I decided that it was time to do something about what’s happening now. So… let’s start again, shall we?”

She held out her hand. “Hello, Sergeant Cross. I’m Elizabeth Gordon. I’m hoping we can be friends.”

Susan looked at her for a moment, then reached out and took it. “Hello, Elizabeth,” she said hesitantly, and, gaining more strength. “I’m Susan Cross. They call me Crosspatch,” she added, with a crooked smile.

“Wonderful!” exclaimed Elizabeth delightedly. “About the nickname, I mean. The best way to take the sting out of it is to claim it as your own! Robert thinks it’s terribly funny. Says your team has adopted it. He’s ridiculously proud of how well you’re doing, by the way. He seems to think it’s all his own doing!” She laughed. By now, Susan was smiling back properly too.

“Right. Time for some action,” said Elizabeth. “Now that we’re friends, let’s go downstairs to see Sergio. We’re going to enjoy a coffee and treat ourselves to a Danish and have a good chat - girl talk, not business - and let everyone see us. We should make a habit of it. We’re going to war against those vile stories. Now, chin up! We have to be seen as being full of confidence and to be good friends - and you know, I think we shall be - good friends, I mean. This will be fun!”

“You are absolutely right,” said Susan, sitting up straight. “It’s about time!”

When the office door opened and Crosspatch and Mrs. Gordon walked out together, laughing, DC Martin Dawson spilled his cold coffee all over the Newcross Assault file. George Andrews, heading back to his desk, tripped and went flat on his face right outside the DCI's office, his carefully collated photocopies flying down the aisle towards the two women.

"Hello, Martin," said Elizabeth cheerfully, waving at him with a bright smile, and "Whoops! Careful George!" as he struggled to get up, and the two waltzed out of the room, leaving everyone staring at each other in confusion.

"Er, what just happened here?" asked Dawson to the room in general.

DS Stevenson stepped out of his office. "I'd say several rather nasty stories just got torpedoed," he said with a broad grin.

* * * * *

"I think the lifts, today," said Elizabeth. "We want to be seen, don't we?" Her eyes were sparkling. The lift doors opened, and she was pleased to see several people she knew. "Good Morning Andrew," she said happily to DI Morrison, "What a lovely day! Susan and I are just popping down for a coffee and a catch up!" Moving to the back of the lift, she winked as Susan joined her. She had to laugh, which of course fitted the situation perfectly. The two stood at the back and giggled like teenagers. There could be no doubt in anyone's mind that they were fast friends.

Arriving at the ground floor, they walked past the front desk towards the coffee shop. Susan waved to the sergeant on duty. As they queued to give their order, Elizabeth felt a prod in her back. It was Pam Morrison.

"Elizabeth," she whispered, "That's *her*," pointing at Crosspatch.

"Who? Oh, Susan? She's Robert's new DS, Susan Cross. Are you all right, Pam? You look a little off colour."

"No, Elizabeth," whispered Pam a bit desperately, "That's *her*. She's the one sleeping with Robert!"

Elizabeth turned and faced her friend. "Rubbish," she said forcefully. "You don't really believe those silly stories, do you? Rubbish, all of them."

Pam subsided, shocked. "You're sure?"

"Positive! Susan would never do that. Have you even met her? If you knew her, you'd know it was nonsense. And Robert? … Honestly!"

"No, no. Of course. I'm sorry," came a mumbled reply. "Well, I'm glad. I didn't believe it at first, but the rumours just kept coming, and everyone has heard them…" and then recovering, "Really, Elizabeth … I'm glad," she said more strongly, and smiled.

Elizabeth turned to Crosspatch. "Susan, have you met Pam Morrison? Andrew Morrison's wife?"

"No, I haven't," she replied. "Hello, Mrs. Morrison. Susan Cross." She held out her hand and Pam stepped forward and took it, looking at her a bit strangely.

"Hello, Susan. Er… it's nice to meet you. I've - umm - heard a lot about you…" she finished gamely. Susan smiled.

"And didn't like what you heard, no doubt!" she said, still smiling. "But I can assure you none of it is true. You know how these rumours can start in tight little communities like ours."

Pam straightened up. "Yes, I do. I'm sorry you had to put up with it, Susan. Some of it has been vicious."

"It hasn't been fun," agreed Susan, "and most unfair to Elizabeth. But she's a clever woman. We're going to show everyone just how ridiculous the stories are!"

"Good for you - both of you," said Pam, smiling suddenly.

"Would you like to join us for coffee, Pam?" asked Elizabeth.

"I would, under other circumstances," said Pam. "But I'm meeting Andrew - oh, here he is," as DI Morrison joined them. "Another time? It would be fun!"

"Yes, it would. Lovely! See you later then, Pam," said Elizabeth, turning back to give her order.

"Hey Crosspatch" Sergio was saying quietly, handing over her preferred latte, "Be careful. That's her!" He glanced at Elizabeth, but getting no reaction from Crosspatch, he added hastily "Mrs. Gordon!" He waggled his eyebrows. Crosspatch looked at him. "Yes, Sergio, thank you. I know. We're friends."

"But the DCI… You and the DCI…"

"Sergio, how many times do I have to tell you that I am *not* the DCI's girlfriend?"

"Ma - of course you must say that…"

"Hello, Sergio," said Elizabeth, joining them. "Doesn't he make just the best coffee?" she said to Susan. "We'll have two of those wicked pastries as well, please. Would you be a darling and bring them to our table when you have a moment?" For once Sergio seemed bereft of words. He looked at the two of them, gave an exaggerated shrug, and turned back to his machines.

As Elizabeth and Susan moved together towards a small table over by the front windows the quiet buzz of conversation died away. Silence.

"Goodness," exclaimed Elizabeth. "I think I just heard a pin drop!" Susan burst out laughing, and a swell of new conversation rushed in to fill the void. They sat down facing each other. Elizabeth looked around with a bright, beaming smile and waved at a couple of acquaintances a few tables away. The buzz got louder. Elizabeth looked at Susan and they laughed, softly.

"Whoever started these rumours didn't know who they were up against. They're going to seem ridiculous." Susan shook her head. "You're amazing, Elizabeth, amazing!"

"I am, aren't I," the DCI's wife replied, deadpan, and the two clinked mugs in a latte toast.

* * * * *

Back in her office, Susan was still smiling. She had been almost in despair at the vicious rumour campaign. It *was* a campaign, she realised, and instead of meeting it head-on, she'd been letting them win. It had been in the back of her mind, a constant worry, and it had been distracting her from the case. But Elizabeth had known exactly what to do and had the courage to stand up and do it. *Well, behind every great man...* She laughed to herself. They'd made plans to meet for coffee again on Friday, and she was looking forward to it… Yes, looking forward to meeting a friend for coffee. Such an ordinary thing, but she couldn't remember when that had happened last. Certainly not since she had joined the Centre. It was like waking from a bad dream! She smiled again. Giving herself a mental shake, she looked at the files in front of her. The whole office seemed somehow brighter. Two new friends. First Mandy, and now Elizabeth. "OK," she thought. "Now I'm ready."

Her phone buzzed. It was Sean. "Morning ma'am" he said.

"Sean" she said cheerfully. "How are things in the world of the theatre? Are our thespians busy spilling all the beans about their trials and tribulations?"

"Things are a bit confused at the moment," he said. "Their 'Lord and Master' - their words - hasn't turned up yet this morning, so they're a bit disorganised. What is interesting is that one of the cast has disappeared…

"Apparently Davison asked her to stay back for a few minutes after the rehearsal finished yesterday evening, and she hasn't been seen since. The first couple of people in this morning thought it looked as though there had been a scuffle outside Davison's office. One of the props had been knocked over. A guillotine, would you believe?

"What?"

"Yes. Completely non-functional, and only about a quarter scale. Creepy though, and Sandeep has found what she thinks may be bloodstains on it - and on the floor. Nose like a bloodhound, that girl."

She thought about that. "I don't like the sound of bloodstains. Could be stage blood, of course, but we need to be interested in anything that's even slightly unusual at this stage. Get forensics to check it. Get all the information you can on whoever is missing. Let's hope she turns up, and not as a floater in the Thames! Anything else so far?"

"Nothing definite yet, but I had a word with Davison's bookkeeper. He says they are funded by an anonymous group of investors, but that Davison was in a bit of a flap late last week ranting that they wanted to be paid back. He felt betrayed by them, apparently. Oh hullo, he's just turned up. Looks rather the worse for wear. Must have had a bad morning – or maybe a bad night. It might be sinking in about Laura, of course, poor bastard. I'll call you later."

She sat back. A girl gone missing. Last person to see her? Apparently Davison. Was he though? Well, she had only really been gone a short while… Nevertheless, it smelt wrong… Better follow up on that straight away. And what had happened with the investors the previous week? She'd let Sean dig into that.

"Back to the grindstone ..." and the phone rattled again. Grabbing it before it vibrated itself right off the desk, she answered.

"Stuart! Don't tell me you two have worked through the mysteries of a corporate accounting system already?"

He grunted. "Fat chance! But their system is an off the shelf one, nothing fancy or particularly complicated. We spoke to the chief accountant here. Explained what we were looking for and he understood exactly what we were talking about. Apparently lots of shopfront operations get shaken down for protection. He says that both his previous jobs were with companies like this one. In fact, one of them was the last company taken over by Laura's. He said they showed the protection as just another form of insurance. They had all the usual ones, you know, public liability, then fire and flood and earthquake cover…"

"What? No, seriously, in England? Earthquakes?"

"Yeah. And against cyber-attacks. Well, I suppose that's more understandable, but honestly, it's amazing how many things there are to be protected against! And then there's everyday theft and vandalism.

"He says it's usually cheaper to pay protection than to get the theft and vandalism cover… Without the protection, vandalism becomes such a problem that the insurance company often won't cover them anyway. So they pay for a small, nominal vandalism and theft policy which basically covers them from shoplifting, and just add the protection fee to it. They even get smart looking invoices, and the payments are made to what seems to be an actual Insurance company!

"But here's the funny bit. Laura's doesn't do that. In fact, when Laura's took over his previous company, they stopped paying the protection there, and just kept their nominal vandalism and theft policy. He thought there was going to be a lot of trouble, but it just didn't happen. He knows it's weird.

"Then yesterday they had that incident that you broke up. He's been with Laura's for four years - loves it. Says she was a great boss, very hands-on with the operations. She gets - got - involved in the purchasing and in the shop design, and he reckons she's the real reason that her chain seems - seemed - to be on the way to being the biggest independent in the industry in the UK. He's really gutted about what's happened."

Susan sat back. No protection paid before Laura's death. Then immediate demands. Well, they were looking for something out of the ordinary. If Laura was considered critical to her company's success, could a competitor have seen an advantage in removing her from the picture? She'd better get an idea who Laura's competitors were.

"OK Stuart. We need to check that story out. See if you can get one of those protection invoices from the previous company. They have to keep records for years, so that shouldn't be a problem. Find out where those records are and get Dave hunting them down. Then leave him up there to carry on. It smacks to me of organised crime. I think the Yard will be interested in anything we can give them and may well take over that aspect of it.

"But I suspect it won't be central to our case. I still feel that this murder was too personal. Someone really had it in for Laura Davison. A major crime syndicate sophisticated enough to set up an extensive protection scheme that successfully mimics an insurance company having some poor woman hacked to death like that? It just doesn't make sense. look, get yourself back to the Centre tomorrow. I think I'm going to need you here."

"Sean has something breaking at the theatre, Ma'am?"

"Not really, but there may be something else I need you to follow up on. Could be nothing, but it just doesn't smell right. Sean and Sandeep don't have anything new for us yet, but I think they will. I'll be at the mortuary with Ellie in the morning, but I'll be back here after lunch.

"Crosspatch out," and she hung up on a surprised DC McLean.

Back to the theatre end of it, she thought. That felt more promising. One of the troupe missing, after being held back by Davison? Could she have known something? *Come on! Let's not jump to conclusions... She'll probably turn up right as rain tomorrow.*

She returned to her review of Laura and Ian Davison's careers determined to find out everything there was to know about them. There was no class that evening and with everything quiet for once, she and Mandy seized the moment and drove out for supper at a pretty country pub near Tunbridge Wells. They stopped at her flat on the way back and Susan grabbed some clothes for the next day, but they spent the rest of the night in the little flat above Laura's.

*   *   *   *   *

A Serial Killer?

Susan arrived at the mortuary a little early. It was not her first time attending an autopsy, and she had found it advisable to allow herself to get used to the smell pervading the building before joining Ellie in the autopsy room. She told herself it helped her stomach settle down before the awful stuff began.

A dab of Vicks just under the nose - that always helped a bit. *Time to stiffen up the sinews,* she thought, *summon up the blood and all that – no,* she brought herself up short. *A case involving the theatre provokes the oddest thoughts! Right... Let's to it! (There we go again....) Without more ado... Oh for heaven's sake...* She pushed through the doors and went into the theatre (*Oh stop it!).*

The FP was there, all kitted up and ready to go.

"Morning Ellie," Susan greeted her. "What's going to be the procedure today?"

Ellie looked up, "Good morning, Susan. You're in a sunny mood today! I'm sorry we've taken so long over this, but we've virtually had to do an autopsy in reverse. The body was so hacked about that our challenge was to put it back together, not open it up." Susan grimaced, sympathetically.

"You wouldn't have thought there could be any doubt about the cause of death, would you? There must be fifteen, twenty or more wounds, any of which could have been fatal. But interestingly, those weren't the cause of death!"

"What?" That was a shocker! "Are you saying she was dead when she went into the bath? That the killer did all this to her body just to disguise what really happened? What did kill her, then?"

"I'll show you," said Ellie. "Look here, at her throat. You can see quite clearly where he grabbed her. He hauled her straight up. He must be very strong indeed. But she was covered in bath oil, and she must have been struggling like a fish on a line! He must have lost his grip letting her fall back into the bath. But both she and the bath were slick with oil. I think she slipped and fell backwards, cracking her head on the side of the bath. It's solid hard-stone, not acrylic and the rim's narrow - almost sharp. That's what killed her. It almost smashed through the lower skull, here."

"But why the repeated stabbing? Why do anything, at that point. He already had a kill, with a believable scene for an accident. He might have got clean away with no one suspecting a murder at all."

"I just don't see this as the work of a cold killer, Susan. I said that when we were at the scene. I'd say our killer was unhinged, a very dangerous man; one who gets off, not so much on killing, but on inflicting the maximum pain and terror. She fell and was killed by the fall, so I think he felt cheated. That's what brought on the rage, and the butchery. It sounds awful, but if I'm right, she was lucky that it killed her. It probably saved her unspeakable terror and agony."

Susan thought back to that terrible bathroom at Nettle Lane. Yes, she could imagine it happening exactly as Ellie described. She was right. Laura had been desperately unlucky that the intruder had got in, but she had also been lucky that death had come quickly. The alternative didn't bear thinking of.

"Thank you, Ellie… Anything else that you can tell us? … Rape?"

"No. No evidence of that. If he'd planned it, he may have been holding that back, waiting for the right moment.

"Something very odd, though. There was something in the back of her throat; something sprayed into her mouth. I didn't know exactly what it was, and I had to send some swabs for analysis. I don't know if it means much, and it really doesn't make much sense to me. It turns out it was Johnson's Bitch Spray - or one of those sprays anyway. It's a mixture of herbal oils that disguises the scent of a bitch in heat. It's not poisonous, although it wouldn't be pleasant - certainly not sprayed into your mouth when you were breathing in to scream! But what an odd thing to appear here!"

"Bitch Spray? Damn, that rings a bell. But you're right. That is odd. Thanks, Ellie. Oh! Do you have an approximate time of death?

"I think it was as early as about 9pm, probably not much later. I'd say between 9pm and 10pm."

"OK, that helps. Do you think the spray was significant? You'll get your report to us?"

"Mostly done, you'll have it tomorrow. As for the spray, I really don't know. It was just something unusual. A killer's comment on the female sex?"

"That makes a perverted sort of sense. I wish it didn't. Anyway, time I got back to the Centre. We need to find this bastard!"

"Do you have a few minutes before you go?" asked Ellie.

"Of course."

"Let's go upstairs. The smell won't worry you as much up there. I'd like to discuss a few things about this case with you. Do you remember I said something was bothering me about it, but I wasn't sure what it was? Well, I know now. Come on up and I'll explain."

"Anything to get out of this smell," she said, taking a good sniff at her Vicks.

* * * * *

Instead of heading back to the Centre, Susan decided a detour to the theatre was needed. It was starting to assume critical importance in her mind, and she hadn't been there yet. She'd paid the congestion charge for the day - might as well make full use of it. She wanted to get a feel for the place; talk to some of the actors.

Just how good was Ian Davison's alibi? He had told Sean that he had been rehearsing until late, and then joined the cast for a nightcap at the local pub before going back to his flat in Pimlico. He had gone straight from there to rehearsals the next morning. So far that was the same story other cast members had given, and it was backed up by their review of CCTV cameras near the theatre. It seemed solid.

The theatre was well situated for access to the underground, bus services and of course the trains from Elephant and Castle, Waterloo and London Bridge. The area also seemed to be up and coming; a mix of commercial and residential with high rises towering above the older buildings, housing ground floor businesses with flats above. Susan spotted a Pret and pulled over. She hadn't had any breakfast. Food and the mortuary just weren't compatible, and a latte and bacon and egg roll were calling. She dialled Sean.

"Good morning," she announced cheerily. "I'm inbound to the theatre. I've just been to see Ellie, who's finished the post-mortem, and there's an interesting development there. Join me at the Pret around the corner. I'll bring you up to date. I don't want to talk about it at the theatre… No, leave Sandeep there… She's doing what? Rehearsing one of the roles? No, that's excellent. It'll make it easier for her to blend in… yes, ten minutes is fine, and I need to grab something to eat… You too? What?... OK, see you there."

Spotting a miraculously empty space at the curb, she parked - a bit close to a yellow line at one end, which was probably why the space was there. She put her auxiliary blue light up on the dashboard where it could be seen and pulled the "On Duty" sign out of the glove compartment and sat it alongside. You never knew when a traffic warden might decide to ruin someone's day, and she thought she might be parked there for a while. Sliding out, she ran across the road and into the restaurant.

Mid-morning… well after the breakfast crowd grabbing something on the way to work, and before the lunchtime rush, but quite a few of the tables were occupied, some singly or by groups all huddled over computers. Freelancers. Self-employed. Lining up, she gave her order and within minutes she was making for one of the tables near the windows carrying a tray with both her and Sean's breakfasts. She had barely sat down when her DC arrived.

"You owe me for these," she said, pushing his share across the table, "but I'll call it quits if you have anything interesting to tell me!"

"Not really anything new since we spoke yesterday. Sandeep did hear from a couple of the actresses - two of the witches - that Ian had told them all that the theatre had almost gone bankrupt, but that Laura had bailed them out. That would be the second time, as the known bailout from Laura's was about eighteen months ago - old news.

"He told them the other day, just after the DCI came to inform him of Laura's death. They'd been expecting him to send them home, for the day at least, if not call off the whole production. Instead, he used Laura's death as a sort of rallying call - 'The show must go on!' Stirring stuff. She'd rescued the play, and they couldn't let it fail now. They thought it was quite touching at the time, especially as he then started working them like a man possessed. Afterwards, though, they wondered if it wasn't a bit cold. Who could focus like that when you had just been told that your wife had been killed? And he's been acting almost as if nothing had happened ever since. It's as though he's put it behind him and just got on with the job!"

"Yes, it does seem cold, doesn't it? He's a method actor of course. It could be that I suppose, nothing else quite real outside the role. He may not have grasped it yet. And he's playing Macbeth himself … that could do your head in if you got too far into the part.

"Anyway, that brings me to this morning. Guess what? Laura wasn't killed by being stabbed!"

"What? She must have been. The woman was virtually hacked in two! How could that *not* have killed her?"

"Oh, it would have killed her, unquestionably. But Ellie thinks she was dead before the stabbing began. She thinks the killer had her up by the throat but she slipped out of his grasp, so she fell and cracked her skull open on the bath. Not wanting to sound callous, but with all that oil in the water, and all over her, she'd have been slipperier than a greased pig!"

"Well, yes, a bit callous, but graphic. I can see that. But if she was already dead, why not stop? Clean up any evidence of another person being there and it's quite possible the whole thing would have been classed as an unfortunate accident."

"Exactly. So, what does it mean? We know it wasn't Davison himself, and if he'd paid a contract killer, it would have looked like an accident. No need for a criminal investigation. Professionals like to keep things clean and neat, don't they? This was anything but. It was extremely vicious, suggesting a killer almost out of control. So, unlikely that the husband had anything to do with it. Ellie thinks it has the markings of a serial killer who's losing it."

“But if that’s the case, Ma’am, where are the other murders? We haven’t been made aware of anything like this.”

“No, but this may not have been his signature style. He could have botched it. She thinks he had something really nasty in mind. Probably a torture scenario, killing Laura slowly, to maximise the turn-on he got from it and then raping her or not depending on whether he still needed that thrill. But the knife was significant. It was unusually big. Probably featured in previous murders. You can imagine it, him gloating over Laura, maybe even telling her what he was going to do to her. Getting off on that. Then, when she slipped out of his grasp and died, he'd have felt she had cheated him, and what we saw was the result… melt down! A murderous frenzy. If he had had any earlier kills, he probably took more time over them, and was able to ‘enjoy’ the kill more.

“Unimaginably worse for the victims. And it may be those are people who have simply gone missing. The bodies may never have been found. But even if they have, the MO would be completely different from what happened here. I’m going to put Stuart on to chasing the theory through the National Database”.

“Yeah. Shit - That really does open it up, doesn’t it? Do you want Sandeep and me to pull back from here?”

“No. Keep following the thread here for now. Did the missing actress appear today? Has anyone tried to contact her?”

“One of the actors tried calling her, but got no answer. She only had a very small part - it’s what Sandeep is helping out with at the moment. Davison just says she quit, let him down. Otherwise, he doesn't seem interested."

"OK, but have you pushed him on that?"

"Yes. He admits he asked her to stay back, wanted to discuss it, see if she'd stay, but says that she just pissed off. She's barely more than a walk on, so they can replace her easily. He really doesn't seem to care."

"Did you get the blood Sandeep found in the back sent for testing?"

"Yes, forensics came in late yesterday afternoon. I don't think they were very hopeful. Made a few jokes about the Phantom of the Opera, suggested that there were probably more fake bloodstains in a theatre than there were muddy footprints. But they took it, of course, and it genuinely was blood, both on the floor and on that creepy guillotine. Fairly fresh too. They took it a bit more seriously then and promised they'd get back to us quickly."

"Good. Don't let that be pushed into the background. If you are tied up with any other issues, give it to Sandeep to follow up. We're a little light on the ground, and she has real promise.

"Also follow up on the financing issue you mentioned. If he was worried that his backers were pulling out last week, what's the situation now? That just doesn't sound right." She stood up, picking up her coffee. "Let's go back to the theatre and see what's happening there?"

* * * * *

Susan was impressed. Ian's theatre wasn't big, but she liked its intimate atmosphere. The audience would feel practically part of the action. With a full house, the atmosphere would be electric. She could imagine it; the actors feeding off of the audience - immersed in their roles - still living the emotions well after the performance. Nice! Yet she could feel it. Something was not quite right, she thought. *Something is rotten in the state of - er ... wherever this is?* She shook herself. *No, let's not start that again!*

Rehearsal was in progress, and there was Sandeep, coming onto the stage with another actor. Both stopped to watch a tall, distraught looking woman come stumbling out of the wings, scrubbing at her hands, her face twisted, a cross between fear and rage. "Out, damned spot!" came the famous line. Sandeep appeared fascinated. Not the usual reaction for the waiting woman, yet somehow it seemed to fit. *Oh no, Sandeep, don't get lost in the play. We need you to have your wits about you.*

And suddenly out of the darkness, there he was... A slim man, perhaps five ten, dark haired, and already showing a five o'clock shadow, stepped up from the seats. "You, Gentlewoman, what's your name?"

Sandeep jerked, startled. "Oh, er, Sandeep, sir"

"You'll do. You're not conventional, but that makes you interesting. You've got your Equity card?"

"Er, no, Sir."

"No? No what? You don't want the part? Why are you here then?"

"Er, No Sir, I don't have an Equity card, and I'm here because I was asked to do this just until the regular girl gets back."

"No card? Bugger! Then we can't use you. What do you mean 'until the regular girl gets back?' You mean Alison Johnson? She's not coming back… Duncan?"

The other actor who had come onto the stage with Sandeep peered across at him. "Yes, Ian?"

"Why haven't we got another Gentlewoman yet? We're almost out of time."

"We thought Ali would be back. We can give the role to Anna; she's earned a chance at a part."

"Good. Sort her out. Get onto it, will you. Right people, on we go."

* * * * *

Susan could feel his magnetism, his charisma. So, this was Ian, the grieving husband. But was there a darkness there, a coldness? She could feel it, but she couldn't explain it. No matter, it strengthened her instinct. This part of the investigation definitely needed to go on.

Ian sensed the unknown in his house. He turned from the stage towards the two detectives. "Who are you?" he barked "Oh, it's you, the policeman. Who's your companion?"

Susan stepped forward. "Mr. Davison? I'm Detective Sergeant Cross. I'm the Senior Investigating Officer on this part of our investigation. I am very sorry for your loss."

She thought she could see the wheels turning in his head, see him toning it down, silently. A subtle change came over him. He seemed to shrink in on himself, and the arrogant look in his face morphed into one of someone bearing up under a great burden. He held up his hand.

"Thank you, Sergeant Cross, I do appreciate that. I hope you'll run down this … this," he seemed at a loss for words, "this lunatic." A catch in the throat, eyes down. "They say it was a vagrant who broke in and killed her. He can't have gone far, surely?"

Then the rest of her statement registered. "This part of the investigation? What other part can there be?"

"I'm afraid I can't say, Mr. Davison. But any murder investigation must involve investigation on many levels." *Hello, he didn't like that!* "Your wife was the head of a successful business with operations over a wide area. We must see if this could have resulted from her business affairs." He relaxed a bit on that, she thought, so where was his concern? "Similarly, it could have something to do with your business affairs…" *Aha! A hit ...a palpable hit? I wonder.* "It's just routine, but it does take time."

"I understand. Anything I can do to help, you have only to ask."

"Well," she smiled, "I know you've been asked already, but can you think of anyone who might have done this?" She spoke lightly and gave an apologetic shrug. "Can you think of anyone who might have wanted her dead?" she asked. *Boom! Good God, he knows! Or at least he thinks he knows!* But…

"I only wish I did," came his response. "Probably a good thing I don't though. I would understand vigilante justice right now. And then you'd be after me!" he said with a wistful smile. "But really, why are you here? Why aren't you out hunting for this maniac? None of us can have done it. We were all here."

"We won't need to be here much longer, Mr. Davison. We're hoping your missing cast member will show up. It's only a very tenuous lead, but when someone in the immediate entourage suddenly disappears, straight after the police deliver the news of the murder, it leads us to wonder what that person knows, or knew," … *and again! He knows something about that! God, I hope she's not in the mud at the bottom of the Thames…*

"You're certain that she isn't coming back. Why is that?" she asked. *Again, a nerve.*

"Oh, that's straightforward. Said she'd been offered a major part in rep up in, oh, Newcastle I think it was, and as her part here was little better than a walk-on, she felt she couldn't afford to turn it down. They wanted her right away… She'll be easy to replace here, so I wished her luck and bon voyage".

"Can you recall the theatre group up there? We'd really like to have a few words with her." *Now that annoyed him…*

"No, I can't remember. Just that it was up north somewhere."

"Well, if it comes back to you please let us know." She smiled. *Definitely something to follow up.*

Susan thanked him, and he turned away immediately. It was almost as though he were no longer with them at all. She saw him make a conscious effort, pull himself back into the present and then into himself again ... "Right then, you lot, on we go…"

Stepping back, they moved to the back of the auditorium. "Well, this trip wasn't wasted," she said quietly. "That's not quite the story he gave you, Sean.

"I'm heading back to the Centre. Stuart should be there this afternoon. I had him wrapping up his part of the investigation at Laura's. He'll leave Dave Crewe to follow some matters of interest there, but I want the rest of the team at Sevenoaks. If you can do without Sandeep, send her back on the train. Finish up what you need to do and then come on in too. I need to talk to the DCI...

"Do follow up on the situation over the funding that had Davison upset last week, and try to find out whatever you can about the missing girl. It may mean nothing, but I don't like it."

Back in her car, she triggered her phone. She remembered where she'd seen the name Bitch Spray.

"Stuart," she jumped in quickly the moment he answered. "Have Forensics finished with all the fingerprint work at Nettle Lane?"

"Yes, all done. No unexplained prints, though. Nothing to help us at all. There's evidence that someone's cleaned up in places, but nothing more."

"Did anyone check that dog spray can at the front door?"

Stuart thought about that. "I really don't know. It was still sitting to the side of the front step when I left, but they must have bagged it."

"Well, if they missed it, get someone down there now with an evidence bag, and get it back to the Centre. I want all the fingerprints on that. I think it may be important."

"The Bitch Spray can? Really?" He sounded unconvinced. "OK, I'll see to it."

"If possible, I want the results by the time I get back to the Centre. I'm serious. It's important."

"You're the boss. See you in an hour or two."

What on earth had she found, Stuart wondered? He remembered the spray can and wondering if Laura had a dog. Thinking about it more, yes, of course she had. Empty bowls on the floor in the kitchen, a dog bed under the stairs, yet there'd been no dog, and no dog had been found wandering about loose in the area… Mind you, he thought, if it was a bitch in heat she could be anywhere. He'd pass that on to the Tonbridge team who were still patrolling the area in case the mysterious tramp should break cover. In the meantime, he'd get the Bitch Spray can brought in – shouldn't have missed that.

* * * * *

Tom had driven back down to St Leonard's especially carefully, avoiding anything that might attract attention. He arrived at Clare's expecting to find Ali in a panic. She'd be imagining his battered body dumped in a ditch, or dropped into the Thames in a weighted sack, and Boris hot on her trail with orders to kill her, Clare and Olivia.

When he'd called, she'd been pretty angry. Switch off her mobile? She'd thought of that already - but how the hell did he think he'd have been able to tell her where he was if she had? And what was he doing disappearing back to London without even telling her? He'd explained. She wasn't angry anymore, now she was worrying.

When the news that he was on his way back penetrated, she'd done what he'd asked her to do. Then she spent the next hour and a half pacing until Clare had invoked the privilege of friendship.

"For Christ's sake, Ali, you're tense. I'm tense, but leave the demons outside, will you? Settle down."

She'd done her best then, only checking her watch every 10 minutes and the news every fifteen. But when Tom arrived, he found them sitting quietly drinking tea. They were watching Olivia, back from kindergarten, busy drawing enormous monsters with bright yellow mop heads being flattened by a stick figure with wild red curls and enormous black boots. Super Ali. At least that was how she explained it. He'd never know about the sudden excitement he'd caused when he pulled up in front of the house. Clare had let him in, as though everything was completely normal, and Ali looked up at him nonchalantly. "Hi, Tom. Good drive down? How was the traffic?"

We're playing it cool, are we? Probably better that way, especially in front of Olivia. He put his bags down, leaned over and gave Ali a kiss. Then all the frustration and anxiety came rushing in and pulling her up on to her feet he enveloped her in a crushing hug, and kissed her again, properly.

"Oi, you two!" interjected Clare, "Get a room!"

"Jealous?" He smiled, then pulled her in for a hug too.

"Hey," called out Olivia. "Me too!" and jumped down from her chair at the table to join in. They all stood together in the middle of the room.

"Ali, I'm so sorry. I did believe you. It just didn't sink in properly. I mean, these things don't happen in real life. Not to people like us." He paused. Took a couple of breaths. Then he hugged them all again. "But they do, don't they? I saw him, Ali. My God, he's huge. Terrifying. He was in our flat, and I nearly walked in on him!" This time his hug was just for Ali.

Clare stepped back and took Olivia by the hand. "Come on Olivia. Let's give Ali and Tom a moment, shall we?"

"Is he going to kiss her again?" asked Olivia.

Clare smiled. "I expect he will, don't you?"

Olivia looked past Clare. "You're right Mummy. He is. He's still kissing her! Why is Ali crying though? Doesn't she like Tom kissing her?"

"Come on, poppet. Yes, she does. Let's leave them alone for a few minutes. They've had a difficult day," and holding her daughter's hand she led her off to the kitchen to try to explain the unexplainable.

* * * * *

They waited until after supper to discuss Tom's trip to London. Tom had phoned Charlie, as arranged, and given him the number of his burner, and Charlie said he'd call again if anything happened at Jermyns. He said Geoff had warned his staff that someone might be coming around asking questions, and they'd let him know.

Olivia had been a bit subdued during the meal. "Are you still cross with Tom, Ali? I thought you were happy to see him, but you're supposed to smile, or laugh when you're happy!"

Ali assured her that, yes, she was happy, and that no, she promised she wasn't going to cry again. Olivia still watched her doubtfully though, all through the meal. When Tom came in to read her a story before she went to sleep, she made him promise solemnly that he wouldn't do anything to make Ali cry again. Twice, before she drifted off to sleep.

Coming back downstairs he met an amused Clare at the foot of the stairs. "She isn't sure that Ali really is happy. It's hard to explain these things to a young child. She says she believes me, but she isn't sure."

"Well, I'm not so sure Ali is all that happy with me either. Christ, Clare, that giant had his hands on her. The man could probably pull her apart! But she got away from him. Call me 'Doubting Thomas,' but until I saw him myself, I just didn't get it at all. I knew something had happened, sure, but I really hadn't believed, not deep down." They went back into the kitchen to join Ali and sat around the table holding their council of war.

After discussing the events of the day, they agreed that they'd wait until they heard from Charlie the next day.

If the police turned up at Jermyns they'd stay where they were. If it was someone else, they were all going to have to disappear.

*   *   *   *   *

Stuart McLean was at his desk finishing up his report on the findings so far at Laura's head office when Susan came in. She went through to her office, took off her coat, hung it on the hook on the wall, and sat down with a satisfied sigh. She still had no confirmed suspects, but she felt they were making progress.

She got up again and walked back out into the common area and along to Stuart's desk. He looked up.

"Did you manage to get the Bitch Spray?"

He nodded. "Helen took it to forensics. She should be up with it any moment."

He'd hardly said that when Constable Jarvis came in. She had the Bitch Spray can in an evidence bag, and the report on what it showed.

"Oh, hello Ma'am. I was just bringing this up from Forensics. Is it important?"

"Thanks, Helen. Let's have a look." She took the report and skimmed what it had to say, then looked at the two with a satisfied smile. "I think we finally have a break. There are two different sets of prints on the can. One is Laura's, but the other hasn't been seen anywhere else. It overlays Laura's, so it's more recent. I think we've got the killer's fingerprints here!"

She went back to her office and took a long gulp of her coffee. She looked through the glass partitions between her and the DCI's office. He was in, and alone. Carrying her mug, she walked along to his office, knocked on the door.

"Come in" came his voice, and she pushed the door open.

"Crosspatch!" he said, caught himself and smiled an apology. "Sorry, Susan. I'm glad you wandered over. I need a break from this file I'm reviewing."

Wincing at his use of her nickname, even though she'd got quite used to it from her team, she stepped in, carefully leaving the door wide open. "I wondered if you'd like a quick update on the Nettle Lane case, Sir. A few interesting things have come up, and I'd like to see if your opinion is close to mine."

"Definitely." She sat down facing his desk. "Elizabeth told me about the campaign the two of you are running against the rumours that have been pervading the Centre. Both of the other DIs have mentioned it to me too. Passed it off as a great joke. Of course, they hadn't believed any of those ridiculous stories - ha! - and they thought it was a masterful way to squash the rumour machine. They even congratulated me! I said I wished I had thought of it myself, but that the credit lay with the two of you." He laughed.

"With Elizabeth, really," smiled Susan. "It was all her idea. I'm glad it's working. We are going to meet quite often - all part of her masterplan. It'll depend on how this case goes, of course. We're having coffee again on Friday just to let it be seen that we're not going to let up."

"Excellent! All right, tell me what's come to light."

Susan took the Laura's end of the case first, explaining how the protection 'insurance' worked. "I think this goes far beyond the local gang we thought we were dealing with. It seems to be a highly organised and extensive scheme so I expect the Yard will want to take over on that. We have two unanswered questions. First, someone knew in advance that there was about to be a change in management at Laura's. That is relevant to us. I expect we'll find that whoever runs this scheme on a national level subcontracts local enforcement to local gangs. So, someone local knew this was going down. If only the two thugs we arrested hadn't been released… Mind you, we'd probably have had to send them to Guantanamo Bay to get much out of them!

"The second question is why Laura's seemed to have protection but was paying no 'premium'. They were on the protected list but weren't paying for it. Someone assumed that with a change in management, protection would no longer be there. So that must have been something to do with Laura herself. I was thrashing around all night on that one, and the only answer I could come up with was her father. He's on a watch list for Organised Crime. If he were high enough up in the umbrella organisation, he could protect his daughter's company… Perhaps without her even knowing. That could be a link to our case, and it would be interesting to find out."

"I agree with you there. The Yard will want to take this part of the investigation over now. I won't fight it. We're stretched thin enough as it is. If they do step in, though, I will try to have them include DC Crewe on their investigation and allow him to focus on your first question… Go on with your findings."

"The other line of investigation has centred on the theatre. DC Murphy and PC Varma have been up there for two days just sniffing around." She smiled, amused. "Actually, that's very apt for PC Varma… DC Murphy says she has the nose of a bloodhound! But I'm getting ahead of myself."

She took a long swallow of her coffee. "After you and DC Crewe informed Mr. Davison of the death of his wife, you know he informed the cast. A couple of them told PC Varma that they'd all expected him to send them home, at least for the day, if not cancel the entire production. But no. He did break down a bit apparently, and locked himself in his office, but only for a few minutes and when he came out, he was all energy again, full of 'the show must go on'. He ran them through rehearsals for about another two hours.

"When he let them go, he asked one of them to stay behind. They wouldn't have noticed if it had been someone playing a major role, but this was a fairly new girl, Alison Johnson. She had a minor role, only a few lines to speak. Anyway, he asked her to wait in his office. One of them wondered if he might have been looking for a quick - er - shag, but they all shouted him down on that because she didn't seem the type and… well… his wife had just been murdered. But the point is, Alison Johnson hasn't been seen since."

The DCI sat up straight. "That was two days ago. No one's seen her?"

"No. Sean is getting as much information as he can. We're trying to track her down. Davison hasn't been completely consistent on this. First it was that if she didn't turn up, she was fired; then that she had just quit. When I asked him directly what had happened, he said she was gone when he went back to his office. She'd told him she had had an offer of a good role up in Newcastle and had taken it. He says he wished her well, no skin off his nose. We'll see what Sean and Sandeep come up with, but we need to resolve this fast. I'm just hoping she doesn't re-appear as a 'floater' in the Thames…

"You remember Sandeep's bloodhound nose? She found splashes of blood and an overturned model guillotine outside Davison's office, also with blood on it. They got forensics in, and they have taken samples. We should get answers – with luck – tomorrow."

"Make sure we follow up on that. Check with any rep companies up there and see if anyone knows about it," said the DCI. "It may be there was something totally different going on there, but it feels suspicious, and it needs investigation. So far, we've got a lot of information and a lot of good questions, but do we have anything that is definitely connected with the murder?"

"I was leaving that for last. Some facts, some suppositions, some guesses.

"Number one. I was at the morgue this morning to see what Ellie had for us. We should get her report tomorrow, but the first point is perhaps the most important. The cause of death wasn't a knife wound!"

"What? The woman was almost torn apart! How could that *not* have been the cause of death?"

"That's what we've all asked, Sir. But in fact, she slipped and smashed her head on the side of the bath. It's solid hard stone, and it proved quite lethal!"

"That was prior to the knife work?"

"Yes. Ellie believes he's a very large and strong man, and that he grabbed her by the throat - the bruises are quite clear - and hauled her straight up in the air. But she was very slippery from the bath oil and when she struggled, he lost his grip - and she fell back into the bath and smashed her head. Ellie thinks she was very lucky..."

"Lucky?" interjected the DCI.

"I know! But she believes the killer had far worse things planned for her. A quick death was a mercy. "

"Good God!" sighed the DCI. "What a world we live in!"

"Well, yes, but brutality isn't exactly new, is it? But what if there is a mob connection, with an enforcer who developed a taste for killing? And now he can't stop? Ellie thinks this could be a serial killer, and he's getting careless."

"Why would she think that? If it is a serial killer, there should be a string of other earlier murders that are similar, and this one seems to be unique."

"Not necessarily. Not if this was a botched job. It could well have been, a break in pattern. I'm going to have the team go over records of any particularly nasty, unsolved knife murders in the past few years. Ellie thinks the knife is his chosen weapon. That he planned to murder Laura with one, taking his time over it. Rape could well be an element, but she doesn't think that was what was important to him."

"Ellie seems to be a bit more than a Forensic Pathologist. Is she auditioning for 'Silent Witness'? She's almost profiled the Killer."

"She's seen a lot of dead bodies, I suppose. You must get a sense of the mind behind the killings after a while. My own feeling is that she's right, but I'm not sure where it leaves us or how it started. I can't let go of the feeling that Davison must have something to do with it. But I'm damned if I can see how or why. If that's the case we should find a transfer of a fairly large sum to someone, somewhere, because contract killers don't usually work on credit.

"They are also careful and meticulous; try to make the kill look like an accident. They really don't want a police investigation. This one is the very antithesis of that; screaming out to be investigated. A serial killer who is losing control, yes, that's possible… But that tosses out the idea of a contract killing and clears Davison.

"I think we have to pursue the serial killer thread, but I want to keep investigating Davison's business. I don't know what it is, but something's not right there. DC Murphy heard there was a panic last week, and that his investors were pulling out. We need to know a bit more about that.

"Beyond that, Sir - I got several strange vibes off Ian Davison."

"Vibes, Susan?"

"Yes, Sir. I know it's an outdated term, but it fits. He's not happy about us looking into his business. He doesn't really care if we check out Laura's. It could just be some little tax fiddle. Maybe nothing to do with the murder at all. But I'm sure he's concealing something he knows about Alison Johnson's disappearance too. I don't know what, but he really doesn't like being questioned about it."

"Lastly, I think he thinks he knows who the killer may be. But he's not saying anything at all."

"I see," said the DCI. "Well, these 'vibes' are interesting. Tell me you're not psychic!"

"I can't explain it, Sir. I've never had any 'psychic' episodes - don't believe in it, really. And I can't say I've ever experienced anything similar before, but I feel fairly certain about this."

The DCI was silent for a few moments, looking at her. "All right. Don't ignore these feelings or 'vibes' as you call them. They're intuition, as opposed to logic and have been known to break cases wide open. I agree that you should carry on looking at Davison. You will have to back them up with solid evidence, but if you can establish a connection between him and the killer, that will make things very interesting. If he thinks he knows the killer, they must have met, and he, in turn, may have picked up 'vibes' suggesting the man was a killer. Or perhaps it's simply part of his unease over his own business affairs. It could also just be his way of reacting to the death… in the middle of playing a psychologically disturbing role. How did Macbeth react to Duncan's death ...?"

Susan waited and that thought lay heavy on the air. Then the DCI returned to practicalities.

"I also agree that we see if we can find a link to other knife murders where torture and perhaps rape were involved. And make sure you follow up on the missing actress. I think our separate leads just may be taking us in the same direction.

"Keep me updated, Susan. This case is starting to get very interesting indeed. Get the report on the protection insurance to DI Crawford at the Yard. I'm sure he'll come back to me very quickly. I'll be glad to hand that one over to them.

"Now, I think you described all that as Number One. What's Number Two?"

"Right. Number two. Forensics finished their sweep of the Nettle Lane house and found no unexplained fingerprints. The killer obviously wore gloves and was careful, apart from the killing itself. No prints in the bathroom and no unexplained DNA that we've found. So we didn't have any definite proof tying him to the house. Only to the lay-by where the shirt and jacket were found."

"Didn't have…?"

"That's right. Ellie found something very odd. Something had been sprayed into the back of Laura's throat. She didn't know what it was, but she sent it for analysis, and they got an answer back really quickly, for once. Someone must owe her a favour! It was something called Bitch Spray."

Gordon nodded. "You use it if you have a bitch in heat. It keeps other dogs away."

"Right. I'm beginning to wonder if I'm the only one who didn't know that. Anyway, it was sprayed into Laura's mouth during the killing. It's not something that your average murderer would bring along, so it must have been something he picked up on site. Stuart found a can of it sitting by the step at the front door. We have it in evidence. It's been checked, and there are very clear prints on the can. Laura's, of course, but there's another set overlying Laura's. They are currently unidentified but given the spray in Laura's throat it suggests that these are the killer's prints.

"He's made a mistake! If we find him, it'll tie him to the murder."

*   *   *   *   *

"Jermyns of Hastings" was not a large operation. They relied on their reputation as one of the top Jaguar garages in the country to bring them a steady stream of business from well-heeled enthusiasts. They maintained this by an insistence on excellence from their small but loyal workforce. Officially, they closed at five pm, but two mechanics had stayed late to spend a few hours on an E-Type that had just come in.

It was in serious need of work. The owner had let it sit for several years before deciding what to do with it. The result was corrosion throughout the vehicle. Bolts frozen in place, Brake disks badly pitted, and rubber grease seals simply cracking up. They reckoned that the longest part of the job would be just getting things apart, so they'd stayed on to make a start on that. They had the car up on a hoist and had managed to get the wire-spoked wheels off. Bruce was wrestling with the dismantling of one of the front brakes and hub when he felt someone tapping him on his shoulder. Looking round, he found himself looking up at a massive bear of a man.

"Hello mate, what can we do for you, then?"

"I'm trying to find a friend of mine," came the reply in a deep, resonating voice. "Tom O'Malley. He and his girlfriend brought a Jaguar here from Classic Cars in Wandsworth this morning. I need to know where they went."

"Oh yeah. Mr. Gregson's car. That's right, we sent it up to Classic to sort out the bodywork after he had a nasty accident with it, and Tom delivered it back to us. Beautiful job they did, too. He was really pleased."

"That would be the one. Where did they go?"

"Who did you say you were?" asked Bruce, feeling a little intimidated, and beginning to resent it. He'd been told the police might be coming by asking questions about Tom, and they were to stick to the simple truth.

"I'm a friend of Tom's." The answer came back in almost a snarl, and the big man stepped closer.

No way was this the police! Backing up against the hoist, Bruce was not about to be bullied. "So, call him on his mobile."

"He's not answering, so I'm asking you. Where did they say they were going?"

"Didn't see any girl. It was just Tom."

"Just answer the bloody question," said the giant, and he stepped forward again, his enormous hand reaching out for Bruce, but stopped as he heard a scratching noise behind him followed by a 'whoosh'. Looking back over his shoulder, he saw Jerry advancing on him with a welding torch with a two-foot flame shooting out of the nozzle. Taking advantage of his distraction, Bruce ducked under the hoist and out the other side towards a big tool chest.

"Whoa there," the big man said, raising his hands. "I don't think you understand. All I want to do is find my friend. He's not answering his mobile, and I'm worried about him. He didn't come back to work. The last place he was seen was here."

"No," said Jerry. "I think we understand just fine. Maybe Tom doesn't want to speak to you."

"He does," said the giant, advancing towards Jerry, who fiddled with the torch. The flame was shorter, now, and hissing with a searing blue/white cone at its centre. Behind him he heard a cough. Turning, he saw Bruce rounding the hoist with a heavy crowbar in his fists. Looking back at Jerry, he recognised the blue and white flame… Hot enough to take his hand off if he made the wrong move.

"No," said Jerry. "I don't think he does. It's time for you to leave."

The giant looked at the two mechanics. The bastards didn't look like they were going to back down, and he wouldn't be able to reach the one with the welding torch without getting seriously burned. He could feel the vicious heat from several steps back. If he turned to deal with his mate, he'd just step back around the hoist, and he could do real damage with that crowbar… And the one with the welding torch would be behind him…

He looked around wildly, and then with a snarl of rage he rushed back out of the raised workshop door to his pickup parked just outside. Wrenching open the door he pulled himself in. His keys were already in the ignition. The engine started, and with a squeal of tires he was off down the narrow street, mounting the pavement to avoid the rush hour jams, scattering pedestrians in all directions as he went. Turning onto the seafront he went racing west out of town. He could hear police sirens behind him. No problem. They would likely be snarled up in the traffic themselves.

*   *   *   *   *

Walworth

Entering her office, Susan found the rest of her team ready and waiting, Sean and Sandeep having finished at the theatre. "Sorry, everyone, I was just updating the DCI on what we've found." She sat down behind her desk.

"Stuart, the DCI agrees that the Yard is going to take over the 'Protection' investigation, but he'll ask them to keep Dave Crewe on it to see if anything ties back to our case. As long as they're in charge, they'll probably go for it. That frees you up for an interesting little job I need you to do.

"Sean, we're going to keep the investigation at the theatre active, but low profile, ok? If you're asked, you're just dotting the i's and crossing the t's. Come back in when you think you've got everything you can. Our biggest question at the theatre is what happened to the actress who went missing, but a secondary one is to find out what the flap was last week over their funding. Something smells wrong with Davison; we need to know what it is. I know we can't see a motive yet, but we still can't ignore the possibility that he contracted out his wife's killing. Mind you, if Stuart comes up with what he's going to be looking for, I don't think you'll find anything."

"Sandeep, you'll be here for now. For a start find out how many Rep companies are up in the Newcastle area. There won't be many. Then call them and ask if they know of our missing actress. Then you can help Stuart. Something is going to break soon, I'm just not sure which of you is going to find it first."

"Rep companies Ma'am?"

"Yes. Local theatrical companies." Then she turned to Ellie's concern about a serial killer who was coming unhinged. "Ellie's theory is that he likes to play with his knife and keep the victim alive as long as possible. We're looking for unsolved cases - and they could be anywhere because this bloke hasn't been caught yet. He may not even know most of his victims. He may just like killing. He kidnaps them and tucks them away somewhere to have his fun. Not all the cases will be recognisable. They may just be missing person's reports. But I'm hoping some of the bodies have been found. That's your job, Stuart. See what you can find."

"Sandeep, but please keep a watch out for anything coming in on the Alison Johnson situation. I think that's mixed up in it.

"By the way, did we get back an analysis on the blood on that shirt and jacket you found?"

"Yes," came Sandeep's quick answer. "The blood is all the victim's, Ma'am, just as we expected. But they were able to get another trace from the shirt. The wearer had sweated into the collar, and they have a DNA stream from it. They also matched the same DNA with those cigarette ends we found."

"I don't suppose it came up with a match in the system, did it? "

"No, Ma'am, sorry."

"Pity. Still, if that DNA crops up somewhere else later, it'll show a match that could tell us a lot. Keep an eye open for the other bits we've sent for analysis. You never know."

"OK Team, you know what to do. I'm popping downstairs for another coffee. This one's gone cold!"

* * * * *

The M&Ms went back to their desks with PC Varma in tow. "Right, then, Sandeep, we'd better see what you already know about searching the database," said Stuart, sitting down at his computer. "You've got a log-in, haven't you?"

"Yes, of course. Shall I put it in?"

"No, not on this one. I'll be using it." Stuart got up again and they moved to the next desk. "Log in on this one." Sandeep did so and sat back, looking at him expectantly. "Now, scroll down to 'Murders - Unsolved', and now we have to select 'All' or specify a region. Select this region. Now it's asking for 'All' again, or you can put in additional factors you want to narrow down your search. So, let's narrow it down. Put in 'Female Victim' and knife as 'weapon'. OK… Search. There we go… and look at that 'Nettle Lane, Nr. Tonbridge, Victim Laura Handley-Davison, SIO DCI Gordon/DS Cross, Sevenoaks'. But look at this, there are others. There's that nasty one two years ago in Brighton, and an even older one, over by Horsham almost five years ago. Bit before my time, that one. Click on it"

The two officers read through the story. Mrs. Audrey Rogers, from Crawley. Thirty-three years old, two children, eight and eleven years old, and husband George Rogers, 35. Mrs. Rogers had been out with two of her friends, a 'Girls Night Out'. She was described as a pretty woman, light brown hair, friendly and cheerful. They were a fairly well-off couple, nice house, about half the mortgage paid off.

Sometime during the evening, the other two women had taken themselves off to the Ladies, and left Audrey sitting at their table nursing a glass of wine and watching over the others' drinks for them. Her friends said it had taken them perhaps ten or fifteen minutes, as they had had to queue. When they got back, she was gone. Their drinks were still on the table, but it looked like hers had been finished. They were a bit surprised but just assumed she had given up on them and gone home.

Her body was found about two months later, lightly covered up under the hedge in a field along the A24, between Horsham and Kingsfold, naked and with a wound from a large knife through her lower belly. The body was partially decomposed, but it was apparent that there had been multiple cuts all over her torso and legs, few of which would have proved fatal if attended to. There was no evidence of rape. She had been gagged and both hands and feet had been bound.

The coroner's opinion was that she had been tortured before being killed with the knife through the belly. It was his opinion that the killer had plunged his knife home and then watched as she died, writhing in agony. He described it as one of the most horrific killings he had ever had to examine.

There was a note that this murder had been linked to one outside Brighton two years later, but no connection other than the 'MO' had been found.

"I remember the Brighton murder," said Stuart. "I was a DC attached to Eastbourne before they opened the Sevenoaks Centre. I'd only been with them a few weeks when it happened. We all heard about it. Much the same." They opened the file. A pretty woman, single in her case, in her mid-twenties. She'd been out with her boyfriend, but the evening hadn't gone very well. They had gone to a pub, but when some of his friends had turned up, he'd basically joined them, leaving her on her own. She'd been pretty fed up and gone out to her car to drive home. Her car was still in the car park the next morning, but she wasn't seen alive again.

Her body was found a few days later by a man walking his dog down one of the country lanes north of the town. Naked, gagged, hands and feet bound, and with knife wounds all over the torso and legs. There was one definite killing blow, again through the belly, but several other wounds fairly deep into the belly, all of which would have been agonising, and eventually fatal.

They looked at each other. "Really?" asked Sandeep. "We've only just started, and we have two murders that fit what we're looking for. Why weren't these put together as serial murders?"

"Good question. They were linked. But they were almost three years apart, and there hadn't been others like it before, or since. Generally we don't announce that there is a serial murderer on the loose until there have been more.

Don't want to start a panic. It doesn't look like there are any others like it in this region, and Brighton was two years ago. Let's take these to Crosspatch, and then we'll spread our search."

Susan was sipping her coffee and leafing through the forensic report on the items found at Nettle Lane. Nothing really useful, and they might not get another sniff of this man in months, even years. They needed more.

Stuart and Sandeep were at her door. "What? Don't tell me you found something already? You've only been at it for twenty minutes!" she exclaimed.

Stuart responded. "Well, we have two, fairly local. They are old, and of course, they don't match Nettle Lane. But they are almost exactly what Ellie reckoned we'd find."

"Seriously? This was only a theory we were testing. Let me look at them, and you two widen your search area. Let's see how far our boy travels."

Susan brought both files up on her computer, showing them side by side with half a screen each. No wonder they'd been matched before. Woman alone in the pub, or leaving alone, and never seen again. Body found days or weeks later, as much by luck as anything. On one, by the farmer doing a round of his fields before letting his horses loose in them, and the other an older man walking his dog. Had others not been found and classified as simply 'missing'?

Did this get them anywhere closer to finding the killer? Neither case had any clear suspects. In the older one, the Horsham one, the victim's two friends said they'd noticed someone who seemed to be keeping his eye on them, but the only description had been that he was 'maybe late twenties' and that he was 'huge'. No one had been able to identify him, although several people remembered seeing him, but again the only description was 'really big'.

After the Brighton murder there had been no mention anywhere of someone like that, although one of the barmaids did remember serving someone 'very big', but she couldn't remember which day that had been.

Well, it matched Ellie's conjecture that the killer must have been big and strong. But it didn't help much. They knew they were looking for someone really powerful, and 'really big' usually went along with that.

Sandeep burst in through the door. "Sergeant Cross," she said excitedly, "we've got one!"

"Got what, Sandeep?" she asked.

"A DNA match!" She was almost bouncing. "It's just been flagged. Walworth Police Station sent in some samples for analysis, and as soon as forensics put the results into the database, they matched with ours!"

"What case were they investigating?"

Sandeep slowed down a moment. "There doesn't appear to be one. A file was opened but it seems to be blank."

"OK, Sandeep, give Walworth a ring, and see what you can find out. We need to know what's going on there. Get back to me as soon as you have some details."

"Yes Ma'am," she said, and she was gone.

Susan sat back. Now what? She thought about it for a minute. Wait a minute, where's Walworth? She looked it up. South London. Near the theatre where another woman had gone missing. Much the same time line? Her pulse picked up. Was this the break they'd been waiting for? She wanted it, a connection through the theatre to two deaths… No. Hang on, Alison Johnson was only missing, so far. What was it that Walworth had?

Sandeep was back in just a few minutes. "They say they don't know what it's all about. It was on the night shift a couple of days ago. But the night sergeant will be on in another couple of hours, and he may be able to tell us."

"Grab your coat, Sandeep. We're going to Walworth!"

* * * * *

Getting up to Walworth took a little longer than she'd expected, although most of the traffic was going the other way. They broke for a quick supper en route, stopping at one of the seemingly hundreds of Indian restaurants along the way. By the time they arrived at the police station in Walworth, night had fallen, and traffic had thinned out considerably. Putting up the 'On Duty' sign, they parked around the corner and walked in. The sergeant behind the counter was drinking a large mug of dubiously coloured tea. They announced themselves and produced their identification.

"Something happened on Monday evening that led you to submit some samples for analysis to forensics. Yet when the file is opened, the forensics analysis is there but with no details of why the analysis was requested. We need to know what happened. What were the samples you sent for analysis?"

"Monday? Just a second… You from Kent?"

"Yes, Sevenoaks"

"Got it. A girl came in, a bit roughed up. Said she knew who'd killed someone and that someone else was after her."

Crosspatch could hardly believe her luck. "Who was she? Where is she now?"

"An actress I think she said. Can't remember her name. Hang about though, Constable Pandya took her statement, and she sent the stuff off to forensics before she went off shift. She'll remember." He went back to one of the first of the cubicles in the open space behind, his counter then shook his head and walked down the aisle between the cubicles. "Anyone seen Pandy?" he asked in a loud voice.

"Here Sergeant," came a voice from near the back, and a tall woman popped up, and made her way up to the front. "Sorry Sarge. I was just helping PC Lane get his notes sorted out."

"Harpee!" burst out PC Varma.

"Sandy?" PC Pandya, walked up to the counter. "I thought you were down in one of the South East stations."

"Yes, I am." She turned to Crosspatch. "Sergeant Cross, this is my cousin, Harpee." And then to PC Pandya "We're here because of the file you opened on the actress who came in on Monday night."

Constable Pandya nodded towards Susan, who took over the narrative.

"That's right, Constable. There's nothing in the file you opened that evening."

"There must be," said Pandya. "I remember setting it up and then I sent in her dress and boots to forensics. Has the analysis come through? Let me look." She settled herself in front of the computer and began to tap. "Here it is," she said, opening it. Sure enough, though, only the forensics analysis was there. "Well, it was there when I went off shift." She looked at the desk sergeant. "You had called the South East Policing Centre, Sergeant, and they were sending someone to pick her up."

"That's right!" said the Sergeant. "I spoke to their duty officer that night, and he said she was a 'person of interest' in a murder case. Said he'd come up and get her. He came himself, which was a bit odd, but when he got here, she'd gone. She had been waiting with Nurse Ryan, but she wasn't there. Nurse Ryan said she thought she'd gone to the Ladies, but she wasn't there either. Just disappeared. He was a bit narked, and asked to see what we had on file, so I sat him down to read what Pandy had put in. The next thing I knew he'd closed it up and was off again. Still, it was his case, not ours, so I didn't question it."

"I'm SIO on that case, Sergeant. That woman may have had crucial information. Now we're no better off than we were before," she said dispiritedly.

"No. Wait!" It was PC Pandya. "Let me check something." She disappeared into one of the cubicles and reappeared with a small tablet. She switched it on and punched in a few words. "Here it is. These are my notes from when I spoke to her. And I should still have her story recorded." She pushed it across the counter to Crosspatch.

As she read it, Susan felt her eyes getting bigger and bigger! It was all here. If Alison Johnson was right, Davison *had* contracted the killing - *But why, for God's sake*? - and Alison accidentally picked up his phone when the killer reported it done. If so, had Davison realised what had happened and set her up in turn for the killer? But she had escaped - *God, she must have courage to spare* - and made it to the police station and told her story. No, she didn't know who the killer was, but she'd probably seen him - up close! She could identify him!

Without Alison herself, though, they had nothing. They had to find her. PC Pandya had met her; she'd spoken to her. She handed the tablet to PC Varma to read.

"PC Pandya, I need you on our team. You've met this girl." She turned to the desk sergeant. "Who do I need to speak to, to get a temporary transfer and have Constable Pandya seconded to our team?"

"Well, I … you won't be able to talk to him until tomorrow…" faltered the sergeant. Susan turned back to Pandya.

"PC Pandya, can I keep your tablet for now?" A nodded assent. "You can expect to hear from us tomorrow. Will you be able to get down to Sevenoaks?"

"I can take the train."

"That's terrific. I can't thank both of you enough. If we can find this girl, we may be able to close a few cases."

"You think this Ian Davison has killed several people?"

"No. But we think the actual killer may have. Thank you for your help, Sergeant. PC Pandya, I hope to see you tomorrow afternoon."

* * * * *

"Ma'am" said Sandeep quietly in the car on the way back to Sevenoaks, "Harpee - I mean PC Pandya - had the whole story. The duty officer that night must have read the file. Why has no-one told us?"

"Good question," Susan replied, "and one I'm going to leave to the DCI."

"Why would you do that, Ma'am? Can't we ask him?"

"The duty officer that night was DI Featherstone. He and I don't see eye to eye on – well – anything, really. And he outranks me. But he doesn't outrank the DCI."

"I see. He might not answer you. But if the DCI asked, he would have to." Susan nodded. She was beginning to have a bad feeling about her former superior.

When they got back to Sevenoaks, Susan dropped Sandeep off at her parents' home. It was after 10pm, too late to drop by and see Mandy? She phoned. "Mandy, it's Susan. How are you?"

"Susan? Sorry, I'm half asleep. I'm fine, thanks. Are you coming over?"

"Can I? It's late, but I'd like to."

"Yes, of course. Please. Shall I rustle up an omelette?"

"That sounds wonderful. Shall I pick up a bottle of plonk?"

"Our Aussie red? Yes please…"

*   *   *   *   *

Susan had a couple of things she wanted to see the DCI about on Friday morning. Item #1, she needed him to persuade the Met to release PC Pandya to her for a few days. Item #2, she wanted him to find out what Featherstone was up to.

Scratch that, she thought. Item #1 was a visit to Sergio for her morning caffeine hit! Then, she would tackle the DCI.

Revised Item #1 taken care of, she made straight for the DCI's office. *Damn!* Someone was already in talking to him. She went to her own office instead, hung up her coat, and sat back, sipping her coffee and watching to see when the DCI was free.

It took a while, but eventually the DCI and his visitor stood up, shook hands and the DCI walked him to the door. *Must be someone important.* As soon as the visitor had left, she put her head around Gordon's door.

"Morning, Susan," he smiled. "I don't have much time, but if it's quick?"

"We've got a big break in the case, Sir, and I need you to - er - extend some influence."

“Terrific! Come in. Let’s hear what you’ve got.” He sat down expectantly, waving her towards another seat.

“I’ll be brief, Sir. Late yesterday afternoon we got a match on the DNA that we found at the lay-by on Nettle Lane… Er … Sir?” The DCI was looking past her, out of his office.

“PC Varma seems to be trying to get our attention,” he said. Swivelling round, she saw Sandeep waving her arms enthusiastically in their direction. “Perhaps we should bring her in?”

Susan got up, went to the door, and told Sandeep to come in. The little PC looked a little alarmed. “It’s fine, Sandeep. Come in. You were with me last night, so it’s partly your story anyway.”

Sandeep hesitated in the doorway. “Ma’am,” she whispered, “I needed to tell you. We have another DNA match!”

Susan looked at her. A moment’s thought. “The blood you found at the theatre.”

“Yes, but how did you know? It just this minute appeared! You couldn’t have known, so I needed to tell you!”

“Elementary, my dear Sandeep,” said Susan with a wide grin. “I’ve been dying for the opportunity to say that to someone! Come on in, you can tell the DCI.”

“I shouldn’t,” Sandeep whispered, “but you need to know so you can tell him”.

"Oh no you don't… It's your news, and it supports what we already know," and she ushered her in, pointed to another chair in front of the DCI, and sat down herself, still chuckling.

"Good morning, PC Varma," said the DCI. "It looked as though you had something you needed to tell us?"

"Yes, Sir," she said, anxiously looking at Crosspatch, who - quite unhelpfully, she thought - indicated she should carry on. "You see, Sir, there have been several samples with possible DNA from different places sent to forensics for analysis, and now we have all three showing the same DNA".

"That would include the blood that you found at the theatre on Tuesday, then, wouldn't it?" asked the DCI.

Sandeep looked at Crosspatch questioningly, then turned back to the DCI. "Yes, sir, and the DNA from the shirt and the cigarette ends at Nettle Lane, and from samples sent in by Walworth."

Suddenly the DCI sat straighter. He looked at Crosspatch.

"You've got a connection between the theatre and the crime scene?" he asked. "What does Walworth have to do with it?"

"Yes! That's why I wanted to talk to you, Sir. PC Varma spotted our first match late yesterday afternoon. I asked about the Walworth connection too. The strange thing was that it was linked to a blank file, as though someone had opened a file and sent the samples in under that number but had then forgotten to add any details. We called Walworth, but they said we would need to wait for the officers who had been on shift that night.

"So, we drove up and talked to the night sergeant there. He remembered that a girl had come in saying she knew who had killed Laura Handley-Davison and that they were trying to kill her too. One of his PC's had taken her statement and there was blood on her clothes, so she had sent them to forensics for testing. The sergeant knew Nettle Lane was on our patch, so he called the Centre. Our duty officer said that she was a POI and he would collect her himself, right away.

"When he got there, though, the girl had skipped. All he could do was look at her statement, which he was apparently able to access but which then disappeared. But the PC who had interviewed her produced this." She held out PC Pandya's tablet, with the relevant file open. "You need to read it. There's also a recording of her telling her story."

The DCI took the tablet and sat back to read. Susan watched and waited. Finally, he put the tablet down on his desk carefully. He looked at Susan. "Your 'vibe' looks to have been right, doesn't it? Where's Alison Johnson? She may be the key to everything!"

"That's the problem Sir. I think our maximum effort needs to go into finding her. She's vanished. We have no idea where to find her. We have her personnel file from the theatre, but the photo in that is a studio shot so we don't know how reliable that image is. However, PC Pandya, at Walworth, has not only seen her, she sat down and talked to her. She can identify her for us. I thought you might be able to persuade the Met to second Pandya to us for a while. I think we need her."

The DCI thought about that for a moment. "I agree. Would she object to being asked to uproot for a couple of weeks and work with us? It's Friday, almost the weekend, and you will have to go at this without a break now until she's found. The killer will be after this actress too, but he should have a harder job of it. We have far more resources than he's likely to have. On the other hand, he has two or three days start on us. We need to catch up fast."

"Sir," spoke up PC Varma. "PC Pandya is my cousin. She'll be very happy to help us with this for as long as we need her. She's very smart, especially with computers."

"Thank you, PC Varma." Looking at Susan he said, "We may have a lever. That was DCI Crawford from the Yard here just before you came in. He seems pleased with what you've found at Laura's. I'll see what he can do to get PC Pandya for us. He should still be in the building. I'll call his mobile now. Leave this with me. Was there anything else?"

"Yes, sir, but it can wait until you've spoken with DCI Crawford."

"Right. I'll do that right away. See if we can get her down here this afternoon. Then I have one more thing I must do, but I'll come and find you after that. Good work, both of you."

Susan retrieved the tablet from the desk and hurried back to her own office, reminding Sandeep to check with

Stuart. That side of the hunt was more important than ever now.

We need to find Alison, she thought, *and please God we find her alive. She may be the only person to have escaped from this brute. And she seems to have understood that something was off about Featherstone coming up to collect her. She deserves to survive.* But there was the image of a huge man with a long knife in her mind. They had to move quickly.

Fifteen minutes later, her mobile chattered on her desk. The DCI. "Susan, Crawford is still here. He was in talking to DI Featherstone. Apparently, they go back a long way. He was quite happy to oblige. He spoke to her superior at Walworth, and everything is in hand. I called her myself. If she can make it on time, she'll be in on the 11:43 from London Bridge. She has your number, and she'll phone to confirm as soon as she's on the train. Can you have someone meet her off the train?"

"Yes, Sir, I'll set that up right away."

"I'll be up to see you in a while. I have to talk to DI Featherstone first."

"Sir, if you are talking to DI Featherstone, that was the other thing I was going to ask you about."

"Go on…"

"DI Featherstone was duty officer on Monday night. He was the one who went up to Walworth to interview Alison Johnson. I was hoping you would ask him why and what he's been doing. He was gone for two days. I'm hoping he may have something useful to tell us."

"I see. I was going to ask him why he recommended the release of those two prisoners that you brought in from the boutique incident, but I'll add that to my list."

"Thank you, Sir. I'll see you in a while, then."

Disconnecting, she went to her office door again. "Sandeep!" she called to her PC who was sitting with Stuart, looking at another file.

"Ma'am" said Sandeep, jumping to her feet and hurrying towards her. The two went back into the office.

"Do you drive, Sandeep?" she asked.

"Yes, I love it. But I don't have a car. My father thinks I'm too young!" she said, looking mournful.

"He thinks you're too young to have a car, but he was OK with your joining the police?"

"He says the responsibility will be good for me. He says it may calm me down!" She rolled her eyes dramatically.

"Well, he may have a point." Then she continued. "But I need you to do something for me. PC Pandya is coming down from London on the train. As soon as we know she is on the way, I need you to go and pick her up at the station."

A big smile lit up Sandeep's face. "That's great. I can do that for you, Ma'am. Which car do you want me to use?"

"Let's see if there is something available from the pool." Susan picked up the office phone and punched in a number. "Hello, DS Cross here. One of my staff needs a car for a few days… No, nothing special, whatever you have… yes, that will do fine. I'll send her down… It'll be PC Varma… Yes, PC Sandeep Varma. How many Varma's do we have? … Oh! That many? It must be a large family… What? You just told me you had a Toyota… Maintenance have listed it as unsafe to drive? Well, no, of course I wouldn't want one of my staff driving an unsafe vehicle. What else do you have? ... Nothing right now? Nothing at all? Who am I speaking to, please? ... Motor Specialist Varma. I see. You wouldn't be related to Sandeep, would you? ... Her brother… Well, Motor Specialist Varma, I suggest you be a very good brother to your sister and find her a car. Now! I'll send her down in a few minutes."

She looked at Sandeep. "Your brother doesn't want to provide you with a car. Just for the record, can I see your license?" PC Varma dug into her jacket pocket and pulled out a small cardholder. Leafing through it, she stopped after the first couple and presented it to Crosspatch. A bright shiny, new driver's license.

"Why doesn't he want you driving?"

"He knows my father doesn't think I should have a car yet. He's just being a good son."

Susan felt that perhaps there was more to this. "That's all?"

"He doesn't think I'm a good driver?" ventured Sandeep. Then a bit scornfully, "He thinks women should stay at home and make babies. He's very old-fashioned!"

"Well, right now you only need to drive from the Centre to the station and back, so you can't get into too much trouble. Just remember you *are* a police officer and need to set a good example to the public. Go on down and get your car. I'll tell you as soon as I hear from PC Pandya."

*　　*　　*　　*　　*

Charlie called just before 10:00 am.

"Tom, it was the big'un that showed up at Jermyns. Two of the mechanics were working late, and he came right into the shop. Geoff says they're big boys, and can look after themselves, and they did see him off… But they said he was bloody intimidating. He was trying to find out where you were heading. They didn't tell him anything - didn't have anything to tell him of course - but they've reported the incident to the local coppers, and they've got the staff on full alert.

"We were right about that copper from yesterday. He was the only one we told about Hastings, and yet it's some bloody great thug that turns up asking questions, not a policeman. He's bent.

"You be careful, lad, bloody careful. He really is an Inspector, so he's got all sorts of ways to track you. Get Simon out of sight; only use those burners; keep off the net. No credit cards or bankcards. Don't let anyone know where you are. Not anyone. I'll call you if I hear anything. We'll see you soon. This can't go on for long."

"Ok." Tom looked at the others; "So, it's not just Boris - maybe one or two more. There's a bent policeman in it too, and he may be able to track us if we're not careful."

Ali turned to Clare. "This is worse than I thought. If he gets onto my Facebook account, he'll look for friends that we might have gone to for help. He knows we're down this way. We've put you and Olivia in danger! I'm so sorry, Clare. We've got to move but I think you'll have to hide now too!"

Clare had paled. The monster was at her door, and Olivia was at risk. She had already been at risk, of course, they just hadn't realised it. She looked at Ali and Tom. "No one knew, so there's no blame to go around. We're in this together. And I know where to go."

*   *   *   *   *

Under attack!

PC Pandya raced onto the platform, relieved to see the train was still there. It had been a rush to get ready, even though she had been expecting the call from Sevenoaks. She had already had a small suitcase packed with the main essentials she'd need for a stay. Of course she hadn't known how long to pack for. Still, she was only going to be an hour or so from home. She could always pop back one evening if she needed to.

When the call came, it had been simply to inform her that a request for her assistance had come through. She was to report to Detective Sergeant Cross at the Regional Police Centre, Sevenoaks, as quickly as possible. But on the heels of that call, she had had another surprising and slightly disturbing one. It was from a DCI Crawford at Scotland Yard who informed her that the father of the Nettle Lane murder victim was on the Yard's Organised Crime watch list. He didn't go into detail, but he thought it was unlikely that the murder itself had anything to do with his case. However – and her skin prickled a bit here - if she came up with any leads that seemed to indicate that a major crime syndicate might be involved, she was to contact him immediately.

"Surely this has been mentioned to Sergeant Cross?" she'd asked.

"She's aware of the possible tie in," came the reply, "But a word of warning, Constable. I have recommended your secondment to DS Cross at Sevenoaks, but I need you also to liaise, unofficially, with DI Featherstone there. A good man. He's expected to take over the Nettle Lane case. DCI Gordon of Major Crimes and Sergeant Cross are compromised. My report is that Cross is not competent for a case of this gravity; that she is only in her current position because of an inappropriate relationship with the DCI. Very unfortunate. You should look to Featherstone for any help you need. Keep him informed of anything that comes up on the case."

That's nasty. I can't believe this is how things are supposed to work. No. He's hedging his bets. He's playing both sides of what sounds like a power struggle. Well, she'd reserve judgement on that. The request for her secondment had come from Sergeant Cross directly and she had seemed very much on the right track. She'd followed up on the DNA analysis with lightning speed, and was moving to bring her aboard without delay. That didn't sound like incompetence.

Barely had Crawford hung up than DCI Gordon was on the phone too, thanking her for her willingness to assist, and asking how soon she'd be in Sevenoaks. She'd looked up the timetable quickly and there was a train at 10:08 - no, too late for that one - probably best to aim for the 11:08 - yes, she could make that if she hurried. She told him she'd try for that one. Putting the phone down, she jettisoned the rest of her breakfast – it had gone soggy - and rushed to finish dressing. Done, in record time! Now where was the other shoe? *Oh no... where...? Work backwards...* She had come in just before midnight, tired but super excited about the chance to join a murder investigation... That's what she'd become a police officer for, not to be a desk sergeant's clerical assistant. *Aaugh! Where IS that shoe?* Found, finally, hiding underneath the radiator by the window.

Grabbing her coat and suitcase, she was out of the door before she remembered her phone, still sitting on the kitchen table. Back inside, grab the phone, out again, lock the door! Finally, a breath. Had she closed the window in the bathroom? Well, if she hadn't it was just too bad! Now, London Bridge Station. Fifteen minutes before the train left! She'd have to run.

She came haring into the Station. *Thank goodness, no line up at the ticket office. No time to bother with the machines!* Fumble for her credit card, pay the man. *Aaugh!* 'Tap' wasn't working. Insert the card, bump in her number, and wait while it digested the request. *Hah!* "Remove Card" … *done* … take the ticket and *go.* She was half a minute late… But it hadn't left yet. Rushing to the first door she came to she leapt inside just moments before the train started moving. Leaning against the bulkhead in sheer relief, she looked down the carriage. Barely anyone else aboard. She wandered down the aisle and took a seat near the window - a table seat and she had it all to herself. She put her bag up on the rack, sat down and leaned back.

Looking out it was another bright, clear, autumn day, and the sun, shining warm through the window, was a wonderful antidote to stress. Here she was, heading out to take part in a genuine murder mystery. She smiled. Suddenly life felt extraordinarily good. She opened her phone and called Sergeant Cross.

"Hello Ma'am, it's PC Pandya. I'm on the train… Yes, ETA 11:31… Thank you Ma'am, I'm looking forward to it… PC Varma will be there to meet me? That's excellent, Ma'am… Yes, I'll see you shortly." She sat back and enjoyed the sunshine, watching suburban England slide by. *It's Friday. We'll be working right through the weekend.* She realised she was looking forward to it enormously!

* * * * *

Sandeep Varma looked at the old Ford Focus sadly. Really, this was not what she'd imagined as her first car, even if it would only be hers for the day. She looked at her brother reproachfully.

"Suresh, is this really the best you can do? I'm your sister! Surely you can do better than this? For me?"

"No" came the reply. "I've driven with you before, and I know how you drive. I agree with Abba. You're too young to have a car. At least with this you're not likely to get into too much trouble and you can't hurt our budget too much. I don't even know why we still have this relic. It was parked at the back and hasn't been used in months. If you damage it no-one will miss it".

"I'm a responsible police officer, now. I've calmed down."

"You might fool your sergeant, but you don't fool me. The car has an up-to-date MOT - although how it passed that I can't imagine. Use this car."

Sandeep sighed, took the keys, and got in. "Wait, sign this," said her brother, pushing a clipboard through the window with a form and a big X showing where her signature had to go.

"What is it?"

"It's the form acknowledging we have provided you with this car to aid you in your duties."

She sighed again but signed and rolled up the window - not even electric windows! Another, bigger sigh.

She started the car, and it caught promptly, running smoothly, with perhaps a bit of a rumble to it. Hmm, a six-speed gearbox… Six? Well, she had driven a manual gearbox when learning to drive, so she pushed down on the clutch, gave the throttle a little blip, put it into first gear, and, remembering her driving lessons, gave it a bit more throttle as she brought up the clutch. Wonder of all wonders, she pulled up the ramp and out of the entrance to the motor pool looking as though she'd been doing this for years. *Thank you*, she thought to the car, patting it on the dashboard. Perhaps she had been too harsh. The car was better than she had expected. She drove sedately around to the staff car park, found a space, and went back upstairs to see if Stuart had unearthed any more unsolved murders. Arriving in the third level squad room, she reported back to Crosspatch.

"Still no word from Pandya, but the train doesn't leave for another ten minutes. We asked her to call once she was aboard, so I'll give you a call when she does. Did you get a car?"

"Yes Ma'am. It's an old Ford Focus. It must be twenty years old or more, but it runs well. I didn't like it at first, but I think I might like it better once I've got used to it. No one would take it for a police car, though."

"An old Focus? Twenty years old? Why would they even have… wait a minute, I think I may have heard of that car. When you have a chance, get Stuart to have a look at it. Your brother may have made a mistake. You may have something quite interesting there… Could be useful too, who knows, something that doesn't look like a police car." Crosspatch smiled.

Sandeep went back to her desk, a little mystified. “Stuart,” she said quietly to her neighbour, “Crosspatch sent me to the pool to get a car. She said you should look at it. Apparently, you’ll know if it’s ‘interesting’. My brother gave me the car, and he thought he was being clever. It’s an old Ford Focus, really old, but it does seem to run well.”

“A Focus? Really old? I didn’t think they had any cars that were old. Yes, I’d love to look at it. After work?” She nodded.

“Sandeep!” It was Crosspatch. “Your cousin is on the train. She’ll be getting in just after 11:30. Make sure you have an ‘On Duty’ sign you can put up if you have to park somewhere that’s restricted. Off you go.”

“I’m on it Ma’am,” and she was gone.

‘Stuart.”

“Yes Ma’am?”

“Let’s look at what else you’ve got.”

“Coming Ma’am.”

* * * * *

Sandeep looked at the Google Maps directions, shook her head and asked the constable at the front desk for the quickest way to the station instead. She listened carefully as he told her, nodded her thanks and was out of the door before anyone could change their minds.

A tall, distinguished looking sergeant came out of the back room. “Was that Sandeep?” he asked.

“Yes, she was asking the way to the station.”

"She's driving? Oh dear, I hope my brother doesn't hear of this."

Sandeep was already around the side of the building and making for the carpark. She got into *her* Ford Focus and started it up. That slight rumble in its idle was endearing; a character trait, she thought. Driving out onto the A25 she turned and headed towards town. There wasn't much traffic, she had a clear road ahead of her. Prepared for a sedate run up to the station, she pressed the accelerator… and … *wah!* … the Ford leaped forward, pushing her back into her seat! *The gears. Change the gear!* she thought in a panic, *and again! and again!* She realised she still had her foot pressed hard on the accelerator… The speedometer was showing that she was well over the speed limit. She lifted her foot and slowed down to just below the speed limit. *Oh, my goodness,* she thought, calming down. W*here did that come from?* She eased off a little more. *I am a responsible member of the police, and I will set a good example.* She patted the dashboard again.

"I'm sorry if I insulted you before," she said, a delighted grin dawning. "You're wonderful. We'll find somewhere you can show me what you can do… But not today. We're going to pick up Harpee from the station and bring her back to the Centre. We'll show her how good we can be. Then I'll see if Sergeant Crosspatch will let us keep you for a while." She patted the steering wheel this time, her big smile wider than ever.

* * * * *

Constable Pandya stepped out of the train, almost sorry the trip had been so short. It had been a pleasant, peaceful ride, but she was here, and excitement bubbled. For at least a short while she would be doing the job of a real police officer, not a uniformed clerk glued to a computer! Exiting the station, she looked around. No police car to meet her? Wait, over by the curb, there was Sandeep waving to her by an old Ford. Where on earth had she found that? She hurried over. Sandeep opened the back door and pushed her suitcase inside, and then the two got into the front.

"Sandy, where did you get this old clunker?"

Sandeep smiled at her cousin. "Clunker?" she smiled. "It's old, but it has character. I love it. You wouldn't believe how fast it is! But we're going to be two responsible police officers and set a good example to the public."

"In this old thing? I doubt you could do anything else! I don't suppose you could push it over 50 if you tried!"

Sandeep patted the dash, speaking into the steering wheel. "Don't you pay any attention. She doesn't know you. She will learn to love you too."

"I really doubt that. Let's go. Sergeant Cross will be waiting."

Going back the way she had come, Sandeep drove carefully and very correctly, living proof that she was a responsible police officer! There would be no reason for anyone to take this treasure away from her!

As they arrived at the Centre, Pandya looked around. A large modern building with lawns, trees, and spacious car parks. Sandeep took her through the front doors, into a bright atrium with a ceiling that seemed to go all the way to the roof. Fifty feet ahead of them was the front desk.

Inside it was hushed compared to the noise of the traffic going by on the main road outside. Looking around, she realised that the surfaces had been lined with a soft, sound absorbing material. To one side of the front desk a wide stairway led up to the first floor. To the right, double doors of frosted glass closed off a corridor leading to the right wing of the building. To the left, the first thing she noticed was the coffee shop, again, behind frosted glass doors. Beyond that, the frosted door theme continued, closing off another corridor running behind the coffee shop and into the left wing.

A coffee shop! With a barista! Sandwiches, pastries, good quality soft drinks! In a police station? Her stomach rumbled, reminding her of her discarded breakfast. "Sandeep, can we grab a quick something here? I was in such a hurry this morning that I missed breakfast, and I haven't had more than a cup of tea all day."

"Of course. Crosspatch won't mind... oh," seeing the alarmed look on Pandya's face, "no, it's ok. We call her that... not to her face, of course, but she doesn't mind. We're known unofficially as 'Team Crosspatch'. She's even been known to call it that herself! She's a terrific Guv." They pushed through the doors into the coffee shop. It was bright, fresh, and sparkling and had that wonderful aroma of freshly brewed coffee.

"A terrific Guv? Really?" she said to Sandeep. "That's not what I heard. I was told that she may not be good enough for this job."

"What? No! From what I've seen, and from what her two DC's say, she's brilliant. Just wait until you meet her!

Oh, you have met her, haven't you? You'll see. Let me introduce you to Sergio, our barista."

They lined up to order their drinks. Latte for Sandeep, while Pandy opted for a Chai. She also ordered a vegetarian wrap and a pastry. While their drinks were being attended to, Sandeep introduced her cousin.

"It is a pleasure to meet you, PC Pandya," said Sergio.

"You too, Sergio. I got used to being called 'Pandy' in London, so please call me that."

"Then we shall call you that too, so you will not get the homesick," he said with a smile. Turning to Sandeep, he was more serious. "You need to warn Crosspatch, Sandeep. DI Featherstone is back today and again he is saying bad things about her. His mood is very bad."

"Thank you, Sergio, I'll tell her." The two cousins picked up their trays and walked across to the tables. "Look… there's Crosspatch!" Pandy looked towards the windows, where two women were waving at them. "We'd better go and join them."

Both women stood up as they arrived. Susan greeted them with a smile. "PC Pandya, I'm so glad you could make it today. Please join us, both of you." As they all sat down, Crosspatch introduced her companion. "I don't think either of you have met Elizabeth Gordon. Elizabeth, this is the redoubtable PC Varma, and this is PC Pandya who's come down from London to help us catch the Nettle Lane killer."

Elizabeth looked at them, smiling. "It's lovely to meet you both. Sandeep, isn't it? We have you to thank for pulling Susan's chestnuts out of the fire earlier this week! She does dive into things headfirst, doesn't she?"

Sandeep was a little abashed. "I… Well… It's nice to meet you, Mrs. Gordon. I'm very glad I could help."

"And PC Pandya… Sergeant Cross tells me you have the key to the entire mystery!"

Pandy too found herself unusually tongue tied. "M… M… Mrs. Gordon? It's very nice to meet you too. Er… Please call me Pandy. I've grown used to it."

"Pandy it is. Do you really have all the answers?"

"Well, honestly, not at all, Ma'am. I had some information that Sergeant Cross didn't have, but I think we have a lot of work to do before we get all the rest of it."

"Well, with you and Susan working on it, I'm sure you'll get there."

She looked at her watch. "I'm sorry, Susan, I'm going to have to fly. I have a meeting with my son's form teacher, and I mustn't be late. Try not to work too hard over the weekend. You're looking much perkier today, but I'm still concerned you'll burn out if you keep going at this rate."

"Don't worry, Elizabeth," said Susan, standing up. "I'm loving it. When things start coming in hot and fast it's incredibly energising. But we're really waiting for some of the lines of investigation to pop. So, we may be flat out or we may just be hanging about. I'll walk out with you." She turned back to her two Constables. "I'll be back in a minute."

Elizabeth smiled at the two as she stood up. "You two look after her. She's a great friend, and I don't want her run ragged!" She linked arms with Susan, and they walked out together, Elizabeth waving to the front desk as they went.

"Have a lovely weekend, Elizabeth. We'll try not to bother the DCI. I'm not really expecting major excitement," said Susan as they were walking across to Elizabeth's parked car.

"Hah… if he doesn't hear from you at least twice a day he'll be starting to fret. He thinks you're close to a breakthrough. But, seriously, try to get some downtime yourself."

Susan nodded, a bit distracted. She had noticed a silver-coloured car that was circling the car park for the second time. "Yes, I will, of course." The car was moving to circle a third time, and it set her senses tingling. "Elizabeth, get in your car and drive straight out. Don't stop."

"What? Susan, you're looking worried."

"I've got a bad feeling about that car. Please go! Now - See you next week." Elizabeth took another look at her face, then got into the car, started it and was moving away in short order. Susan turned and hurried back inside.

*　　*　　*　　*　　*

In the coffee shop Pandy turned to Sandeep. "What was that about a DI Featherstone? Why does Sergio want to warn Sergeant Cross?"

"It's something that has been going on for a while, I think. Featherstone is bad news. Stay away from him! Crosspatch was put into Featherstone's squad when she was transferred here from Maidstone. I don't know what happened, but it wasn't good. Some of the other girls have warned me about him. They say don't be in a room alone with him. Crosspatch had no choice. She had to work for him. Something must have happened, and now he's badmouthing her. He's the one saying she isn't good enough to be a sergeant."

"Well, that's what I heard too."

"It's not true. Anyway, the DCI didn't listen. She had scored very high in the sergeants' exams, and her old boss still said she was really good, so he took her out of Featherstone's squad and put her in charge of a team in major crimes. She's done well there. Featherstone doesn't like that and keeps trying to make her sound bad again. He says she seduced the DCI. That's why she's in major crimes."

"Are you sure she didn't? That story seems to be all over Scotland Yard!"

"Oh, that's just stupid. She did not. You just saw, she's a good friend of the DCI's wife. Do you think they'd be friends if it were true?"

"Perhaps Mrs. Gordon doesn't know?"

"Harpee! You've just met her. How could you think that? Crosspatch likes the DCI, but that's all. We all do – you couldn't not! But Crosspatch told me - he pulled her out of a bad situation with Featherstone and she's grateful, but she would never steal another woman's husband. She's brave, too. You should have seen her the other day. She took on a big thug when he attacked someone at a shop we were at. That's where she got that shiner. She's very good with people too. She was so kind to the poor sales assistant who got attacked.

"And there's something weird about Featherstone. He seems popular with some of the senior people, but not with most of the lower ranks."

They watched as Crosspatch came back in through the front doors. She hurried straight to the front desk and then went to the side door to the security room behind.

"That's odd," commented Sandeep. "She looks worried."

* * * * *

Susan knocked on the side door to the front desk office. It opened, and in she went, heading straight for the senior sergeant's desk. Sergeant Surinder Varma was watching a security camera showing the front parking area on the display on his desk.

"Surinder, there's a car circling the car park outside. I've got a bad feeling..."

"We've got it right here, Susan. We're going to clear the Atrium. Sergeant Grissom has been alerted."

The speaker system in the lobby came to life. "Please clear the Atrium. This is not a drill. Please clear the Atrium." The few people coming through hesitated fractionally, then hurried either into the coffee shop or up the stairs to the first floor.

"Let's see what they intend doing, shall we?" said the desk sergeant. They watched as the car finally pulled up outside the front doors. Two young men leaped out and rushed through the front doors. One had a pistol in his hand. They hesitated, finding themselves alone in the wide area. Then the doors closed behind them…

There was an audible 'click' as the locks engaged on the doors from the coffee shop into the atrium. The same was happening on all the doors leading out of the atrium. Red lights were flashing, and screens rose up out of the front counter to protect those behind them. Near the front doors, the two men stood transfixed. The alarm continued to blare, until suddenly it was replaced by the amplified voice of Sergeant Varma.

"Armed Police! You two, by the doors, do not move." The two men, little more than teenagers, turned and bolted back to the front doors, but found them shut tight. They turned, their backs to the doors, now pinned in a spotlight from several floors up. Sgt. Varma's booming voice came again. "I repeat, do not move. There will be no more warnings!"

Looking around wildly, one of them saw people watching from behind the glass doors in the coffee shop. He ran towards them, waving the pistol that looked somehow far too big for him. As he stopped at the doors trying to force them open, a single shot rang out, loud yet muffled in the confined space. He jerked backwards, off balance, swung around still waving his gun, then seemed to fold up and fell flat on his face.

"Thank you, Mr. Smith. I think we have control now," came Sergeant Varma's voice. "Medical team to the Atrium, please. You, by the door, on your knees with both hands on your head."

Susan had watched everything on the monitor on Sergeant Varma's desk. *They're so young! Bloody ISIS. Calling for random attacks, anywhere, anytime... Something like this was bound to happen.* She remembered the warning the DCI had passed on to them all. So here it was. *These idiots are going to get themselves killed!*

There was a short delay during which absolute silence reigned, then "Opening for Medical. Subject is down in front of the coffee shop. Sergeant Grissom, we have a subject for you at the front doors. Subject may still be armed. Mr. Smith is covering."

There was another short delay, and then the doors into the corridor to the right wing opened. Four medics in full protective gear hurried out towards the unconscious boy by the coffee shop doors. Four other men in protective armour placed themselves between the medics and the boy near the front doors. Once the first one had been loaded onto a stretcher and carried out, the security detail started to move towards the young man by the door. He looked terrified.

Crosspatch spoke quietly to Sergeant Varma. His voice came again.

"Sergeant Grissom, Sergeant Cross is joining you. Mr. Smith on alert please."

Crosspatch slipped out of the office. The door closed behind her and the lock snapped closed again. She crossed to join Sergeant Grissom and his men.

"You shouldn't be here Susan," said the squad leader. "You're not in protective gear. We have the situation under control."

Crosspatch shook her head. "Come on, George! The boy's petrified. He's on his knees, hands on his head. All he sees right now are four big, armoured men advancing on him like devils from hell. He's like a cornered animal. He thinks his friend has just been shot down in front of him. He's probably seen films of people being killed in situations like this. He's shown no aggression since the alarm went off… but he's not in a rational state right now. Let me try and talk him down." Sergeant Grissom looked at the boy. He paused for a few seconds.

"Not on your own, Susan. I'm not going to let you risk yourself alone. I'll do this with you, but I'll try to look less threatening." He took off his helmet, took his pistol out of its holster and handed it to one of his men. "Right then," he said, "we'll do this together. Let's try *not* to get someone killed today." He turned to his team. "Just give us a little space," and together they walked towards the boy.

"Hello," said Susan, stopping about six paces away. "I'm Sergeant Cross, and this is Sergeant Grissom. What's your name?"

The boy looked at her. He was trembling. He wasn't sure if his legs might not collapse altogether. If he moved, he would die, and he realised he didn't want to die. He was only really there as a witness for his friend. Mohammed had said he must shoot people here but then they could escape. Jamal was waiting, in the car, outside. He said it would be easy. The Caliphate would be pleased. But Mohammad had been shot down - right in front of him. He couldn't escape. *Mohammed is dead and now they are going to kill me…*

The woman was talking again. She wasn't wearing armour. She didn't have a weapon. She didn't look like police. She had a nasty black eye. Someone had hit her. What was she saying? That he hadn't killed or hurt anyone? He was not in big trouble? What was his name? She asked again. He tried to speak but found he couldn't.

"Y…Y…" He swallowed and tried again. "Y… Yusuf," he finally managed, hoarsely.

She was speaking again.

"Yusuf, these men don't want to hurt you, but we need to know if you are armed."

He shook his head.

"Well Yusuf, I need you to hold your arms straight up in the air, like this." She lifted her arms straight up over her head. He did it, still shaking.

"Now Yusuf, Sergeant Grissom is going to check that you are telling the truth. He will confirm that you are really unarmed. I am sorry, but your friend had a gun, and we need to know."

They will find the knife and then they will kill me! Yusuf remained as still as he could. Grissom walked up to him; empty handed. The policeman was unarmed, but he was armoured. The knife would be useless against him, but the woman… He was dead, no matter what happened now…

As Grissom reached out to pat him down, Yusuf lunged under his arms, and leaped towards the woman, reaching for the knife tucked into his belt behind his back. Shockingly though, the woman held her ground, dropping to one knee and crossing her wrists in front of her, blocking his arm's downward sweep. The next second he was down, hard, as the big sergeant had him flat down on the floor.

Grissom looked up at Susan. "Good block, but this is why you shouldn't be here without armour!"

She looked a little pale but was otherwise steady. "I know, George. You're right. I just didn't want to see anyone killed."

As Grissom hauled Yusuf to his feet, she stepped up again.

"Yusuf, why did you do that? You knew you didn't have a chance."

Yusuf looked at her miserably. "I had no choice," he whispered. "If you didn't kill me, they would. It made no difference."

"Who would kill you, Yusuf?" she asked. "Who wanted you to do this?"

"I can't tell you. At least they will know I tried. Perhaps they will leave me alone now."

"Go with Sergeant Grissom. There will be people who need you to answer some questions. That's all they are going to do. They won't hurt you. Just be patient for a while."

"Y…You killed Mohammed!" His voice was raised.

"No, he was just put to sleep for a while. He's being looked after in our medical room. Don't worry, he'll live. He'll probably have a monstrous headache for a few hours when he wakes up though. You'll see him again, but not for a while."

"You shot him like a wild animal" He shouted it out, wanting to be heard.

"You'd prefer we had killed him?" she responded quietly.

He paused, then looked at her and shook his head. "No. He is not a bad man. He knew this was his only chance."

"Go with Sergeant Grissom. You will be all right, Yusuf. Good luck. You haven't hurt anyone. You tried, but I don't think you really wanted to. You'll need to tell us what this was all about, though."

She turned to thank Sergeant Grissom. He was smiling at her and touched her arm - "Not by the book, Susan, but you may have saved that kid today. Nicely done."

Susan's whole body tingled at his touch. She felt herself go cold and then hot, felt her stomach contract, knew she was blushing, and found herself smiling back at him. She couldn't help herself. *Phew! What's this? Stress reaction? Post stress turn-on? But God, he's gorgeous with his hair all messed up like that ...* Somehow, she damped it down, breathed for a moment and pulled a quiet, professional answer out from somewhere.

"There are too many images out there of young men being killed by the police. We don't want any more if we can help it."

"No, that we don't." He smiled again. He'd felt her warmth and reaction. Liked it, but now was not the time. "Come on, then, lad. Let's go and get this over with," and they took Yusuf away down the corridor.

Susan watched them go, stood quite still for a moment and then turned and started back towards the coffee shop. Everyone was on their feet, staring. *What?* She came in through the now open doors and suddenly everyone was applauding. She looked back, but there was no one behind her. The applause was for her? Blushing furiously, she waved an arm at them and hurried over to her team who were also clapping enthusiastically. "Oh, stop that," she said, horribly embarrassed, and flung herself back into her chair. They sat down too. She picked up her coffee. *Bugger!* It was cold. "Would you two stop staring at me? Where were we?"

PC Pandya - no, 'Pandy' - cleared her throat and asked, hesitantly, "Why did you go out there, Ma'am? He was still dangerous. You saw how careful the security detail was. They knew he could still be armed. He had a knife… You went out there unarmed … with no protection."

"Pandy, the boy was terrified. To many teenagers the police are their enemy. He's no different. He was seconds away from complete meltdown. Animals attack when cornered. What else can they do? Think about it. If he had attacked Sergeant Grissom's men with that knife, their training would have kicked in, and that could have ended in him being killed. We don't need that."

Pandy sniffed, and then nodded. "Yes, you're right. Perhaps I'm a bit biased. My aunt was killed by a terrorist in Kabul, two years ago. She was working with a relief organisation."

Crosspatch touched her arm. "I'm sorry!"

She shrugged, deflecting the sympathy. "I thought my one chance of being a real member of the force had walked out into the atrium with you."

"That's rather dramatic! I had George Grissom with me. He's worth a whole platoon all by himself! Anyway," she grinned, trying to lighten the mood, "the DCI wouldn't have let you go that easily. You're our best chance of tracking down Alison Johnson."

"After seeing that," Pandy pointed out towards the front doors, "I'd just as soon work with you, not your successor."

Sergio broke in on their conversation. He carried three fresh coffees, and three of the pastries that he knew Crosspatch and Sandeep liked.

"Crosspatch! Brava! Brava! I have never seen something like that. I was very frightened. Here, I have fresh coffees for you all, and something else to enjoy. On the house. Team Crosspatch! You will be legends!"

"Oh really, Sergio, you're being silly, but thank you." Susan was eyeing the coffees proprietarily and already reaching for one.

"Ladies, since Sergio is being so accommodating, let's stay here for now." She turned to Pandy.

"How was your trip down from London?" she asked.

"Too short! I didn't get much sleep last night then I was up early and had to rush to get to London Bridge. But despite what everyone says about the railways, it was warm and peaceful. I'd have been happy for it to last longer."

"Yes," laughed Susan. "I feel the same way every time I take the train back from London. Everything is such a rush up there, and then you fall into that peaceful oasis on the train."

"Exactly," said Pandy, and then segued away. "This seems a really nice place. I'm amazed people get any work done. I'd be tempted to sit here half the day enjoying a coffee or a chai, which is excellent here. Sergio is going to save the reputation of police station hot drinks singlehanded!"

"We all feel that way when we first get here! But in the end we are here to work. Our efficiency rating is at least as good as anywhere else. Better than most, although I'll admit to possible bias on that."

"Well, I'm definitely here to work ma'am. Just tell me what you need me to do."

Crosspatch looked her directly in the eye and smiled. "Find Alison Johnson. Find her before the killer does."

PC Pandya returned her gaze. "Oh. Right. Find her before the killer does? Is that all? How am I supposed to do that, Ma'am?"

Susan smiled, took a sip of her coffee, held up one finger, and turned to Sandeep. "We've been getting calls on Laura's mobile. It's being monitored by Helen Jarvis in the Incident room. It's about a dog. There were signs at Laura's that she had a dog – but no dog. When we're finished here, can you follow up on that and see what it's all about?"

Then she turned back to Pandy, leaning across the table and speaking intently.

“Now, Pandy. Those DNA samples you sent in to Forensics after Alison filed her statement at Walworth matched ones we have from Nettle Lane, and the DNA Sandeep got from the Classic Theatre. That pretty much confirms her story, and that it was the Nettle Lane killer she ran into at the theatre. She may be the only woman who has escaped from him - ever, that we know of! We may be tracking a multiple killer and Laura Handley-Davison could be just one of many women he has murdered. Sandeep also got a second sample of blood from the theatre, by the way. I’m guessing it was Alison’s, which might help us in identifying her if we don’t find her soon enough!

“But how do you expect me to find Alison, Ma’am?”

Susan paused, organising her thoughts, then continued. “You are the only one of us who has actually met her. The only one who’s seen her and talked to her. You may not think you know her, but you know her better than anyone else here. So, tell me about her.”

“Well,” said Pandy after a slight pause, “she just came in off the street. She seemed almost high, and I thought she might have had a bit too much to drink - but looking back I would say it was adrenaline. I didn’t really believe her - oh, I could see she’d been roughed up a bit. She had a graze on her chin, and she was limping slightly, but the rest of the story seemed so bizarre. Then she showed me the bloodstains on her skirt, where she said she’d kneed him in the face, and others on her boot - she’d kicked him too. I could see then that it was serious. But now you’re saying this may be a serial killer? He’s killed several women?”

“We think he may have been at this for several years. He doesn’t fit the classic type, doesn’t seem to have a particular choice of victim. Just women, as far as we know. And he appears to have made a mistake with Laura.

“But, that can be a pattern with some killers. Slow and careful at first, making it very hard to unmask them, but then the kills become more frequent, and they start to make mistakes. I think that’s where our man is on the curve. Our thinking is that it’s not so much that he got arrogant and believed himself too clever to be caught. It’s more a sort of hunger. He started to live for the kill, and each time he did, he wanted - no, needed - to do it again. It’s like an addiction.

“In this case we think he botched it at Nettle Lane. If we’re right, he’s taken his time with his other victims, killed them slowly, painfully. We think he gets off on that. He doesn’t seem to rape, he just kills, slowly. At Nettle Lane, the victim fell and died hitting her head. So, no slow torture. He didn’t even kill her himself. Not the way he wanted to, anyway. So, failure. Frustration. And then Alison… She could have been his consolation prize, but he failed again. This time his prey not only escaped, she even hurt him in the process. He’ll need to kill again soon, but I’m sure he’s after Alison. She beat him. He’d find that intolerable. He’ll go after her with every resource he has. So, we *must* find her first. The thought of what he’d do to her if he got to her first is … well … unthinkable!”

“And you think I can find her? Save her?”

“That’s what it comes down to, because if we don’t find her, he very likely will and I doubt she’ll escape him again. We need to use everything we’ve got, Pandy - and that includes you. No, I don't expect you to do it alone. We're a team, and we work as a team. We are going to find her."

"Ma'am, she could be anywhere."

"OK, try this. Imagine it's a fictional investigation. You're a 'private eye' - what would you do?"

Pandy sat back. "Me?" Susan nodded. Surprised, Pandy thought for a minute. "OK … I'd start by doing a search on the Internet. Try to get onto her Social Media accounts, her email, and see if she is talking to someone. Secondly, or - no, this should come first. We have her address … She gave it to me. Have we sent someone there to see whatever there is to see? There may be clues to where she might have gone. Does she have a partner? If so, who are they? Where do they live? Work? Does either of them have a car? Can we track them by that?"

She looked surprised and more than a little pleased. "I see what you're telling me. There are lots of things we can do. I've just never thought it through like that, step by step. Constables aren't supposed to. We're a bit like soldiers in the army… Just do what you're told to do!" She was starting to see the possibilities as her mind woke up to the task.

"Her friends. Who are they? Has anyone spoken to them? If there is a boyfriend or girlfriend, then their friends too." She stopped suddenly. "Wait. She spoke to someone else that night. She told me. When she bolted, she tried to hide herself in a crowd and it started to rain. Several people peeled off into a pub, and she went in with them. It was a pub they often went to after rehearsals. She said she watched Mr. Davison from inside. She had a glass of wine - someone she knew there bought it for her… a woman... Madeleine! That was her name. Madeleine. She may know something."

"Hang on a second, Pandy. Keep thinking, though." Crosspatch had her phone out. "Sean," she said, when her DC answered. "Are you still at the theatre? Really? They've moved the opening forward to this weekend? That's odd. I thought it was two weeks away. OK, let me think about that. In the meantime, find out from the actors which pub or pubs they usually hang out at after rehearsals. Then call me back… What? No, nothing significant. But I may want you to join them there after rehearsals are done for the day… I'll explain later. Crosspatch out."

Pandy was looking at her strangely. "Sorry Pandy. You've just come up with something we didn't know, and I wanted to get moving on it right away. 'No stone unturned' and all that… What?"

"I'm sorry. Ma'am. I was fed an image of you before I came, but you aren't like that at all. You're not what they say."

"Oh dear. Someone's been telling you stories about me, haven't they? It's amazing how fast and far bad news spreads. Go ahead. Ask. Whatever you need to know."

Pandy looked across to Sandeep who had been sitting and listening, quietly. Getting no help there but an 'I told you so' look from under raised eyebrows, Pandy took the plunge.

"They say you shouldn't be in charge of a case like this. That you only got this position … sorry… by sleeping with the DCI. They say you are too inexperienced and even perhaps… incompetent." She took a deep breath, wincing internally. How would her temporary 'Guv' take that? But getting no reaction, she continued.

"But I don't see that. I don't know you, so I can't judge if you are sleeping with the DCI, but after seeing you with Mrs. Gordon I really doubt it. The same as far as competency is concerned. You've already made me remember more than I thought I could about Alison Johnson, and you're moving to make use of that even before we've stopped speaking."

Susan sighed. "How far has the sleeping with the DCI rumour gone?"

"I heard it from someone at Scotland Yard. He said you were incompetent, and making no progress and DI Featherstone was expected to take over. I'm supposed to liaise with him."

Featherstone! It always comes back to Featherstone. What did Featherstone know about the case? Two full days he'd been missing this week. Did the DCI get the full story? She knew Featherstone had been to Walworth in an attempt to pick up Alison. *Why?* Trying to get one over on her team? *Wait ... could he have cleared the Walworth file? Would he have been able to do that*? He must have been to Scotland Yard too, she realised, spreading his poison through his old cronies' network.

He's still after the DCI position, she realised. *He'd ruin the whole experiment towards "new policing" if he got into such a senior position. Just look at the mockery of modern policing that he fashioned his squad into on the second floor.*

Her phone buzzed. "Sean, what news? They're packing up? Their lord and master must be feeling benevolent today… Ah, it was a full dress rehearsal? They're opening tomorrow evening? OK, priority one, see if any of them are going to the pub. Go with them. Alison Johnson, the girl who disappeared, met up with a friend of hers called Madeleine at the pub when she escaped from the theatre on Monday evening. Apparently they often meet at that pub, which suggests she's a regular. Ask the bar staff if they've seen Madeleine recently. It's a Friday, so if she usually stops in for a drink after work there's a chance she'll be there after work this evening. Try to meet her, talk to her.

"We're still building up our understanding of Alison Johnson and this Madeleine will know a lot more than we do. Use that Irish charm on her, Sean. Explain that Alison's not wanted for any crime, but we believe she's a witness with important information, and we're concerned that she may be in danger… Get her to give you as much information on our girl as she can.

"Call me later if you get the chance to speak to her…

"OK, don't overdo it, but see what you can learn. The actors may have something to say about her too…

"Yes, I know it's Saturday tomorrow, but I want to bring the whole team together for a full briefing. Let's say here at the Centre at 10:00, in the incident room. I'm afraid we may be at this all weekend…

"Right, call me tonight if anything interesting comes up. Crosspatch out."

“You don’t mind that people call you ‘Crosspatch’?” asked Pandy?

“What’s the point? There are far worse things to be called. Might as well embrace it!”

Pandy thought about that. “You’re right. I used to hate it when the others at the station called me ‘Pandy’, but after a while I realised they weren’t being disrespectful. It was because they’d accepted me. I was one of them. I think I even became a bit proud of it. I’m glad to be a member of Team Crosspatch, even if it is only for one case.”

Susan wasn’t sure what to say to that, but there was no need. Seeing Robert Gordon striding across the room towards them she sat up straighter.

“Susan, you nearly gave me a heart attack when you waltzed out there with Sergeant Grissom’s men and that boy pulled the knife! Well done, but be warned, PR are going to want you now. The whole thing was captured on our security cameras, and they’re going to use it. I’m afraid you’ll probably be on the news tonight.” He pulled up another chair and sat down...

She groaned. “Really? Can’t they just keep me out of it? It could be a real nuisance.”

“Yes, but it’ll be wonderful publicity. It showed the human side to policing that the public seldom gets a chance to see.

“Besides, ‘Don’t do anything great if you can’t take the congratulations.’ They say that in American Football. Have you ever seen it? When someone makes a great catch or scores, the congratulations can get quite rough. Their players are big - six foot five, maybe six, and some weigh about as much as a Sumo wrestler," he added by way of explanation. "I suspect they aren't gentle."

"No, I imagine not," she replied, wincing.

"PC Varma," he said turning towards Sandeep. "Are you enjoying life as a plains clothes officer?"

"Very much, thank you Sir."

He turned to the third member of Crosspatch's team. "You must be PC Pandya. Welcome to Sevenoaks. I expect this all seems a little different from London."

"Yes, Sir, very different." She looked around. "I think it's great. Your officers must love working here. I'll be sorry when I have to go back to the Met."

"Well, do me a favour, both of you" he asked, looking at them. They nodded, earnest and keen. "Don't let her pull too many stunts like the one we have just seen. We would like to keep her around a little longer!" He chuckled and turned to Crosspatch.

"Susan. Something just popped up on the net. Apparently a 'really big man' turned up at a repair garage in Hastings two evenings ago, enquiring about a couple who had dropped a car off there that morning. There is no clear description of the man. The two mechanics he threatened just concentrated on his size. There is no proof that it was our man, but it sounds a lot like it. Have a look on the net. I marked it for updating to your case file. Now, I'll leave you to your meeting," and he was up and off again.

"Right," said Susan, "We'd better move our meeting upstairs. Bring your drinks and pastries, we can finish them there. I want to see that Hastings report. Then we'll plan how we are going to find Alison Johnson."

*   *   *   *   *

The Calm before the Storm

Back in her office, Susan wasted no time in looking up the incident. As promised, it had been linked to her file. 'Jermyns', a garage in Hastings, had reported an incident that had occurred the previous evening. They had received a call from a company in Wandsworth they often worked with, warning them that someone might come around looking for information on one of their own staff who had delivered a refurbished Jaguar to them that morning. They were asked to let them know if that happened.

Someone had indeed turned up that evening… and tried to intimidate two of the mechanics but they had driven him off. The only description they had was that he was a very big man. There was one new piece of information: he was driving an older model, green Toyota Hilux - a pickup. Unfortunately, they hadn't got the number. But it was something! She agreed with the DCI. That sounded like their man. But how on earth did it fit? She felt sure it had something to do with their case, but what? She highlighted it as something to follow up on, but as she walked over to the incident room, it hit her. He was looking for something or someone. She looked up the number and called Jermyns for more information. It turned out he'd been looking for a Tom O'Malley. She smiled at that, wondering if he had long whiskers. But who on earth was he?

* * * * *

"I had no idea you knew my uncle so well," said Sandeep.

"I had to get all his stories about you once you joined my team, Sandeep!" Crosspatch smiled.

"All of them?" asked Sandeep a little worried.

"All that he was willing to tell me. He rang me when you went off to the station to fetch Pandy. It seems your driving is legendary at home! I said that was OK, I'd just make sure you never drove me! He laughed at that, but to be fair, he also said you hadn't killed anyone yet; hadn't even had a bump. But your passengers all seemed terrified that you were about to kill them. So, no worries."

Pandy looked accusingly at Sandeep. "It was you who made our old Auntie swear she would never to get into a car again, wasn't it? Crosspatch, are you trying to scare me off the team?"

Sandeep came back on that. "Old Auntie was afraid of anyone driving. She was just looking for an excuse to stay at home! Anyway, Harpee, you're tougher than that." A sardonic grin appeared. "You're a Metropolitan Police officer. You're not afraid of anything! Besides," turning back to Crosspatch, in a very formal tone she proclaimed "I am a responsible officer of the law, and it is my duty to set a good example to the public. I would never dream of doing anything outside the law!

"Anyway, it's just an old Ford. How much trouble could we get into?"

Susan looked at her sternly. "Funny! I had a report of one of my team doing the ton on the A25 heading up into town… In an old Ford!"

A look of alarm crossed her face. "Oh no… no, that must have been a mistake. It couldn't have been me. I mean, it's just an old Focus." She paused. "The ton? Really?" She couldn't keep a look of smiling speculation from creeping over her face.

Susan laughed. "Next time put your police lights on. It was reported again going much more sedately on the way back. I did a little checking on that car, though, Sandeep. It's not really ours. Supposedly it belongs to the Thames Valley Police. It seems to be here on loan. That way it doesn't actually appear on our books, and I bet it doesn't show up on theirs either. Under the rules, it should have been sold or scrapped years ago, but someone wanted to keep it for some reason. Look after it, Sandeep, it may prove very useful. We'll see what happens. Now, can you go and check how Stuart is doing on other kills?"

Sandeep was up and out of the room in a flash. "Good grief, that girl has boundless energy," she said to Pandy. "Let me know what you think of Sandeep's driving. Can you keep her under control?"

"I don't know if anyone can keep Sandy under control. But she obviously respects you a lot. She's been on her best behaviour, from what I've seen."

"Well, long may that last.

"Now... We have some details of DI Featherstone's meanderings over the last couple of days on the net, now. You know that he was the one who drove to Walworth to pick Alison up last Monday night?" Pandy nodded. "Well, the DCI had a chat with him today. Featherstone was missing for two days until he rolled up here again yesterday afternoon. The DCI wanted to know where he'd been and what he's been doing. What he told him was that he went to the theatre on Tuesday and looked through Alison's personnel file. He got her contact details and some publicity photos that were in it along with her CV. She wasn't answering her phone, so he went to her flat. There was no one there, so he had the concierge let him in. He says there were no signs of a hurried departure, so he waited there hoping she'd come back. It seems he had some idea he could bring her in for questioning - not sure what for though. She wasn't under arrest at Walworth, and there was no reason to detain her.

"Featherstone believes she may have 'absconded' - his word - in a car. Apparently he spent much of Wednesday alternately watching her apartment, questioning her neighbours, her parents, and trying to get details of the car so we could put out a trace on it. If we had the details of this car, we could put out an alert for us to be notified anywhere it's seen."

"DI Featherstone didn't find the details of her car? Is a car even registered in her name?"

"No, I checked that. She hasn't rented one either as far as we can tell. I've applied to get her credit card and bank records, but we don't have them yet. Same for her phone. Hopefully we'll get them this afternoon; otherwise, we probably won't get anything before Monday."

"If there is a car, we need the details," said Pandy. "She was on foot when she came to Walworth. She joked about her boots, saying that she wore them so that her feet didn't get trampled on the train in rush hour… So, she didn't drive to work, and she didn't have a car when she left Walworth. Why *did* she leave Walworth? She knew someone was coming to talk to her from Sevenoaks. What made her run? Nurse Ryan said she was worried about getting hold of her boyfriend…"

"*Boyfriend*!" Pandy and Susan exclaimed together.

"She has a boyfriend!" said Susan. "That's why she left Walworth. She knew that Davison had her address on file at the theatre. She was afraid her boyfriend would walk into a trap at home! And I bet the boyfriend has a car! Now… Who is this boyfriend? DI Featherstone didn't say."

"We need her phone records," said Pandy, her eyes dancing.

"I'll try to expedite that," said Susan. "Some of the other actors might know - or her mother! Most mothers know who their daughters are going out with. Do we have a contact number for her? Featherstone was trying to trace her through her parents. He must have it. Damn the man! We should have that on his report, but it's bloody skimpy and that's putting it mildly. There's not nearly enough there to have kept him busy for two days."

"The theatre, then! Personnel records! Next of Kin!" Pandy was excited. "Did your DC get a copy for the file?"

Susan was at the door. "Sandeep, Stuart. In here!"

"I've got three others for you, ma'am. They're all over the country, though," said Stuart coming in.

"Great, Stuart, we'll look at them in a minute. Sorry - I know it's important - very - but we're onto something. Do you know where all Sean's things are for the file on the theatre?"

"Yes." It was Sandeep. "He gave me the things he had put together. They're on my desk." She returned quickly with a file.

"Is the info from Alison's personnel file there?"

"Here," and she pulled out a sheet of paper and put it on Susan's desk. Susan and Pandy both reached for it, but Pandy pulled back and Susan grabbed it and skimmed through it. Yes! Next of Kin! Marjorie Johnson, an Exeter address, and - Bingo! - a telephone number.

Pandy was already handing her the phone. She punched in the number, and after a few seconds it found the connection, and everyone could hear the phone ringing at the other end… and ringing… and ringing. Crosspatch and Pandy were looking at each other, anticipating disappointment, when it was picked up.

"Hello, Johnson residence."

"Hello" Crosspatch had the phone again. "Mrs. Johnson?"

"Yes, this is she." Eyebrows rose around the room.

"Mrs. Johnson, this is Detective Sergeant Cross from Sevenoaks Police Centre. Is your daughter Alison with you?"

"Alison? No. She doesn't live here."

"Can you tell me when you saw her last?"

“Saw her last? Alison? I haven’t seen her in weeks... Months. She’s in London. She’s an actress. She’s living with… a boy.”

“I see. Do you know his name?”

“His name? Why are you asking me all this again? I’ve already given all this information to the detective who phoned earlier. Why do you need it again?”

“The other detective? Which detective was that Mrs. Johnson? … You wrote his name down? Yes, I can wait while you find it… Yes, I’m still here Mrs. Johnson… Inspector Featherstone! When was that, Mrs. Johnson? … Tuesday afternoon! … Do you still have the name of Alison’s boyfriend?”… Suddenly she knew the answer! “Thomas O’Malley! Of course. And he works at a garage in Wandsworth. Do you recall the name? … That’s very helpful, Mrs. Johnson. Thank you very much indeed ... What’s that? No, she’s not in trouble with us … Yes, of course, Mrs. Johnson. As soon as we find her, we’ll let you know. Thank you again. Goodbye, now.”

“Pandy, get hold of Classic Cars in Wandsworth and find out all you can about Thomas O’Malley. I can already tell you he’s the boyfriend, and I think he and Alison delivered an E-type Jaguar to Jermyns in Hastings on Tuesday morning. Our killer knows that, and he tried to find out where they went from there – but either they didn’t know, or they weren’t letting on. That’s the connection with that file the DCI linked to our case file. That also means we know he hadn’t found them by Tuesday evening, so there’s an excellent chance they are both still alive.”

Before anyone could move, Crosspatch's phone started vibrating across the desk. Susan reached for it with shaky hands "Crosspatch… Sean, yes, what do you have for us?" She sat up straight. "You've found Madeleine? Go on," She grabbed a pen and a small notepad and started writing. "OK, Sean that's brilliant… One of the other actors? Duncan? Isn't he a part in the play? … Ah, both an actor and a part, but Duncan isn't playing Duncan. That must keep things simple over there! OK, he knew Alison better than most? Refers to her as 'Gentlewoman'? I doubt the killer would use the same name! She was hardly gentle with him… Yes, buy him a drink and let him talk. We'll see you in the morning. Yes, 10am tomorrow! Crosspatch out."

"Right," she said, looking Stuart in the eye. "His name is Thomas O'Malley. He drives a classic car, a Jensen Interceptor, whatever that is, from the sixties or seventies. She says he's a Saint. I'm not sure what she means by that. And we got all that from a memory that Pandy had of someone that Alison had met on her way to Walworth last Monday night. Pandy, I told you you'd find her for us!"

"We haven't found her just yet, Crosspatch!" said Pandy. Stuart blinked, *'Crosspatch?'* He looked at the two women, then shrugged.

"Perhaps not," she agreed. "But we're a lot closer than we were four hours ago."

"Sandeep, I want the registration plate of that Jensen and I want it out on the net as a 'report but do not detain' before we call it quits for today. Use the incident room number for notification purposes. I'm warning you all now, if we get a location, I want to be on the road tonight. A very brave young woman's life is at stake. She's been on the run for four days now, with a killer on the hunt for her. We're behind on this and we need to catch up. Alison isn't going to know who she can trust. The only one of us who really helped her last Monday night was Pandy. I'm hoping if she sees her, she'll recognise her and won't run away again. But that means we have to get Pandy there. That's likely to be your job, Sandeep, so stay together tonight. You can stay at my flat."

"Pandy, I'm going to go and see the DCI. We need a 24-hour watch on Mr. Davison. He's to be detained if he tries to leave the country, but other than that we'll leave him alone and see if he leads us to someone else. In the meantime, see what you can learn from that Classic Cars place."

"Stuart, put together what you've got on our serial killer. Finding Alison is priority number one, but your work tracking the killer can't fall behind. Alison will be able to identify him when we find him, but we still have to find him for her to do that. I'm pretty sure Davison won't tell us where he is voluntarily, but you never know. He might still lead us to him."

"A few hours ago, we were just fishing at random, Team. Now we have a fairly good idea of what happened and it's time to cast some nets. We need some hard evidence to back it up with." She stood up, but as she went out, she turned.

"Pandy, we know that Thomas O'Malley took a Jaguar down to Jermyn's - a garage in Hastings - on Tuesday morning. But how did the killer know? I want to know just how many people knew about that. Come and find me in my office when you've spoken to Classic Cars. I may have a special little job for you." She went off in search of the DCI. Would he sanction what she had in mind?

* * * * *

"That's odd", said PC Varma. "There's another notice out on O'Malley's car." How could that be? They'd only discovered that he even existed in the last hour. Yet this had been posted… on Wednesday? It too was '*report but do not detain*', but the phone number that was to be notified wasn't one she recognised. Who else was on this case? This had to be reported back to Crosspatch. Then she and Pandy should go and pick up the dog!

Crosspatch seemed unsurprised when Sandeep dropped her little bomb. "That's what I thought you'd find, Sandeep. See if there's been a request out for Alison's phone records, and her bank and credit card records too. And the same for Thomas O'Malley. I'll bet there has. Please see if we can be copied on whatever comes in, directly to our case file - and on anything that's come in already."

Now the next thing. Classic Cars in Wandsworth… Pandy had just learned that DI Featherstone had paid them a visit last Tuesday, and he knew O'Malley had taken the car down to Jermyns, yet it had not been in the scanty report he had reluctantly given the DCI …

She thought she knew where Alison and her boyfriend had gone. She'd been checking friends and relatives on Alison's Facebook account, but until she knew which direction she'd run in they had just been names to be tackled in any order. Now she believed she knew that she and O'Malley had gone south to Hastings. Three days ago! She and Tom had friends in St Leonard's, barely a mile west along the coast. That moved them to the top of the list to be spoken to. She'd have been off to St Leonard's like a flash, but now she had a TV thing to deal with first.

Damn and Blast! Why did everything seem to be coming to a head at the weekend? It was going to be hard to track people down. But she would ask the local police down there to go and check on them; a songwriter, his photographer wife and little daughter. She made it clear that these people were not criminals in any sense of the word and were to be treated with the utmost respect. If Alison Johnson were there too, they were to inform her or the DCI directly and in any case a watch was to be put on their home.

* * * * *

Detective Inspector Featherstone had been watching any alerts that went out, in the hope that Sergeant Cross's team might latch onto something. He knew who Thomas O'Malley was. At least he knew he was Alison Johnson's boyfriend. Once he had got the name, he'd tracked down the registration number of his car, so he knew he was looking for a 1970, metallic blue Jensen Interceptor. He knew where O'Malley worked - Classic Cars, where they had given him the run around. Clearly, they didn't like coppers. He had called to enquire if Thomas was at work on the Wednesday, and every day since, but had been told that Thomas was still away, and no one knew when he'd be back. Some family crisis, they thought. He had put out a "*report but do not detain*" notice on the car, but nothing had come of it yet.

With luck he would get notification ahead of Cross if it was spotted somewhere.

Bloody woman! She was obviously catching up! He'd hoped that his efforts to discredit her and the DCI would have resulted in some changes by now, but Elizabeth Gordon had stuck her nose in and put up a damnably effective roadblock on it locally, and now, after Cross's performance with the would-be terrorists, PR wanted her to appear on an early morning TV chat show. Unless she bungled that completely, even Scotland Yard wasn't going to get in her way now! In the meantime, the trace had gone completely cold.

'Lennox' had bungled it in Hastings and stirred up a hornets' nest! There'd be no information coming from there. All he knew was that the boyfriend had gone down to Hastings on a job for his boss. The girl might - or might not - have gone with him. O'Malley had come back to London, probably by train. Had they both come back together? Had the girl stayed down there? Or was she still somewhere in London, with the Hastings trip only a red herring?

He'd just have to be quicker off the mark than Cross as soon as anything came in. He did have the advantage of knowing it was a race, while she did not. That should give his man a chance to get in first once they had a location. But he really needed someone closer to her team in case they picked up something that he didn't know.

He looked up as someone knocked on his office door. A tall young woman. Intrigued, he waved his hand for her to come in.

"Detective Inspector Featherstone? I'm PC Pandya. I've been seconded from the Met to help with the Nettle Lane Murder. I'm working with Sergeant Cross' team. DCI Crawford said I should check in with you and keep you informed on how the case was going."

It must be Christmas, he thought, grinning inwardly like a Cheshire Cat.

*   *   *   *   *

Susan was on her way home. It was all beginning to catch up with her. She recognised that she'd been on a bit of an adrenaline spike through the terrorist incident and was now on the downside of that, but she really wasn't looking forward to the morning. Henry Cavill, the PR officer, had been quite adamant. Be at the local TV station by 07:00, dressed smartly. Yes, he knew it was a Saturday. However, the video of the terrorist attack would be on the national news tonight, and the local Morning show had been delighted at the chance to have her on to talk about it and, of course, the "New Policing" experiment that the Sevenoaks Centre represented - but it had to be tomorrow. By next week it would be old news!

This was not an opportunity to be missed, and he made it quite clear that **it would not be missed**. Yes, he knew she was at a critical part of her investigation, but it would only take a few hours, and he was sure a team as competent as hers could carry it themselves for a short while. She couldn't really argue with that, so she'd left them all to it and bunked off promptly. It was going to be a horribly early start.

But it just might also be an opportunity to advance the case a little.

Feeling a bit more cheerful she decided to drop by to see Mandy. All in the line of duty. Just to ensure that all was OK there now.

It was Friday evening, and people were on their way home. Laura's was still open but things were quiet in the boutique. There was just one employee on the floor, Mandy. She was wearing a deep red, fitted jacket, skinny black jeans and over the knee boots, Susan thought she was the loveliest thing she'd seen in months.

She saw Susan and wrapped her in a hug.

"So good to see you. But you're a bit early, tonight. I can't close until six."

"That's ok. I was surprised to see you open, actually. Has your head office done something about security? And how are you managing?"

"A man from head office came down to see me this morning. He said I could open up again if I felt ready to, and he assured me that this would never happen again. Apparently, they've made special arrangements, so I should feel quite safe. He said I might not see anyone, but their security company would be around the area. Very unobtrusive but effective."

She pulled up a small push button attached to a thin golden chain from inside her shirt. "All I have to do is push this, and help will be here in no time at all. I can use it 24/7, so it's to keep me safe at night, too."

So, the full "protection" screen was up again. Susan smiled at her friend. "That's great. I'm glad they thought to keep you safe at night, too."

"You look like you've had a rough day, today." Mandy touched her cheek, gently. "Do you have to go home tonight?"

"Yes, damn it," said Susan. "A couple of my team are staying at mine, and I've got to be up early and dressed really smartly. They want me at the TV studio by seven. I'll have to get home to find something to wear… Not that I've got much that our PR man will approve of," she added glumly.

"No, stay here," said Mandy. "Please stay. We've got lots of stuff here. Just the thing for your TV interview, too. I'll dress you. You'll look fabulous: Detective Cross, stern and competent, yet warm. You'll be a knock-out! I've still got some nice wine here, and we'll get a take-away and have a lovely evening. You look like you need that!"

It just sounded too good. Susan knew she had lost before she even opened her mouth to argue. "Sold!" she sighed. "It sounds wonderful!"

She had one last thing to do. She called Sandeep. "You are staying at my place tonight with Pandy. I won't be in after all. You've got a key. Just let yourselves in. You'll have to get yourselves some supper. I've got nothing in the fridge, so just order in whatever you want. I have that TV interview in the morning, but it's being taped early so I should be in by 10:00."

There were some odd snuffling noises coming over the phone. “Have the pair of you got someone else with you?”

“Someone else? No, just Pandy and me.” She was sure she could hear Pandy in the background though, saying something that sounded like “Ergh, get off!” She didn’t sound panicked or even very disturbed though. Then she heard her laugh.

Really? Well, who was she to say what they should or shouldn’t do on their own time. “OK, enjoy your evening, both of you. I’ll call if we get an alert on that car.”

On their way to Crosspatch’s apartment, Sandeep looked at Pandy and grinned. “Crosspatch has a boyfriend!”

“Lucky Crosspatch. After being on the night shift for the past six months my love life is non-existent!”

“Mine too,” mourned Sandeep. “Living with Baba and Maji and an over-protective brother makes sure of that. They’re probably dreaming of arranging a marriage for me soon.” She scowled. “They’ll be sadly disappointed if they try! Let’s find something exciting to watch tonight. Crosspatch has a nice big screen!”

“Let’s do that… But I think I might prefer being in Crosspatch’s shoes right now.”

But no-one was in Crosspatch’s shoes. She was happily cuddled up with Mandy in front of the fire, watching a Netflix film. Mandy had dug out a blanket for them to snuggle under. She would pop down to take in their meal when it was delivered, but after that it would be just the two of them, wine, a chicken curry, and each other. Perfect.

The Morning Show

Susan arrived at the TV station punctually the next morning. Wide-awake and ready to go, she was feeling amazingly good and surprisingly confident. She was in a very smart suit, a subtle shade of yellow, cut to flatter her figure. Her hair was freshly washed and expertly blow-dried, and her eyebrows had been shaped to bring out her eyes. *Well, one of them anyway*, she thought wryly. The other remained something of a disaster, so dark glasses were still de rigueur. She'd hardly recognised herself when Mandy stopped primping and let her look in the mirror.

"Is that really me?" She turned and hugged Mandy hard. "The show is at nine," she said. "Will you watch it? It'll give me confidence knowing you are."

"Of course I will. You'll be great. They want you on the show because you're the latest hero," said Mandy. "They'll make sure you come across brilliantly!"

They had watched the 'News at Nine' and there it was. The whole video of the raid, which had, surprisingly, lasted less than five minutes. In Crosspatch's memory, it seemed to have taken far longer. Then there'd been Henry Cavill describing how Sergeant Cross and Sergeant Grissom had acted "in the best traditions of the force to minimise any casualties." Mandy had been a most appreciative audience. It had been a good night, despite that early start looming over her.

"Will you be back tonight?" she'd asked hesitantly as she saw Susan off at the door.

"I'll try," Susan said. "If the show's over quickly I'll come back with some breakfast before I go back to work. If not - well, I'll be back when I can. Thanks!" She'd reached out, hugged her, kissed her on the cheek, and then ran out to her car.

She presented herself at the reception desk, and a bright-young-thing invited her into a large, cheerfully furnished waiting room. Scarcely had the door closed behind her when it was flung open again and in breezed Henry Cavill.

"Ah, Sergeant Cross, you're here." He looked her over. "Stand up," he ordered, and walked around her, looking her up and down. "Yes, you'll do. In fact, you'll do very well indeed. They'll need you in for make-up of course, but that's routine. I'm just here for support if you need it. Just remember, be gracious. Perhaps play it down a bit. 'Anyone would have done the same' - that sort of thing. I've primed Ralph. He'll go easy on you."

"Sergeant Cross," said a man hurrying in to usher her off to the inner recesses of the studio. "I'm George Somerby. I do appreciate your being on time. We're in a bit of a rush, I'm afraid. We've had to completely revise this morning's show! We usually record a day or two in advance, but when the news of the attack came through yesterday, and the Centre offered to allow you to appear on our show, well, there was no choice really, was there? I mean… the hero of the hour! How could we pass that up? This will quite likely go National!" They were walking rapidly down a corridor towards a brightly lit area ahead. "We'll just pop you in here," he said, stopping at a glass door on the right marked 'Hair & Make-Up'. "We have to get you camera ready. It's the lights, you see. They leave you looking completely washed out if we don't."

A slim young man in cropped white jeans and a black T-shirt rushed forward. "Sergeant Cross," he said. "I'm Julian, I'm just going to get you tidy for the show." He sat her down and chatted happily as he swept a gown around her shoulders. "We saw the news last night. I thought you were in for it when you walked out there, cool as could be, but no helmet or bulletproof vest. Then when he came at you with the knife… I think I screamed! We were so excited when George said you were coming in." Two older ladies waved from behind him, obviously very excited too. He spun her around to face the mirror and beamed at her.

"Well, aren't you beautiful? This won't take long. Now just take off the sunglasses, lovie… Oooh! What a shiner! George, look at this!" George obligingly moved from the door to peer at her.

"I didn't see you get hit on the news," Julian said.

George leaned over. "No, this is a few days old. Is there a story behind this Sergeant?"

"I suppose there is," said Susan, "but it had nothing to do with the attack on the Centre."

"Well, you just sit there and tell me all about it while Julian gets you ready."

"There's not much to tell, really. Two of my team and I were in a shop the other day making enquiries regarding a case we're dealing with, when a couple of thugs came in and started demanding payment with menaces – protection racket stuff. They attacked the poor sales assistant, but they hadn't noticed us. We were all in plain clothes, and out of view. I called for back-up, but it wouldn't get there quickly enough, so I'm afraid I just waded in. When PC Varma and DC Murphy did too, we managed to restrain them, but not before I'd collected this," she said wryly. "I've been wearing the sunglasses ever since!"

"Well, it's a good thing you had two large constables with you, then," said George sagely. "A policeman's job and all that, I suppose!"

"Hardly two large constables," she smiled. "PC Varma is a young woman and she's not big at all. DC Murphy is strong and fit, but there was only one of him."

"Wait", said George. "Two girls - sorry, young women - and one man took down two villains?"

"I thought we were in trouble, actually. But we couldn't just stand by and do nothing!"

"Excuse me, a moment," said George. "I'll be back for you in a second." He spoke to Julian. "Don't cover up that eye. It'll make great television," and he shot out the door.

"Where's he going?" asked Susan.

"Oh, he's off to tell Ralph," said Julian, applying foundation to her face. "You don't wear much make up usually, do you lovie? Don't worry, this comes off easily enough. Just remember not to wipe your hand over your face. We'll do the back of your hands too, which will remind you to leave your face alone. He thinks Ralph will want to ask you about it," he added, changing subject rapidly. "I bet he does, too. Not one for missing a story, our Ralph. He'll ignore the script and just go for it. It's a good story, too. Menacing mobsters taken down by two girls and a young, hunky, male colleague! Thrilling!" He clapped his hands together and stood back to admire his handy work.

"There you are, lovie! You're done. George will be back in a moment to take you through to Ralph. Don't be nervous. Anyone who can face down a terrorist and two big thugs can handle Ralph any day."

A moment later George was back, and they headed down towards the bright lights. "We'll just pin this mike to your lapel here… Put your sunglasses on again, but be careful not to smudge your makeup." Looking around she saw the brightly lit stage, with a bright red sofa and an armchair. "You'll come in from the side, here, when Ralph introduces you. Go towards him, shake hands carefully, and then move to the sofa. Sit at the end closest to the other chair. Ralph will sit there. We'll be starting with a replay of the video from last night's news, and then Ralph will introduce you. Don't be nervous, you'll be terrific!"

She looked around. There were seats for an audience, but the only person seated there was Henry Cavill who gave her what he no doubt thought was an encouraging smile and a 'thumbs up'.

"No audience today?" she asked.

"No. We bring in an audience for sessions we pre-tape, but not for last minute, early morning pieces. We'll dub that in."

"Well, that makes it much less frightening." She smiled.

“Here we go,” said George, and all the lights dimmed except those on the stage. Ralph walked on, waving to an imaginary audience.

“Good morning the South East! Good morning! How are you all today? It’s early Saturday morning and many of you will still be in bed, but we have a real treat for you today. Yesterday afternoon there was an attack on the Policing Centre just up the road from Sevenoaks. Some of you may have seen it on the News last night. It’s remarkable! For those who didn’t see it, here it is now.” A large screen behind him came alive and started replaying the video.

“Viewers will see this direct on their screens,” said Somerby quietly to Susan. “We do it this way to reinforce the idea that there’s an audience watching in the studio,” and they watched it through again. She had a feeling she was going to get very tired of it very quickly… Then the lights came up on the stage, and Ralph was still standing centre stage.

“How often have we seen scenes like this end with people being seriously hurt or even killed? Yet here we saw our police, while under considerable stress, make a very clear and deliberate effort *not* to let that happen. We have here with us in the studio this morning Detective Sergeant Cross, the very brave officer who led this effort from the front.”

George gave her a prod, “Off you go.”

“Ladies and Gentlemen, Detective Sergeant Susan Cross!”

Taking a deep breath, Crosspatch stepped forward into the lights, and walked towards Ralph. Smiling and shaking hands, she then moved to the sofa and sat down, Ralph taking the armchair.

"Well," he said, "and how are you after all that? I doubt I'd have had the courage to walk out there the way you did. But if I had, I think I'd have needed a stiff drink afterwards! Even two or three! How do you get your equilibrium back after something like that?"

She smiled. "Well, I'll admit to a couple of glasses of wine when I got home yesterday evening, but it was over so fast, I don't think it hit me for quite a while afterwards. We really just wanted to prevent it ending up with someone getting hurt. That young man was terrified. He'd probably been pressured and frightened into being there in the first place. Then when it turned into a horrifying reality... He could easily have panicked and tried to attack the security detail. Even with the number of knife attacks we've seen lately, no one would have tried to injure him deliberately, but when you have to subdue someone who is armed and frantic and probably expecting to be killed, well, you follow your training, and people can get hurt. It happens."

"Yes, I think we've seen that. Now, I've checked into this, and both you and Sergeant Grissom broke police protocol in doing what you did. So why did you do it?"

Susan paused for a moment, collecting her thoughts. "Police protocol lays down a set of procedures to be followed in circumstances like these. But every case is different, and sometimes it can be too overbearing and perhaps brutal. You have to understand that the rules are there primarily to protect the police officers from being hurt themselves, and we take them very seriously. In 90% of all cases, nothing else can be done. But officers always have a small amount of leeway if they think it can lead to a better outcome."

"What if it doesn't lead to a better outcome?"

"Then at best you'll get a reprimand on your file." She smiled and added, "If you survive, of course."

"I see. It's a case of don't break the rules unless you succeed?"

She laughed. "Yes, I suppose it is."

Ralph sat back. "You came out of last night's situation with no one hurt other than the boy brandishing the gun, and even he was deliberately taken down in a non-lethal manner, no actual damage. The one with the knife was too – both neutralised but essentially unhurt."

She sobered. "Yes. But, if there had been more of them … well, it certainly could have had a more serious outcome. Our security teams include army-trained snipers. With one or two targets they can use the tranquilisers but with more than that, or against more powerful weapons they would have no choice but to use live ammunition."

"Why didn't they simply tranquilise the second attacker?"

"If he'd been acting violently, they would have done. But tranquilising someone is not quite as easy as it is portrayed in films. To be quite safe you need to know a lot about the person to be taken down. You need to know their weight and have an idea of their metabolism to know how quickly their system will recover from it. Then on top of that you need to know of any allergies. In emergency circumstances like that our tranquillisers are set to work on an average person, but a dose that is safe for one person might kill another, so there is a degree of risk involved. If the person isn't resisting, it's actually safer to stick to normal arrest procedures. The downside is the risk that they are still armed and might panic and attack the arresting officer. That boy was still armed, and he was right on the edge of panic, as you saw. So, while we took a risk, we were aware of the danger."

"You weren't in the security detail, though. You came through from the rear of the atrium."

"Yes, I did. I was in the office behind the front desk. I saw what was happening, and I felt that I could present a less threatening face in that situation. Fortunately, it worked!"

"Indeed, it did. Ever since the New Policing Centre was opened, there have been people questioning whether it was secure enough in an age of terrorism. I think we can say that it's more secure than it looks?"

"It's not something that I can talk about, but yes. The Centre, and the philosophy behind it is an attempt to bring the police back in touch with the people they are here to protect, while still remaining secure from attack."

Ralph sat forward again. "Yesterday you came away completely unscathed. Thank God for that. But it doesn't always work that way, does it?"

Susan paused. "Well, it can be a dangerous job, and a few knocks and scratches are inevitable." She smiled. "Of course we try to avoid it."

"But sometimes you can get hurt, can't you? Susan, would you mind taking off your sunglasses?"

"Must I?" she asked, clearly reluctant.

"I think you should. It does the public good to be reminded that keeping us all safe comes at a price." With a sigh, Susan took off the sunglasses. "Now look straight into the camera," said Ralph. She could almost sense the camera zoom in on her eye. "Thank you, Susan. Tell us the story behind that."

It looked as if this was another story she'd be telling again and again! She sighed, and told it again. Ralph then closed the interview with some more generalised questions about policing and the New Policing Centre and asked her if she had anything further she wanted to say.

"Yes, I have, actually. Thank you. There is someone we're looking for and I'd like to leave her a message in case she sees this."

"Go right ahead."

She thought about it for a moment, and then looked straight at the camera. "This message is for Ali. Alison and Thomas. We know what happened, and we believe you are in considerable danger. We can help you. Please contact me at the Policing Centre in Sevenoaks, or call me on this number," and she gave her own personal mobile number. It meant she'd have to get a new number, but it was one more chance to keep Alison alive.

"No doubt there's a story behind that too?"

"Yes, Ralph, there is. But I'm afraid it's an ongoing case, and I can't talk about it."

"Well, thank you very much for taking the time, and at the weekend, to come in and tell us about last night's incident and your previous encounter too." He turned towards the supposed audience. "Ladies and Gentlemen, Sergeant Susan Cross, one of our brave police officers from right here in Sevenoaks!"

She smiled out towards Henry Cavill, who also wore a big smile. "Is that it?" she asked Ralph. "Can I get back to work now? We're on a very hot case."

"That's it, Susan. It went very well. Good luck with your case."

She got up and stepped down from the stage towards Cavill. "Will that do? I really do have to get back."

"It was excellent, Sergeant Cross. Very natural. You speak well to the camera, so don't be surprised if we ask you to appear again. I'll give you as much warning as I can. This story is likely to be picked up nationwide, and we need ones with happy endings. You surprised me with the second story - I hadn't heard that one. But it really helped."

"I realise we need to do everything we can to polish our image, Henry, and I'm happy to do my bit … but I do have real police work to do, too."

"Of course! Of course. But the police need a face that the public can relate to. You have just given them that and they are going to want more. And the public do pay your salary, Susan."

Susan pulled a face. She touched his arm and smiled at him disarmingly

"I know they do, and I get it, really. I'll do what I can. But frankly, they pay me that salary to do genuine police work. So please, can we keep it to a minimum?"

"I'll do my best."

* * * * *

It was still only 08:00, so Susan stopped into a Pret and bought two large take-out lattes and a couple of freshly baked croissants. Then it was back to Mandy's flat to change into her normal working clothes of slacks, shirt, and comfortable blazer. But as she handed back her borrowed finery she hesitated.

"Mandy, the PR officer says I may have to do some other interviews. Can I buy these and leave them with you for when I need them?"

"You're going to be doing more? Don't worry about these, then. I'll use them on a display. I'll pair it with a wig with your hairstyle and colour, and a set of sunglasses! With any luck, people will recognise the outfit and want to copy the look. I bet you looked gorgeous! I can't wait to see it! I'll tell Head Office that you came to me for advice on what to wear, and I lent these to you especially for the show. I wouldn't be surprised if they got on to your PR people asking to be your official wardrobe provider! It would be great advertising! Then I can dress you up every time you have to go on TV, a bit differently each time." She smiled, "I'd love that." They sat quietly at the little table looking out over the street, enjoying their breakfast.

Susan looked at her watch. 09:00. "The show should be on. Shall we watch?"

Mandy leaped up. "I'll turn it on." The TV lit up just in time to catch Ralph's introduction, and to watch the news footage again. Then on she came. Mandy grabbed her hand tight, and they sat back and watched. Susan marvelled at how professionally the show was put together. They had dubbed in a studio audience, and she almost laughed at the "Oooh!" that came from them when she took off her sunglasses and the camera zeroed in on her rainbow-coloured eye. She suspected that had been embellished a bit too, as she was certain it hadn't looked so vivid when she looked in the mirror that morning. But they were right, it did make good television. When it was over, Mandy hugged her tight.

"You were fabulous!" she said. "I knew you would be!"

But time was moving on… "Got to go" she sighed. "I'm meeting my team in half an hour."

"Will you come back this evening?"

"I'd like to, love, but I'm not sure. We're expecting to be working right through the weekend. The case is at a really tense point at the moment, and something could break open anytime. If it does, we need to be ready to move."

"Let's play it by ear, then. See what the situation is tonight."

"Done. I'll give you a ring."

*   *   *   *   *

Susan walked into the third level conference room to find her team crowded around a large computer monitor. Before she could say anything, she tripped over a large but apparently friendly dog, that rose to its feet, then onto its back legs, put its front paws on her shoulders and gave her a tentative lick, looking anxiously into her face.

"Gaah!" She staggered backwards, pushing the dog off and trying to wipe her face at the same time. "Where did this come from?" she asked as she pushed the animal down. "He shouldn't be in here. Who does he belong to?"

Sandeep leaped up from her seat beside Pandy. "He's a she, Ma'am," she said with a bright smile, "and she's part of the case!"

"Run that past me again? How can he - I mean she - be part of the case?"

"It was those calls you asked me to check into. The ones from 'Jennings & Co'. They're breeders, and they specialise in English Pointers," explained Sandeep.

"What's an English Pointer when it's at home?" she asked, "and what has it got to do with all this?"

"Her, Ma'am. She's an English Pointer. She's Laura's." Sandeep slowed down, suddenly. "Or she *was* Laura's."

"Wait… This was Laura's dog? Why was she at Jennings?"

"Er, she's a valuable pedigree bitch, and she was just bred last Monday."

"Last Monday? Pull the other one! Look at the size of her! She was never just bred this week!"

"Sorry Ma'am, I mean she was mated with a 'him' last Monday. They told me that with pedigrees they like to keep them in the kennels in isolation for a few days and then at the right moment they introduce them to the chosen male dog to mate. She was mated last Monday, and they've been trying to get through to Laura to come and bring her home. They said she couldn't stay at their kennels any longer as they didn't have any room. I suppose she belongs to her husband now, but Ma'am, I couldn't take her to him. I mean he may be a murderer. He had Laura killed! She can't go to him!"

"What ever happened to innocent until proven guilty Sandeep? But I know how you feel. So, you brought him here? I mean you brought her here. How did you get her past reception? Or the constable at the back door?"

"I told the constable that she was an important piece of evidence that you needed to see," said Sandeep, deliberately not looking her in the eye.

"And he let that go?"

"I think he thought it was a joke, Ma'am. He certainly seemed to think it was funny. He was laughing," she said, her face darkening a bit.

"OK, we'll sort her out later. Actually, that's interesting. It explains the Bitch Spray, doesn't it? How did the killer know the dog wasn't there? A dog this size would have made a lot of noise," … as the dog started barking at her… "if he just barged in. What does she want now?"

"Er… I don't know. I've never had a dog before."

Stuart McLean spoke up. "Sandeep, when did you last take her out to relieve herself?"

Sandeep looked at him blankly. "Relieve herself?"

"Yes," said Stuart "oh damn, like that!" The dog had retired to the corner and was quietly depositing a seemingly enormous and very smelly package on the floor. "How long have you had her, Sandeep?"

"Since about 16:30 yesterday."

"And you haven't taken her outside even once?"

"Er, no… we stayed at Sergeant Cross's place last night. She seemed a little lost, but I think she was OK."

"Ma'am, you may need some room freshener when you get home. She almost certainly peed during the night. You'll have to find where she did and clean it - spray it. You may have to get the carpet cleaned."

"Bugger." She took a deep breath." OK, I'll check. Better still, you can check it this evening, Sandeep. Pick up an air freshener and a carpet cleaner-spray on your way back there. Then make sure you walk her around the building a couple of times early in the evening, and again before you turn in for the night. First thing in the morning too! Make sure you have several plastic bags. You need a bag now, and some paper towels, too."

"a bag, Ma'am?" Susan pointed at the mess in the corner. "Oh. I see. Yes, shall I clean that up?"

"Good idea, Sandeep."

Pandy broke in. "You won't be there again tonight. Ma'am?"

"No, I'm staying with a friend. It gives the two of you a bit more room."

Sandeep looked across at Pandy and grinned. Pandy nodded and grinned back. Susan closed her eyes, shook her head and decided not to go there. She looked at the dog. No. Not dog, bitch, she thought, but that was such a derogatory term. "Does anyone know her name? We can't really just call her 'Dog', and certainly not 'Bitch'."

She took a good look at the dog. Perhaps not as big as she'd thought. She was a shorthaired breed, predominantly white with orange-brown markings above her eyes, her ears, her shoulders and along her flanks. What made her seem so big were those long thin legs. Built for speed she thought? She really had no idea what the breed was known for. But she had huge, soulful, expressive eyes. You couldn't get cross with an animal that looked at you that way.

"I think the name was on the paper they sent back with her. It's a receipt, as the - er - service was paid in advance. It's in the car, ma'am."

"OK, Sandeep, go and get it. Take her with you and walk her around the car park a few times in case she's got any more where that came from," nodding at the mess Sandeep was trying to shovel into a liner from one of the wastepaper baskets. "And take that away with you. There must be a bin outside you can dump it into. Oh, and find a bowl or something to give her some water."

"Yes, Ma'am," and Sandeep, grabbing the dog's lead, and heading off towards the stairs. All the way down the hall they could hear her scolding the dog.

"How could you do that? She'd just walked in, and you had to disgrace yourself, didn't you? Stop looking at me like that. I didn't know you needed to go. We'll just have to get used to each other, then you can tell…" and the door into the stairwell closed behind them.

"Right. Comedy hour's over. What have you lot been up to on the computer while you've been waiting for me?"

Pandy spoke up. "We watched your TV interview. Have you done anything like that before?"

"No, I've never even spoken to a reporter."

"Really? Well, after that performance, I think you'd better be prepared. You came over really well. I bet the publicity people will be all over you now!"

"Hell! I mean, thank you! But I hope not. Mr. Cavill suggested I might have to do it again, but he did promise to try to keep it to a minimum."

"Perhaps get a new phone and stay out of the office as much as you can?" suggested Pandy with a grin. "At least this case gives you lots of excuses to do that."

"I can try," sighed Crosspatch. "OK, what else have you all been doing?"

Pandy indicated the large computer monitor at the end of the table. "I did a lot of work in London checking out information to see if it was confirmed by the CCTV system in the area. So, I downloaded recordings from the area around The Classic last Monday night. Helen helped me with it," she said, nodding towards one of the uniforms handling the phones, "as she had already found the files for Sunday. Those told us that Ian Davison was at the theatre when his wife was killed. There was no reason after that to look there again - but now we know about Alison Johnson, and she was at the theatre on Monday. We know when Ali got to Walworth so we can estimate when she must have left the theatre. Look at what we found."

Pandy keyed in some instructions, and up came an overhead map of the area around the theatre. "There's a camera here," she pointed at the corner of the alleyway leading back past the stage door. "Watch."

She clicked on the camera icon and the alley sprang into life on the screen. The stage door opened, and the cast members straggled out and dispersed. A minute later, Ian Davison came out too, but didn't follow the others. Hands in his pockets, he ambled off further down the alley. After a few minutes, he wandered back, looked at his watch, and then did his little walk down the alley again. Just as he was turning back again, the stage door burst open and out came Alison. She looked, saw Davison, and turned and ran as though the hounds of hell were after her. He shouted at her, and ran after her, but she had a good lead as she swung around the front of the theatre and raced down the road in the opposite direction to that taken by the cast. A little way ahead people were bustling out of an office tower and setting off in both directions.

"Here's the next camera." The scene came into focus again, but a little further down the road. You could see

Alison haring around the corner and then merging with the crowd. It must have started raining, because almost immediately a forest of umbrellas opened up and effectively hid everyone. Davison could be seen in the background scanning the crowd.

"Watch here." A small group peeled away from the crowd and took refuge in a pub, while the rest kept going. "Alison was in that group that went into the pub."

"Yes," this from Sean. "That's the pub we went to last night."

They watched Davison walk down towards the pub. He gave it a cursory glance, but his eyes were tracking the sea of umbrellas as it meandered on down the pavement. "Now watch the window, above the half curtain." They watched, and after a few moments, a face appeared at the edge, carefully at first. It was Alison, watching Ian. Susan thought she had never seen a face portray such an utter sense of betrayal and anger.

"He done her wrong," drawled Stuart. No one disagreed.

Alison watched as Davison twisted around, apparently in an agony of indecision, until he finally realised how wet he was getting and headed back towards the theatre and back out of the picture.

"I can take you back and watch on the other camera again, but it's on file. We won't lose it. Let's just move this forward about ten minutes." The screen flickered and then steadied again, now showing Davison and another man - a giant of a man - coming back down the road towards them.

The giant was limping a little, and clearly in a foul mood. Davison was yelling at him, gesticulating, his hair a wild mop now. The giant was shouting back. Suddenly Susan realised what she was seeing. She wondered if Ian had any idea of the violence that could erupt from the other man. They stood outside the pub, arguing.

"There," said Sean. "In the window. That's Madeleine, and almost hidden behind her, there's Alison again." They watched as Davison and the giant continued to argue, and then separated, Ian making for the theatre, and the giant limping off in the direction the crowd had taken earlier.

Pandy moved the time forward again. They saw Alison leave the pub, cross the road, and then turn down another road that she knew led to Walworth. With another three switches of cameras, they saw her arrive at the police station and disappear inside. Again, time moved forward, and they saw her re-appear from the back of the building and head off towards Waterloo. Then she stopped and seemed to be doing something with her phone. Shortly afterwards a car pulled up and they saw her get into it, and she was gone.

"Must have called an Uber. Did you get the number," asked Susan?

"Yes, we've got the number and the time. We were about to call Uber and ask for the destination on that run when you arrived. We'll get on to it right away."

Susan sat down. She felt quite winded, as though she'd run behind Alison all the way.

"She went to find her boyfriend. Then the two of them drove down to Hastings … She told us everything, exactly as it happened. On Monday. Today's Saturday. How did our communications get so tangled?"

She thought for a minute. "Right. Let's get some pictures of her the way she was dressed when she left Walworth. And someone call Uber. Confirm where she went."

She turned to Pandy. "That was brilliantly done. I think you've found the killer! Get some pictures of him printed out for me too, will you?"

"Stuart, as soon as Pandy can get them in a suitable format, get pictures out to all the teams that investigated the previous murders we think he's responsible for. Maybe some of their witnesses will be able to recognise him. He certainly looks hard to forget! Get some out to the local and the Met squads dealing with gang violence too. See if they can give us a name. It's time to put some heat under him. Once we can get him out in the open, we can close the net. If the DCI approves, I want his picture released to the press as a "Person of Interest" in the Nettle Lane murder.

"And we've got a direct link to Ian Davison. Bloody marvellous! Well done all of you. I thought we'd just be waiting for something to break this weekend, and you've already done it!"

* * * * *

DCI Gordon liked dogs. He wasn't expecting to find one in the lobby of the Police Centre, but it rather brightened his day.

"Hello Sandeep! Beautiful pointer. Yours? What's her name?"

"Luna, Sir. Actually, she's Laura Handley-Davison's dog, Sir."

His expression sharpened and he looked at her questioningly. "Really?"

"Yes, Sir. She was in kennels, but they needed her to be collected and had been leaving messages on Laura's phone for a couple of days. So, I picked her up." She hesitated. "She's not very happy being here, Sir. I think, she's not very happy, full stop."

"Thoroughly confused and rather frightened I'd imagine. Poor old thing. I suppose Ian Davison is her owner, now."

"But sir, he may be a murderer. How can we leave her with him? And he's busy at the theatre anyway." Gordon stroked the pointers head, running the silky ears through his fingers and then reached for his phone.

"Elizabeth," he said when it was answered. "Could you do something for me?"

He turned away as he spoke to his wife, but his hands were still caressing the dog and he signalled an apology to the young PC. The exchange was brief and as he rang off, he turned back with a smile.

"I'm so sorry - that was rude of me. I knew my wife was about to go out and I wanted to catch her before she did. I've asked her to collect Luna from you here. Perhaps she can go to Laura's mother, but we'll have to let Davison know we have her. He's wrapped up in his play's opening weekend though, so I doubt he'll even be interested. We have a large dog already, so it won't be hard to have another for the weekend. But we'll have to turn her over to the family next week. I'll speak to Sergeant Cross. Would you keep her with you till Elizabeth gets here? Were you just taking her out?"

Sandeep nodded. She'd got rather fond of the dog and that seemed a sound solution. "I'll take her out now Sir, but I'll bring her up to you as soon as your wife gets here."

"Come on Luna," she said. "Looks like you'll be going back to luxury living - lucky you." And she led her off chatting to her brightly as the elegant dog paced along beside her with that graceful racehorse stride.

Gordon watched her go and smiled. Luna would probably go to Laura's parents in the end, if they'd take her, but he'd leave all that until the weekend was over.

He walked up the stairs and into the incident room. The team was all there, and busy. Crosspatch got up from her chair as the DCI came in and walked forward with a big smile. "Good morning, Sir. I hope we're not the cause of getting you out on a Saturday morning?"

"Good morning, Susan. No, or only indirectly. I came to congratulate you on an excellent job on that TV interview. It seems DI Featherstone severely underestimated your communication skills! Risky, though, giving out your mobile number like that. You're going to have to get a new one now. You'll be bombarded with calls, many of them very unpleasant. Have you already turned it over to one of the uniforms here?"

"Yes, Sir. I picked one up on my way in and had the shop clone it to my old phone. So, I still have my contacts on it, but under a different number. My team all have the new number. Scotty's got the old one," she said, pointing to one of the three uniforms sitting at the other end of the room with a battery of phones. "He'll alert me if we get a genuine call. I know it's only a faint chance, but it was worth trying, I think.

"But while I was doing that, the team made some giant strides. They've got pictures of the killer, Sir. Clear as daylight on CCTV. We don't know who he is yet, but now we can release his picture to the press, someone will come forward who does. And we've got a link to Ian Davison too."

Gordon's wide smile embraced them all as he sat down by the monitor. He was immensely proud of how this team had come together. "Well done!" he said. "Someone show me the CCTV footage. I really want to see our killer."

"Pandy? Can you show the DCI?"

Leaping up, Pandy hurried forward to work the screen. Susan stayed to watch in case he had any questions.

"Oh, Ma'am, before I forget…" It was Sean. "I did check into what the fuss Davison was making the week before. He told the bookkeeper that the investors wanted their money back, and he was quite upset about it. But he must have got it sorted out over the weekend, because he told the bookkeeper everything was OK when he saw him this week."

"OK, Sean. Do we know who the investors are?"

"They're a group that lends money to 'worthy enterprises' that run short of working capital."

"Have you checked with them?"

"Yes. I spoke to a representative of the group. He says there had been a misunderstanding, but that it had been resolved. He said the investors were actually quite happy with the way things were going."

"OK. All that is in the file?" He nodded.

*   *   *   *   *

Elizabeth Gordon wasted no time. She hated the idea of an animal in distress and was delighted to be asked to help. She made a few calls to free up her afternoon, backed the car out of the garage, tossed in a rug and drove to the Centre to meet her new charge.

Luna looked up at Elizabeth with soft, questioning brown eyes that held a hint that she was not a little aggrieved. Nothing had been right for days now. Where was Laura? Where was her bed? Her toys? Why no walks, no food, no water? The indignity of being forced to squat in that office! Her world had been rocked, her faith in people shaken. Where was Laura? Would this woman take her home to Laura?

Elizabeth smiled and crouched down to stroke her and the dog moved hesitantly towards her, then put her nose into her hand and whimpered. Elizabeth was lost. "Poor Luna" she crooned "Poor girl! That's all right now, sweetheart, you'll be fine!" She stroked her and fondled her head and the pointer moved as close to her as she could get and slowly wagged her tail.

Sandeep was outraged. "Luna! What a diva! Anyone would think we'd beaten you!"

*   *   *   *   *

Classic Cars was not a volume sales operation, and its customers weren't generally the type that had to make their major purchases on the weekends, so there was only a small staff on duty on Saturdays. Charlie reckoned his best value to the company was on the golf course at weekends, always turning up in traditional golf paraphernalia and driving one of their classic restorations. He'd made more sales on the golf course than in the office! The weather was holding, and the sun was quite warm by mid-morning. There were several foursomes on the course.

Doris didn't work weekends. They had another girl who just came in on Saturdays, and Ron Brown usually wandered in for a few hours, but it was always a quiet time. Doris liked to stay in bed late and watch the South East morning show on television while sipping a coffee that her adoring husband got up to make for her. That morning, she was watching when Susan Cross appeared on the show. She enjoyed it. Someone at that new Police Centre was bright enough to hire an intelligent woman and give her a responsible role! So many places didn't, and that was their loss. She knew Charlie valued her work and her salary reflected it.

"That's a tough girl," she said to herself when the TV picked up on the sergeant's shiner. Two women cops taking down two big gangland enforcers – ok with one bloke. Still, definitely tough, and competent, too. She felt proud of them. Then right at the end was the appeal to "Alison and Thomas." She sat up at that, and listened. Before she heard the phone number, she was scrabbling at the bedside table for a pen to write it down. This was something Charlie needed to know about.

Charlie was in mid swing at the third tee when his phone buzzed.

"Bloody hell!" he burst out as he sliced his drive well off to the right. This had better be important or someone was going to get an earful! Stepping aside, he grimaced apologetically at his companions, who were all grinning widely. Damn! That was probably going to cost him the game. He pulled the phone out of his pocket. Doris? His irritation disappeared. If Doris called, it was something important. He stepped away from the others and called her back.

"Doris, you just put my drive so far out into the rough I'll never find it! What's happened?"

"Charlie, you remember that copper who was looking for the Cat?"

"Yes, an Inspector Featherweight or something from the South-East Constabulary."

"Yes, that one. Did you think he was on the level?"

"Not a chance, love. Bent as a paper clip. It wasn't police who turned up in Hastings looking for Tommy. It was some giant bruiser, and he wasn't playing nice. Really put the wind up the lads at Jermyns. Tommy's been warned to keep his head down until this gets sorted out."

"Good. So you know where he is?"

"No, and I don't want to know. That way I can't tell anyone."

"But you can get hold of him?"

Charlie spoke very quietly. "Look Doris, that's not something you want to know either. Why?"

"Charlie, I just saw an interview with a copper on the Morning Show. She was the one on the news last night, talking down that terrorist kid. She's genuine, I'd swear to it. She's working a case at the moment that she can't talk about, but she made an appeal. She said it was for Alison and Thomas. Her words. She said she knows what happened. Said they were in danger. Asked them to call her, either at the Policing Centre in Sevenoaks, or at this number. I'm going to text it to you. I think someone should make sure the Cat hears about it. If you have any doubts about her, listen to the interview yourself. It should be on the ITV South-East website by now. I think it's important."

Charlie thought about it. Doris had an uncanny nose for spotting important things on the news, and he'd never known her to get anyone's character wrong. "OK. I'll take a dekko and if it looks right Tommy will hear about it."

"Thanks Charlie. I'd hate it if something happened to those two. They're sort of sweet!"

"Sweet? Yeah… OK, Doris. Thanks for the heads up. Looks like I'm going to have to forfeit this game and go somewhere I can watch that interview."

He turned back to the other players. "Sorry, lads. That was an important call. I'm going to have to cut out. Business, I'm afraid."

"Come on Charlie. No! That's not on! You can't walk away just because you bollixed up that drive!"

"No! Finish the round, Wanker!"

"Come on, lads, I'll pay up, course I will. But I really do have to deal with this. I'll win it back next week if the weather holds, anyway!" He grinned. He knew he would, and so did they. But despite the teasing, they were somewhat mollified. It wasn't like Charlie to back out of a game.

"Right, then. Settle up next week?" They agreed and went back to their round while Charlie made his way back to the Clubhouse. Once in his car, he pulled a headset out of the glovebox, and did a quick search on his phone. He found it and settled back to watch the show. Then he watched it again. Yes, he agreed with Doris. This girl was the real thing. Time to call Tommy.

*   *   *   *   *

Scotty sat up with a jerk. He'd been monitoring the calls coming in on Crosspatch's phone. There had been a number of bully calls. The ones where someone would call in and just scream abuse at the person answering. All recorded, and the numbers logged. He'd smiled. They would take their time over it, but if things ever got slow, the people who had made those calls might receive a visit from their friendly local copper to discuss them. But this one wasn't one of those. It was a quiet call. It simply said that if Sergeant Cross would like to call this number someone might be able to help with her request. He waved his arm and within moments Crosspatch was with him. Taking a headset, she listened to the recording of the call. She nodded at Scotty. She'd follow up on this one.

She went back to her seat and dialled the number using one of the incident room lines.

"Hello," a male voice answered. A hint of a Northern burr? "Who is this?"

"Good morning, this is Detective Sergeant Cross calling from the Sevenoaks Policing Centre. I'm answering your call."

"You aren't calling on the number you gave out on TV."

"No, I'm not. I'm afraid that line is tied up right now. You did say you might be of help?"

"Tell me one thing. Is there an Inspector Turkey - oh, sorry, I mean Featherweight - on the investigation team?"

"I'm curious to know why you ask that. No. I do know an Inspector Featherstone, but he is not associated with this investigation."

"Why is he asking questions about Thomas O'Malley if he's not on the investigation?"

"I'm afraid I can't answer that," she replied. "He has his own cases that he's working on. But he's aware of this case. It's possibly the biggest one that's happening at the moment, so if he got wind of something, he'd certainly ask questions, and then pass the answers on to the investigation team."

"So, if he got some pertinent information, he'd pass it on to you?"

"Yes, that's the way the system works."

“So, you know where Thomas was last Tuesday morning?”

“We may know that. I can’t give out information about the case.”

“Featherstone was asking questions last Tuesday. He was told that Thomas delivered a car to Jermyns in Hastings. He told you that? But it wasn’t a policeman who turned up asking questions in Hastings, was it?”

“No,” she said quietly. “It wasn’t. And if you have any information on who it was that did appear and start asking questions, I’d be very interested.”

“Sergeant Cross, I’m on my way to have lunch at the Alma in Wandsworth. Can you find it?”

“I can.”

“Meet me there in an hour. But don’t bring Featherstone.”

“I’ll do my best, but I’m coming from Sevenoaks. How will I recognise you?”

“Oh, don’t worry about that. I’ll recognise you. You’re the television star!”

* * * * *

Contact

"Are we calling you Crosspatch now, then?" asked Stuart as they pulled out of the car park and motored down to the main road.

"Not in any formal situations," replied Susan, "but as long as it's just within the team, and there's no agenda behind it, I don't mind. I know you all call me that anyway, at least amongst yourselves, and it's better than having you all being careful when you talk to me. If it gets out of hand, I'll slap it down. In the meantime, I'll live with it."

"Got it," he said with a smile. "Oh, by the way, Sandeep asked me to check out that old Ford she's been given to drive. I took a look at it this morning when we came in. It looks like a heap of old rubbish, but that's deliberate, isn't it?"

"Go on…"

"Well, for a start that's not the wimpy little motor that most of those cars had. That's a full Cosworth two litre twin cam unit, and it has a six-speed gearbox, not five. It's got all the stuff to make it a really potent package! It's an all-wheel drive, too. That thing could be entered into a historic car rally and probably win! Where on earth did it come from? Does her brother have any idea what he's given her?"

Susan blinked. She had no idea what any of that meant, except that the car had been souped up well beyond the norm.

"OK. That raises a few questions, doesn't it? I had heard something about it. It's just been stuck away in the back of the pool. It's not on our books at all. Someone knew they had something special and didn't want to lose it. So, we maintain it, and MOT it, and here it's sat for quite some time. Every few weeks Roger Dean from the carpool takes it out for a drive to keep the oil circulating, and the suspension and brakes moving, and then it gets tucked in the back again. Her brother thought he was pulling a fast one when he was told that he had to find her something to drive. He looked around for something harmless, spotted an old clunker mouldering in the back and decided that would do." She grinned. "When Dean finds out what's happened, he'll have a fit."

Stuart laughed. "No wonder she's so protective of it. She obviously has an idea of what it can do and likes that. I hope she doesn't wreck it, though. I wouldn't mind borrowing it myself for a few hours – preferably somewhere quiet, like in the Welsh mountains!

"Back to business, though. What are we hoping to find in Wandsworth?"

"I'm hoping it's going to be someone who knows where Alison and Thomas are. But whoever called is being really cagey. He knows Featherstone is interfering with this investigation. He thinks Featherstone's bent, and, before he tells us anything, he's going to make sure we aren't too. I want you and Sandeep to go in ahead. You can check the place out. See if anything looks strange. If it looks like a set-up, just walk out. I'll take Pandy with me."

They pulled up and parked on a side road, a discreet distance from the pub, Sandeep pulling the Ford in behind them. The team paired off, with Sandeep and Stuart going ahead and Susan and Pandy taking their time. Susan stopped, suddenly. “Look, Pandy. Up the road. It’s Classic Cars! We’re definitely on the right track here.”

Stuart and Sandeep didn’t come back out, so they went into the pub and walked up to the bar. Better keep things light, thought Susan, ordering an alcohol-free lager. Pandy opted for a mineral water, and when Sandeep came over to join them, she followed her Guv’s example with the lager. While the two constables were studying the lunch menu chalked up on the board, Susan leaned back against the bar and looked around the room.

Over by the wall, a group of three seemed to be waiting for someone. Interesting. Two men, she guessed both to be in their late fifties, and a younger woman with a mass of bright blonde hair and glossy, red lipstick. The men pulled the eye too; one was dressed as though he’d just come off the golf course and the other looked like a pastiche of a 1950’s used car salesman.

Nothing alarming there. If her contact was one of them, she’d find out in due course. Then, as Susan turned to look at the menu herself, there was a squeal behind her. All three detectives swung round, suddenly tense. It was the blonde, who had jumped up from her seat, and was hurrying over to them - or more particularly, to Susan!

“It’s you, isn’t it? You’re her! You were on the telly this morning and now you’re here! Ooh, it’s so exciting! To actually *see* you!” She flapped her hands at her companions who were all watching. “Look Charlie, it’s her. That policeman - sorry, police girl that was on telly this morning. She’s a star!”

Oh lord, thought Susan, this is precisely why she hadn't wanted to do that damn TV interview. She'd kill bloody Henry Cavill and his bright ideas. The blonde bounced up onto the bar stool next to her.

"I'm Doris," she said. "And I know your name. Sergeant Cross! So, what's your real name? I know they have to change people's names on TV. Actors always have totally different names in real life! So go on, what's your real name when you aren't on TV?"

She groaned inwardly. *How do I get out of this without hurting her feelings? She's only being friendly! But - really bad timing.*

"Hello, Doris," she managed. "Lovely to meet you. Actually, that is my real name. We only use false names on undercover work."

"Get off… you don't do undercover work! You're a policeman - sorry, police girl! You have to be FBI to go undercover."

Police GIRL? FBI?

Susan looked across at her two constables. Stuart had joined them at the bar now. The *girls* seemed to be finding this hilarious! A lot of help they were! Or maybe they could be? Stuart was obviously trying to catch up with what was going on!

"I see you know your police, Doris. Let me introduce you to these two. They're police girls too," and lowering her voice to a whisper "they're undercover. They're my bodyguards so I don't get attacked when we're outside the station! You don't want to mess with them, they can be fierce!"

Doris sat back and looked at them. "They think this is funny, don't they? That's not very nice. And why aren't they stopping me from talking to you? I could be a Russian assassin out to poison you!"

"That's ok, Doris. They can see you're friendly. It's been lovely to meet you. Say hello to your friends from me, but" dropping her voice again "I'm on duty. I'm waiting for someone with a secret message for me, and they won't come near me while you're here. So please, help me out. If you go back to your table, then I can make it look like I'm just having lunch here with my friends."

Doris looked at her. "You're pulling my leg, aren't you?" She sighed. "This one," pointing at Stuart, "He's your bodyguard, if any." Then she looked over at her companions and spoke in a completely different voice.

"She's OK, Charlie. If she's bent, I can't see it," Then to Susan, "Why don't you join us at our table, Sergeant Cross? If you can convince us, maybe we'll have a story for you!" She looked at the three constables consideringly. "The small one, Charlie. I reckon she's the one who took down that bruiser at Sevenoaks." Then to Sandeep, "That was well done, girl! Underestimated you, didn't he?"

Charlie was the man in golfing gear. He introduced himself as the owner of Classic Cars. The 1950's car salesman type introduced himself as Ron Brown, assistant manager.

"So, Sergeant Cross. Are you going to tell us what's going on? Or are we supposed to tell you?" came from Charlie.

They shuffled around to make room for extra chairs, and Susan started the exchange. "You must understand that this is an ongoing case and there's very little I can tell you other than what the press has already put out. You clearly know it's about the Nettle Lane murder." They all nodded. "The victim was Laura Handley-Davison. She was married to Ian Davison, a well-known actor and director. Davison is getting a play ready to open at the Classic Theatre near Elephant and Castle. Your employee Thomas O'Malley's girlfriend, Alison Johnson, was going to be acting in that play.

"Ms. Johnson made a statement to the police last Monday evening about an assault at the theatre, but then she disappeared. We're trying to find her. I'm hoping you can put us in touch with her. We believe she is with Thomas O'Malley. If you know where they are, or can contact them, please help us. We believe they are in serious danger!"

"Nice one, Sergeant, but I think you've left a few bits out there," said Charlie. Susan sat back. OK. That's what she'd come for… To hear what they had to say.

"Then fill in the gaps for me."

Charlie paused for a moment, organising his thoughts. "OK, the Nettle Lane Murder. I bet the killer just walked right in. That Laura lady, she didn't have a chance. That fucker Davison found a hit man to do it for him. Bastard! Then, after he killed her, the hit man phoned in to say the job was done. But it was Ali that picked up the phone, wasn't it?" Susan could only nod. Charlie knew as much - and perhaps more - than they did.

"Davison must have realised that Ali had heard the phone message. Called his hit man in again and set her up too. Only, she escaped. She's got guts, that girl. She got to Walworth Police Station and told them all about it.

"But here's the kicker… What I want to know is, if you lot knew about this back on Monday night, what the hell have you been doing all week? That Inspector bloody Featherweight came poncing in demanding to know where Tommy was back last Tuesday! It's Saturday, today." No-one spoke.

"Well," Charlie continued after a moment. "Doris figured him. Bent as a paperclip! So, we tested him. Jermyns was a dead end by then, but he didn't know it. So, we told him the truth. We'd sent Tommy down there to deliver a Jag. If the police turned up there asking questions, well, no harm done. But it wasn't the police, was it? It was some big goon who tried to intimidate a couple of Geoff's mechanics into saying where Tommy had gone.

"But, we only gave that information to Featherwhatsit, and look what happened. Proved Doris right - for the umpteenth time, I might add! - He's a policeman all right, we looked him up, but he's passing on information to a killer. So, we need to be really careful who we speak to." He looked around at his audience, but no-one had anything to say.

"OK, what you don't seem to know, then. After he'd dropped the E-Type off, Tommy took the train back from Hastings. He went back to their flat and almost ran smack into the killer. He got away though, and he came here and talked to me. Told me about it. He'd left his car here, so he took it and went back down to Hastings. Ali stayed down there with friends. The plan was to see who turned up at Jermyns. If it was the police, they'd talk to them. If it wasn't, he and Ali were going into hiding - and no, before you ask, I don't know where.

"So... What have you lot been doing over the last three or four days if you're only just catching up to Hastings?"

"I can answer part of that," said Susan. "We weren't aware of the statement at Walworth until Thursday evening. Walworth is a Met station and we're the South-East Constabulary, but we do talk to each other. I don't know why our communications broke down on this. Usually, an open file like that would be highlighted as needing follow up daily until it was closed. But it didn't get flagged. Not until they got the results of the DNA analysis Walworth requested from Alison's clothes. That can take days to process."

Pandy took up the story. "I'm from Walworth. I was the one who took Ali's statement and opened the file. I put all of her story into it directly from her statement. But she was talking about a murder that took place near Tonbridge. That case was being handled by Sevenoaks. Our Sergeant called Sevenoaks and spoke to the duty officer there. He told us that Ali was a Person of Interest in the case and that they wanted to speak to her. He drove up personally to get her, but by the time he got there she was gone. I'm told he opened the file and read it. He told our Sergeant that he would take it from there. He even took her signed statement with him. It wasn't our investigation, and no one looked at it again until

Sergeant Cross came in to find out what was going on. We can only guess that the Sevenoaks duty officer accidentally deleted the file, perhaps intending to transfer all the data to his own file."

"I don't think you believe that any more than I do," said Charlie. "It was deliberate."

"We will be investigating that. But in the meantime we need to make sure Alison and Thomas are safe."

"There we agree. So, what do we do now?" asked Charlie.

*   *   *   *   *

Tom jumped when the burner phone buzzed at him. It could only be Charlie, but Charlie had said he'd only call if he really had to, so it was in his thickest Irish accent that he answered

"Hello there. Is that you, Patrick?"

"No, you git. It's Charlie. It's almost time to come home!"

*   *   *   *   *

Inspector Featherstone's mobile rang. It was 6 o'clock on a Saturday evening, from a number he didn't recognise. "Featherstone…"

"Oh Inspector, I'm glad I was able to get you. I used the number on your card. It's Ron Brown."

Ron Brown? The name was familiar, but he couldn't put a face or place to it.

"Assistant Manager at Classic Cars in Wandsworth? I spoke to you last Tuesday."

Got it, the anachronistic salesman who'd given him the useless information about Hastings and then tried to sell him a car.

"Yes, Mr. Brown, I remember now. You told me that our fugitive on the Nettle Lane case had driven down to Hastings. Quite true, but the trail stopped there. Do you have any further information?"

"Well, yes, I do. That's why I'm calling you. I've just seen him! Thomas O'Malley! He has his girlfriend with him. They're staying here. Charlie's putting them up in the guest suite upstairs."

"He's there now, Mr. Brown?" he asked excitedly. But then he remembered the run-around they had given him before. "Hang about. Why are you telling me this? I got the feeling that no one there wanted to cooperate with the police."

"Well, yes. I'm afraid it was a bit like that. But that's not the way I think we should behave. It's our duty to provide all the help we can. After all, you police officers dedicate your lives to our protection. That's why I made sure you had the truth when you were here. I'm sorry if it didn't turn out to be useful, but it was all that I knew at the time. Anyway, I thought that if Thomas was involved in some way in that awful murder, then I ought to call you."

"Mr. Brown, you may be helping us detain a very dangerous man."

“Oh I say, do you really think so? Thomas? Dangerous? He’s always so pleasant. He’s worked for us for over three years! Don’t tell me we’ve had a murderer right under our noses and we didn’t know it?”

“Criminals can be very clever, Mr. Brown. Some conceal their true nature so well that no-one suspects it until it is too late. But thank you for this information. We will take it from here. Mr. O’Malley may be dangerous, Mr. Brown, so please don’t approach him. Leave it to us!”

“Of course, Inspector. I’ll keep well clear!”

“Goodbye, Mr. Brown. Thank you again.”

Scarcely had he put down his phone than it buzzed again.

“It’s PC Pandya, Inspector. You asked me to keep you updated on any news on the Nettle Lane case.”

“Yes. Has something come up?”

“I’m not sure how significant it is, Sir, but Sergeant Cross said we had a big break in the case. She’s found the girl we’ve been trying to trace - an actress from Mr. Davison’s theatre. She’s been in hiding for some reason, but she heard Sergeant Cross’s appeal on television this morning and she’s coming up to town, tonight, I think. We’re to meet her at Classic Cars in Wandsworth, tomorrow at 10:00.”

Featherstone sat back for a minute or two. He could almost believe there was a God! He punched in the number for ‘Paul Lennox’. “We’ve got them! They’ll be in Wandsworth tonight.”

* * * * *

George Grissom… Susan could still feel the burn that had surged through her as he had touched her arm at the end of the terrorist takedown. Damn! She'd fancied him ever since she first met him when she transferred in from Maidstone and was being given a tour of the Centre's facilities, but she'd never had the opportunity to get to know him. Certainly never thought it might be more than - well - a fancy. Then once the problem of dealing with - or even surviving - Featherstone's squad became her paramount concern, she'd hardly given him - or anyone else - a thought. But now… He'd felt it too, she knew he had. He was just what she needed… and he just might be interested. She thought about it. Yes, it was worth a try. She got out her phone again and punched in his number.

"George," she said as soon as he answered. "It's Susan Cross. Do you have any plans for this evening?"

*   *   *   *   *

"DC MacLean? DI Bishop from Luton here. You sent us some photographs asking if anyone could identify the subject. We know who he is. That's Stan Bellamy. He's known to be involved with the Leytonstone gang up here, although we've never been able to bring him in on anything. The one time we did have a case against him, our witness disappeared, apparently frightened off, as she's never been seen since."

"Inspector Bishop, if she disappeared, you'll probably find her body under a hedge or in a field somewhere not too far away. This man does a lot more than frighten people! We suspect he is a multiple killer."

*   *   *   *   *

Confrontation

"Tom!" Ali was shaking him.

"What?" He jerked awake. Again. He felt under his pillow, flipped his phone over. "Al, it's after one a.m. Get some sleep. Come on, love. We're safe here. It'll all be over tomorrow... Today." he corrected. "But later. Much later." He rolled back over.

"No, really. I'm sure I heard something!"

"You've been hearing things for two days straight. Go back to sleep. Please, Al. You'll wake Olivia across the way, and then none of us will get any sleep. She's been feeding off everyone's anxiety ever since we got here, and if she starts into her 'Where's Daddy?' routine again, Clare will probably kill you. Slowly. Her nerves are stretched tight too."

She muttered a bit, then cuddled up close. He turned into her arms and kissed her lightly. "You're not the only one on edge, love. My imagination's been in overdrive too. But Charlie says this detective is straight. She has everything under control. We'll meet her in the morning."

"Yes, but she hasn't got that monster yet. He's still out there looking for us." She breathed him in, each taking comfort from the other. But for Ali, that monster loomed, larger than life every time she closed her eyes. It was going to be another sleepless night. Outside, the room, she was sure something was moving.

* * * * *

Stan Bellamy - known to some as 'Boris' or 'Lennox' - looked up at the building. The car showroom was on the ground floor, at the front. Above it, on the first floor was a long balcony stretching the length of the building. Behind that were offices, and from the plans Featherstone had sent him, the three at the end had been converted into accommodation: a sitting room with a bedroom on each side. He smiled. The curtains were drawn, but he could see the faint glow of a night light behind the one at the end. He'd been watching for an hour. There had been no movement. They were asleep.

There was bound to be an alarm, but that would cover the entrance to the showroom and the workshops behind. There were probably motion detectors on the ground floor too, but there wouldn't be anything upstairs. This was going to be easy. His luck hadn't deserted him after all. Knock out the lock on the balcony doors quickly and once inside take out the man fast. Then he'd have hours with the girl before he had to be away. His heartbeat quickened, remembering her; remembering, particularly, how she'd hurt him. She was going to regret that. He'd learned how to stretch it out, to prolong it without killing. She'd be begging for death long before the finale, when she'd die writhing around the knife pinning her to the floor. Or perhaps to the wall this time? He hadn't done that in a while. He was breathing fast, now.

He manoeuvred his pickup onto the forecourt and parked it sideways on. He could step up from the load bed onto its roof and reach the lowest rung of the balcony railing. A quick heave and he was up and over and ducking down so as not to cast a shadow onto the windows from the lamppost across the road. Now, the end one, where the night light glowed. Check the door… and it slid back silently. *They haven't even locked it! People are such fools...*

He was in, closing the door behind him… A double bed. Two bodies, just stirring…

* * * * *

Ali started awake again. Someone *was* in the room. The door had opened, a shadow, and it was moving…

* * * * *

Stan lunged forward only to find his arms wrapped in bedclothes. He missed the larger silhouette completely, as both occupants of the bed suddenly shot up and out of his reach. Swivelling around, and trying to untangle himself, he found himself facing two people. A man and woman as he had been expecting, but fully dressed! A warning bell clanged dully in the back of his mind. They'd been expecting him?

"Give it up, Stan. End of the line."

They knew his name? The warning bell clanged louder. Were they from the Organisation? From Georgiades? Were they here to erase the problem he'd created? No matter. He'd just kill them and then disappear for a while. With a grunt of frustration, he launched himself at the man, again reaching out to grapple. Once he had his hands on him he knew he could end it. The woman moved aside as he charged, and the man stepped back a pace. He had him now! But he missed again! The man, spinning lightly on his feet, grabbed his outstretched arm and using his own momentum propelled him face first into the wall! Bouncing back, he roared and charged again.

He didn't even see how it was done, but suddenly he was flying straight over the man's shoulder to go crashing to the floor behind him. As he twisted in mid-air there was an agonising tearing as his left shoulder dislocated, his arm trapped in a vicelike grip behind him. He got to his feet again, breathing in hoarse gasps, one arm now hanging uselessly at his side and sending pulses of agony across his shoulders. How? No one stood up to him. He was bigger, stronger. He always won! But now he hesitated.

The woman! A hostage! Grab her and he could get away, take her with him. She was his target, anyway. He lunged in her direction, but with only one arm he couldn't get hold of her properly. She spun away from him, but he grasped her wrist and pulled her to him. She tucked in tightly, holding onto his damaged arm. Wait! This wasn't the woman from the theatre!

What the fuck?

"Another mistake, Stan! I think you'd better let go."

What?

She was blocking him at the front and the man was behind him now. He struggled but couldn't get any leverage. Fingers of dread walked up his spine as the man's hand came around from behind to lock on his jaw, the other behind his head… He froze.

"Hold absolutely still, Sunshine, or I'll break your neck." It was said quietly, but with total conviction, and Stan

Bellamy, the man who dealt in terror and pain, felt icy terror freeze his own veins. He let the woman go.

"We've got him!" she called. The lights came on and the bedroom door opened to show others waiting outside. He was handcuffed quickly and efficiently, with cheerful disregard of his dislocated shoulder. Then, to complete his ignominy, leg shackles clicked around his ankles. He wasn't getting out of this one easily!

* * * * *

Robert Gordon sat at home, watching his phone. He knew it was Featherstone in the BMW at the end of the lane. He wanted to be out with Crosspatch and her team tonight, but he couldn't risk letting Featherstone know something was happening. It had to seem like a perfectly ordinary Saturday evening.

He and Elizabeth had taken the children out to supper at a nice restaurant in town, celebrating young Jamie's glowing report from school. Now everyone was bedded down quietly at home. But not Robert. He needed to be awake, ready to call in extra back-up if it was needed. Crosspatch had a clever operation going though, and he was confident that she'd be calling in with news of success, not asking for help. How that woman had blossomed in confidence over the past few months, as she was allowed to spread her wings! She was exceeding all his expectations.

"Robbie." It was Elizabeth. She'd slipped down quietly and came over to sit beside him. She hadn't turned on any lights. She snuggled up to him, and he put his arm around her and drew her in. He gave her a soft kiss, and she pulled in tighter and sighed.

"I haven't seen you so twitchy in years. Something's going on, isn't it? Is it the car at the end of the lane? Is he watching us or guarding us?"

"Watching us. It's Featherstone. He's making sure I stay quietly at home."

"Why?" she asked. "We've had a lovely evening. Jamie really enjoyed it. He was in good form. But it's been a bluff, hasn't it? What is that bastard up to?"

"Just what I said. He's watching to see that I stay quietly at home because he has something going down, and he wants to be sure I stay out of the way. He can't believe I'd let one of my teams do anything without being there to take any possible credit for it."

"Susan's onto something, isn't she?"

"Yes, she's found the woman that can identify the Nettle Lane killer for us. Constable Pandya and DC McLean are running protection for the woman overnight and they're coming into the Centre tomorrow."

"There's more to it than that, though, isn't there? Something's happening tonight, and you don't want Featherstone to twig, do you?"

"You always were too clever, Mrs. Gordon."

"I know," she smiled. "That's why you love me!"

"I love you for all sorts of reasons," he said, gathering her to him.

“So, Susan is up to something tonight! And you’re running camouflage!”

“Definitely too clever, my love. Yes, and I’m waiting to hear how it goes.”

“Right. Let me get a blanket, and then we’ll both tuck down here on the sofa and wait for Susan to report success. Far more fun waiting it out together!”

The Gordons were warm and cozy on the sofa when Crosspatch’s call came through.

* * * * *

Stan’s mind was whirling with pain and shock. What the fuck had just happened? Who were these people? The woman from the bedroom stepped forward.

“I’m Detective Sergeant Cross, from Sevenoaks, Stan. This gentleman,” indicating the man who’d tossed him around like a rag doll, “is Sergeant Grissom, also from Sevenoaks. We’ve been looking forward to meeting you. In fact, there are several police departments all over the country who want to see you, but we’ve got you first. It’s about the Nettle Lane murder. So say goodbye to these nice people, thank them for their generous hospitality, and we’ll take you back to Sevenoaks with us.”

There was a man taking photographs on his mobile and a tall, flashy blonde, who eyed him up dismissively and then said. “I’ll send the pics down to Jermyns. Their lads will get a kick out of them. We could put them in the ‘before and after’ album on our website, too, Charlie. We got some beautiful shots of him on the security cameras as he came up over the balcony. Show our customers how well our security system works!" They grinned at each other. "You'd better phone the Cat in the morning and tell him we've taken care of his little problem. No need to wake him up yet."

Susan turned to the others, including two more of Grissom's Security team.

"Caution him and call in the van. DC Murphy will be shadowing your van just to make sure nothing happens, and Sandeep and I will catch up on the way. One of you, drive his Ute back to the Centre, too. It can't stay here."

* * * * *

"Susan!" answered Elizabeth, who'd beaten her husband to the phone on the coffee table. "You're out slaying dragons tonight! Did you get him? ... Hooray for George! Hah, I'd love to have seen that. I'll have to tease him about it next time I see him! Yes! George and the Dragon! Anyway, well done! Now I suppose you'll want to speak to Robert?... Yes, you should really. We have to let him think he's in charge, don't we? Oops, talk to you later. There's a senior police officer here who wants to speak to you. Better mind your p's and q's!" and she offered her husband his phone.

"She did it!" she said, her eyes dancing. "Oh, I'd *so* like to see that idiot Featherstone's face when he realises what you've done!" Then, laughing, she pulled the phone back!

"Susan, well done!" said the DCI when he finally got the phone from his wife, who was taking delight in making him snatch for it. In the end he'd simply grabbed her, given her a very thorough kiss, and taken the phone while she was distracted.

"You sound a little breathless Sir," said Susan. "We're a bit that way ourselves… No, Sir, no trouble, but that man really is big. I'm glad we didn't have to fall back on a tranquiliser shot. I'm not sure we'd have had one strong enough! But we have him in the van now and we're travelling back in convoy!

"The security boys seem quite happy. Tonight's exercise was right up their street. They keep suggesting that George shouldn't have had all the fun, and that we should let Stan loose again for a 'bit of exercise'. They're arguing over which of them should have first go at him!

"I could almost feel sorry for him, but then I remember what he did to Laura, and to those women in Brighton and Horsham, and others that we haven't even found yet. I think I could turn a blind eye if our boys took him apart. Not to worry though - they won't.

"By the way, could you have a doctor on hand at the Centre? He seems to have dislocated his shoulder… Oh, he was trying to kill George, Sir. He didn't try to run when he realised we were expecting him. Just launched right at us. It's pretty clear he had plans for me. Or Alison, I suppose. Bastard! But he found George was rather different from his usual victims. I'm afraid we're none of us feeling very merciful, so if it hurts, well ... His confidence has taken a hit, though. I'd say he's always just depended on his size and strength, and it didn't work this time. He never bothered to learn to fight - not properly, anyway. George reckons any one of his people would have been able to handle him."

“Slow down, Susan, I think you’re still running a little high on adrenaline yourself. Where are you?”

“Sorry, Sir. Am I babbling? I do feel a little lightheaded, but that could be Sandeep’s driving, which is er - rather exhilarating, actually. Um, we’re on the M25, just past Oxted. Should be there in about half an hour. Traffic’s really light, as you’d expect at this time on a Sunday morning. Just a few lorries heading for the Chunnel.”

“Terrific. Well done, all of you. I’ll meet you at the Centre. DI Featherstone’s been watching me all evening to make sure I stay out of the way while his boy is at play! He’s likely to have a heart attack when you bring him in.”

“* * *”

“I didn’t quite catch what you said there, Susan…”

“Er… I said it would serve the … er… serve him right, Sir.”

*   *   *   *   *

Featherstone was tucked into a small break in the hedge on the Gordons’ lane. It was an excellent spot for surveillance, as he could see the house between a pair of trees, while he could only be seen himself if someone was actively searching for him. He’d been on site since about 20:00. Shortly after that the DCI had arrived home with his whole family. An hour or so later the lights had gone out in the children’s bedrooms, and in the rest of the house at about 22:30. There’d been no movement since. Nevertheless, he thought, he’d better stay put until ‘Lennox’ called to report the job was finally complete. Looking at his watch, he saw it was now 02:00. He should be hearing from him any moment now.

Suddenly there were lights on in the Gordons' house! Something was happening. A few minutes later the DCI's car came flying past, lights flashing. He barely paused at the end of the lane and then took off at speed in the direction of the Centre. Featherstone smiled to himself. *Looks like the DCI has just lost his key witness!* He started his car. He wanted to watch their humiliation! A healthy payday, and a black mark against that bastard Gordon and that bitch. He could almost taste his promotion. It wouldn't matter if he couldn't close the case… He could claim they'd made such a mess of it that it couldn't be resolved now! Not long…

Arriving a few minutes before Crosspatch's convoy, the DCI chivvied the night staff into opening the entrance to the underground levels and made sure the way was clear from there straight to the cells. Shortly afterwards the convoy arrived and drove straight down the ramp. Grissom and two of his men heaved their cuffed and shackled prisoner out of the van and marched him through to custody. Susan stood back and let the security team be recorded as bringing him in. They'd made a risky situation look routine.

The doctor arrived a few minutes later, venting shocked displeasure that 'her patient' had not had his dislocated shoulder tended to sooner. Susan took her aside and had a few words with her, after which she came back to the counter and wrote up her report. *Resisting arrest, shoulder dislocated. Doctor summoned to put it right immediately he was brought into the Centre.*

"What did you say to her?" asked Sandeep, sitting beside her as they waited for the prisoner to be charged and the paperwork to be completed. "She was all upset, but she's completely changed her tune now!"

"Remember the Brighton case? This doctor's name was on the file. She was working with the pathologist on that one and had added a note to the file about the atrocities that the killer had inflicted on the victim. I told her this was almost certainly the Brighton killer, and before that the Horsham one too. I think she'd have condoned anything done to him after that. I feel a bit that way myself. That woman from Crawley … her kids will be thirteen and sixteen now. Maybe this'll make things a bit easier for them."

She noticed when DI Featherstone arrived. The DCI noticed too.

"Maurice! What are you doing here at this time of night?"

"I was driving by, and I saw all the lights and vehicles arriving and wondered what was happening. Bad news, I take it?"

"On the contrary! Sergeant Cross has just brought in the Nettle Lane killer! Excellent news, I'd say."

Featherstone glanced around. There seemed to be people everywhere, and there was Sergeant Grissom just leading his prisoner out of the medical room and down towards the cells. The prisoner looked over, saw Featherstone, and scowled. The Inspector swallowed. It was 'Lennox'.

"All this for one man?" he asked Gordon sourly. "You'd better be very sure you have the right man."

"Maurice, you should have faith in Sergeant Cross. She's a credit to your mentoring! No wonder you didn't want to give her up!"

Featherstone knew when it was time to leave…

Gordon turned to Crosspatch. "Excellent work, Susan. Is there anything else I need to know?"

"Yes, sir. When he was being taken down to the van one of George's men just happened to say that it had gone down just the way DI Featherstone had planned… Bellamy had a lot to say about that before he suddenly clammed up. It confirmed what we knew, and in front of very credible witnesses too."

She looked around. Everyone was here except for Stuart and Pandy. They were down at the coast, liaising with the local police who had the Holiday Chalets, where Clare, Olivia, Tom and Ali were sheltering, under observation in case their hiding place had been compromised.

"Can we hold off on a debrief until later today? Stuart and Pandy are going to be escorting Tom O'Malley and Alison Johnson up here in the morning and I'd like to hear from them and get Alison to identify Bellamy as her attacker. In addition, we'll need to interview him and see what he has to say. Perhaps a full team meeting after lunch?

"One more thing though. Should we put a "Detain" order out to the Ports and Airports on Featherstone? In case he decides to run for it."

"I don't think that's necessary. It would confirm his guilt, and he knows we can track him through Interpol. I think he'll sit tight and just try to brazen it out. He'll try to use his Old Boys' network to get him out of trouble. I don't think he realises how deep the trouble is that he's in.

"We'll need to alert the PR boys sharpish, though. We want an announcement of the arrest on the news and in the papers as soon as possible. I'm most interested to see what Ian Davison's reaction to it is. If all this really was his idea he may panic - give himself away."

"Yes, sir. He just might. Perhaps we should go and give him the news ourselves!"

"Yes, good idea." The DCI was thoughtful. "That's something that is still troubling me though. I still can't see why Davison would have wanted his wife dead. But whether he did or not, it's only right that the investigating officer should inform the victim's grieving spouse that the killer has been caught! Let's see how he reacts. Do you want to go to him, or call him in?"

"I think his Macbeth opened tonight at the Classic. Perhaps you and Elizabeth could go tomorrow? Oh, sorry, tonight? You could inform him immediately after the play?"

The DCI thought about it. "You know, I'd enjoy that. I wonder if O'Malley and Alison Johnson would like to accompany us as our guests? Should we include you and Sergeant Grissom too?"

Crosspatch looked at him, and then burst out laughing! "That would be cruel!" Then she sobered. "No, I don't think Sergeant Grissom and I should be included. After the terrorist incident, and now this, I'm not sure that it would be fair to George to have our names linked too often. My reputation at the Centre might cause him a few problems."

"Perhaps that should be left up to him to decide? I get the impression he rather enjoyed tonight's exercise. Think about it. I doubt your reputation is going to be a problem after this!"

* * * * *

Crosspatch's car was still in the car park. She and Sandeep left together - Sandeep to Crosspatch's apartment. She thought she might have it to herself for a few hours, at least until Pandy got back from the coast. She wondered if Crosspatch would come in, or if she would go to her boyfriend's. She knew which she would choose!

Susan sat in her car, tired after a very long day, the adrenaline from the night long since faded. She looked at her watch - almost 06:00! She'd been up for over twenty-four hours straight! No wonder she was tired. Time to go home. She started the car and pulled out onto the main road. Quite unconsciously she found herself driving into town. She turned up Otford Rd, then right, and then around the roundabout to the McDonalds. Who else would be open at 06:00 on a Sunday morning? Sure enough, they had just opened, and she could smell the coffee, and the eggs and bacon on the griddle. She wandered in, loaded up with lattes and McMuffins, and then it was back down Otford Rd.

Next thing she knew she was at the back door of 'Laura's'. When Mandy opened the door, she practically fell in. Mandy got her upstairs to the flat, helped her off with her jacket and boots, and sat her down at the table with their breakfast while Susan told her about the night's happenings. "We got him," she said with a tired smile as her head went down on the table.

"Oh no you don't!" said Mandy leaping up and coming around the table! She got Susan's arm across her shoulder, heaved her up and staggered into the bedroom with her. Jeans, shirt and fleece all came off, and she tucked the exhausted sergeant under the duvet. "Sleep well, Hun. No bed bugs to bite - you've beaten them!"

* * * * *

Ali was up quite early. She stretched as she waited for the kettle to boil so that she could make some tea, and some hot chocolate for Olivia, who was awake but yawning widely, sitting at the table.

"Oh Olly, don't yawn like that! You'll have me doing it too," as a big yawn stretched across her own face. "There, see what you've done?" She smiled at her little goddaughter. Actually, they had all got to sleep quite quickly after Olivia had crept into their room in the middle of the night, scaring them both half to death. Ali had been convinced that it was Boris, until Olivia had piped up from the doorway saying she couldn't sleep.

"Mummy won't wake up. She keeps telling me to go to sleep, but I can't." Then the little girl had hopped into bed and curled up between them while Tom tried valiantly to tell her a story - but he kept losing track. Ali couldn't even remember what story it was, but it did the trick. After a few minutes Olivia's breathing had smoothed out and softened, and not long later both Ali and Tom were asleep again too.

Olivia woke up early. She needed the loo. Then she was hungry. So, she prodded Ali to see if she was hungry too. Tom was still firmly asleep. "Better go and see if Mummy is awake, poppet. She'll be wondering what's happened to you." Olivia trotted off to check on Clare, and Ali snuggled down into the warmth of the bed again. But a minute later Olivia was back. "Mummy's still asleep. She doesn't want to wake up! Come on Ali. I'm hungry."

Recognising the inevitable, Ali pulled herself out of her cocoon. "OK, torment. What would you like?"

"I usually have yogurt and honey at home, but I don't like the ones we have here - they're a funny colour and they taste funny too. Perhaps cereal instead?"

"I don't think the Holiday Park shop has much to choose from - but let's go and see what we've got in the cupboard," and the two girls went hand in hand into the little kitchen.

"Umm," said Ali looking into the cupboard. "I bet it was Tom who did the shopping! It looks like we have Weetabix and Corn Flakes."

"Weetabix," said Olivia. "With lots of milk so it goes soggy!"

"One Weetabix coming up! With sugar?"

"Only brown sugar, Ali. Mummy says it's healthier."

"Does she? I expect she's right," said Ali, wondering if that was what happened when one had children. She was just getting down a small bowl, and reaching into the fridge for the milk when the little scene was interrupted by someone knocking on the door.

"The Monster!" screeched Olivia leaping down from the chair and racing off into her mother's bedroom.

Ali's heart was beating fast. *No, it couldn't be.* Charlie had said they'd be dealing with him last night. He had told Tom they were going to arrest him. He'd sounded very confident. But she remembered how big he was, and the strength in his hands and her stomach contracted.

The knock sounded on the door again. This time she could hear a woman's voice. "Alison Johnson! Thomas O'Malley! It's the police!" That voice! She'd heard it before! Where?

The knock came again. "Ms. Johnson! Mr. O'Malley!" Suddenly she knew who it was. She reached hesitantly for the handle, pulled back the deadbolt, and opened the door a few inches.

"Constable Pandya? Is that really you?" Looking out she could see the tall constable she had last seen in Walworth. But in plainclothes, not in uniform! She opened the door wider, and yes, it was constable Pandya, with a man beside her. "What are you doing here?"

"Hello, Ali," Pandy was smiling broadly. "I'm so glad to see you again! We've been worried about you. This is DC McLean," she said, indicating the man standing next to her. "We're here to escort you back to the Policing Centre in Sevenoaks when you're ready. You'll be glad to know that we arrested your 'Boris' last night. He's in custody."

Tom came through from the bedroom, wearing just a pair of boxers, his mobile phone to his ear. "Ali, it's Charlie. They got Boris last night! … Hey, close the door, it's freezing out here!" Then waking up a bit more, "Who're you talking to?"

She looked at him and laughed. "I know!" She turned to Pandy outside the door "Come on in, both of you. You haven't met Tom. Tom, it's Constable Pandya from the police station at Walworth! Come in. I'd just put the kettle on. Olivia, Clare," she called out. "It's OK, it's the police. They got Boris last night!"

* * * * *

By 13:00 Team Crosspatch had assembled in the incident room, joined in this instance by George Grissom's security team from the previous night - all there, except for Crosspatch herself. There was a lively discussion going on about the type of hand-to-hand skills that George had used against Stan Bellamy, with Sandeep in particular asking for a demonstration. That, of course led to two of the security team squaring off against each other and demonstrating the type of moves that their sergeant had so ably displayed the night before.

"Simple Jiu Jitsu," explained Grissom. "Let your opponent come at you and just deflect his movements so that his speed and aggression work against him." It was not long before the security team were working with Team Crosspatch who had had only a brief introduction to the martial arts during police training. Then there was Sandeep. A few moves from her showed that she knew and had mastered many of those techniques, and it went from there to her demonstrating some of her Savate skills to the burly sergeant.

The desks had been pushed back to create a wide demonstration area in the middle, and when Crosspatch walked in a few minutes later she could have been forgiven for thinking a pitched battle had broken out between the two teams. Carefully guarding her latte grande, she moved down the side-lines, found a seat and sat back to watch. Shortly afterwards, the DCI arrived on the scene, took in what was happening and moved quietly across to join her.

"Morning, Susan." He gestured towards the battle in the middle of the room. "Your idea on updating their training?"

She shook her head. "No, this was already under way when I arrived, so I thought they could let off some steam while I finished my coffee. Mind you, it wouldn't be a bad idea. I could use some extra training in hand-to-hand myself! But not this morning. I just don't have the energy. Yesterday was brutal. I'm surprised that they do! But," she turned to him with an urchin grin, "we did it, didn't we? We got him! And it's not just Laura. We should be able to close a lot of cold cases now." She sobered up. "We haven't got Davison yet - or I don't think we have. Everything we have so far looks compelling but there's nothing conclusive. Could he possibly not have known what Bellamy was?

"We haven't found any indication of his having paid Bellamy, and we haven't got a strong motive. Why was

Laura killed? I'm wondering if Bellamy realised Laura would be alone at home, and simply selected her as a convenient next victim. No contract, no payment, simply the opportunity to hunt down another attractive woman!"

"That's almost certainly what a good lawyer will argue, and he could very well win with it," commented the DCI. "It could even be true. It doesn't explain the phone call that Alison picked up though, or why the killer then came after her. But the phone call is just her word against his since we don't have Davison's phone. That may be easier once we get his phone records, but we haven't seen them yet. Do you have any other lines you can follow that may give us a bit more?"

"Sean asked Davison if he would allow us to go through his phone, 'as a means of eliminating him from our enquiries,' and he handed it over quite happily. It turned out it was only about three days old… He said he was so sorry, but he'd accidentally dropped his old one getting out of a taxi a few days before, and the taxi ran over it as it was leaving!

"I talked to Bellamy, before coming up here this morning. He's showing no signs of being helpful at all. All he offered were "colourful metaphors" as Mr. Spock would describe them, and he wouldn't answer any questions. I don't think he feels any particular loyalty to Davison, but he isn't going to give us anything unless he sees an advantage for himself. Without some completely unrealistic 'deal' by the CPS, he may just spit in our eye and tell us to go to hell."

"Yes, that's my impression too. And as far as the CPS is concerned, they aren't going to offer him any kind of deal. To their minds he's the one they want, the real killer. Given his history, I can understand that. He is the big catch. He's possibly a killer many times over. We just don't know about Davison yet. With regard to Nettle Lane I doubt we could make a good case, but he's vulnerable when it comes to the Alison Johnson assault. Of course, that's a far lesser charge."

Looking up, they saw that the melee had ended, and everyone was taking their place in a ring of seats around their two leaders. The DCI looked around at the ring of expectant faces.

"All right, everyone. First let me give you all my congratulations. George," looking over at Grissom, "my wife wishes me to inform you that you are to be known forthwith as 'George the Dragon Slayer'!" The room broke into laughter, especially when George stood up and bowed in all directions! "Well done indeed, George. Alas, your partner will still have to suffer under the name of 'Crosspatch'." Grissom turned and bowed again, this time to Susan. "Wear it with pride, Sergeant," bringing on another round of laughter!

"Now we start a different phase of the investigation. Sergeant Cross and I will be presenting our case to the Crown Prosecution Service tomorrow morning. Our case against Stan Bellamy is rock solid. Not only can we tie him absolutely to the murder scene, he was carrying the murder weapon when he was arrested. He didn't use it in resisting arrest. Early psychological input has it that it is because he doesn't see it as a weapon. It's more like a musical instrument to him, to be used when he's performing. That wouldn't have come into play until he had beaten our two sergeants into virtual insensibility. He fights with his hands…

"We also have him for assault on Ms. Johnson at the theatre both by her witness statement and through his DNA found both at the theatre and on Ms. Johnson's clothes. I suppose he could try to claim that in fact she assaulted him, but given the other charges against him, that one would probably be laughed out of court! We also have him threatening two mechanics at Jermyns in Hastings, trying to get information on the whereabouts of Ms. Johnson, which links into another aspect of this investigation which I am unable to talk about at present." That was greeted with mutterings, and some questioning faces.

"Featherstone," said Pandy quietly, and everyone nodded.

The DCI went on. "Most of you know that the position of Ian Davison remains unclear but suspicious. It appears probable that he instigated the murder of his wife, that Stan Bellamy carried out that murder and that Davison also tried to have Alison Johnson killed because she had become aware of his involvement. But our case is weak. We have evidence against him, certainly, but it is all circumstantial. Bellamy is not currently cooperating with our investigation, so we don't have a corroborating statement from him.

"If we can find anything else, we may be able to strengthen our case, and we will be working on that now. The CPS has considerable depth in prosecution, and they may see things we have missed. We will follow their advice if some is proffered. In the meantime I think we'll be busy for a while yet.

"Now, we have a further task for you all. Sergeant Cross will explain."

Susan stood up. "Ok everyone, this is perhaps a little outside your normal roles. I hope you all love Shakespeare… You're going to the theatre tonight!"

*   *   *   *   *

One down

The foyer was bright, every light gleaming, spilling out of the doors and into the early November night. The crowds inside the foyer and those outside too, waiting for the crush around the doors and box office to dissipate so that they could push inside, seemed to pulse with excitement. There was a queue stretching around the corner. The atmosphere was intense, almost brittle, and DCI Gordon, looking out across the floor from the steps into the stalls bar, felt the anticipation rise.

"They're all here tonight," he remarked to his wife, and she agreed.

"Yes, they are. Not all Shakespeare buffs, either. They want to see Ian. They're the murder watchers aren't they, half of them? The guillotine crowd."

"Mmm. Not surprising though is it? The news has been full of the murder."

"Yes. But the opening reviews were amazing too, weren't they?"

And they had been.

Despite everything, despite the sudden rush that had brought the soft opening forward by a week, perhaps even because of it, the play had come together and gelled. The emotions of fear, anger, pity, and confusion had fused into a desperate energy that pulled out performances that were raw and vivid. Ian seemed touched with a sort of madness that fitted his role and made Macbeth live as none of his audience, nor indeed his cast, had ever previously experienced. The thane's ambition, the dilemma of loyalty and love pushed aside by greed, a weakness exploited and urged on by promises and coercion, and the dreadful sense of a hubris that couldn't be escaped - it was all there. The critics had seen and felt it and written about the actor whose own tragedy had inspired his work and brought a greatness to it that should not, could not be missed. Ticket sales were roaring.

"Look," said Elizabeth, "they're here." They watched as Ali and Tom pushed through the door. They showed their tickets to the usher who did a classic double-take as she recognised Ali and pulled her back for a rather startled exchange. They saw Ali shrug and smile and disengage. Saw the usher call across to a colleague, who waved at Ali, and knew that it wouldn't take long for the news to percolate down to the dressing rooms that she was there.

Gordon waved across and they saw him and made their way over to join him and Elizabeth. Together they pushed through to the bar.

Sean, with a brightly dressed and almost bouncing Sandeep on his arm spoke quietly into his mobile. "They made it. They've been clocked." He smiled, a slightly crooked smile. "Let the revels begin."

The bell sounded and the audience moved into the auditorium, those with seats in the middle, inevitably later than those at the ends of the row and squeezing themselves along with muttered apologies as eyebrows were raised, seats pushed up and programmes dropped. Then as the final rustles stilled, the lights dimmed, and the curtains swept aside.

They had plain clothes and uniforms scattered around both inside and outside the theatre, as they'd half expected him to bolt, but Ian was in the grip of the play and his own success. Word had filtered down that Ali had suddenly turned up in the audience, that she was with the police inspector who'd come about Laura, but they'd known better than to burst into his dressing room to tell him. Ian's dressing, make-up and warm-up routines were sacrosanct. But her name and the buzzing of speculation were rife backstage.

The actors acted their hearts out. For a few short hours nothing existed beyond the cold stones of the castle, the dreams and despair, the malign magic of the heath and the horror of the moment that a forest came to life and marched against a murdering king. At the end there was a heartbeat of profound stillness and then a roar. The audience rose and cheered and clapped and stamped. The cast, in that no-man's-land between role and reality, smiled and bowed, clasped each other's hands, and bowed some more. Off, and on again, surging forward in a rush, standing back to let the principals come forward - and always Ian, bloody, sweating, blazing with vitality.

They went down to his dressing room together, DCI Gordon leading the way and Ali behind him. His dresser stepped aside and, as they hesitated briefly in the dark corridor, they saw him, illuminated in the glare of the make-up lights, drenched in sweat, the congealing stage blood streaked on his face and shirt, his hair wet and rat tailed, sitting back in his chair, legs thrust out, his boots half on, half off, his chest still heaving, laughing in the triumph of the night.

He saw them, and in a moment recognised Gordon and pulled himself to his feet. “Chief inspector?” It was a welcome and a question.

Gordon came forward but didn’t shake his hand. “We have made an arrest Mr. Davison.”

Ian stared at him and shook his head. “An arrest?”

“We’ve arrested the man who killed your wife.”

“Laura? The man who killed Laura?” Ian was visibly pulling himself back to reality. He stared at Gordon for a moment, expressionless, then “You’ve found the vagrant? But that’s wonderful news. Can I tell the cast? This play, it’s for her, all for her, so I can go on, this theatre can go on - as she’d have wanted.”

Gordon shook his head. “There was no vagrant, Mr Davison. The man we have arrested is a known mob enforcer, Stan Bellamy. It seems that Bellamy is no stranger to murder. We are investigating his movements in regard to other, earlier murders of young women.”

Ian was shocked and it showed. Gordon paused and looked at him keenly.

“We understand he is known to you, Sir.” There was silence. Ian stood, unmoving, then he brought his fingers up to his face, pulled at his lower lip, pulled his hand down across his forehead and rubbed his eyes.

“Known to me? I’m not sure I… what do you mean?”

Ali stepped forward now. “Hello Ian”

He stared at her, recognised her. There was a slight hesitation, then "Alison! You disappeared. What happened? We were supposed to be talking about the play and you just ran away. I wondered what the hell was up and practically tripped over a bloody great giant roaming around and he said he was looking for you. Said he was your boyfriend. Said you'd had a fight. I told him to piss off out of my theatre and he scarpered. I couldn't find you. I was furious - not the best timing. I was pretty pissed off with you." He stopped. "What are you doing here?"

Oh God. Could some of that be true? Ali simply stared at Ian; conflicted, uncertain, half of her wanting desperately to believe. The other half nearly choked with anger.

"That was the killer. You sent me right into his arms, Ian."

Gordon stepped in. He put his hand on her arm and gave a slight shake of his head.

"Alison ran for her life, Mr. Davison. That giant was the man we've arrested for killing your wife. He was caught trying to kill Ms. Johnson - perhaps I should say trying again to kill her - last night. You may have saved her life when you - er- tripped over him here at the theatre that evening. We don't know yet why he was so interested in her."

He paused and smiled blandly. "Early days though. I'm sure he'll tell us in due course."

Ian said nothing for a moment. Then he shook his head and smiled apologetically. "I'm sorry. I'm very tired. Congratulations on your arrest Chief Inspector. Thank you for telling me. Alison …" he shrugged a little, "I'm tired! Glad you're safe."

"Of course." Gordon kept his restraining hand on Ali's arm, pressing slightly, reassuring her but warning; they'd done enough.

"Thank you for a remarkable evening. Definitely the best Macbeth I've ever seen. You have an extraordinary talent, Sir. Goodnight."

And taking a still churning Ali by the arm, he turned, and they left.

As they did so, Ian's dresser went silently into the dressing room behind them and closed the door.

* * * * *

Watchers stood motionless until Ian had turned the corner and was seen hurrying to catch up with the group that was headed to the pub. They stepped forward, phones in hand. A lighter flared, a cigarette lit. The smoker inhaled deeply, blew out a ring and spoke softly.

"We let him go for tonight. Murphy and Varma are at the pub and McLean has him covered overnight in case he gets any funny ideas. The chief wants us back at base in the morning."

When the dresser left an hour or so later, the alley was empty of watchers and the theatre seemed finally to sleep.

Ian tossed back the Laphroaig Duncan had waiting for him and bought a round himself, with a toast to the Scottish Play and a "bloody brilliant performance, all of you!" He saw Sandeep and Sean, raised a glass in their direction, and noted that while they seemed upbeat themselves, the acknowledgement of his toast looked a little less than friendly. So… He was still considered a suspect?

They'd got Bellamy. Apparently he'd killed before? Ian closed his eyes and felt his world tilting. Heard the witches. Felt fear and frustration, alone in a world where mists swirled, and forests walked. What had happened? Why? Would Bellamy sing? Of course he would. The question was what song sheet he would be singing from and would he be believed? Ian wasn't even sure now that he had ever really known the tune himself. Had he just danced to Bellamy's direction? A puppet, not the puppet master in the end?

"We're heading up to Soho, Ian. Anna's booked a table for dinner. You joining us? You're looking a bit done in, old son." It was Duncan, concerned, but not about to push the sympathy. Careful. Caring.

"Thanks, mate. I'm totally done in actually... Hadn't realised but I think it's all just beginning to hit. Look - I'll just slip off. Can you explain? Make my excuses? I may have to do some family stuff in the morning - sort things for me if I'm late, ok?"

And with a rueful punch on Duncan's arm, he was gone. A picture of exhaustion, with a shadow trailing behind him, in the shadows.

*   *   *   *   *

Ian worried and fretted about it all night. Or at least it felt as though he'd been at it all night. He'd seen his in-laws in the audience. He had slept but only once he'd decided on his strategy, the role he'd play with his father-in-law. He scarcely considered Mary. A mistake that men often made… once.

In the morning, he texted Gerald. "You came last night. Saw you in the audience. Thank you. I haven't been able to face you - couldn't bear your grief on top of my own. Cowardly of me. Your coming to Laura's play makes me realise how much. May I come to see you this morning?"

Gerald Handley read it, pushed his coffee cup aside and passed his phone across to his wife.

"What do you think?" he asked.

Mary glanced at it. "Laura loved him." She buttered a fragment of sourdough toast, scraped a smear of Rosa's sharp, sliver fine marmalade across it and bit thoughtfully, scarcely a taste. "I was never sure about him." A thin cashmere covered shoulder rose, fractionally.

"We should see him. Then the Detective is coming to see us this afternoon. I want to hear what she has to say. Then we can decide."

* * * * *

He rang the bell at 10, gave Rosa the lightest of hugs along with his coat and went in to Gerald's study. The scene was emotional. Ian spoke of his earliest feelings for Laura and Gerald listened as Ian poured out a paean to Laura's beauty, intelligence, and love. As he spoke, he brought her image to mind. Laura, long legs drawn up as she sat in the deep warmth of the sofa, a whisky swirling in the facets of a crystal tumbler. Her smile, surprised, sceptical, warming to delight. Her hair, hints of amber in the gold. Her support. Her care. Her patience.

When Mary came in, he was the soft, caring, grief filled husband; emotions too raw to share, contrite in his negligence of them, needing forgiveness, wanting their love. It seemed enough.

He left a little lighter and stopped for a coffee on his way - where? Home or the theatre? One ordeal dealt with. He'd brushed through it well enough he felt. Better than well enough. He'd won that skirmish, but there'd be more ahead. He stirred sugar into his espresso and brooded, frowning into his cup. How safe was he from Stan? His own phone was clear. His computer - clear. Nothing incriminating in his paperwork. And Ali had bought his take on the fiasco with Stan at the theatre, he thought. That was the story. He had to believe it himself, grow into it. Live it. He didn't want to think about how an investment in his theatre had ended in the death of his wife. He had to protect himself now – a new act, a new play. He looked at his hands – blinked away the illusion of blood. Closed his ears to the witches' whispers. He'd be fine.

*   *   *   *   *

The day hadn't started well. Susan and the DCI had spent most of the morning presenting their case to the CPS, but they hadn't got the go ahead to charge Davison formally as an accessory in the murder. They acknowledged that the case against him was incomplete. Where was the motive? Ali's testimony was their main strength, but was she even sure about it now? A good legal defence team coupled with the skills of a superlative actor could create enough doubt in the minds of the jury that a successful prosecution was more than unlikely.

The CPS spokesperson summed up their opinion succinctly. "The case hinges on the word of the young actress. She heard the message on a phone left in the wings that the job was done, and 'she' was dead. But we don't have anything to corroborate that. And as to his calling Bellamy in to deal with her - well there is no proof of that either. Just seeing Davison and Bellamy together outside the Pub isn't enough. No-one heard what they were saying.

"Davison's story is leaky given the CCTV video of him coming out of the theatre with Bellamy that night. It's fairly obvious that they knew each other, but that could be attributed to Bellamy being a messenger from Davison's investors. That his old phone was crushed under the wheels of a taxi can't be disproved, and getting a new phone is what any normal person would do. So, nothing useful there. It would be Alison's word against his, and there's the celebrity factor. People want to love him. He'd come across to the jury as a victim in all this." Since both the DCI and Crosspatch agreed with them, there wasn't much else to do.

The prosecutor continued. "You need to find more evidence, and you need to show a motive. Get Bellamy to rat on Davison, or perhaps find Bellamy's phone. That may not have been destroyed, and it may have the other end of any communications between them. It's only a little over a week since the murder, so keep the file open. You've done well in a commendably short time. We'll proceed against Bellamy. I suggest you keep looking into Davison. If he did aim

Bellamy at his wife, you'll find out. He won't get away with it."

Ending the meeting, Crosspatch went back to her team to give them the news. The case was still on.

"Sean, do we know why the opening date for the play was suddenly moved forward by a week?"

"Yes, I asked Ian about that. He said it was at the insistence of his investors - his backers. The investors were concerned that the costs were getting too high and insisted that enough preparation had been done. They wanted the play opening right away. Ian wasn't happy about it, but I don't think he had a choice."

"Do we know who these investors are?"

"Not really. It is a known investment group, but little is known about them. I was going to bring it up, but that's when everything suddenly went into emergency mode, and we were following up on the information from Classic Cars."

"OK, I understand. But the emergency is over. We have the killer, but Davison's role is still unclear. We have a motive, but it's sketchy. His bookkeeper says he was in a panic the week before because he said the investors were demanding their money back. He told the bookkeeper he was going to ask Laura to bail him out, but then he found out later that it had been a misunderstanding. I confirmed that with a Mr. Georgiades. They didn't want their money back, they wanted the project to move faster and stop wasting their money. We can say it was a motive, because he was looking at the potential collapse of his theatre, and at the time of the murder he didn't know it was just a misunderstanding. So he was under financial pressure, but would that be sufficient motive? Especially when it was just a misunderstanding, in the end."

"Anyone else have anything that could be considered unusual?"

Stuart spoke up. "He turned up at Laura's Group head office while I was still there. Apparently he announced that he would be taking over as CEO as his wife had died. But Laura had put succession plans in place that didn't include him. No way was the Board of Directors going to pass control over to him."

"That was quick off the mark, wasn't it? Must have been the morning Sean said he was late coming in. Get hold of Dave Crewe see if he can find out anything more."

Pandy spoke up. "If he was looking for money, he would have gone to the bank too wouldn't he? Have we checked that?"

"No, I don't believe we have. Sean, see if we can get anything more on the investment group. Pandy, follow up on whether he spoke to his bank if you can - and if he did, what about."

"You know, the CPS raised a good point," added Pandy. "We don't have Ian's phone. That got destroyed - remarkably conveniently, but Bellamy's phone? Where's that? It should have the other end of any conversations they had. He certainly wasn't expecting to be caught, or even questioned. And we're still waiting for Davison's phone records. They may show what was on the destroyed phone. We have to find it."

The room was silent. Then Crosspatch spoke. "Why haven't we checked for Bellamy's phone? Pandy's absolutely right. We need that phone. Do we know where it is?"

No one spoke. Then Stuart broke the silence. "He didn't have a phone on him. It's not listed on the items he had on him when he was arrested. But he must have had a phone. That's almost certainly how Featherstone communicated with him. He's been under close guard ever since George flattened him, so he can't have destroyed it."

Pandy stepped in. "It must be in his pickup. We've impounded that. The forensics people are just looking at it today. I'll go down and see what they have."

"Right people. We need that phone. Find it. I've got another job to do this afternoon, so I'll leave it in your hands. Find that mobile. Stuart's right, it has to be somewhere. Find it! And call me as soon as we have it!"

* * * * *

Rosa was waiting at the door when they drew up at the Handley's Wimbledon house.

"Mrs. Gordon and Detective Sergeant Cross? Oh, and Miss Laura's Luna." She squatted down in front of the dog. "I'm so happy to see you, Luna." She stroked her, put her hand in her pocket and gave her a treat. "I look after her sometimes, when Miss Laura is away working," she explained, looking up at the visitors. Then she realised what she'd said. "I used to look after her," she added sadly.

Luna waved her tail and her eyes brightened, recognising the compact woman in her navy dress and white apron, and she pawed her foot for another treat, which was instantly forthcoming.

Standing up, Rosa turned back to the visitors. "Please - come in," she said to Elizabeth, a gesture including Susan in her welcome. "Lady Mary is expecting you." She led them through to a sunny room overlooking the garden, opened the French windows to let Luna out and motioned to them to sit down.

"I'll tell Lady Mary you are here," and she disappeared back out of the room.

They were watching Luna sniff her way around the perimeter of the garden when Lady Mary joined them.

"Mrs. Gordon! And Detective Sergeant Cross. Thank you both for coming!"

"Lady Mary." Elizabeth went across the room with her hands held out to take the other woman's hands in hers. "I can't tell you how sorry I am for your loss."

Mary had herself rigidly under control. She gave a tight smile, returned the pressure of the hand clasp briefly but then pulled away.

"Thank you. I'm afraid I am still not quite myself. Tea? Coffee? You can stay?" She turned to look out into the garden and a spasm passed across her face.

"Laura's dog." It was as though she was confirming the pointer's identity. There seemed little warmth in her as she stared across at the pretty bitch, frozen in full point as a squirrel leapt for the safety of a tree.

A tray was brought in, and the three women sat and stirred milk or lemon into their tea and a silence began to grow and spread through the room.

Mary turned towards Elizabeth. "DCI Gordon told us that they have made an arrest. You think this man is my daughter's killer?"

Both nodded and Susan added "We are very confident that we have the killer, Lady Mary. A dangerous, very violent man. We believe he has killed a number of women."

"Not just my daughter then?" Lady Mary looked up sharply. "More women? A serial killer? So, this did not have more personal implications?"

Elizabeth and Susan held their breath. What was she asking them? Was this the Ian question?

The door opened suddenly, and Sir Gerald came in. He was not a tall man, perhaps three inches short of six feet, and casually dressed in a navy cardigan over a blue shirt and dark cords, but he exuded an indefinable air of authority. His white hair was slightly longer than was fashionable among his generation, and bushy eyebrows shaded sharp grey eyes.

"Ladies - oh. Sorry. May I say that? Mrs Gordon! And the famous Detective Sergeant Cross. We saw your interview on television. Thank you for your hard work on our behalf. On Laura's behalf."

He looked into the garden. Saw Luna. "You've brought her dog. Yes. Mary said you were going to do that. Why? Surely our son-in-law would want their dog?" He looked at them under those heavy brows.

"Sir Gerald." Susan hesitated. She put down her cup. How to answer? "Mr. Davison is an extremely busy man at present with his play, and he is still helping us with our inquiries. His life is in turmoil. When we found Luna, my team felt that she might be happier with you, at least for now."

Laura's parents looked at each other and looked away again. Quickly. Then Mary spoke, quietly.

"You suspect Ian of some involvement?"

Susan looked at the two of them. No, she thought, they aren't shocked. They were grieving, but not shocked. "Lady Mary, Mr. Davison was at his theatre when the murder was committed. He certainly did not kill your daughter. I'm sorry I can't comment further, as this case is still ongoing."

"Of course," came the reply. "Well, thank you. Both of you. Thank you!"

And the interview, if that was what it had been, was over. As Elizabeth drew out of the gates and pointed the car in the direction of Tonbridge, she broke the silence.

"They suspect him, don't they Susan?"

"I'd bet my life on it. But what could we say? Despite their impeccable manners and control, I'm not sure I'd want to have them wondering about me." Susan shivered. "No, I really wouldn't."

Her mobile chirped. Looking at the display she saw it was Pandy. She accepted the call. "Pandy, what have you got for me?"

"I've got the phone! Forensics found it in his truck. Its password was ridiculously simple. I can access everything! It's here. Davison is on his contacts list, and it shows several calls and perhaps more importantly texts going both ways. There's even a voice message from Ian. Nothing conclusive, but I think we've got him! Oh, and we have Davison's phone records now, which corroborate it all."

It was as though a great weight had lifted from her shoulders. "Well done, Pandy. Call the DCI. He needs to know."

She turned, smiled at Elizabeth. "I think we've got him! You know, overall, this has been a pretty good day." She smiled all the way back to Sevenoaks.

* * * * *

"What do you think? Will they arrest Ian, Gerald?"

"They may, but they're not certain they have enough to make it watertight. There is no obvious motive, and the murderer seems to have killed before, just for the sake of killing. That Sergeant Cross is a very determined young lady. If a solid case can be made, I think she'll make it. But I don't think they have it yet. What do you want to do?"

"We have cut ourselves off from many of the more unpleasant activities that we carried on in the past, and we have been successful. But every time I think of our lovely daughter and what the killer did, I want to take anyone involved apart, piece by piece. I want them to die screaming - screaming for a long time." She hesitated. "If Ian was complicit in any way, I want to know."

She looked at her husband and there was ice in her eyes. “I have observed people for a long time. I recognise insincerity and that’s what I saw when Ian was here this morning. He may not have killed Laura himself, but he was definitely involved. He’s trying to cover his tracks.” Her fists clenched, and she took a deep, ragged breath, “Ian had something to do with Laura’s death, Gerald. His wife. Our lovely Laura. If he did, I want him to pay.”

“We don’t know, Mary. I don’t know. Let me have someone ask a few questions and find out just what happened.”

“Thank you, Gerald. Yes, we should be sure.”

Sir Gerald Handley took out his mobile and punched in a number…

* * * * *

Susan was sitting at her desk, still worrying at the case. The proof in Bellamy’s phone tied the two together. The one thing they lacked was still a clear motive. She pulled up the file again on her computer. Sean Murphy had it right in that Ian Davison was looking at the imminent collapse of his theatre. There was little doubt that was the most important thing in his life. More than his wife? Perhaps, but it had proved to be unfounded. His theatre was safe. Then it hit her. The timing. What was the timing? It was in the file. She looked carefully.

Davison had been worrying about it and had discussed it with the bookkeeper. When? Early in the week before the murder. He’d told the bookkeeper that he’d get a bailout from his wife. But he'd still been worrying about it later in the week. She called in Pandy.

"Can you and Helen check the CCTV around the theatre again on the Thursday and Friday before the murder? We know Bellamy came in to see Davison on the Tuesday of that week. He must have come in again. I need to know when."

She went back to the file. Did Laura refuse to bail him out this time? Could that have sparked it? He hadn't learned that it had all been a misunderstanding until the Tuesday after the murder, after he'd been in to Laura's LLC expecting to take over. When Laura had been killed, he still believed his theatre was at risk. If she was right, that was a clear motive. Now, did everything else fit with that?

It took Pandy several hours, then she was back.

"We found him. He first came in on the Tuesday. I think that was when Davison started to panic. He came in again the following day, clearly in an impatient mood. There's an interesting bit where he comes out again with Davison and the two of them were arguing. It doesn't look like Davison convinced him of anything, but when he left he was looking quite pleased, and Davison looked quite shaken. Then he came in again late on the Friday evening. He seemed to be in quite a jovial mood when he came in, but he left about half an hour later looking positively excited!"

"When did Davison decide to schedule the Sunday rehearsal?"

It had been announced on the Saturday morning, and was a surprise to the cast…

* * * * *

DS Cross and DCI Gordon arrested Davison the next morning. He was shocked, the outraged victim of police incompetence. He would nonetheless do his civic duty, of course, and cooperate.

* * * * *

Gerald Handley sighed and hung up the phone. He stood up, squared his shoulders and went through to the drawing room to find his wife.

"Mary," he hesitated. "Mary, you know we were using Ian's theatre as a test site for the laundry project… It wasn't going well. Ian was wasting large amounts of money in interminable rehearsals - dragging things out, making change after change, spending money on ever more lavish settings for his play. Georgiades needed to speed things up. But he's also at a critical point in negotiations with the Belgians on the Europe project, so he just sent one of the Leytonstone boys with a message instead of dealing with it himself. That *boy* was Stan Bellamy, and Bellamy got the message wrong. He told Ian that the investment was revoked and that repayment was required at once.

"We got someone in to talk to Bellamy. He says Ian suggested he lean on Laura as a way to get the money. He said Ian knew what that meant and he told him when Laura would be alone. He may not specifically have ordered her death, Mary, but he facilitated it. We know Bellamy too - he's gone off half-cocked before, and there have been rumours about his appetites. He was taken off the active list because of it.

He watched the impact his words had on his wife. Saw her absorb, consider and then condemn, although it was a careless mistake by a member of their own organisation that had led to their daughter's death. Gerald sighed, and leaving the room he went into the cloakroom and washed his hands.

*   *   *   *   *

Something had happened. Had Bellamy broken down? Admitted everything and implicated him? Inspector Gordon and that woman detective had been waiting when he arrived at the theatre that morning, and with hardly a chance for him to protest, he'd been cautioned, charged as an accessory to the murder of his wife and then driven down to the Policing Centre in Sevenoaks.

Fucking Hell! He fought to keep his breathing under control. They thought *he'd* sent Bellamy to kill Laura. Couldn't he make them understand that the whole thing had been a misunderstanding? Then Alison - Bellamy had said he'd sort it… He hadn't known… but of course he had. After Laura's death, he knew precisely how Bellamy solved problems.

But he stamped on the knowledge that had lurked beneath the surface from the beginning. His head was swimming. Ever the actor, though, he saw a script; a new role, a way through the mists and the forest. There had been no financial squeeze, he knew that now - so there was no motive! He'd just have to play it out. He brightened a little, he could see it now; the innocent victim of police harassment! Plodding bloody police, unable to see past their own noses. The jury would understand. He'd have them eating out of his hand!

They'd asked if he wanted a lawyer. An innocent man had no need of a lawyer! But Antonio had needed a lawyer to save him from Shylock - no shame in that. He did need someone, someone with presence, to work with him to convince a jury of his innocence. But it would cost a fortune to hire a lawyer of that calibre. So, for now he was simply sitting in a cell. They'd even taken his belt away! Did they think he would hang himself? Seriously?

His arraignment was scheduled for early afternoon. He'd have the opportunity to apply for bail, but he had almost no money!

He heard footsteps outside, and a muffled 'clunk' as his cell door unlocked. Outside he saw the custody sergeant, and with him an attractive woman, in her early thirties he guessed. Expensively and very professionally dressed, she thanked the sergeant and stepped inside.

"That's all right, Sergeant, I'll call once we're done. I just need some time with my client."

She turned to Davison. "Hello, Mr. Davison. My firm has sent me down here to represent you." She handed him a card,

Oatley, Elliott and Daniel
Solicitors
Portia S. Daniel, MA, LLB

No, really, this had to be a joke!

She smiled at him. "You can call me Portia. That really is my name! You'll probably be one of the few clients I've had to see the irony in it. Our firm has been engaged to represent you. We are on a retainer to the Handley family. I knew Laura well. She thought my name was hilarious! I was so sorry to hear of her death."

He was still trying to collect his thoughts.

“Ms. Daniel - Portia - I’m very glad to meet you. I… I still haven’t been able to grasp this. They think I killed her, or that I paid someone to kill her! It’s … ridiculous!”

“That’s all right, Mr. Davison. I’m sure we can sort it out. The first thing to do is get you out of here. We’ll apply for bail at your arraignment, which should be only an hour or so from now.”

“Bail… I can’t… I don’t …”

“Don’t worry about that, Mr. Davison. The Handley’s will put up whatever is required. Let’s take things one step at a time. We need to discuss what you’ll say, how you’ll say it - your attitude in court. The judge has to believe you will obey whatever restrictions they choose to impose and that you’ll turn up for trial once a date is set. That won’t be a problem, will it? No. So let’s do this properly and you’ll be able to go back to the theatre, pick up your role as Macbeth and scarcely miss a day.

“Think of the effect all this will have on ticket sales. An accused murderer playing the role of the wicked usurper of the throne of Scotland? It’ll be a sensation!”

That thought got through. “Yes, it will, won’t it? And the trial… what an incredible role!” His enthusiasm was building…

“Of course. But as I said, one step at a time. Act one, the arraignment and bail hearing. I need you to be at your absolute best.”

And he would be. Portia was right. This was just the first act in what would be the most challenging role of his life! He felt Ian slip, reality fading as his professional persona took over.

Portia saw it, the moment that he understood. He would give a superb performance. All she need do was offer him the right prompts. This was going to be easy.

* * * * *

Susan and DCI Gordon were meeting with representatives of the Independent Office for Police Conduct. Superintendent Atkinson had been advised of the proceedings by the DCI. As the officer in command of all detectives at the Policing Centre he was furious that one of his Inspectors had been reported to the IOPC and intended to make his displeasure known. He was waiting outside the conference room when Gordon and Sergeant Cross came up the stairs.

"We should be dealing with this internally, Gordon. Why did we have to involve these bastards? We could have resolved this quietly without ruining a good man's reputation! What if any other of our officers or detectives are involved?"

"We couldn't handle this internally, and you know it, Geoffrey," said the DCI. "This was no mere peccadillo. This was cooperation with a violent killer, to help him kill again, and deliberate interference with a murder investigation. If it involves other officers, we need to know."

"I don't believe it, Gordon. You can't blame the man for defending his own patch. He should have been in charge of the investigation from the start, not a mere Sergeant. Now these bastards are going to hound him, perhaps even send him down. Not right to do that to one of our own!"

"I can't tell you how disappointed I am to hear you say that, Sir. I thought better of you. Perhaps you should sit in and hear the case against him?"

"Humph. Don't have much choice, do I, now they're here? I'm staying to make sure Maurice gets a fair shake."

"I wouldn't expect anything else, Sir. Shall we?" and he led them in to face the inquisitors.

There were three investigators, two men and one woman, sitting along one side of the table. The superintendent and his two detectives sat opposite them. Susan looked at them curiously. This was the dreaded IOPC, the ones who answered to the age-old question 'Quis custodiet ipsos custodes'. Who guards the guards? In America an actual branch of the police known as 'Internal Affairs' had this role, but in the UK, it was a totally independent body drawn from people with many different backgrounds.

Few knew much about them, and to many in the force they were the bogeyman, an enemy, to be despised and feared. Susan had never been afraid of them though, believing that they, like her, were only interested in getting to the truth of their investigations. They seemed very ordinary - just people; but these people had the power to investigate misdeeds by the police themselves, and to prosecute them to the full extent of the law if it was justified. This would be no internal investigation with misdeeds quietly swept under the carpet 'in the interest of maintaining the public's trust in the policing services.' No, she thought, it was by the very existence of these people that the public's trust in the police was maintained.

She smiled at them as introductions were made all round. Then came the statement of the implied offences and the hearing of the evidence. If the evidence warranted it, the IOPC would then move the case forward. Those who had been accused would have their say, and the IOPC would also review those who collected the evidence - both their competence and their motives.

She and the DCI presented their case on what Inspector Featherstone had done. They gave a summary of the evidence they had to support the case. Others would be available to give information on how Featherstone had tried to take Alison from Walworth, and later looked to obtain inside information on a case he was not involved in.

The group from Classic Cars would attend if required to give personal accounts of how Featherstone had demanded information on the movements of Tom and Alison, and it was now a matter of public record that it had been the supposed murderer that had appeared in Hastings following up on information given only to Featherstone. Finally, how Ron Brown had informed Featherstone that Tom and Alison were staying in the guest suite at the dealership, and yet it had been a killer that had broken in and attacked the couple supposedly sleeping there. Lastly there was the damning evidence from Stan Bellamy's phone showing the contacts and timing with Featherstone, which really left little doubt.

After an exhaustive series of questions, the IOPC investigators thanked the three police officers, who were then dismissed, leaving the investigation team to discuss it amongst themselves. If they deemed the case sufficient to proceed, Inspector Featherstone would have his chance to present his side of the case to them the next day.

Superintendent Atkinson stopped them at the top of the stairs before heading to his own office.

"Robert," he said, and looking at Crosspatch, "Susan. I owe you both an apology. I had not realised how serious this case was, and knowing you, Robert, I should have. You were right. This was no minor slip. This was a full-blown crime, and it hints at others that we may not even have been aware of in the past. I'm not happy about it, but that's not your fault. It's mine. I didn't see what I didn't want to see. We're going to have to tighten up around here. Give me a few days - I intend to sit in and hear both sides of this story, but I have no doubt that you two have the right of it. Let's get this over and done with and we'll take a look at our structure and our policies. We can, and must, do better."

"Yes, we can, Geoffrey. We need a thorough shake up here, as I'm sure we'll hear from the IOPC investigators. But we've also proved we can do an excellent job, as Sergeant Cross has demonstrated."

"Yes. Well done indeed, Sergeant. I saw that television interview. Excellent. And you've proved that you're a first-class police officer not just a television personality! I hope we'll see more of both!"

"Thank you. It was a team effort, Sir. We aren't exactly typical, but my team plays to several different strengths, and we work well together."

"Yes, well congratulations. You too Gordon, for seeing the potential and guiding it along. We'll talk in a few days."

*   *   *   *   *

Word had got around quickly, it seemed. He'd only been arrested a few hours ago, but already a crowd had gathered. As he stepped out of the building alongside Ms. Daniel the babble of the press erupted into calls and questions. He faced a sea of cameras, their flashes popping. The cool, humiliating insolence of police protocol was forgotten. He was back in his own world. The camera had always loved him and here was an audience begging him to speak.

"You ok Ian?"

"They going to lock you up, Ian?"

"What news on the killer, Ian?"

"Ian!"

"Ian?"

"Look this way, Ian!"

He straightened his shoulders and gazed straight out at the pack.

"My wife," he said, and his voice thrummed with emotion. "My beautiful wife is ... dead. Murdered. Brutally, horribly murdered. The police have arrested her killer…" a pause, "and yet they haul me in to their interrogation rooms, insinuate the unspeakable…

"Oh yes, I'm guilty."

There were gasps from the crowd. More flash bulbs popped.

"I was at the theatre when it happened, not at home to protect my wife. That is the guilt I'll always carry. I wasn't there. I was rehearsing a play, one dedicated to Laura, my wife.

"Lady Macbeth *was* an accessory to murder. She could never wash the stain of blood from her hands, from her heart." He held up his hands, a slight tremor in the fingers, no more. "Do you see a stain? Look! My hands are clean. But my heart…" He looked down a moment and then spoke in little more than a whisper, but one that carried clearly through the autumn morning. "My heart is in pieces."

Questions erupted around him, but Portia took him by the arm and helped push a way through to the car she'd told him was waiting.

"It's a mistake," she said, facing the crowd. "Mr. Davison is free for now, and we are confident he will be fully exonerated in court." She joined him in the backseat of the limousine.

"That was brilliant. Keep that up throughout the trial and you won't have a thing to worry about. Juries are easier to convince than a judge. They're generally less cynical. Now you can sit back and relax. As long as they know where you are, the police won't bother you. Try not to upset them, though, or they will be a nuisance.

"Here," she pointed, "I made sure the drinks cabinet was stocked with your favourite, Laphroaig. Pour yourself one, you deserve it. That was a masterful performance." She handed him a tumbler from a cabinet in the wall between the driver and passenger compartments, then tapped on the partition glass.

"Drop me at the office will you, Wilson? Then take Mr. Davison wherever he wants to go." She smiled at him. "I need you to present the perfect image of the wronged and responsible citizen for the next few weeks - months possibly - before we go to trial. We'll be in touch as soon as a date is set, and we'll plan how we approach the trial. I'll make sure you understand exactly what's going to happen, and coach you through it."

"Thank you," he said accepting the glass. He poured himself a large one and sat back. The nightmare was over - or almost over. He could handle what remained - it was what he did on stage every night. Easy. He sipped the whisky *God that was good.* Just what he needed. His troupe would be delighted to see him. He looked at his watch. He could even make tonight's performance. His eyes closed.

The car was slowing down. Must be Portia's office. He opened his eyes. Tried to sit up, thank her… but he felt dizzy suddenly. She was getting out, then she looked back at him from the open door.

"She was my friend, you bastard! I hope you fry in hell!" She slammed the door and was gone.

"What…? What…?" but no words came.

The mists engulfed him, the witches' laughter a mere whisper as he slumped sideways, unconscious.

The chauffeur drove on.

*   *   *   *   *

"Susan… Got a minute?" It was the DCI, looking in at her door.

She looked up from her computer. "Of course, Sir. Come in."

He came in and sat down opposite her, looking tired. "It's about the Nettle Lane case. Davison hasn't been seen in several days.

"We've had a Panda check the house every couple of days. The Met have done the same for his flat in Pimlico. He hasn't shown up at either place. We've checked with his lawyers. They say that their limousine dropped Ms. Daniel at her office and was then going to take him to the theatre. They had agreed to be in touch once a trial date was announced, but she wasn't expecting to hear from him before that.

"But he hasn't been seen at the theatre either.

"Apparently the limo driver returned the car that afternoon but hasn't been seen since. He was a temporary replacement for their regular driver who called in sick, and it seems its navigation system memory has been wiped. It looks as though our man has done a bunk, and had help to do it."

Susan sat back, unsure what her feelings were. "We're sure he hasn't just gone to ground somewhere? If he has done a runner, it'll make our case virtually watertight. I must admit I wasn't looking forward to facing him in court. With his acting skills, matched with a good barrister - and Oatley and Daniel have connections with very good ones -

he might still run rings around us. Have we launched a search?"

"We have." He shrugged. "Hopefully he'll be found. The restrictions on his leaving the country are in force so it's unlikely he simply turned up at an airport and flew off to South America. In the meantime, brief your team."

She nodded.

"We aren't going to make any announcements until we're quite sure. We're going to be seen in a poor light no matter which way this falls. He was free on bail, so we couldn't keep too close a watch without it being seen as harassment. At the same time, there will be plenty who will see it as our incompetence. If he *has* just gone to ground for a while and shows up when he's supposed to, we'll be accused of that very harassment anyway. So, we'll try to find him quietly, and see what happens."

Susan agreed and then asked "Is there anything my team can do to help? We're working with the other police jurisdictions at the moment trying to clear up the cold cases that we think Bellamy is responsible for. He's still being uncooperative, but we've tied him, fairly definitively, to at least seven other murders all over the country. I'm off to Manchester tomorrow - they've just found another body up there that their FP reckons is only a month or so old. She may have been Bellamy's last kill before Laura Handley."

"Poor woman. Let's hope we can bring some closure there."

She nodded. "Pandy is down in Brighton with Stuart, talking to witnesses on the case down there, and

Sandeep is with Sean in Crawley. The pictures of Bellamy have triggered memories. They visited the families of the two murdered women to let them know we believe we finally have the killer. Sean tells me that when they were talking to the family in Crawley, the daughter, who's sixteen now, suddenly burst into tears, jumped up and hugged them both. Sean said that Sandeep was crying, and he nearly bawled too. Sometimes we forget how these things affect the ones left behind." Gordon saw that Susan's eyes, too, were damp. "They should be back tomorrow."

Gordon smiled. "Well, at least we still have Bellamy. We may be able to close the door on some very nasty memories for several families. Let's hope that he'll decide to cooperate and help us find the ones that are still listed as missing?"

"I hope so. Maybe not till the trial is over though," said Susan.

After he left, Susan sat quietly thinking about what had happened.

Given his personality, Davison would have stayed and fought it out in court. By running he'd convict himself. Was he guilty? Yes, she believed so. There was a faint possibility that he was not in the case of Laura, but she was quite certain on the attempted murder of Alison Johnson. Someone else had no doubt, though, and wasn't going to let him get away with it. Her mind snapped back to her visit to the Handleys. Lady Mary's eyes, cold and hard. She would not forgive Laura's death.

The Handleys had provided the lawyer for Davison. The father and mother providing help for their beleaguered son-in law? She'd been a bit doubtful when she heard that and wondered if the lawyer had been primed to lose the case.

No. All she had to do was get him out of police custody. Then he'd be an easy target. I don't think he made it to freedom at all. He isn't sipping margaritas on a tropical beach somewhere. He's dead.

And when she reported her suspicions to the DCI, he didn't seem surprised.

"Did Ian Davison deliberately set a serial killer on his wife? Did he set the same killer on another young woman who just might have known too much? We may believe that, Susan, and the evidence points that way. But, would a jury have convicted him?

"Your theory is that someone was convinced he was guilty and made sure that he'd pay for what he'd done. A mother avenging the death of a much-loved daughter perhaps? I wouldn't be surprised. I would even agree. But your chances of proving it? I just don't see it happening.

"Would you say justice had been served though?

" It's not what we've been brought up to believe in, but the ancient Greeks would have seen it as most appropriate. And they were the founders of our modern civilization!" He sat back and looked at her sadly.

"But that's just between the two of us…"

*   *   *   *   *

Team Crosspatch will be back… Watch for XP2!

About the Author

'Helen M. Barton' is the pen name of Ren Carroll and Anne Carroll Marshall - a brother and sister writing partnership. After careers living and working in various places around the world, one now lives in Kamloops, British Columbia, Canada, and the other in St Leonards on the south coast of England. The name is a tip of the hat to the person who instilled in them both a love of reading from a very early age.

Acknowledgements:

We'd like to express our thanks to the many people without whose very constructive criticisms - and encouragement - this book may never have seen the light of day. Particular mention should be made of Janet Gyenes, who provided a very professional review of an early draft and Judy O'Neill, who helped with reviews of later ones in Canada. Similarly, thanks in England to Kathy Doyle, Kirsty Ranger and Julie Stringer, not to mention all those whose questions "How is the book coming along?" spurred on the muse!

Finally, of course, to Angela and Roger who were always there providing support, advice, the time to write and to hear a read through of yet another version.

Manufactured by Amazon.ca
Bolton, ON

43848581R00213